ROGUE FORCE

(A TROY STARK THRILLER—BOOK 1)

JACK MARS

Jack Mars

Jack Mars is the USA Today bestselling author of the LUKE STONE thriller series, which includes seven books. He is also the author of the new FORGING OF LUKE STONE prequel series, comprising six books; of the AGENT ZERO spy thriller series, comprising twelve books; and of the TROY STARK thriller series, comprising three books (and counting).

Jack loves to hear from you, so please feel free to visit www.Jackmarsauthor.com to join the email list, receive a free book, receive free giveaways, connect on Facebook and Twitter, and stay in touch!

ISBN: 978-1-0943-7664-6

BOOKS BY JACK MARS

TROY STARK THRILLER SERIES
ROGUE FORCE (Book #1)
ROGUE COMMAND (Book #2)
ROGUE TARGET (Book #3)

LUKE STONE THRILLER SERIES
ANY MEANS NECESSARY (Book #1)
OATH OF OFFICE (Book #2)
SITUATION ROOM (Book #3)
OPPOSE ANY FOE (Book #4)
PRESIDENT ELECT (Book #5)
OUR SACRED HONOR (Book #6)
HOUSE DIVIDED (Book #7)

FORGING OF LUKE STONE PREQUEL SERIES
PRIMARY TARGET (Book #1)
PRIMARY COMMAND (Book #2)
PRIMARY THREAT (Book #3)
PRIMARY GLORY (Book #4)
PRIMARY VALOR (Book #5)
PRIMARY DUTY (Book #6)

AN AGENT ZERO SPY THRILLER SERIES
AGENT ZERO (Book #1)
TARGET ZERO (Book #2)
HUNTING ZERO (Book #3)
TRAPPING ZERO (Book #4)
FILE ZERO (Book #5)
RECALL ZERO (Book #6)
ASSASSIN ZERO (Book #7)
DECOY ZERO (Book #8)
CHASING ZERO (Book #9)
VENGEANCE ZERO (Book #10)
ZERO ZERO (Book #11)
ABSOLUTE ZERO (Book #12)

PROLOGUE

October 15
1:35 pm Eastern Daylight Time
Ross Dock Picnic Area
Fort Lee, New Jersey

Almost nothing about the man was as it appeared.

He seemed tall, a bit over six feet, but he was wearing two-inch lifts inside his fine leather boots, which themselves had one-inch heels. He seemed to have a thick blonde beard. In fact, it was a cleverly crafted fake, glued to his face with the skill and care that Hollywood cosmetic specialists use when working on film actors.

He seemed to have long blonde hair, tied in a ponytail. Same. The wig was as high-quality as the beard and affixed to his head with equal care. In fact, his head was closely shaven, his real hair was dark and, if allowed to grow out, would show him to be a victim of early male pattern balding. He wore colored contact lenses to make his brown eyes seem pale blue. His eyebrows were dyed blonde and could easily and quickly be dyed back to their normal color.

He often went by the name "Sven." He had no idea why, but he found this amusing. Perhaps because he was as far from a Nordic Sven as humanly possible, both physically and in outlook. He also found it amusing how a man like him, what some might call a true believer, even a religious extremist, could find common cause with a nihilistic businessman, a man who was happy to tell you that he believed in nothing but the material world that he could touch and see.

He shook his head and smiled. It helped that the pay was good. Very good.

He left the car in the parking lot and walked across the grass to the far southeastern corner of the park. He skirted the edge of a large family gathering, which he supposed had about 30 people, and was monopolizing four picnic tables and two charcoal grills. The adults stood around, drank beer, and ate hotdogs and hamburgers. The children chased each other in circles. A couple of dogs jumped and barked. A few of the older kids were messing with a small toy drone.

It was a lovely fall day, great for a barbecue.

1

The park was just north of, and well below, the George Washington Bridge. The bridge loomed overhead in the near distance, cutting across the pale blue sky. Sven could see the westbound cars and trucks crossing it on the upper level, moving from New York City to New Jersey. Below the bridge, on the distant side of the Hudson River, the skyline of Manhattan marched south.

This was a good spot. He had considered Liberty State Park, but it was too close to the target. Impact would happen much more quickly from there, which would have given him no time to disappear. Yes, there was more chance of interference when launching from this distance, but how much chance was there really?

Not much. Not much at all.

Sven was carrying a large, heavy pack, which weighed on his shoulder. When he was close to the water's edge, he set it down. Then he went back to the car, and got another heavy pack, nearly identical to the first. He glanced back at the family. No one over there was looking at him. Soon, he was alone by the water again. He opened both packs and pulled out the various parts of the drone. They tended to fasten together with relative ease.

It was much larger than the toy drone that the kids had, but it was still relatively small as drones went. He connected the four sections of the fuselage, making the body about two meters in overall length, and quite bulbous. Along the inside of each side of the fuselage was a closed compartment, which contained the drone's payload, and to which he had no access. They were by far the heaviest parts.

He slowly and meticulously connected the drone's four arms and eight rotors. At the end of each arm, the rotors were attached horizontally both above and below the bracket there. When he was finished, the drone looked like a very large, very scary, very pregnant spider. It was all black, with two sensors on top, and nine cameras mounted on an appendage from the bottom. Eight of the cameras were multi-directional, and could move autonomously, including both up and down. The ninth camera faced down and was also multi-directional. The thing had a field of vision that no living creature could match.

Sven took out the controller, opened it, turned it on, and let it run through its diagnostic tests. The controller was simply a small black laptop with a few buttons and a tiny readout. It had to be close, within about ten meters, to launch the drone. It was really more of a launcher, and a navigator, than a controller.

Once the device was in flight, no more input from the human end user was necessary. The system would become fully autonomous. The destination of the drone was pre-programmed. The navigator would remain in contact and guide it there. The drone's actions when it arrived at the destination would depend on how the targets presented themselves.

"Wow!" a voice said behind him. "Can we see your drone?"

Sven was on his knees. He turned and two small children were there, a boy and a girl. The children were brown-skinned, with dark hair. The boy was about a head taller than the girl.

Sven would have preferred if no one had come this close. But it didn't matter. He was a tall, blonde-haired, blue-eyed man who flew drones as a hobby. He would be long gone, and his appearance would have changed, before it occurred to anyone to think differently about him. He smiled and stood. He made sure to raise himself to his full augmented height.

"He was very tall," he could imagine the children saying.

"Sure, kids," Sven said. "It's a good one, isn't it?"

English was not his first language, but he had studied for years to eliminate any hint of an accent in his voice.

"It's awesome!" the little boy said.

The girl was silent, staring at the thing in wonder.

The controller had finished its tests. Of course, everything on the drone was operational. It had been tested and re-tested just this morning. The man had brought it here with nearly infinite care. Now it was ready.

"Watch it fly," he said.

He pressed the green button on his controller. The rotors spun, making a low whining noise. After a moment, the thing tentatively lifted from the ground. For a few seconds, it almost seemed to struggle with the weight of the payload it was carrying. Then it went up about one or two stories, hovered for a moment, and headed toward the bridge.

"Wow!" the boy said.

"Wow!" the girl echoed.

The man, whose real name was not Sven, reached down, picked up the empty black bags, closed the controller, and slipped it under his arm. "Well," he said. "That's it for me. Have a nice day, kids."

"Mister, what about your drone?" the boy said. He pointed south, where the drone was now a dark speck, about to fly under the George Washington Bridge.

"Don't you want it?"

Both the boy and the girl's faces said they were disturbed that the man would launch such a wonderful toy, then simply walk away and forget about it.

He smiled brightly again, to reassure them that there was no problem.

"Oh, it'll be fine. It's going to meet some friends on the other side of that bridge."

* * *

The drone flew south above the Hudson River.

Within two minutes, it had passed beneath the George Washington Bridge. It stayed low, skimming just five meters over the water, its giant span a shadow looming above it. Once past the bridge, it ascended to 20 meters and continued on.

It was on its own. It had no mind in the way humans might think of one. It had no memory of the past, and no real anticipation of the future. It had no loved ones. It had no fear, and no courage in the face of fear. It was not capable of guilt or remorse. It had no preferences. It didn't judge anything as good or bad. It had no opinion of what it was about to do. It wasn't excited, nor did it have any second thoughts. There was no sick feeling of anxiety deep inside its belly.

But its computer brain was more than enough to guide it. It absorbed and adjusted to a steady stream of data about its environment - height, wind speed and direction, along with visual data about objects in its path, such as large ships, or any potential hostile intervention that might stop it from carrying out its directive.

There was no such intervention, nor was any going to come. Given the vast scope of the river, and the city, and the drone's height above the water, it was nearly invisible out here. If it appeared on anyone's radar, it would seem to be the toy of an obsessed hobbyist. People had not yet begun to think of drone attacks against civilians as something to worry about.

Its destination was now 7.4 miles south, southeast. The tall buildings of New York City were directly to its east, passing by at approximately 28 miles per hour. It was a sunny, breezy day, and the drone was very stable in flight. It began to accelerate, its speed increasing rapidly. In the final seconds before contact, it should top out at a little over 100 miles per hour.

Visibility was excellent. In another few seconds, it should receive its first visual data on the target. Its destination was known as Vessel, a

4

popular tourist attraction in the Hudson Yards neighborhood of Manhattan.

It would arrive there momentarily.

CHAPTER ONE

2:05 pm Eastern Daylight Time
Vessel
Hudson Yards
New York City

"What a beautiful day!" Kate said. "What a view."

"Gorgeous," Adam said.

He didn't know where he had gotten that word, but he said it a lot nowadays. "Gorgeous." It was almost a mechanical response, but it seemed to fit much of the time.

He and Kate had come in to Manhattan on the PATH train from their waterfront condo over in Jersey City. Kate was certainly gorgeous, nearly fashion model tier, in fact. She was tall, with long blonde hair, high cheekbones, and an upturned nose. Today she was wearing skinny jeans and a light jacket and fuzzy boots. When she was excited, like now, her face and smile would light up the world. When she was sad, or bored, which she often was, you would do anything to make her happy again. With eight years in selling bonds at Stifel, Adam was making real money these days. He hoped money would be enough to keep her.

And the day, of course, was gorgeous. Wide open blue skies, breezy, with a hint of the coming winter in the air, and thin white clouds skidding across the sky. And the view from this strange… he wasn't sure what to call it. Building? Sculpture? Monument? It was basically an interlocking honeycomb of stairs and landings, stairs and landings, stairs and landings, in a sort of circular pattern, 16 stories high. It was as if an architect was smoking pot while staring at an MC Escher sketch and decided to build what he saw.

The view from here, near the very top, looking back toward the wide expanse of river, with the steel and glass towers of Hudson Yards in the foreground, and the old train yards still visible below street level was… gorgeous.

There was no better word for it.

"Gorgeous, hon," Adam said. "Really gorgeous."

6

Kate laughed. Maybe she was delighted by the day. Maybe she was delighted by the word that he kept saying. Whatever delighted her, she was laughing as she leaned against the railing and clear panel of glass, and that was enough. When she laughed, everyone around her faded and then disappeared. That was the raw power of her beauty. And it was crowded here today - a lot of folks were quietly melting into the background.

Vessel had only reopened a week ago. Some angst-ridden teenager had thrown himself off from the top a few months back, and it was a long way down. The owners had closed the place to study what to do about that. Apparently, the answer was nothing. People jumped from high places sometimes. So now Vessel was open again, and there was a lot of pent-up demand. People wanted to be here. Adam and Kate wanted to be here. It was a place to be.

Maybe it was *THE* place to be. Adam liked the thought of that.

"Let me get some pictures of you," he said.

His phone was never far from his hand. It was a new model, expensive, and encased in bright blue rubber to protect it from drops, spills, and all the other dangers that smart phones were vulnerable to. This one had a super high-definition camera, with the ability to instantly upload photos and video to cloud storage. The TV ads would lead you to believe that somewhere, right now, entire crews were shooting feature films with this telephone. Maybe they were.

He didn't have to ask her twice. Kate was a natural ham. She loved to be photographed. He turned the video on, as she moved fluidly from pose to pose, like a fashion model. It was disconcerting the ease with which she did it, going from a pout to a bright smile, to a searing come hither look with no break in between. For a split second, it occurred to Adam that she must practice these moves, maybe in front of a mirror.

But then something else caught his eye. Behind Kate, a sort of black speck appeared. No, it was more than a speck. A second ago, it had been a speck. A second before that, it wasn't even noticeable.

Now it was larger, coming from the direction of the river, and rising as though it had emerged from the surface of the water. Adam's eyes tried to formulate it into a shape he recognized. Was it a bird? It was coming kind of fast for a bird. On the screen, Kate threw her head back, causing her luxurious hair to make a wave-like motion. Behind her, that thing was still coming.

What was it?

Now other people had started to notice. A man in a dark blue windbreaker pointed at it. Adam noticed the white logo on the man's jacket: North Face.

A woman picked up her blonde-haired toddler and clutched him.

Three bored teenagers, all in black, and with skin as white as alabaster, were sitting on one of the many staircases. Now they turned to look at the approaching thing.

As Adam watched, it resolved into a shape he recognized - it looked like a sort of flying spider. His brain could make sense of that.

"It's a drone," he said.

"What?" Kate said, still smiling, still moving, still going for it.

Adam gestured behind her with his chin. "There's kind of a funny drone coming."

It was the speed that had caught his attention. Less than ten seconds ago, the thing hadn't existed at all. Now it was almost here. It was coming in this direction. There was no doubt about that. It was almost as if it was making a beeline for Vessel itself.

Kate turned to look at it.

"Weird."

Adam could hear it now. It made that whining noise a lot of drones made.

Someone nearby gasped. The drone suddenly lurched straight upwards, above their heads. The abrupt change and steep climb made it whine even louder. It was going to pass right over the top of them.

Adam followed the arc of the flight with his camera. He didn't know why. Because it was interesting. Because it was disturbing. Because the thing was moving so fast it was an actual challenge to follow it.

Then the drone stopped. It hovered, maybe four stories above the crowd, everyone watching it now.

"I guess somebody thinks they're pretty clever," a man said.

Sure. Some idiot was fooling around with a high-end drone, probably filming, and thought he'd give a bunch of people a scare.

Then the drone broke apart.

A woman screamed, sending an involuntary shiver through Adam's body.

The drone seemed to split down the middle and fall away as two fat pieces. But then those pieces seemed to disintegrate and become dozens of much smaller fragments. The whining increased in intensity.

The fragments weren't falling so much as flying themselves. They were like a cloud of black insects. They were. They were like tiny dragonflies. Lots of them. And they were coming down.

"Kate. We better…"

People started to run.

"Kate!"

The man in the windbreaker burst for the nearest stairs and bumped into Kate, knocking her to the walkway.

"Hey!" Adam screamed. "Hey!"

The woman who had picked up her child got hit with something. A burst of red exploded from her forehead, her eyes went blank, and she sank to the ground, folding over on top of her child. The boy was under her body, screaming.

Adam couldn't seem to move. He was frozen in place.

His mind played back what had happened to the woman, watching it again. A tiny dragonfly had come down at lightning speed and crashed into her forehead. When it did, a sort of POP happened, like a mini firecracker going off. It was like she had been shot in the head with a bullet.

He glanced at her again. Her eyes were wide open and staring. She hadn't moved at all since she had fallen. Her head was at an odd, boneless angle from her body. A narrow stream of blood pulsed down, dripping to the concrete walkway. Her child squirmed beneath her, hugging her and shrieking now.

Adam watched the scene unfold in a sort of slow motion.

North Face was down now. He had reached the stairs but had only gotten up two or three of them. He was spread out, face down.

Kate, on all fours, crawled toward the man for some reason. Maybe she was crawling for the stairs. As she did, a black speck hit her in the back of the head. A small mist of pink fluid sprayed upward, and Kate dropped like a broken doll. Instantly, she stopped moving.

A small sound escaped from Adam.

"Unh."

It was too horrible. It couldn't be. How could this be? He took a tentative step toward her. She was not moving at all. The back of her head, her beautiful hair, was streaked with red. Her arms were splayed out on either side of her. Her face was against the ground. Did she move? For a second, it almost seemed like she did. Maybe she was okay. Maybe she was still…

"Kate?"

He took a step, and another. He seemed to float above her. People were screaming. Everywhere, all across the top floors, there were bodies strewn. Adam approached Kate. Blood was pooling around her head now.

"Oh God." He felt, and almost saw, a small black shadow hit his own head with incredible force.

CHAPTER TWO

2:15 pm Eastern Daylight Time
E. 239th Street
Woodlawn, The Bronx
New York City

"Well, I see the international man of mystery is back."

"You're very observant," Troy Stark said. He stood across the back porch from his brother Donnie. There was a barbecue going on. The four Stark brothers, a couple of cousins, wives, and children were all here.

Donnie had just arrived and come out the kitchen door. He was the eldest brother in the clan, nearly a decade older than Troy. And he was big. They were all big, and broad, but Donnie was the biggest. The group of them on the porch made the thing seem tiny and cramped, like it was originally built for Lilliputians.

"It's one of your finer personality traits," Troy said.

Eddie Stark, another of the brothers, smiled. "Yeah? What's another one?"

Eddie was the second oldest. He was big - big across the chest, big shoulders, big arms, legs like tree trunks. He was a gym rat, always pumping iron. He wore jeans and a dark blue t-shirt with NYPD in white across the front. Eddie had worked undercover Narcotics for a long time. Now he was a homicide detective. He claimed he did it so his mom, and his wife, could sleep better. Maybe he slept a little better, too. He was holding a can of Miller Lite. The guy was a throwback to the days of bad beer. The can looked like a toy in his hand.

Troy shook his head sadly. "Come to think of it, there aren't any."

Donnie grinned. He came across the porch and gave Troy a bear hug. Donnie, at six foot six, was about four inches taller than his youngest brother. It was a funny thing. Nowhere he went on Earth was Troy Stark considered a small man. Nowhere, except in the house where he grew up.

He once asked his mother why she figured he had been shortchanged on size. She considered it a moment, then shrugged and said, "You were the last one. I was already 32 years old when I had you. My eggs were no good anymore."

The two brothers broke their embrace. Donnie gazed down at Troy. He touched a hand to Troy's face.

"What have you been doing since you got back? You even shave today?"

Troy shrugged. "Yeah, I shaved." He hadn't but that was beside the point.

"Well, stand a little closer to the razor next time."

That got a few laughs going. In addition to being the oldest, and the biggest, Donnie often took it upon himself to be the master of ceremonies.

He turned and addressed the crowd. "What's this kid do for a living, anyway?" That was always a fun one. Kick the sore spot. It was part of coming home. Troy knew that. It just wasn't his favorite part.

"He'd tell ya…," Eddie said.

Donnie finished off the punch line. "But he'd have to kill me."

Yuk, yuk, yuk. They all knew what Troy had done for a living. If not the specifics of it, the overall outline. He'd gone into the Navy through the SEAL challenge contract, right out of high school. He was in boot camp in Great Lakes, Illinois, two weeks after graduation. Spent a year preparing for BUD/S and became a SEAL at 19.

Two tours in Afghanistan. More training. A couple of classified deployments with Joint Special Operations Command. Further training. Then things got a little squirrelly. He was on loan to the CIA for a while, bouncing back and forth between there and the SEALs. Then he went on loan to another agency, if you could call it that, a black budget line item that didn't even have a name.

In the Pentagon, they called the group "The Metal Shop." Or often, just "The Shop."

Troy had been in war zones and under deep cover in a lot of places, for a long time. He was 32 years old. Now he was on his way out, staring down the barrel of a general discharge. That was not ideal, but he was coming to terms with it. People who liked him had pulled strings to get him that. It was better than an OTH by a lot, and a hundred miles better than a bad conduct discharge.

He'd given his entire adult life to his country. Now…

He shrugged it away. Instead, he joined in on the fun and raised the index and middle finger of his right hand. He took a sip of his beer to hide his smile.

"And he'd do it with just two fingers," Eddie said.

12

And he would, too. These guys were all coppers, and way past the Police Academy. Donnie had risen to Inspector. He'd been riding a desk the past several years, and it showed. He was living fat nowadays across the Hudson River in Piermont. He didn't wear a trench coat to work because it looked cool. He wore it to hide the chub.

"Leave him alone," their mother said.

She came out onto the porch carrying a big tray with bowls of macaroni salad and chicken salad on it. Troy let the sight of her wash over him. Mary Stark. She had aged quite a bit in the years he had been away.

Her hair was gray, and she didn't bother to color it. The skin on her face was wrinkled like old parchment now. According to Eddie, it was lined with worry. She worried because two out of the three boys who had stayed home were cops, and the other was with the fire department. But she mostly worried, and stayed up late at night, because her baby was some kind of special forces secret agent and was just gone much of the time. Gone, and out of contact. He could be alive, he could be dead, and no one knew which.

"Ma, let me get that," Donnie said.

She turned away from him. "Get out of here. The day I can't carry a tray of food is the day I go to Gate of Heaven."

Troy's smiled widened. She'd been talking about going to Gate of Heaven since he was a kid. It was a giant cemetery on rolling hills up in the suburbs. Everybody from Babe Ruth to Mrs. O'Malley from around the corner was buried there. In fact, Troy's father was up there too, not that anybody missed him.

What cracked up Troy the most was that his mom never talked about going to heaven, she talked about going to Gate of Heaven. There was a big difference.

Pat Stark came out on the porch now. He was the third brother. Until Troy came along, Patty had been the rebel. He turned his back on the police and joined the fire department instead. He was Emergency Medical Services.

He walked out holding his phone to his ear. He was just signing off with someone. His face showed confusion, mixed with something else. Troy had seen the look many times, in many places. He wouldn't expect this look from a guy like Pat, who by now had seen just about every blood and guts thing there was to see.

It was the look of shock.

"Have you guys heard about this?" he said. "There's been some kind of thing downtown. Hudson Yards."

"What kind of thing?" Donnie said.

Pat glanced down at two toddlers on the floor, and a nine-year-old currently hugging her mother. It was clear he was reluctant to come out and say it in front of children. "I don't know. They're saying it was maybe... you know. Like an explosion, but not exactly. They think it was a drone. They're not even sure what happened."

"When?" Troy said.

Pat shrugged. "Maybe ten minutes ago. I just got called in." He looked at the beer in his hand. At least it was an IPA. Then he looked at his wife Holly and shook his head. Holly's eyes had become big. "Not to go there. They're moving resources around, putting people who were already on in the impact zone. I'm taking a replacement shift at a firehouse in Long Island City."

Donnie was already on his phone and going into the house.

Eddie shook his head. "Not my department."

Troy looked at Pat. "Is it bad?"

Pat downed the last of his beer and nodded. "I think so, yeah."

Troy thought about that. A drone. Like an explosion, but not really. Pat was talking about a terrorist attack. In Manhattan.

Donnie came back out onto the deck. "It's not my department, either. At least, not yet. It sounds like a real mess, though. Here we go again. That's what my boss said." Donnie pointed at Troy. "You coming to the bar tonight?"

Troy nodded. "Yeah. I think so."

"Good. I want to talk to you."

"Don't get your brother in trouble," their mother said. "He just got back."

"Don't worry," Donnie said. "I'll keep him safe. I know he's only a baby."

* * *

"So look," Donnie said. "How many years do you have in?"

They were belly up, at the far end of the bar at Michael Collins, a place they had been to many, many times over the years. They each had an empty shot glass and a half-drunk pint of Guinness in front of them. It was dark in here. Behind them, Eddie was with their cousin Marty, at a corner table, talking to a bunch of guys Troy didn't know.

The TVs above the bar played nonstop coverage of the terrorist attack in Manhattan earlier that day. It was indeed bad. At least 40 people had died. Others were in critical condition in area hospitals. The best thing about the coverage was that the sound was down. The jukebox here was loud, and tended to play things like the Pogues and the Dropkick Murphys. Currently, it was playing a fast version of "Come Out Ye Black and Tans," by the Battering Ram.

This place was Irish Republican to its core. Back in the 1990s, when the Stark boys were kids, the owner had been indicted on charges of running guns to the IRA. Kenny Dolan. That fact still lent an air of mystery to the joint, as though gun-heavy ships were sailing out of New York harbor, and deals were going down just beyond the reach of your hearing.

Kenny was still around; in fact he was here tonight. He was an old man now, heavyset, with a swollen face and white hair. He hadn't spent one minute in jail on the gun running indictment. Word was he had too many friends among the cops, and the prosecutors.

Troy shrugged. "Fourteen. I'm in the Navy 14 years."

The thought of that number made Troy sag just a little bit, like a weight was pressing down on him. He didn't like to catalog the many ways it was a waste. Troy Stark was hard, even as a boy. And he had become an even harder man. He had seen and done a lot of ugly things on behalf of his country. His brothers had stayed here, built careers, and started families. Troy had gone out there, to the edge, and then beyond it.

What was that old saying?

See the world! Meet interesting people. And kill them.

Donnie was nodding. Donnie was the eldest, and therefore the voice of reason. "It's good. It's all right. You're vested. You'll get a small pension out of them. You get lifetime healthcare. Mom told me you're interviewing with the Department tomorrow. Some former commanding officer of yours…"

Troy nodded. "Of course she told you." He had asked her not to tell anyone, which was like asking her to broadcast it on national TV.

"So she told me. So what? Listen, you've already got a pension, like we said. You have your VA benefits. If you take this job tomorrow…"

Troy shook his head. "I don't want to be a cop, Donnie. I don't want to start over."

Donnie raised a meaty hand. "There's nothing wrong with being a cop."

"No offense," Troy said. "I didn't say there was something wrong with it. I said I don't want to be one."

"Anyway," Donnie said, "Hear the guy out. You take this job, you put your 20 in, you walk away with a very nice pension on top of the naval pension, and you're only 52 years old at that point. You're still a young man."

Troy smiled. "Said the 42-year-old."

Donnie smiled and shook his head. He gestured at the bartender, then at the empty shot glasses. "Two more, Vinny? Thanks man."

"Anyway, I don't think this is a 20-year offer. The guy sees me in a bad spot, and he's throwing me a rope. Not sure if he wants me to grab it or hang myself with it."

One of Troy's old SEAL commanders, Colonel Stuart Persons, had retired from the Navy a few years back. He had turned up in New York, attached to a special task force of some kind. Port and harbor security.

It was under the aegis of the NYPD, but it included elements from the Fire Department, the Coast Guard, the Port Authority of New York and New Jersey, the Metropolitan Transit Authority, and about a dozen other agencies. It was supposed to identify emerging threats and neutralize them before they arose. It seemed to Troy like a sort of blue-ribbon commission. It looked okay on paper, but a lot of good it had done earlier today. Troy was going in tomorrow, basically to be polite.

"It sounds like a desk job," he said now.

Donnie raised an eyebrow. Thankfully, he didn't try to defend the sanctity of desk jobs. "It sounds like you can make it anything you want it to be."

"Yeah," Troy said. "Maybe. Like I said, I'll talk to him."

The shots came and they both pounded them without another word. Troy felt the heat go down his throat to his stomach. His eyes watered.

"Amen," Donnie said.

They turned around with their beers and looked out at the action in the bar. It was getting late, and the place was filling up. The music seemed louder than before. A group of young folks were starting to jump around on the dance floor, such as it was. The crowd around Eddie's table had grown.

Troy had a buzz on now, and it put a bit of a glow around everything that was going on. He didn't want to get too drunk, even though it was Saturday night and his mom's house was a five-minute walk from here. Both Eddie and Donnie were staying over there tonight. It was supposed to seem like old times.

"Who are Eddie's new friends?" he said, shouting a little.

Donnie shrugged. "Knuckle draggers. Mount Vernon cops. I don't know why they hang out here. Not really friends. Eddie suspects

16

they're dirty, a couple of them. Holding up the dealers, taking the money, doing the drugs. He hangs with them to get close, see if he's right."

"And then what?"

"Eddie's a crusader," Donnie said. "You know that. I think he also misses the rush of undercover. I tell him don't get killed. He's got a wife and a daughter now. It's irresponsible. Does he listen?"

"Looks like he's still alive," Troy said.

Donnie shook his head as if already lamenting his brother's death. "Barely."

It was as though Donnie's words had just given the signal. One of the crew cut guys at Eddie's table suddenly stood up, turned his beer bottle upside down, and tried to hit Eddie in the head with it. Eddie got an arm up and blocked it. The bottle shattered, glass and beer spraying all over him.

"I guess he's not as undercover as he thinks," Donnie said.

Troy took a sip from his pint. "He doesn't seem to be fooling anyone."

Donnie shook his head. "No."

A second later, another of the goons, who was already standing, punched a defenseless Marty in the face. The punch connected perfectly. Marty fell backwards, his arms flying into the air. His chair went over, and he was on the floor. Two guys were on top of him in a flash.

People started yelling. A high-pitched voice screamed.

Troy stared at the melee for a long second. He counted six guys attacking Eddie and Marty. Eddie was on his feet, trading punches with three of them. Marty was on the floor, getting kicked and punched by the other three.

Poor Marty. The guy worked in banking - mortgages, that sort of thing. Young families. Old people and their retirement accounts. Troy couldn't see anything left of Marty but his feet. Shoes, mind you. Black leather shoes. Don't come to a bar like this one wearing shoes.

Troy glanced down at his own steel-toed work boots. Force of habit.

Donnie took a final slug of his beer, then set the pint glass on the bar. He sighed. "Welcome home, kid."

Troy nodded. "Yeah."

They crossed the space between the bar and the table. Troy waded in, nothing heroic about it. The three guys fighting Eddie had their backs to him. He didn't tap anyone to get his attention. He just walked up, grabbed the middle guy by his head and punched him, a hard right hand, in the back of the neck.

BAM!

The guy's head snapped backwards. He did a sort of half-turn, nearly out on his feet. Troy's left came around and hit the guy squarely in the jaw. The guy's head snapped back around the other way. He did a sort of pirouette, spinning and collapsing onto the table.

In the corner of Troy's eye, huge, immensely strong Donnie grabbed one of the guys kicking Marty and bum rushed him, head first into the wall. A large glass New York Yankees mirror crashed to the floor, shattering everywhere. Donnie rammed the guy's head into the wall again, and then dropped the guy onto the glass.

The guy who started the fight punched Troy in the face. That woke Troy up. *Don't look at Donnie. Focus on what you're doing.*

They went toe to toe. The guy was BIG, broad, a gym rat like Eddie, but one who was probably doing steroids. His eyes were hard. His face perfectly clean shaven. His arms were so big, he had trouble punching forward. His punches came around like a windmill.

Troy stepped inside, very close. The rule of thumb for a smaller man was to stay out of the bigger opponent's grasp, but that rule didn't consider Troy Stark. He pushed the guy's face back with his left, exposing the throat. The guy grabbed Troy in a powerful clinch. His arms were strong. He pulled Troy tight. They were too close for Troy to get a clean punch. They were close enough to kiss.

Troy's knee came up like a rocket. Ferocious shot to the balls.

The guy's eyes went wide.

Troy did it again.

The guy's mouth opened.

"Dirty," the guy grunted. "Dirty mother…"

"Yeah," Troy said. Now the guy's arms had loosened. Troy stepped back and hammered the right into the guy's face. Broke his nose with the first punch.

Hit him again.

The guy's head snapped sideways.

His eyes were still hard, defiant. He wasn't out, but he wasn't defending himself either. Troy grabbed him by the little bit of hair in the front. This one would finish him.

Something jabbed into Troy's side. Hard.

He turned to see what had done it. It was old, white-haired Kenny Dolan, the infamous gun runner. He had jabbed Troy in the side with a sawed-off pool cue. His eyes were bleary, bloodshot with the drink.

"Get out! Get out ye Stark boys, and don't bust up me place!"

"Sorry Mr. Dolan," Troy said.

He turned back to the steroid guy. The guy was waking up. Troy lined him up and punched him in the nose again.

BAM!

The guy dropped to the floor as if a trap door had opened beneath him.

"Get out, I said!"

Dolan jabbed Troy again.

"Okay! I'm going!" Troy said.

A side door was open to the alley. Troy headed that way, Kenny Dolan behind him.

"Which Stark one are you?" Dolan said.

"Troy. Don't you remember me?"

"Troy? Troy. Where you been?"

"I was in the Navy."

"The Navy, eh? Well, welcome home."

"Thank you."

Eddie was helping Marty out into the alleyway. Marty's face was a bloody wreck.

Donnie was coming through the door. He stopped for a second and shook hands with Kenny Dolan. He loomed over the older man.

"Don't bust up me pub, Donnie. All right?"

Donnie nodded. "I'll come back during the week. You let me know the tab, okay?"

Dolan shook his head and smiled. "Get out. All the mobile phones in here, ten people have called the coppers by now."

"We are the coppers," Donnie said. He gestured with his head back inside. "So are they."

Dolan jabbed him with the pool cue.

"Get out, ye punks."

They moved up the alley toward the main drag. Donnie was breathing hard and holding his side. He sounded like some kind of pneumatic machine, wheezing through the end of its manufactured lifespan. He was carrying too much weight.

Eddie was at the mouth of the alley, glancing both ways for any cops before going out onto the street. He was holding up one hand in a STOP gesture. But the coast was clear, and he waved them on.

They walked down the sidewalk of the wide boulevard, the four of them in a row. All around them, the shops were closed, corrugated metal pulled down over the windows. Marty wiped the blood from his face with his dress shirt. He looked at Troy. "I thought you guys had outgrown this kind of thing."

Troy's blood was up. The fight had ended before he was ready. He shook his head. "Nah."

They had gotten in a scrape at the bar. Troy was drunk, he was walking down the quiet late-night streets with his brothers, and he had to be up early in the morning for a job interview.

"We never outgrow anything," he said.

CHAPTER THREE

October 16
8:05 am Eastern Daylight Time
New York City Police Department Counterterrorism Bureau
One Police Plaza
Lower Manhattan, New York City

The place was chaos.

It was early Sunday morning, and Troy imagined that most Sundays, there'd barely be anyone around.

Not today. The terrorist attack on the day before meant that it was all hands on deck. Security was tight just getting into the building. The line was out the double doors, and onto the plaza in front of the 13-story, squat, Stalin-esque concrete monstrosity that was the headquarters of the NYPD.

Troy waited in a long line to first get into the building, then pass through the metal detector, the guards pulling every other person aside and giving them an extra swipe with the handheld wand. He had a pounding headache and what seemed like a slight tremor in his entire body. He was dressed in what he thought of as "uppity," - boots, khaki slacks, a blue open-throated dress shirt, and a wind breaker jacket.

This wasn't a wedding, or a funeral. It wasn't an interview. It was a just a chat.

He was drinking his third cup of coffee in one of those heavy paper cups that were everywhere in New York City. The cup was blue with Greek columns on it. You saw it in every coffee shop, every concession near a subway stop, in every hand, everywhere you looked. He stared at it. It seemed to shimmer and shake. The coffee had already gone cold. He'd gotten about four hours of lousy sleep.

Eventually he got through, rode an elevator to the 12th floor, and a girl he found at a reception desk walked him through a warren of tight corridors to a back room. The wooden door, unmarked - no words, no number, nothing - was the dead end of the hallway. This wasn't what Troy was expecting. He thought that Colonel Persons...

"Right through there," the girl said. "It should be open."

He went in. The man himself sat at a desk in a cramped space directly across from the door. Boxes were piled up on the floor around him. The desk itself was covered in paperwork. He had a laptop computer, which sat on top of various papers.

The only thing the office had going for it was a wide, tall window behind the desk, giving a view directly out toward the Brooklyn Bridge. The map in Troy's brain suggested that this meant the tiny office was tucked away in the back of the building.

The man stood. Troy knew the guy in his bones.

Colonel Stuart Persons. Retired. Former United States Army Special Forces. Former Joint Special Operations Command. Troy guessed he was just about 50 years old. He was tall, and slim, with sharp edges to his face. His singular feature was the black eyepatch that he wore, the band tight to his mostly bald head. Nowadays, the patch was situated under a pair of glasses. The setup made Persons look older than his years.

Persons had never said what happened to his eye. Rumors had abounded. He lost it in combat in Fallujah. He lost it in a paratrooper training gone wrong in the Arizona desert - his primary chute had failed, he hit hard and plunged face-first into a cactus. A prostitute in the Philippines had gouged it out with a knife during a drunken argument. It could have been none of these, or all of them. Persons certainly had that reputation - some people referred to him as "Missing" Persons (though never to his face). Either way, the eye was gone when Troy first met him.

They shook hands across the desk. "Stark. Thanks for coming."

"Colonel," Troy said. "What happened to your eye?"

Persons smiled and shook his head.

It was an old joke. Saying "What happened to your eye?" to Missing Persons was like saying "How have you been?" to a normal human.

"It's a long story," Persons said. "Why don't you sit down?" He gestured to the chair on Troy's side of the desk. "And call me Stu. All that colonel stuff is over with."

Troy sat down. The idea of calling this guy "Stu" was about as far-fetched as calling the owner of the Michael Collins bar "Kenny." Or calling Mrs. Lynch, who lived across the alley from his mother, "Margaret." None of that was going to happen.

Persons nodded to Troy's big hands. "How's your hands?"

Troy looked at them. He hadn't noticed until now that they were scraped raw along the knuckles from last night's fight. No. That wasn't true. He had noticed, felt the soreness there, but had been too tired and hungover to really look at them. The right was worse than the left. That was usually the case. The right was his power hand.

He moved and stretched the fingers. "Uh, fine. Fine. Just a little fishing accident."

Persons raised an eyebrow. "Little fishing accident, eh? On R&R?"

Troy shrugged. "It's all R&R these days."

"I was sorry to hear about what happened," Persons said.

Troy nodded. "Thank you. I appreciate that." This wasn't something he wanted to talk about, not with Persons, not really with anyone. Not now, anyway. It was still too painful. Thankfully, Persons didn't seem to want to talk about it, either.

"Military life can be a long way from fair. You're an exceptional soldier, Stark. Among the best. I've always said that to anyone who would listen. That's why I invited you in today."

He raised his arms and looked around the room. "Welcome to my empire. This is only the beginning."

Troy eyed him. "I had the idea that you were in the Counterterrorism Unit. Maybe even running it. I was kind of expecting a big room with a bunch of surveillance display screens on the wall, and a row of hackers cracking code. A bunch of guys with headsets on. People running in and out. Something along those lines."

Persons nodded. "I might have given you that impression. Those guys are down on the eighth floor. Pretty much as you describe. Also, not really my bailiwick."

"So what are you doing here... in that case?"

Persons spoke slowly, as if carefully choosing his words. "It's a lot like counterterrorism. You might even say we should be part of that unit. But we're not."

Troy glanced around the room, wondering who "we" referred to. There were two people in the room, and Persons was the only one who worked here.

"So..."

"You were part of that unit some people called the Metal Shop."

Now Troy was the one being careful, suddenly walking in a minefield. "What was I? I've never heard of that. The... what?"

Persons smiled, nearly laughed. "I've seen your file, Stark. You don't have any secrets in here."

"Colonel, I have no knowledge of a unit known as the Metal Shop. Nor if I did have knowledge of such a unit, would I be at liberty to..."

Persons raised a hand. "I know. It's classified. But it's why you're here. I have a job for you, if you want it. It's not the counterterrorism unit. It's not a desk job. Your paychecks would come from the NYPD, but your connection to the police would be tenuous at best. It's an investigations arm, but it's for people who color outside the lines, so to speak. Do you have any idea what I'm talking about?"

Troy stared at the man. He was locked in on Persons's one remaining, very blue eye.

"I might. Yes."

"If you're willing to start today, your paperwork has already been filled out. Nothing to look over. No orientation. No filmstrips to watch. No one to take your blood pressure or temperature. Nothing to sign. You'd just have to trust me that it's all on the level, and it's been put to bed."

"What would I be doing?" Troy said.

Persons shrugged. "There was a terrorist attack yesterday. You might have heard about it."

Troy said nothing.

"We think it was a warm-up. The target was random, not terribly high value. A bunch of tourists and day trippers at a weird attraction near the river, and not even that many of them."

"I heard 48 dead so far," Troy said.

Persons nodded. "That's right. As I said, not that many. They could kill a lot more than that, believe me. It was sophisticated technology. What we call slaughterbots. An autonomous drone flew south along the river, turned in at Hudson Yards, and released a swarm of much smaller drones. No one was flying these things. They were simply pre-programmed to take people out. They were tiny, a little bigger than dragonflies. In the head of each one was a charge of TNT, just powerful enough to punch through a skull and do catastrophic damage to the person's brain."

"Almost like bullets," Troy said.

"That's right," Persons said. "Autonomous bullets, that pick a target on the fly. But not just any target. Within seconds, they were dropping people all over the place. The whole attack was over in less than 15 seconds. You'd think they were going for a heat signature or something along those lines. But it isn't true. None of them, not one of them, hit a single child."

Troy let that sink in. The bots would have needed advanced sensor technology, instantly determining the size and shape of the targets and weeding out the smaller ones. All of this, aboard autonomous drones that were moving fast and were the size of dragonflies.

"High tech," Troy said. "Probably not a non-state actor."

Persons shook his head. "We don't know that. We can't know that. These technologies are becoming ever more available. Advanced countries could have technology like this. So could advanced corporations. Rag-tag militias? Terrorist organizations? Probably not, not yet. But what we do know is this was a practice run. It showcased their abilities. And we believe something bigger is coming. The clock is ticking."

Again, with the "we." Persons was sitting in a cramped room, all by himself, down the end of a narrow hall at the back of the building. Who were we?

"And we have a person of interest in this case whom we'd like to talk to."

Troy stared at him. There were tens of thousands of cops in this city, plus the FBI, plus the NSA, plus the counterterrorism unit, and God only knew how many weird little sub-agencies like this one. There were the transit cops and the military police units. There were the Port Authority police and the state police, and the state bureau of investigation. There were the National Parks police.

"If that's true, why haven't we picked him up yet? What with the clock ticking and all?"

Persons shrugged. "We'd like to pick him up. We'd like to do that today, in fact. But we need to do it a certain way. People have rights. They have the right to remain silent. They have the right to an attorney. They have the right not to implicate themselves in a crime. They have a right to the assumption of innocence."

Troy began to get it. This wasn't an offer to become a police officer, or anything like that. Persons had access to Troy's classified military record, or at least some of it. There were things in Troy's history that would probably never be recorded in any sort of paperwork, anywhere. But Persons knew enough.

He didn't want Troy to be a cop. He wanted him to be a black operator.

"Bring a guy like the one I'm thinking of in, and he clams up in a hot minute. Then he lawyers up. Then things become protracted, with endless delays, while the guy says nothing. Meanwhile, it's not clear that he's committed any crime. Knowing things isn't necessarily against the law."

Troy and Persons were staring at one another again.

"And the clock, as you indicated, is ticking."

Troy said nothing. He supposed that all along, everything was inevitably leading back to something like this. You didn't hire Troy Stark to be an investigator. You didn't hire him to ride a desk. You didn't hire him to administrate anything, or to be part of some kind of cockamamie task force. You hired Troy Stark...

...to be Troy Stark.

It hurt, a little bit. *This is what they thought of him?*

But on the heels of that, another thought came:

What else would they think?

Everyone was responsible for who they were and what they had done. No one gets off the hook. No one rides for free.

"It's up to you, Stark. The city is in a state of high anxiety, maybe even terror. I'm sure you noticed that on your way in here. I was going to give you a week to think about this gig. But then yesterday happened and we need to act fast. You could do a good thing. We could get information that might stop this from happening again. Or you can tell me I'm wrong and you're not that person. Is that what you're going to tell me?"

"I don't have a weapon," Troy said. And it was true. He didn't own a gun. He certainly wouldn't keep one at his mother's house. He didn't own any non-lethal weapons, like a Taser or bear spray. The only knives he had access to were in his mom's kitchen. "I also don't have a badge."

Persons opened the top drawer of his desk. He pulled out a black Glock 19 nine-millimeter pistol and placed it on top of all his random paperwork. Then he put two 15-round magazines next to it. Then he placed an NYPD badge there. The nameplate said, "Stevens, Tom." There was a serial number above it.

Troy indicated the badge. "Is it real?"

Persons shrugged. "Does it matter?"

Troy looked at the rest of the stuff. "Is that it? A gun, some ammo, and a badge that may or may not be real? Is that all there is?"

Persons went back in the drawer and came out with brass knuckles. The knucks would fit over four fingers of either hand and were spiked along the top. One good punch would do A LOT of damage to an opponent's face.

Persons then placed a four-inch serrated hunting knife and sheath on the desk. The sheath had a strap you could use to wrap it to a leg or upper arm. Then he reached in and came out with a tiny Beretta Nano pocket pistol, with an elastic ankle holster.

He gestured at the Nano. "You never know. Could come down to that."

Then he placed an old blue cell phone, flip-style, on top of it all. Troy hadn't seen one like it in probably a decade or more.

"Never use your own phone. There's a number saved on speed dial in there. Call it when you have something for me."

Troy nodded. He was in. He supposed that Persons had known it would happen this way all along. "Okay. Now who am I picking up?"

CHAPTER FOUR

10:30 am Eastern Daylight Time
Hope Street, near Metropolitan Avenue
Williamsburg, Brooklyn
New York City

"What makes you think the guy is in there?" Troy said.

The man in the driver's seat shrugged. Persons had said to call him Alex. There was no way the guy's actual name was Alex, but so be it. He was a thin guy, with a thick beard, and a dark, almost brown, golden-hued complexion. He was wearing a large blue headwrap, like a turban, with some kind of medallion or coin or button front and center on it, like the medallion was holding the thing together.

Other than that, he was dressed normally, in jeans, a light jacket, and boots. The boots were a kind of soft suede. They were nice. Troy never wore boots like that. His own boots were still the curb-stomper work boots from last night. Yes. He had gone to what was ostensibly a job interview wearing these steel-toed boots. On some level, he must have already known what Colonel Persons had in mind.

Alex was sitting on those beads that a lot of taxi drivers would drape over their seats. Troy had sat on beads like those before. They were comfortable, especially for people who spent long hours sitting in a car, which is apparently what Alex did for a living.

"For one thing, he never leaves the building," Alex said. He spoke English exceptionally well, with a hint of somewhere else hidden in his voice. "You see those two guys standing on the loading dock back there? They're not waiting for some shipment to come in. They're bodyguards. If he's not here, there's no reason to have goons standing around outside, is there?"

Troy tilted the rearview mirror just a touch to get a better look at the guys. The building in question was a large old factory or warehouse building, which took up half of a city block. It had the kind of tall, two-story windows that suggested high ceilings and cavernous internal spaces. Alex had passed the building and parked this car - a beat up

28

Lincoln Town Car - up at the end of the block and across this narrow street.

The only obvious way into the building was the loading dock, which fronted the street. Once upon a time, trucks must have backed up to it. There was a corrugated metal door that was about two stories high, and probably on some kind of pulley system, like a garage door. There was also a door built into the metal. You could open that door and walk inside, without lifting the bay door.

Two big guys with flattop haircuts stood on the dock. One was wearing a blue tracksuit. The other was wearing a black tracksuit. They had sneakers on. They were big guys, with broad chests and shoulders. Even from here, Troy could see the tattoos snaking up their necks, and down their wrists and across their hands.

"What is his story?"

"Constantine Ambramovich," Alex said. He didn't have any paperwork with him. He didn't refer to a phone or a tablet computer. He just had this guy in his head. "He's young, maybe 27 years old. He got his start nearly a decade ago in Russia, putting up and hosting bootleg sports websites, the kind where people can watch the matches without having a TV package. Or watch matches in other countries. Free pay per view, that kind of thing. Tons of pop-up ads, maybe some malware inserted if the viewer doesn't have anti-virus. It helped to start in Russia, where they barely recognize and don't enforce copyright law. The FBI took down sites associated with him over the years, but then he just moved them to new domains in other countries. He made a lot of money at this. No one knows how much. He still has his hand in it, as far as we know, but that's not his focus now."

"And his new focus?" Troy said.

"Technology trading on the dark web. He builds sites where people with tech to sell and people who want to buy it can meet up and make untraceable cryptocurrency transactions. He calls the system the Bazaar, like the old Middle Eastern markets. Delivery details aren't his problem, although there are rumors that some of the shipments pass through this warehouse building. He's certainly got the room for it."

"What kind of tech needs to be traded in the dark?" Troy said. He got it, in one sense, but he also didn't get it.

"You name it," Alex said. "Anything and everything on the cutting edge, that has disturbing moral and ethical ramifications. Gene-editing technology that can be used for illegal cloning operations. Sophisticated drug lab tech that can churn out designer street drugs, while staying one step ahead of the narcotics laws. Diseases. Dried anthrax spores, for example, the kind you could mail to your favorite congressman. Also, mini spy drones, and maybe miniaturized attack drones."

"Russians," Troy said. "I don't believe it. I doubt Russians would risk a drone attack on American soil."

"I don't think that's what Stu is getting at," Alex said. "He thinks Constantine has information, or maybe he'd facilitate a deal."

Troy raised an eyebrow at how easily this guy with the fake name from some other country called Colonel Persons "Stu."

"Stu?"

"That's his name, isn't it?"

"What were you?" Troy said. "Translator? Afghanistan?"

Alex turned slowly to look at Troy. "Do you need to know that?"

"It's nice to know who I'm working with."

"I'm from Kansas," Alex said. "We all wear funny hats out there."

"Well, I guess we better do this," Troy said.

He looked out at their surroundings. Quiet side street of warehouses. Sunday morning, nothing much going on. The bustle of Metropolitan Avenue was a block away. The roar of the Brooklyn-Queens Expressway was a few blocks behind them. They were parked in front of a low-slung, windowless Chinese food product warehouse. It looked like no one had been inside in years.

He could do it. He could do this in broad daylight.

"I'm 50 meters behind you," Alex said. "If you manage to get past those guys and get inside, and Stu says you will, hold the door open an extra five seconds. Then I'll come in. We take the freight elevator to the sixth floor. That's where he lives. Intel suggests the elevator opens directly into his apartment. I have no idea if that's true. I'm going to assume there will be more guards up there."

"You let me worry about the guards," Troy said.

Alex smiled. "That's why you're here."

Troy looked at him. "You keep any kind of knife on you?" He didn't want to go through the trouble of taking his own knife out, then having to put it back again.

Alex shrugged. "Box cutter. Why?"

"You mind if I borrow it a minute? I'll give it right back."

Alex gestured with his head. "It's in the glove box."

Troy opened the door of the glove box. The box cutter was there among some paperwork, a small flashlight, a tire pressure gauge, a few other things. The cutter was bright orange. Troy took it and pushed the lever to expose the razor blade.

"Watch out," Alex said. "It's sharp."

Troy opened his own left hand and ran the blade slowly across the palm. He winced, just a touch. It hurt, like a very bad paper cut. A red line appeared on his flesh, like a smile. The blood welled up, then began to spill out across his hand.

Alex also winced, more than just a touch.

"What did you do that for?"

Troy shrugged. "I don't know. Keeps me sharp, I guess."

He closed the box cutter and tossed it back into the glove compartment.

"See you."

He opened the door and stepped out of the car. It was chilly on this street, in the shadow of the warehouses. He shut the door and walked back toward the loading dock. He didn't look directly at it, not yet. He walked with his hands in his jacket pockets. The Glock was in a shoulder holster under his jacket. In a fight, he would never reach it in time, and so had no intention of using it for this.

As he walked, he slipped the brass knuckles onto his right hand. They fit fine, nice and snug, almost as if they were custom built to...

"...fit my hand," he said out loud.

He grunted, smiled, and shook his head. He looked up. The dock was just ahead. Four concrete steps built into the side led up to it. The guards were coming into better relief now. They were both smoking cigarettes. They were hard looking men. They had the dead eyes that Troy had seen on so many just like them, in so many places.

Troy trotted up the steps. Suddenly, he was standing right with them. They both stared at him. Each of them was two or three inches taller than him, and broader. They were big men; he would give them credit for that.

"Private building," the one in blue said. His tone was flat. There could be no discussion about it. A white plastic digital card hung from his neck on a thin piece of rope, or maybe a thick piece of twine. Troy glanced at the door. It had a digital lock mounted on its side. There was a card reader there. Not the kind that you swipe - the kind you just hold the card up to.

Okay.

"I know," Troy said. "It's private. I was just wondering if you guys could help me out a second."

He held out his bloody left hand. "My hand is bleeding. I cut it a minute ago." Every word he'd said to these guys was true.

The man in the blue tracksuit looked at Troy's hand. He uttered a short bark of laughter as he inspected it. "Yes. You did."

Troy stepped forward and punched him in the face with the sharp brass knuckles. The guy's head snapped backwards, instantly bloody. Troy took another step into him and punched him again. The guy sank to the ground, but Troy was already past him.

The second guy, Black Tracksuit, was reaching under his jacket.

Dumb. He needed his hands free.

Troy put his bloody hand to the guy's face. Then he punched him with the knucks in the side of the head. Once, twice, three times in fast succession.

The guy was still on his feet, but not in any real way. Troy banged his head off the corrugated metal of the giant door, then dropped him to the loading dock.

He glanced back at Blue Tracksuit. The guy was still moving. He was reaching inside his jacket, too.

Troy bent down and clocked him in the side of the head. The sharp knucks sliced across his cheek, ripping the flesh there. The guy's head spun around, and he went all the way down this time.

Troy ripped the plastic card from around the guy's neck.

"Thanks. I'm gonna need this."

He swiped the card by the digital lock. The light on the box went from red to green, and he heard the click as the door unlocked. He pulled the door open, revealing a long, wide, concrete hallway.

Alex came trotting up the stairs.

"Give me a hand with these guys, will you? We can't leave them here."

Alex bent to help move the guards inside. "Who are you?" he said.

"Who are you?" Troy said.

"I'm Alex."

Troy nodded. "Stevens, Tom. NYPD."

Together, they dragged the two heavy Russians into the hallway, and dumped them by the door. Troy looked down the hall. It was dark. There were a couple of sets of heavy double doors along the right side. The walls were cinderblock. The flooring was cement. There was nothing even slightly friendly about the place.

A black half-orb hung from the ceiling about halfway down the hall. Security cameras, for sure. They'd better make this quick. He looked back at the Russians.

Alex was squatting next to them. He was wearing white gloves.

"Freight elevator is down the hall on the left," he said.

As Troy watched, Alex took out a tiny syringe and popped it into Black Tracksuit's thick, tattooed neck. Then he did the same to Blue Tracksuit. He tossed the syringes and the wrappers on the floor.

"What's that?" Troy said.

"It'll help them sleep, keep them under for a few hours. No sense having them wake up and creep up the stairs behind us."

"Get their guns and let's go," Troy said.

Troy watched Alex take the guns from inside the track jackets. Couple of small pistols; Troy guessed Makarovs.

They moved up the hall. No one was around. That overhead security camera gave Troy a bad feeling. He swiped his card at the box mounted on the wall next to the elevator. The door slid open. They got on. The elevator was very wide. The flooring was a thick metal grate. If you peered through it, you could probably see to the bottom.

There were no buttons inside the elevator. Just another card reader. Troy swiped the card at it. The door slowly slid shut again. It closed with a heavy CLANG. The elevator lurched into motion.

Troy took the Glock out.

"The guy lives here?" he said.

Alex nodded. "That's what the intel says."

"Strange place to live, isn't it?"

Alex shrugged. "Brighton Beach is too dangerous for him. Rumor has it the Russian mob wants to shake him down, offer him protection. Supposedly he doesn't want silent partners, so he hides out here. Maybe he's just too young to understand. They're going to get to him sooner or later."

"I'm a little surprised they haven't already," Troy said.

Alex nodded. "Me too."

They were slowly ascending through the building. There was a small rectangular window in the door, reinforced with steel mesh. As they passed each floor, a large black number would appear on the security door across from the elevator. The numbers were clearly visible through the window. 4… 5…

"If I were you, I'd stand over there for a minute," Troy said. He indicated the corner of the elevator away from where the door would open.

Alex moved over.

Troy watched the door. It was moving slowly, slowly. His mind was blank. He took a deep breath. His heart skipped a beat. Those were the only accommodations his nervous system made to the situation. He didn't try to imagine who or what he would encounter behind the door.

He didn't worry that they were already waiting for him. He didn't worry that someone might shoot him. He didn't worry at all.

He had always been like this. Whatever happened, he would simply respond to it.

Inside the window, the number 6 appeared.

"Here we go. Hold on to your biscuits."

The elevator car lurched again, this time to a stop. The door began sliding to Troy's right. He stepped with it, using it as a shield. He spotted two guys sitting in easy chairs, like they were in a living room. They were looking at the door. One was a tracksuit guy, this one red. The other, smaller and thinner, wore a light sweater and jeans.

Troy stepped into the room, his gun held in a two-handed shooter's grip.

"Nobody move."

The guys had drinks in their hands. Clear fluid in small glasses, with ice. There was a blue-tinted bottle of Grey Goose vodka on the table between them. Next to the bottle was an Uzi submachine gun.

The two men barely reacted. They simply stared at Troy. Red Tracksuit was a literal clone of the men downstairs. The other had a shock of white hair, completely white, as if it he had dyed it that color. He wore a gold, loose fitting watch on his right wrist. He took a sip of his vodka.

"My friend. Go back down. You will die here."

"Police," Troy said. He held up the Tom Stevens badge.

The man shrugged. "Yes. Of course."

"You gonna kill a cop?"

Now the man just stared. From the looks of him alone, it would be impossible to guess his age. His skin was youthful, but there was experience in his eyes.

Troy scanned the room. It was nothing like the exterior of the building, nor the interior hallways, nor the freight elevator, would suggest. It was opulent, with rich, deep blue wall-to-wall carpet. The ceiling soared two stories above their heads, and a bank of tall windows gave a staggering view of the Williamsburg Bridge, the East River, and the Manhattan skyline in the distance. It must be quite a view at night, or at sunset.

On the walls were colorful abstract art pieces.

To Troy's right, there was a chef's kitchen, with a large central island, gleaming countertops, a restaurant-style oven with multiple…

There was a man over there with a gun. He moved closer, pointing it at Troy, not quite ready to take his shot.

Troy turned to him. "Police, I said!"

Now he and the guy were pointing guns at each other.

"Drop the gun!" the man screamed.

"Police! Drop your gun!"

Suddenly, Red Tracksuit was behind him. He grabbed Troy in a chokehold. The guy was strong, and his grip was tight. His hot booze breath was on Troy's neck.

"Drop gun, policeman."

BAM! Troy used his own head as a battering ram, slamming the back of it into the guy's face. BAM! He did it again. And:

BAM! Again.

He slipped out of the man's grasp and slid in behind him. He put the gun in his bloody left hand and smashed the back of the man's head with his right.

He was mindful that there was an Uzi behind him somewhere. If the guy with white hair grabbed that Uzi…

"Alex! What are you doing?"

BANG! BANG! BANG!

The guy in the kitchen fired his gun. The shots were loud, echoing around the giant apartment.

The bullets hit Red Tracksuit high in the chest. The guy jittered in Troy's grasp.

BANG!

Troy fired, the gun bucking in his hand.

Across the way, the other guy's head snapped back. A mist of blood sprayed, and the man fell to the kitchen tiles. Troy let go of Red Tracksuit and he oozed to the carpet, still alive for the moment, but on his way out.

Troy turned. The man with white hair was up and moving. There was an opening to a hallway, and the man darted down it. The Uzi was still on the table. Wherever that guy was going, the Uzi didn't interest him.

"Alex!"

Alex peered out from the elevator.

"He has a panic room! There's an emergency exit to the outside! If he gets in there…"

Troy ran for the hallway. The guy was ahead, but not that much. There was a steel door at the far end. He reached it and opened a lid, exposing a keypad. He punched some numbers in.

Troy was running top speed.

The steel door slid open. The man stepped inside. He pounded a button of some kind.

Troy sprinted.

The door was closing again.

Troy ran for it.

He crashed into the door and slid between it and the wall. For an instant, he thought he would be crushed. But the door had a rubber buffer along its edge, and it must also have a sensor. It pushed against Troy for a long second, then opened up again.

Troy walked into the panic room. It was conical in shape. It was appointed much like a living room, with two easy chairs and a table in between. There was what looked like a small refrigerator. There was a sink. There were some drawers. There was even a small metal toilet. There was also a steel door leading to somewhere.

The man stood across from Troy. There was no sense going for the exit.

"Two men just died because of you," Troy said.

The man shook his head. "No. If you hadn't come, they would still be alive."

Troy indicated the living room with his head.

"Come with me, Vladimir."

"Constantine is my name."

Troy grabbed the man by his shock of white hair, then kicked his legs out from under him. The man's legs and torso fell to the floor, but Troy still had his hair.

"Come with me anyway," he said.

He dragged the man by his hair, out of the panic room, and back down the hall.

* * *

"We got two guys knocked out in the hallway downstairs," Troy said. He held the tiny flip phone that Colonel Persons had given him to his ear. "And so far, we got two dead guys up here in the apartment."

He stared at the last guy. This was Constantine. Alex had zip-tied his hands behind his back. Then he had taken a dishtowel from a drawer in the kitchen, stuffed it in the guy's mouth, and taped it in place with some dark gray duct tape he'd either found somewhere, or brought along with him for the occasion.

Alex was okay. He wasn't here for the fighting, but he had his uses.

The effect on Constantine was profound. He was sitting in the same chair he was in before, but this time his face was bright red. His eyes bulged enormously. He wasn't even looking at the corpses on the floor. In fact, he tended to look away from them. He was having a hard day.

"We got a third guy up here, the subject, who's trying to decide if he's going to live or die. Right now, it doesn't look good for him."

There was silence over the line. The pause was a little irritating. Troy understood. He did. The man was digesting the news. But say something. Anything.

A thought occurred to him. "How's the encryption on this thing?"

"It's perfect," Persons said. "Nothing to think about. Just give the phone to Alex when we're done. He'll get rid of it."

Troy nodded. "Okay. And what about all these guys?"

"Not your problem," Persons said. "It'll all be taken care of after you leave there."

"The guys downstairs?"

"They'll sit for a bit with friends of ours. They'll come to understand that nothing happened worth remembering. Then they'll turn up in their home countries at some point in the future. Russia. Ukraine. Wherever."

"Like magic," Troy said. He eyed the man with the duct tape over his mouth. "Now you see me, now you don't."

"Peek-a-boo," Persons said.

"And what about this last guy?" Troy said.

"Find out what he knows."

Troy nodded. "Roger that."

He hung up. He handed the phone to Alex, who was standing a few feet from Constantine. Alex took the phone and slipped it into his jacket.

"What did he say?"

Troy shrugged. He spoke more than loud enough for his words to penetrate Constantine's fevered mind. "He said don't worry about the dead guys. The cleaning crew will stop by later. And he said give this guy one chance to get himself off the hook. If he doesn't take that chance....," Troy shrugged again. "You know."

He sat down just across from Constantine, then pulled his chair closer, so he could reach out and touch the guy.

"Did you hear me, Vladimir? You have one chance here. Just one."

Constantine nodded. He heard.

"Vladimir, I want to tell you something. This is my city. I grew up here. There are a lot of very good people here. I take it personally when someone attacks my city, and my people. It makes me angry. What makes me even more angry is when someone knows something about how the attack took place, or why it happened, or who did it, but refuses to share that information. Now, I'm not suggesting that you had something to do with the attack. I am suggesting that you know something about it and are withholding what you know."

Troy paused and took a deep breath.

"Can you see how angry that might make me?"

Constantine nodded. The tears were still streaming down his face. But there might be defiance in his eyes. Troy had seen that look before. Constantine still wanted to resist. He was trying to protect something here. Maybe he knew who carried out the attack. Or maybe he was just protecting his business. Maybe he was shielding his contacts. Maybe he had a boss, or a silent partner, too dangerous to talk about.

"It's why your friends are dead on the floor right now."

Troy got up and went behind Constantine. He put both his hands on Constantine's head. Constantine released a low moan from his throat, like a wounded animal. Gently but firmly, Troy turned Constantine's head so he could see the bodies on the floor, one laying on the living room rug, the blood soaking into the carpet, the other splayed out in the kitchen with a halo of blood around his head.

"Dead guys," Troy said. Personally, he felt nothing about them. They had chosen to be gunmen for this clown. They had probably thought it was an easy gig. They had also chosen to fight instead of surrender when Troy showed up. That was a mistake… their mistake. Apparently, they had also been drinking on the job. And with their boss. The mistakes piled up, mistake upon mistake. And now here they were.

"You see them?"

Constantine nodded.

"Good. I want you to see them. I want you to get a nice look at them. You're more of a businessman than a gangster, I take it. So it's possible you've never seen anything quite like this before, isn't it?"

Constantine squeezed his eyes shut. His whole body shook.

Troy nodded. "Good."

He went back around, sat down, and faced Constantine again.

"Open your eyes. I'm only going to say that once."

Constantine opened his eyes. They were red and rimmed with tears. If the eyes had been hard before, they were not now. He was a kid who was good at the internet. He had gotten himself in very deep, very quickly, because he thought playing with dangerous people was fun.

Maybe he thought he could be dangerous, if he stayed with it long enough.

And maybe he could. In a sense, creating a marketplace for people to trade weapons and drugs and viruses was a very dangerous thing to be doing.

"This is your only chance, Vladimir. My friend is going to take off that tape in a minute, and the first words out of your mouth are going to be everything you know about the drone strike at Hudson Yards yesterday. Everything. If you hold back anything, if I suspect that you're holding back anything, I'm just going to kill you."

Troy shrugged.

"Then later, when the cleaners come to get those two guys over there, they'll take you, too. Your mother will never even know what happened to you."

Troy let another pause play out, while Constantine absorbed the idea of his corpse simply disappearing, no one knew where.

"This is why they hire people like me. You understand that, right?"

Constantine nodded.

"Okay," Troy said. "Ready to be honest? Ready for full disclosure?"

Constantine nodded again.

"Give me a reason to let you live."

Troy glanced at Alex. He gestured with his head. Constantine seemed ready now. If the tape came off, and he started to blather a bunch of lies, about how he didn't know anything, about how Troy had it all wrong…

Well, then they'd have to start all over again, wouldn't they?

This might turn out to be a long day.

Alex stepped up and pulled the tape off Constantine's face. He did it quickly, with no gentleness or concern or hesitation whatsoever. He just ripped it off. That was the best way to do it, anyway. Constantine winced.

"Spit out the towel," Alex said.

Constantine pushed the dish towel out of his mouth with his tongue. It fell onto his lap. It was wet with his saliva, and a bit of his blood. Troy stared at it. It was kind of disgusting, actually. Constantine barely seemed to notice.

"First and only chance," Troy said.

Constantine nodded. He seemed to prepare himself for the effort. He opened his mouth as if to speak.

Troy raised a large index finger. "One. Chance."

"Drones," Constantine said. "Drones like that one, with the nested mini-drone swarms. Governments may have them, I don't know. China. Russia."

Troy felt genuine anger rising. He took a deep breath. "Vladimir..."

"Please," Constantine said. "Please let me speak. On the black market, they are available. They are manufactured in Western Europe, in the Netherlands. It is a very high-tech country, among the best. I have traced the cryptocurrency transactions. I have tried to trace the IP addresses of certain communications. I like to know who is using the platform, or at least, where. The location may be the famous Van Nelle Factory building in Rotterdam. It seems right. There are many start-ups in that building. The headquarters may be there. A small company... they make..."

He trailed off, as if he was going to end it on that note.

"They make aerospace robotics, maybe."

"What's the name?" Troy said.

Constantine stared at him.

Troy shook his head. "Don't tell me you don't know. You didn't trace these people to a location without finding out a name. You're not protecting anything. Your days of running a computerized weapons bazaar are over, Vlad. Your days of breathing oxygen might also be over."

"SymAero. A very small company. Maybe the Dutch police know them already. Maybe..."

Constantine shook his head and let it hang down. The tears were streaming again.

"You let these be sold on your website?" Troy said.

"They're supposed to be spy drones," Constantine said. "Not murder drones. No dynamite charges were advertised. They must have been added afterwards by the purchaser."

"Or negotiated offline as part of the transaction," Alex said. "Once you open Pandora's box, you don't get to control what comes out."

"Who bought them?" Troy said.

"I don't know."

"Vladimir..."

"I mean it. I don't know. Some people are more sophisticated, impossible to trace. The buyers are a mystery to me."

Troy took a deep breath. He made it loud.

Constantine said something, just barely louder than a whisper. His head was still down. Troy didn't hear it.

"What was that?"

"Please don't kill me," Constantine said.

CHAPTER FIVE

1:45 pm Eastern Daylight Time
New York City Police Department Counterterrorism Bureau
One Police Plaza
Lower Manhattan, New York City

"That was easy."

Troy had returned to the ridiculous back office of Colonel Persons, and he was sitting across from the man himself again. Persons had been talking to someone on yet another flip phone about what to do with Constantine. Now he seemed to be on hold. He raised a hand to Troy. STOP. Talking.

Troy shrugged. He was sipping from a can of Rock Star Zero energy drink. Rock Star was his go-to beverage. He liked the slim cans for some reason. They were like little missiles. He liked the little rush he got from them, and then the extended energy they seemed to give him. He went for the Zero sugar version because the full sugar version was loaded with carbohydrates. He wanted all the energy, without the empty carbs. A man had to stay fit. And he drank a lot of these things.

The Rock Star was basically to get him home. He was still tired from last night. He was tired from this morning's activities. He had been staying at his mom's house in the Bronx since he got back to town, and he was anticipating heading back up there as soon as this little meeting with Persons was over. He figured he'd be home in time to catch the 4 pm football game on TV.

"How was your day?" his mom would probably say when he came in.

"Good," he imagined saying back to her. "It was definitely a full day. I got hired, then I went out to Brooklyn and killed a couple guys. Made another guy tell me what he knew about yesterday's drone attack - the sight of violent death tends to get people talking. Now I'm going to enjoy some of your delicious tater tot and beef casserole, crack open a beer, and watch the Jets get murdered by the Chiefs."

Persons ended his call and placed the outdated phone on the desk.

"Good job today, Stark. Not that I expected anything different from you."

"The bodies?" Troy said.

Persons shrugged. "You know."

"And the rest?"

"They'll go home eventually. Constantine will be looking for a new line of work. We're handing his little dark web bazaar empire over to some friends of ours. It's a good way to keep tabs on people. And he's already expressed a desire to help."

To Troy, "some friends of ours" sounded like the CIA. But that was none of his business. "So we're done today?" he said.

Persons watched Troy. Troy couldn't read his good eye. "There's the little matter of the information you guys acquired."

Troy nodded. "Right. The Netherlands. Amsterdam. German guy, maybe. I don't remember the specific details, but Alex said he recorded it."

Persons nodded. "He did. And we believe it's a solid lead."

"Good." To Troy, this seemed like some strange outfit. So far, it looked like it was Troy himself, the infamous Colonel Missing Persons, some kind of Afghan or Sikh who called himself Alex, and whoever these mysterious "we" people were. But Troy liked it, he had to admit. Alex steered clear of the actual fighting, but otherwise he was a consummate pro out there today. He knew his role and didn't get rattled the least bit. Meanwhile, Persons here was an old-school paratrooper, a combat vet going back to the Central American dirty wars of the 1980s. Troy had the sense you could clobber Persons with a Louisville Slugger, and his facial expression wouldn't change at all.

"I'm glad we could help."

Persons nodded. "Now it becomes a matter for the European Union, the internal security apparatus in the Netherlands, and Interpol."

"Well...," Troy said. "A win is a win. I guess we hand it over, and hope they..."

Now Persons shook his head. "We can't let it go that easily. There's too many cooks over there. Too many chiefs and not enough Indians, if you understand me."

Troy nearly smiled. "I don't think you're allowed to say that anymore."

"We got attacked yesterday, not the Europeans. Not the Dutch. There are so many entities at play, all of them sharing responsibilities, all of them trying not to step on each other's toes. Time is of the essence here, Stark. Another attack is probably coming. You don't like that, and I don't like it. I hate it, in fact. And we need someone over there who doesn't mind stepping on toes."

A long silence drew out between them. Troy was beginning to wonder if he was going to catch that football game after all.

"If something is everyone's responsibility, whose responsibility is it?"

Troy sighed. "No one's."

"That's right," Persons said.

"So we're going to make it our responsibility," Troy said.

"Right again."

"Who are we, Colonel? Can you at least tell me that much?"

Persons shook his head. "We don't have a name. We're a black budget line item. Funds come from the Pentagon for miscellaneous counterterrorism efforts carried out by the NYPD. It's not part of the joint task force. It's not part of the NYPD proper. We're not policemen. We're nobody. Hundreds of millions of dollars, possibly billions, go missing from the Pentagon budget every year, Stark. We're so small, we could be a rounding error. But I would like us to have an impact out of proportion to our size. Does that make sense to you?"

Troy nodded. "Yes, sir. It does."

"Stop with the sir crap. It doesn't fit in this environment. You've worked in clandestine units before."

It wasn't a question, so Troy didn't answer.

"Three days, Stark. Tops. Hit the ground running. Go talk to these SymAero people and see what they know. Find out if they're working for someone else, and then find out who. Maybe they're a front for a mafia of some kind. Find out who they sold the drones to. But if they were involved... make an example of them. Not for public consumption, but for the others like them to see. Interpol will help you, but only to a point. Accept help that doesn't hinder your activities, if you follow me. You do what you need to do. They won't always understand that."

"So I'm supposed to do this alone?" Troy said.

Persons shook his head. "Alex will be nearby. He just won't announce his presence, for obvious reasons. You men seemed to gel pretty well today. He's a resourceful guy. He'll see to it that you have whatever you need."

There was another pause.

"Are you in?"

Troy nodded. "I'm in, but I need to run up to the Bronx to get some stuff."

"Won't be necessary," Persons said. "There's a car waiting downstairs. It'll take you to an airstrip out on Long Island. The plane will have everything you need on board. Clothes, shavers, soap, weapons, food, drink. We know everything about you, Stark. We know your shoe size and your jacket size. We know your inseam."

Persons gestured at the Rock Star in Troy's hand.

"We know you drink those things. We know what weapons you prefer. We know your fighting style. You're government issue, Stark. We've been watching you all along."

"And?" Troy said.

Persons smiled. Troy didn't think he'd ever seen that before. A smile from Missing Persons? "We're impressed. You probably don't know this, but you're one of the highest rated soldiers in both water survival, and especially isolation survival, that this country has produced in the past two decades. You're an exceptional swimmer, and top 5% marksman. The reason they didn't develop you as a sniper was you were too good at other things. A sniper is a sniper, and valuable as far as that goes. But true resilience, true leadership skills, true operational and strategic..."

"And yet they're drumming me out."

Persons raised his hands. "You were insubordinate in a combat zone. You know that. You go in country and countermand direct orders... that's how the machine breaks down."

Troy didn't bother with the fiction that Persons wouldn't have access to his classified records, or the history of classified missions. "What would you have done, in my place?"

"I hope," Persons said, "that I would have done the same as you. But I don't know that for a fact. In any case, people, understand what you were facing, more people than you might think."

"Okay," Troy said. "In the meantime, I guess I'll..."

Persons finished the thought for him. "Go to Europe."

Troy took the stairwell to the ground floor. He called his mother as he walked down the steps.

The realization came to him that she was the only person on Earth for him to contact. She was the only person who worried. He and his brothers loved each other; that much was true. But they knew the deal and didn't worry about him.

Only his mother. He had no wife, no kids, no very close friends. His friendships had faded over the years. What that said about him, he wasn't quite sure. At one time, he thought that it meant he was married to his duty. But what duty? The Navy was going to drum him out, in all likelihood. He wasn't wanted by them anymore.

Persons wanted him, but for what? To use his skills? And his willingness to…

Color outside the lines.

That's the way Persons had put it this morning.

His mother answered after a few rings.

"Hello?"

"Mom. It's Troy."

"Well, hello Troy. How is your day going?" She sounded cheerful.

"I got hired," he said.

"Well, thank God for that. I said a prayer to Saint Jude for you."

Saint Jude. The Catholic saint of desperate cases and lost causes. Troy smiled. Which one of these was he: a desperate case or a lost cause?

"Thank you. The thing is, I need to go out of town for a few days."

"Are you coming back here first, to pack up some things?"

"No. No, I'm not. I just gotta go. It's a last-minute thing. They're putting me on a plane this afternoon, maybe early tonight. They're going to send ahead whatever I need. Some clothes. Toiletries. I don't really need a lot."

"Is it…," his mom said. Then she stopped.

"Is it what?"

"Is it related to the attack yesterday?"

Troy made a grunt, as if that was silliest thing he'd heard in a while. "Oh, no, Ma. I just got hired today. I'm low man on the totem pole around here. We didn't even talk about that."

His mind raced out ahead of him, concocting a story on the fly. It came to him effortlessly and poured like a sweet fluid from his mouth. It was a story about an almost impossibly benign mission, for a guy who was on his first day at the new job. A training wheels mission.

"There's a couple of guys down in Tennessee. Backwoods militia types. Hillbillies… you know. They're like middle-aged, overweight diabetics. One of them can barely see. But they like to play with guns, pretend they're Daniel Boone. I don't know. They don't like stem cell research, I guess, and they've been making what you might call terroristic threats against the owners of a small biochemical, life sciences, whatever you want to call it, engineering company out in Queens."

"Is it dangerous?" she said.

"I doubt it. Nobody really thinks they're going to come up here and do what they're saying. They probably couldn't find their way to New York if they tried. But one of these guys runs an illegal whiskey distillery. ATF is going to take it down. While the guy is in custody, we'll have a chance to question him, and see how serious he is about the threats he's been making. He has no idea that we're coming. And I'll probably just be an observer anyway."

Troy paused. Troy felt like he needed to finish strong. "It's probably a nothing burger," he said.

There was silence over the line.

"You know," his mother said. "Your brother Donnie made Inspector recently."

"Yeah. I know."

Donnie had made Inspector about ten months ago, but okay. Time was malleable to their mother, depending on what kind of axe she was planning to grind. Reality itself could be bent to her will.

"He's involved in some top level… uh… you know."

Troy nodded. "I imagine he is."

"He could help you, maybe."

"He offered," Troy said. "I turned him down. I'll make my own way."

"See? But that was nice of him. So, have you ever sent him anything? To congratulate him? It's a big deal. It was a big promotion. The kids are in private school. He's making a lot of money now."

"Well, if he's making a lot of money, maybe he should send me something. I don't know, maybe a houseplant. Or one of those turtles that lives a long time. Three hundred years. It's a nice gift."

"Troy… I'm being serious."

Troy shook his head. He knew she was. That was the hardest part. This was his mom. Sometimes he wasn't sure whether to laugh or cry.

He had reached the ground floor and was about to open the stairwell door to the lobby. He wanted to end the conversation before he did.

"Mom, look. I gotta run. They're waving me over. I gotta… I don't know, fill out some paperwork. Anyway, let Donnie know I took the job, if you don't mind. That'll make him happy. And listen, don't worry, okay?"

"I won't worry. If it's just Tennessee, and no one is shooting at you, then there's nothing to worry about, right?"

"That's exactly right."

"Do a good job. I love you, Troy. You're my baby."

"I love you too," he said.

CHAPTER SIX

4:35 pm Eastern Daylight Time
A small jet airplane
The skies over the Atlantic Ocean

"It's been a long day."

He almost didn't realize he had spoken.

The six-seat Lear jet screamed north and east across the late afternoon sky. The jet was dark blue with no markings on it. Behind it, the sun began to set. Troy stared out his window to the east. It was already dark ahead of them - it was fall, and the days were getting shorter. Far below, the ocean was vast, endless, and deep green.

He'd been on the plane for about an hour. He was all alone in the passenger cabin. There were two pilots up in the cockpit, but he hadn't spoken to them. The car had simply pulled up to the plane at the airfield somewhere in eastern Long Island, the pilots had climbed aboard, and so had Troy. Then the car had driven away. He had barely spoken to the driver, either.

And it hadn't been a long day, not by his standards. It just seemed long because he'd been out drinking and fighting last night and hadn't really slept. Then he'd been fighting this morning. And now he was leaving on a moment's notice.

He glanced around the tiny plane. Persons hadn't lied. The back of the plane had a horizontal bar going across, like the bar in a closet. Draped on hangers were all sorts of clothing items Troy might need, from jeans and t-shirts, to flannel shirts, to three-piece suits and even a tuxedo. They were all his size. There were shoes, boots, and sneakers. There were a couple of suitcases back there with socks, underwear, shavers, cologne.

There were all kinds of potato chips, coffee drinks, and Rock Stars. Beef jerky. Salami. Those little round cheeses that you grabbed the tiny red string and unzipped, and which didn't really need refrigeration.

Persons knew the kind of food he ate, all right.

Troy still had the Glock, the tiny Beretta, the knife, and the brass knuckles. He didn't know how he was going to enter Europe with all this stuff, but he didn't worry about it, either. He supposed Persons had arranged for that. Or Alex would turn up with a way to do it.

In a side pocket of one of the suitcases, there were four passports. Three were American, one was Irish. Only one of them identified him as Troy Stark.

Troy sat back and let the day wash over him. He glanced out the window again. Up ahead, it was already dark. This was a fast plane, and they were moving into darkness.

These were the times that he hated. Alone, no one to talk to, and nothing to do. No way to distract himself. There were small TVs embedded in each of the seat backs, and there was probably some way to turn them on and watch a movie, but he was never much for entertainment. He hated TV, actually.

Still, he would almost prefer to watch TV than to stew in his own juices and relive the situation that brought him to this. It was a pastime of his, something he couldn't seem to stop himself from doing.

Northern Syria, last spring. Simple enough, or so it seemed.

He was in command of a unit from Joint Special Operations Command, 24 men including himself, basically two 12-man squads. Salted through these squads were guys who could reasonably be considered Metal Shop, the worst of the worst, or the best of the best, depending on how you looked at it. Stone killers. They had dropped in to connect with the Kurdish People's Protection Units, what the Kurds called the YPG.

There was a large group of ISIS that was moving west through a region that some people now referred to as "Rojava." The Kurds wanted their own independent country, and Troy couldn't blame them. Rojava was the start of it. Syria had collapsed, and that gave the Kurds the chance to carve out a little piece for themselves.

The place was scrub desert and low mountains, still cold from the winter. He'd fought alongside Kurds before, and they were good, tough people. The young women went into combat in their own units, called the Women's Protection Units. The Kurds were the primary reason that ISIS was in retreat across northern Syria.

The ISIS force was running away from a massacre they had carried out against a population of civilians. They were moving fast, trying to get away from evidence of their crimes. They were getting picked apart from the rear by the Kurds.

Then Troy and his men landed. The Kurds asked them to move north and then west, parallel to ISIS, without engaging. Okay. There was a group of civilians up there, pinned between ISIS and the border with Turkey.

Troy's small group, along with some of the Kurds, went up to create a buffer against ISIS turning north toward where the civilians were.

It sounded like a plan. Except it didn't go according to plan.

Troy and his combined force dug in outside the village of Manbij, very close to the border with Turkey. That night, they were attacked by squads coming across the border. Stark's crew had ripped them up, thinking they were ISIS. In the light of day, it was clear that the attackers were Turkish military. These jerks were less than a mile away, lining up artillery to fire on Stark's encampment.

Then he got a call on the satellite phone.

"Stark, this is Colonel Roger Manning of JSOC."

"Yes, sir."

"What are you men doing? You were sent on a mission to interdict ISIS forces."

"Yes sir, we were. There were enough Kurdish forces to continue pursuit. We came north to a town called Manbij…"

"We know where you are, Stark."

"Yes, sir."

"What are you doing there?"

"We joined a small force of Kurds up here that had been thinned out in the fighting. They don't have much left. We're protecting a group of maybe three hundred civilians, women and children and old people, who got trapped between ISIS and the border."

"Those are Turkish Kurds, Stark."

"I don't know what kind of Kurds they are, sir. A Kurd is a Kurd to me."

"Incorrect, Stark. A Kurd is not a Kurd. Those are Turkish Kurds you've linked up with. They're none of our affair. You and your men need to pick up stakes and move south. Your assignment is to the south. You engage ISIS, and that's the extent of your engagement."

Troy wasn't quite sure what he was hearing. He couldn't follow it. And he wasn't sure who this O-6 Colonel Manning was. But he did know one thing. He and his men weren't going anywhere.

"Uh… Negative, Colonel. We can't leave here. We were attacked by what appear to be Turkish forces coming from the north. If we go south, we're going to leave a large group of civilians and a very sparse force of YPG…"

"Those aren't YPG, Stark. Those are PKK. Don't you even know who you're with?"

"I'm with Kurds, sir. That's what I know."

The man began to speak slowly, as if he were talking to an imbecile. "Stark. The YPG are the Kurdish Protection Units. Those are the good guys. They're our Kurds."

"I know what they are, sir. We brought some with us, including a few squads of the women's force."

"Stark, listen to me. I don't care who you brought. They pulled a bait and switch on you. The bulk of that force is PKK. Those are Turkish Kurds, and not our Kurds. They're a terrorist organization. The so-called civilians they have with them are terrorist sympathizers. The Turks are trying to eliminate them."

Troy started over again. Colonel Manning couldn't seem to grasp the situation on the ground.

"Uh... sir? There are babies here. Last night, the Turkish military attacked an enclave with women and children inside of it. We beat them back. I think the Kurds lost about 18 fighters, including three women. We could use some reinforcements. I'm anticipating..."

"Stark. Your orders are to leave there. You and your men. Move south."

"We will, sir, but I'm taking these people with me, and to do that I'm going to need more resources."

"Stark! Are you hearing me? You are standing down from that position."

Troy shook his head. "No, sir. I'm not. There are children here. There's no way the Kurds can hold off those Turks. I don't know why they attacked, and I don't really care. Fully a third of the Kurdish forces here are women and girls. And when I say girls, I mean they've got about a dozen female fighters who appear to be younger than 16. There's no way we can just..."

"Stark. The forces there are a problem for Turkey. Turkey is an ally of the United States, in case you've forgotten. We don't fight against Turkey."

Troy was beginning to suspect something about Colonel Manning.

"Sir, are you in touch with those Turkish forces?"

"Yes, I am. They want you out of there."

Troy gazed out at the desert. There was a lot of wreckage out there. The truth was the Turks had run into a buzz saw last night. And Troy's men would be better prepared for the next round. Last night, they hadn't expected an attack from the north.

51

"Can you tell them something for me, sir?"

"What is it, Stark?"

"I have a mixed unit of experienced Navy SEALs and DELTA operators under my command. We have advanced weaponry, and we are loaded down with ammo. We're not going anywhere unless we can safely bring these civilians with us."

"Stark."

"Please listen to me, sir. If the Turks come again tonight, I promise that we are going to send every one of them back to Istanbul in bags. And that's if they can even piece together the bodies."

"Sailor, listen to me very carefully. This is insubordination. If you don't leave there today, now, then you are setting yourself up for a court-martial, a possible prison term, and a dishonorable separation from the service. Is that what you want?"

Troy listened to the words but could barely comprehend their meaning.

"I suppose I'll have to take that chance, sir."

Now, Troy stared out the window again. It was dark outside, and all he saw was his own pale reflection against the darkness. The plane was bucking a bit from turbulence. It was small and moving fast - it felt every bump in the road. The eyes in the reflection seemed sad. If they were truly windows to his soul, then they should be sad.

His military career was over. He was tainted, damaged goods. After what happened, he had no interest in going back. He didn't understand it. He didn't want to understand it. He had joined the military to protect people and save lives.

What had Colonel Manning joined for? To abandon civilians, and leave them to their deaths? Why? Over political considerations?

That wasn't Troy Stark.

"You have to see the big picture," a guy had told him once.

No. No, he didn't.

He would do just fine seeing things on a human scale.

CHAPTER SEVEN

11:50 pm Central European Daylight Time (5:50 pm Eastern Daylight Time)
The Markt of Bruges
Bruges, Belgium

"We must close in ten minutes."

Martin Figler already knew that. He wasn't dumb. He was just drunk.

He was sitting in the outdoor café section of a bar - in English, it was known as the Friends' Bar. The waiter was standing near the door to the inside, basically waiting for Martin to leave. How friendly was that? Not very.

Martin had about half of a 12-ounce glass of beer in front of him. Was it half-full or half-empty? It was very definitely half-empty. It was a Scotch ale, high alcohol content, went straight to your head like a missile. He'd ordered two of these about 15 minutes ago, and now he was down to half of one.

He should have ordered three of them. Now it was too late to order any more. He'd been drinking here for probably four hours, and he was nowhere near as drunk as he wanted to be. And the waiter just wanted to go home. The bartender probably did, too. Martin was the last customer in the place.

Martin waved at the waiter. "Go away. I still have time."

The waiter did as he was told. He went back inside the bar. Probably to call the cops. Martin was a big guy, had played football at Yale, defensive end in fact, and he tended to intimidate people. Especially when he'd been drinking.

"Eh," he said. It was just a sound. Martin wasn't even sure what he meant by it.

He stared out at the lovely medieval market square, lit up for the evening. There were still a few people out and about, but not very many. It was a chilly night and getting late. Europe was supposed to have all this nightlife, wasn't it? In Martin's experience, they rolled up the sidewalks by midnight.

53

So he sat alone, finishing his beer, and about to go home to his tiny flat.

Directly across from him was the central statue, a rendering of two guys who led an obscure Flemish uprising against the French sometime around the year 1300. The history of the United States hadn't even started yet at that point. The best thing about the statue was that the taller of the two guys, Jan Breydel, apparently wasn't at the uprising at all, never mind leading it. The guy was a fraud.

Martin enjoyed history like that.

There was a lot of nice stuff here in Bruges. For one, right here in the Markt, there was the giant Belfry of Bruges, a soaring medieval bell tower and lookout post, which was built in the 1200s. There was a line of colorful medieval buildings, all painted different bright colors; there was the Historium, a neo-Gothic building with its own narrow lookout tower. Then there were all the winding canals from the Middle Ages.

It really was a beautiful city. But if so, why did he hate it here so much? He was here at the College of Europe, studying for his master's in International Relations. The semester was six weeks old, and he was having trouble connecting. Yeah, his French was lousy. "Your French is abysmal," his dad had told him before he left the States. "It's a disgrace. I'm surprised they even let you in."

That was a pretty typical sentiment from dear old Dad. He was just irritated because he thought Martin was looking for an excuse to play student for another year. There was an element of truth to that, of course. Going to a college like Yale, and playing football, was like have two full-time jobs simultaneously. Martin barely had a college experience, as far as he was concerned. And you know what? The College of Europe wasn't cutting the mustard.

So yeah. His French was bad. And okay, his Dutch was pretty much nonexistent. But people here did know how to speak English. They just… They just…

He was having trouble connecting. To guys, girls, anyone. That was it in a nutshell. He was doing okay in school, he was smart (he went to Yale, for the love of God), but his own international relations were sorely lacking right now. Nobody cared that he went to Yale. Nobody cared that he played football. He was beginning to suspect that the students here - and they came from all over the place, not just Belgium - had something against Americans.

"Forget it," he said, and polished off the last of his beer. "Who cares?"

He had already paid the guy, so he didn't bother to say goodnight. He just got up and reeled out of the open-air café. Wow. Those things hit hard. You didn't notice it until you were standing.

He walked across the square toward the central statue. He lived on the other side of the square and several streets down, near the large canal that headed out to the English Channel port. When he was sober, he could just about pronounce the names of the canal and the port. Now? Not a chance.

There was a sound above his head, a sort of high-pitched buzzing. He looked up and caught sight of a small object whizzing by him. It was hardly more than a shadow. Then another one zipped by. He was having trouble focusing on them.

Another zipped by, and now the buzzing was growing louder.

Someone in the square shouted, and a couple began to run. Then another did. And a guy by himself. People were starting to move. A woman screamed. She sounded drunk, certainly, but also afraid.

"Drones," Martin said. "Oh my God. They're drones."

That's why people were running. They were tiny drones, like dragonflies, zipping into the Markt square from all around. There was a swarm of them, coming from different directions.

There must be a hundred of them. But no, there were a lot more than that. They were still coming. The whining grew louder and louder. A black swarm of drones was gathering in the square, about 30 feet off the ground.

Why don't they attack?

There was no one here. Why would they attack? Who would they attack?

Maybe it's not an attack.

That made sense. If the drones were going to attack like they did in New York, then Martin would already be dead. He stared up at them. They had started gathering maybe 15 seconds ago. Now they were a mass above his head, coming together, climbing all over each other in mid-air, congealing into something like a giant ball. They hovered there, the ball growing, stragglers zipping in and attaching themselves to it now.

How does it stay up like that?

Several other people hadn't run. They began to gather near Martin now, as if his size would protect them from whatever was happening here. He glanced to his right and just a few feet away was the surly waiter from the bar. His mad rush to get out of here seemed to have been derailed.

Without warning, the whining went up several notches in volume. It became something like an ear-piercing shriek.

The mass of tiny drones seemed to vibrate. Within the ball, they seemed to be wriggling and writhing, just like real insects.

Suddenly, the thing flew. It made a sound like WHOOOOOOOSSSHHHHHH. It went away so fast, it was hard for Martin to follow it with his eyes.

The crowd released a collective sigh, as if they were watching fireworks. "Aaaaaaaaaaaahhhhhh."

It didn't last long. The mass flew like a missile, directly at the building that housed the Historium. It crashed into the observation tower at high speed. A light flashed, and then a sound rent the night, massive, deafening, a thousand times louder than the previous whining. It was so loud thatMartin clamped his hands to his ears.

The tower blew apart, into what must be a million pieces.

Martin stared as a large chunk of stone masonry flew from where the tower had been. The chunk was on fire, and he could watch its progress against the darkness. It was coming fast. He knew he should run, or duck, or throw himself to the ground, but he seemed frozen in place and rooted to the spot.

He watched the chunk right up until it smashed into his head.

CHAPTER EIGHT

October 17
5:05 am Central European Daylight Time
Interpol Liaison Office - Special Investigations Unit
Europol Headquarters
The Hague, The Netherlands

There was a light brown teddy bear in the back seat with him. It had a purple ribbon tied around its neck.

Troy picked up the bear and held it against his chest with one hand. They were zipping along on mostly empty roads into the city. It was still early, and dark. It looked like the sun wouldn't rise for a while yet.

"I'm tired, man."

The two cops either didn't hear him or didn't understand him. They barely spoke four words to him at the airport. They prattled on quietly in their own language, of which Troy understood nothing. Occasionally a word popped up that he recognized. He caught "water," and "clock," and even "ambulance." Troy seemed to remember learning somewhere that English and German and Dutch were interrelated languages.

Troy was riding with the Dutch National Police. They had been waiting for him on the tarmac when he got off the plane. Two other guys had loaded his luggage and his gear into a van and had driven off with it. Troy didn't know anything about who he was linking up with here but, evidently, they knew he was coming. He had managed to get off the plane and into this car with a couple of guns, a knife and his knucks in a bag, and he had a loop of plastic zip ties in his pocket, but his hosts had everything else.

The car was a modern Volkswagen Beetle, white, with orange and blue diagonal stripes and blue and red flashers up top. There was no barrier between Troy and the cops in the front. They had a bunch of computer screens and other high-tech stuff mounted into the dashboard. There were no weapons in sight. The cops wore black uniforms with bright yellow stripes across the shoulders and chest. They were young guys and seemed content to ignore Troy for the ride in from the airport.

Sure. That was fine.

"What's the bear for?"

The guy in the passenger seat looked back at him. He had close-cropped blonde hair. His cheeks were denuded of stubble. "Yes?"

Troy held up the teddy bear. "The bear. Why do you have it?"

"You're a policeman, aren't you?" the guy said.

Troy shrugged. He no longer knew what he was. If the people here wanted him to be a police officer, he would go with that. But also, the guy could have just answered the question, instead of asking one of his own.

"Sure," Troy said. "I'm a cop. In a sense."

"And you don't carry a teddy bear in your car?"

"Um... I'm more of an investigator, you might say. Interrogator. Don't really drive a police car. I turn up places and people are surprised to see me."

He thought of the incident yesterday with the Russians. It pretty well summed up that little interaction. And it was the only police assignment he had ever gone on.

The guy in the shotgun seat said something to his partner. It ended with a word that sounded like "Ee-meer-eee-kansh." Both cops laughed. Troy took the word to mean "American." He had no idea if that was right or not, so he decided not to judge it.

But he was starting to get annoyed. He was beginning to think this wasn't such a hot idea that Missing Persons had come up with. Troy was wiped out. He'd had trouble sleeping on the plane. Another day was starting, all over again, as if the night had never happened. This was exactly how you got jet lag.

And now these comedians were riding him into town. They obviously could speak English. It would be polite if they spoke English in his presence. But they chose not to do that, for the most part. So they were asking him, without knowing they were doing it, to control his temper. Controlling his temper was not the easiest thing in the world for Troy Stark.

"Guys," he said. "I've had a long night. I'm tired, and my patience is thin. I'm getting a little aggravated. You're not going to like me if I get aggravated."

Blue eyes in the shotgun seat stared back at Troy. His face was blank.

"It's for the children," the driver said. He was looking into the rearview mirror. He had close-cropped blonde hair. His cheeks were chubby. No stubble. These guys could be clones of one another. Is that what they were doing here, in this special high-tech society? Churning out clones?

"The children?"

"Yes. Most of our job is to serve in emergencies. Car crashes. Fires. Things of this nature. Our training is to take care of the most vulnerable first. That's usually a child. A teddy bear helps make them calm. We have three more bears in the boot of the car."

"Guns?" Troy said.

The cop in the shotgun seat shrugged. "We have them, of course. But they're unimportant. I have never discharged my weapon, except at the training range."

The driver cop was still watching Troy in the rearview.

"You?" Troy said.

"I tasered a disturbed man once. He was threatening passersby in the city center with a sword. It was a replica of a traditional Japanese katana sword. It was not well maintained, so it was no longer sharp, but I didn't know that."

They drove on for a moment in silence.

"And you?" the passenger cop said. "Have you shot someone?"

Troy shrugged and shook his head. He sighed. He had shot and killed a man yesterday, in a fight where another man was killed. It was technically his first day on the job. Most cops went their entire careers without shooting anyone. He had no idea how many people he had killed while in the military. During a firefight on an isolated hillside in eastern Afghanistan, he had sprayed the Taliban with an M249 machine gun so much that the gun overheated, jammed, and became too hot to touch.

"Nah. What you hear about Americans is exaggerated. We're not all trigger-happy maniacs. I've never discharged a gun in anger in my life."

"There was an attack in Belgium last night," the driver said. "Did you know that?"

Troy looked into his eyes. "How bad?"

The cop shrugged. "Three dead. Several in hospital. It was a drone attack, but they did it late at night. Similar type of attack, but different in the details."

Troy shook his head. "This is the first I've heard of another attack."

"I'm sure they will tell you all about it," the cop said.

* * *

"It's real pretty, isn't it?" Troy said to himself.

59

The outside of the building had a similar Soviet architectural style to One Police Plaza, as if Joseph Stalin had designed the place himself. It was gray and comprised of three block towers rising from a main building, each tower a different height. The highest tower looked to be about ten stories tall. The lowest tower had the word EUROPOL across its outer wall, in nifty modern lettering.

If the building was called THE TERMINATOR, they could have used the same style of writing. Troy stared up at the word for a moment. EUROPOL. He thought he was meeting with Interpol. That's what Persons seemed to have been saying yesterday. Maybe they were the same thing. Or maybe Troy had heard wrong.

A woman had just opened the glass door to let him in. It was still dark, and probably these were off hours. Troy did notice that there were numerous office lights on in various parts of the building, though.

The woman was small, trim, petite. She was a light-skinned black woman, with braided hair tight to her scalp. Troy towered over her, but that fact didn't seem to interest her. She wore some sort of brown leather jacket and pants ensemble, that must be what passed for stylish around here. She had a badge or pass or some kind of ID clipped to the jacket. It had a photo of her on it. Troy noticed her feet - she was wearing sneakers.

She reached her small hand out and Troy shook it. His hand swallowed hers. He was careful not to squeeze very hard. She didn't smile.

"Agent Stark? I'm Agent Dubois of Interpol. We flew in from Lyon a few hours ago. Time is important, as I'm sure you know."

She spoke English perfectly, with a lilting accent from somewhere else.

She turned and started walking back down the hall. He walked beside her.

They came to the security checkpoint. There was a metal detector to walk through, and a conveyor belt to put his bag on. Most of his stuff had been taken by a porter at the airport and sent on to his hotel.

"Credentials?" one of the sleepy guards said.

Troy gave him his passport, the one with his real name on it, along with his NYPD badge and ID. The guy ran both the passport and the ID through a scanner, and then read a block of text that appeared on his computer screen.

"Weapon?" the other guard said.

Troy took out the Glock, popped out the magazine, and placed both on the table. "There's a small gun in my bag. It's loaded. Also, there's a knife. And some brass knuckles." He figured he should tell them all this before the alarms went off.

"Are you going to a war?"

Troy didn't smile. "If I was, I'd have brought the submachine gun."

On the far side of security, he picked up his bag and they continued on. Inside, the building was a wide-open design, almost like a mall, with catwalks above them running along the outside of office spaces. The visible skeleton of a staircase was ahead of them in the wide hallway, with a glass elevator running up through the center of it. He and his new friend Agent Dubois were walking fast.

"Can you tell me something?" Troy said.

She shrugged. "You're going to be briefed on everything we know in a few moments. But I'll give you the short answer."

"You're from Interpol, right?"

She nodded. "Yes."

"Why does it say Europol on the building?"

She stopped walking abruptly and looked up at him. She seemed to be searching his face for some information that might be found there. Her eyes were dark brown. Her skin was flawless, and a rich bright coffee color.

"You really are an American," she said, then started walking again.

Was everyone here like this? In the United States, people often said, "there are no stupid questions." Sometimes, if they were idiots, they might say, "Ask a stupid question, get a stupid answer."

Apparently if you asked a stupid question here, you didn't get any answer at all. This was especially true when you were American.

They reached the stairs and started up. "Can you tell me something?" she said.

He shrugged. "Sure."

"Why do you require that arsenal you have with you? Do you feel threatened?"

Troy smiled. "You're really... what? French, I guess."

She shook her head.

They moved down a darkened hallway to an office at the end. It had a glass wall and a glass door. There were lights on inside. When they reached the door, Troy noticed small white lettering on it - Interpol Liaison. So... that meant something. She was from Interpol, and this was apparently an Interpol office, inside of a Europol building. He was starting to get it. It might have been easier if she had just taken a moment to explain.

They entered the office. Here was a big guy, very big, at a desk. He had three laptops open in a line across the desk, and two smart phones attached to long wires. He stood as they came in. As he took his feet, he rose to his full height. He was probably six-foot five-inches tall. He was broad across the chest, huge shoulders, his body the V shape that bodybuilders go for. His head was shaved, with just the outline of where the hair would grow if he didn't shave it. He was a guy with male pattern baldness who realized he looked better without any hair at all and went for that look instead.

He wore black jeans painted onto his tree trunk legs, and a tight black t-shirt. It said INTERPOL across the chest in white letters. His ID was clipped to his belt. He grinned as he stuck his big hand out.

They shook. His grip was powerful, and Troy didn't feel the need to shrink from it or go easy on him.

"Troy Stark?" the man said. "I'm Jan Bakker from Interpol. We came in from headquarters in France this morning. I'm from the Netherlands, and in a sense I'm home. So welcome to my country."

Troy nodded. Now they were getting somewhere. If they were going to have to kick some butt today, or intimidate people, this was the right guy for the job.

"Good to meet you, Jan. So you're my partner in this?"

Jan made that big-eyed face of confusion that people made sometimes. Troy got that look a lot. He, Jan, and Agent what's her name were standing in a rough triangle. Jan looked from Troy to the other agent, and back.

"I'm the technology officer. Mari is your partner. Haven't you met?"

Troy looked at the tiny black woman. He guessed you could say she was pretty. Her face was stern. She hadn't cracked anything remotely like a smile so far. Even so, her sternness only went so far. She was decidedly less intimidating than Jan.

"My name is Mariem," she said. "Only my friends call me Mari."

"You have friends?" Troy said.

A door from a back room opened, and another man walked in. He was smaller, middle-aged, with a bushy head of black hair going gray, and a mustache doing the same. He wore dress pants and a rumpled white shirt, with a plain blue tie. His ID was clipped to the pocket of his shirt. A pair of reading glasses were tilted back on top of his head.

"Agent Stark, I'm Miquel Castro-Ruiz. I'm the director of this office. We're the Special Investigations Unit. Thank you for coming."

"Thanks for having me."

The man looked up at Troy. He seemed, for an instant, to be scanning Troy's face for hints of any sarcasm, or wise-assery. Then he nodded.

"Of course. We're always delighted to work with the New York City Police. There are a couple of former NYPD officers who work in the American Liaison office on this floor. Good men, nice guys. I imagine you've heard there was another drone attack late last night, this one in Bruges."

"I heard there was an attack, but I don't know the details." Troy didn't want to get into the fact that the cops in the car had told him the attack took place in Belgium. Maybe Bruges was a place in Belgium. Maybe Belgium was a place in Bruges. Maybe they were code words for each other.

"The details are it was something of a reversal of the New York attack," Castro said. "In this one, the mini-drone swarm gathered, coming from many different directions, convening in the Markt square, which is a popular tourist destination. Rather than use their charges to murder individuals with a shot to the head, they combined themselves to make a bomb, then launched at a famous building there, obliterating the facade, bringing down a lookout tower, and doing extensive damage to much of the interior. Three people in the square were killed, along with a night watchman inside the building. We suspect it was practice, and not a real attack."

Troy nodded. "Because if they wanted to kill a lot of people..."

"That's right. They would have done it in the daytime when the square is packed, and many people would normally be in the lookout tower."

Hmmm. A nighttime attack. As practice. Why practice when you've already carried out a successful, larger attack in New York City?

It was as if Castro had read his mind. "We think both attacks were practice. The big one is still coming."

"We have surveillance video of the drone swarms moving through the streets and along the canals," Jan said. "And coming together in the Markt." He shook his head. "It's unbelievable. It's like a ballet dance. It's almost beautiful, you might say."

Agent Dubois spoke up.

"Miquel, I think Agent Stark and I should go and see about SymAero. After all, that's why he came all this way. He has a lead to follow, and his superiors want him to do that. He can watch videos with Jan later."

Jan smiled sheepishly.

63

Castro nodded his head. "Agreed."

She went on. "Agent Stark is also armed to the teeth, so he should probably relinquish his weapons here."

Castro looked at Troy.

"We're not the police. We're not empowered to make arrests. Our function is data acquisition, analysis, and sharing. We're an informational resource. If you were to discharge your weapon while here, even accidentally...," he shook his head and made a pained face. It was almost a wince.

"It would become an incident, and it would reflect badly on Interpol, on our hosts here at Europol, on the Dutch police, and on the NYPD. I'm sure you understand."

Troy nodded. "Not completely. But I'm beginning to."

CHAPTER NINE

6:25 am Central European Daylight Time
Van Nelle Factory Building
Rotterdam, The Netherlands

"It's flat as a pancake around here," Troy said.

It was still dark. They were sitting in an unmarked blue sedan. They had driven out here from The Hague, maybe 40 minutes. There was barely a hill or an undulation of the earth the entire way.

Traffic was just beginning to pick up. There was the ambient sound of activity rising around them now. They had stopped for coffee at some all-night joint on the way here, and that was a small blessing. Troy was starting to feel human again.

The building in front of them was long and narrow, maybe eight stories high. It was entirely white, with the words VAN NELLE in white stenciled lettering standing on top of it. A handful of lights were on inside the building. There was a parking lot in the back with a few cars already there, and a black, narrow canal ran along the far edge of the lot.

"It's the Netherlands," Dubois said. She shrugged, as if that explained it.

Troy nodded. "You're very talkative."

She gestured at the building with her chin. "I think it's best to focus on the job."

"And what is the job?" Troy said. "We can't arrest anyone. We have no weapons."

"Do you feel vulnerable without your weapons?" she said.

Now Troy smiled. He shook his head. "Lady, you don't know me very well."

"That's what I thought," she said. "They sent you here from New York because you're some kind of tough guy, yes? They want to track down every lead, no matter how tenuous, and rather than go through normal police protocols, they're hoping you will frighten the subjects, or perhaps beat some information out of them."

"There was a terrorist attack in New York City two days ago," he said.

"Yes, I'm familiar."

"People are concerned."

She nodded. "I share their concern."

Troy looked out the window at the darkness. He sipped his coffee. He had bought two. He had pounded the first one down. This was the second one. It was lukewarm and going cold.

"So what is your plan?" he said.

"We go in and interview the subjects, the three men who are the founders and principals of SymAero."

"That's it? Interview them?"

She nodded. "Of course. We have no evidence of wrongdoing. All we have is hearsay from a Russian criminal living in New York, and we suspect his testimony was given under duress."

Troy took a deep breath. It was a mistake to come here. Or maybe coming here wasn't the mistake. Connecting with the Europeans was the mistake. He and that guy Alex should have just come here themselves. They could have quietly worked these guys over, like they did with the Russians, then took another rung up the ladder.

"Okay," he said. "It's a big building. They're just three guys, so you say. How will we know when they arrive?"

She shrugged. "They're already here. We posted an agent in the parking lot all night. They arrived about an hour ago."

Now she smiled. "Everyone was very skeptical of your information, you know. We did go through the motions and research this company. Everything seemed to check out fine. Computer science and engineering graduates from excellent schools, offering cutting edge aerospace tools to industry. It's a new company, and they did nearly two million euros in sales last year. Nothing to see here. No reason to believe they would risk everything - their business, their reputations, their freedom, possibly their lives - selling drones to dangerous people. But then they panicked. Odd to arrive so early, just hours after a terror attack."

Troy felt his heart skip a beat. "If they're already here, what are we doing?"

She spoke slowly, as if to a child. A thug like Troy probably couldn't understand the nuances of police work. "We are allowing them to incriminate themselves."

Troy pointed at the building. He felt like screaming at her, but he tamped his voice down. "They're in there destroying evidence. Emails. Schematics. Web histories. Entire hard drives. Whatever."

She shook her head. "No, they're not. They're not destroying anything. It's too late for that. They're simply digging a hole."

Troy opened his door. "I don't understand. Let's go."

"You met Jan, yes? The big boy you thought of as your partner? He's had the name SymAero since yesterday evening. He's spent the past 12 hours, when we were in France, on the plane, and here at Europol, hacking their systems. He has broken their encryptions and taken copies of their servers and their cloud storage. All of their information. It's too much to sift through at this moment, especially for one man, but we can put a team of analysts on it. Whatever SymAero is deleting, we already have. Later, we can compare what we have with what they deleted and ask them why they did that."

Troy stopped. He was standing in the parking lot now, leaning back into the car. "Paperwork? He couldn't possibly access their paperwork. They could be shredding…"

She shrugged. Then she smiled.

Bingo! It was the first time. She had a nice smile.

"If you were selling drones on the dark web to terrorists, would you keep paper copies of the billing details in your office?"

Okay. Okay. She had a point. "Listen. Agent Dubois. Can we please go talk to these guys? It makes me nervous to have them in there doing whatever they want. I don't want to lose them. I came a long way."

She nodded. "Of course. But remember, we're not here to make arrests. We have no evidence against them. And we have no arresting powers anyway. We're just here to gather information. Maybe they will choose to share that information voluntarily."

Now Troy nearly smiled but didn't. "Yeah. Maybe they will."

They crossed the lot. There was an entryway nearby and an exterior glass stairway that climbed the outside of the building. To their left, the building arced in a near semicircle. To their right, it extended out in a long straight line.

"The building is nearly a hundred years old," Dubois said. "At one time, it was considered a breakthrough, the very height of modernity. Like your Google or Apple campuses are now."

"Are they mine?" he said.

She shook her head and pulled the heavy door. It opened easily.

"High tech," Troy said. "They don't even lock the door. I'll bet the tenants…"

"Jan," she said. "He hacked it and opened it remotely before we came. When he looked at it this morning, he said the lock was very simple. Yes, no. Yes for engaged, no for disengaged. He told it no."

They walked a long hallway, with three-story ceilings and a bank of floor to ceiling windows along one side. They moved quietly. The lighting was dim. Troy would have expected her shoes to clack on this flooring, but then he remembered she was wearing sneakers.

They came to a black spiral staircase.

"Up one floor," she said. "Then down another hall maybe 30 meters." She began to ascend, then looked down at him. "Are you ready? Things sometimes happen quickly."

He stared at her. "Uh… yeah. I think I'm ready."

"Just an interview," she said.

He smiled. "Of course. After you."

At the top of the stairs there was a new hallway, half the width of the one downstairs, sharing the same high ceiling, only two stories above them now. They moved down the hall and reached the SymAero door in seconds.

Troy felt that same feeling he always got. It wasn't butterflies. You could even call it a lack of feeling. There was no sensation in his gut at all. There were no thoughts in his mind. He was here. Everything that had come before had brought him here. He was in the right place.

The door was solid wood, with clear glass panes, floor to ceiling again, next to it. There were lights on inside. The words SymAero were simple, with a stylized SA logo next to them. Beneath that was some slogan or motto in another language; Troy imagined Dutch.

We bring good things to life, maybe.

Be all you can be.

This door was locked. The lock wasn't digital. It was a lock in the knob mechanism, with a metal plate affixed to the door, and a deadbolt that went into the wall. No way to hack that thing remotely.

Troy felt it with his hand. Not the kind of door you could kick in easily. If they had a couple of real cops here with them, and a battering ram, it was the kind of door that might be demolished with some repeated brute force.

Dubois knocked on it. In a few seconds a young male face, with floppy blonde hair, appeared in the window next to the door. Dubois pressed her Interpol identification against the window.

The kid nodded.

"There's nowhere for them to go," she said. "There's no back exit from this office. They must answer."

"Fire escape?" Troy said.

She made a tiny head shake. "No need. There are sprinklers. Extensive, throughout the building. And the whole place was remodeled in the past decade with modern fireproof materials."

The door opened and the kid was standing there. He was sort of tall, but young and thin. Another somewhat identical kid was standing behind him. The Netherlands was a nation of clones. They clustered together. The cops were clones. These guys were clones, but of each other, not the cops. Though come to think of it, there was some resemblance.

"Yes?" the kid said.

"I'm Agent Dubois of Interpol. This is Agent Stark of the New York City Police Department. We'd like to have a small chat, if we may."

The kid shook his head. "No, I'm afraid now is not a good time."

He moved as if to shut the door, but Troy had already slid his boot between the door and the frame. The kid slammed the door against Troy's foot. He pulled it open just a bit and went to slam it again.

Troy put his hands against the door and shoved it open, pushing the kid backwards.

"Now is a perfect time," he said.

He stepped inside. The kid's eyes were wide, as were the eyes of the kid behind him. The New York City part. That must have gotten them.

Behind the door, about a dozen boxes were piled. There were three tall black servers on wheels next to the boxes. None of it was plugged in. They were getting ready to move stuff out. Their office was a long open space, with a high ceiling and just a few desks. At the far side of the office, the lights were not on. It was dark down there.

"Going somewhere, guys?" Troy said. "Seems a little early to leave when you're growing such a nice business here."

"We are... uh... moving the office to Amsterdam."

Stark looked at the guy but didn't say a word.

"It's a better city. More beautiful than Rotterdam."

Dubois was looking at some photographs she had pulled up on her phone. "Are you Peter? Van Gent?"

The guy nodded. "Yes. And you are?"

She was about to speak, but Troy interrupted. "You know who she is. She's from Interpol. She already told you that."

The kid grinned, maybe regaining his composure just a little. Maybe he knew that a visit from Interpol was like a visit from your mean aunt. A little nerve wracking, but her bark was worse than her bite. In fact, she had no teeth and forgot her dentures at home. Whatever the grin meant, Troy didn't like it.

Instantly.

"Well, I have a great deal happening today; as you can see we are very busy, and it seems it has already slipped my..."

BAM!

Troy punched the kid in the face. It was a sharp right hook, and it came without warning. In fact, it happened before Troy even knew he was going to do it.

The right was Troy's power hand. The kid's head snapped back, and he took two stutter-steps backward. The back of his skull connected with the office wall. The sound was like a low THUD. Then the kid oozed down the wall to the floor and sat there.

The other guy gasped.

"Stark!" Dubois shouted. "You can't..."

Troy crouched down by the kid. He raised the kid's chin with one hand. "What were you saying? I don't think I heard you. You have something else to do?"

"Agent Stark! This is inappropriate!"

Troy raised the other hand to her. "Shhhh. Shut up a minute. Let him speak."

"Stark!"

"I will retain a lawyer," the kid said.

"Where you gonna do that from, the hospital?"

The kid nodded. "Yes, and I will have your job."

Troy smiled. He loved it when people said things like that. His job? What job? His career in the Navy, which was about to end? His fake job at the NYPD, which was paid for out of a budget that didn't exist? Or his actual job, the one he was hired to do, where his boss had expressed no qualms at all about him killing people?

"If that's the case, I might as well beat you up a little more, huh? Since I'm gonna be out of a job anyway?"

"Stark, you can't..."

"Shhhhh. Honey, relax."

Now Dubois gasped. "Honey!"

That was the way this was going to go. If Troy did this the way Dubois wanted it to go, they'd be back in the office in a couple of hours, with no answers, and no closer to finding the terrorists. These guys, right here, had very likely built and sold the drones used in the attack. If so, they were going to tell Troy about it. They weren't going to hem and haw and talk about how busy they were.

That probably meant Troy and Dubois were not going to be friends. They weren't even going to be partners. Troy was fine with it.

"Don't you move! Don't you dare hit him again!"

A man appeared to Troy's right, behind the second kid, who had been standing there ineffectually. There had been nobody there a moment ago; now there was. The guy just emerged from the darkness at the far end of the room. He had been hanging back and remaining silent.

It was stupid on Troy's part. He was tired, yes. But he should have asked these guys who else was here. The third man had nearly killed him in Brooklyn just yesterday. And now this guy. Troy was off his feed.

The guy came closer. He was the only one of these three who was slightly different. He was older than the other two, short and stocky, strong looking, with auburn hair that was starting to thin. If the other two were in their mid- to late-twenties, this guy might have been in his late-thirties.

He had a gun in his hand.

"You cannot do this!" he shouted. "You cannot!"

"Gun," Troy said. He sighed. This was supposed to be an unarmed society; he and Dubois were certainly unarmed, and now here was a guy with a gun.

"We are leaving," the man said. "Raise your hands and step away from him. This is police brutality."

"Buddy," Troy said. The gun was pointed directly at his head. He was in a squat position, close to the floor. He had no friends here, and a gun just a few feet from blowing a hole in his skull. But there might be something he could do. If he got lucky, he might be able to...

"Let the record show that you came here and behaved in a manner..."

Behind Troy, a blur streaked by. Dubois.

He caught a glimpse of her, fluid, like a ballerina. She zipped through the air and launched a front kick. Her foot hit the guy's hand, and the gun flew away, back and over his head.

In almost the same movement, she landed and delivered a punch to his throat.

The man grabbed that spot with both hands, his eyes wide.

"GLUH..."

Then she swept a leg behind his two legs, and pushed him hard in the chest, using her whole body and the momentum from her jump.

The guy fell over backwards onto the floor.

Troy popped up from the squat. Now two of these guys were down. He looked at the last guy. This was probably the youngest of the bunch. His eyes said he wanted no part of any fighting.

Troy went over and picked up the gun. It was a Luger pistol, an antique, Troy guessed World War II vintage. It was a beautiful gun, and it seemed like it was in decent shape. He pocketed it in his jacket, then turned and looked at Dubois.

He smiled. "There's my girl. That's what I like to see. A little enthusiasm."

She didn't smile at all. Her face was cold as ice.

"I'm not your girl," she said.

CHAPTER TEN

"Is this the best we can do?"

Dubois's eyes were fierce. They almost seemed to glow in the semi-darkness. She spoke in a low voice, angry, but barely above a whisper. Troy understood why. She didn't want the subject to overhear her.

"I resent that you put me in this position. I will be reprimanded at the very least. I could be demoted. I don't know what's going to happen. You don't seem to care what happens to you. But I care what happens to me. This is my career. I don't know what your career is. But I don't believe that you're a police officer."

Troy shrugged. "I meant the train tracks. Is this all we have?"

They were standing on an elevated train line, which had fallen into disuse. The wood was old and splintered, sections of rail were missing, and weeds grew up from the cinders. They had walked the first blonde guy, Van Gent, down the tracks from a dirt parking lot about three hundred meters back.

Dubois said he was the one in charge. He was currently sitting against a low concrete abutment covered in graffiti. His wrists were zip-tied behind his back. The other two guys, his business partners, were zip-tied and gagged, and lying head to feet inside the trunk of the car. Hog-tied was a better way to put it. Troy had bound both their wrists and ankles. He was going to see where he got with Van Gent, and if it wasn't enough, he would start in on the other two.

Dubois had surprised him a little bit. She was mad at him, but then again, here she was with him on a derelict railway. And she was the one who knew this place. There was more to her than a straight-laced, by the book, "I'm not really a cop," Interpol investigator. Troy didn't think she was play acting. It just wasn't the whole story.

This wasn't a great spot, though. Weak light was beginning to appear in the sky, and there were glass and steel corporate towers probably half a mile away. They could be visible here in a little while.

"Rotterdam is a prosperous city," Dubois said. "There are very few abandoned places left. Even this rail line is scheduled to become a city garden and walking path within a year from now."

"Well, then we don't have a lot of time," Troy said. "I guess we better get to work. Have you ever run the good cop, bad cop?"

A devilish glint almost appeared in her eyes. A ghost of a smile also almost appeared, but then disappeared just as quickly.

"I have no idea what you're talking about."

Troy nodded. "Good. In that case I'll just run the bad cop."

He turned and walked back to Van Gent, Dubois a step behind. Troy reached the guy and crouched down next to him again. The guy's eyes were closed.

"Peter."

The eyes opened. They were bloodshot. They stared into Troy's eyes.

"I know what you did, okay? You can't hide anything from us. Our guys already hacked your computers. Don't you realize that? The first attack was two days ago, and we already found you. See what I mean? There's nowhere to hide."

The man's voice was stable, in that way when someone is trying very hard to control their emotions. "I have no idea what you're talking about."

"Look where we are," Troy said. "We're just out on some abandoned train tracks, right? We're not in a police station, or anything like that. You know why?"

The man shook his head. "No," he said. It was very low. It sounded like he had a lump in his throat.

"Because I'm going to kill you. I'm just going to shoot you in the head, with your friend's gun, and then I'm going to get him out of the trunk of the car, bring him out here and show him what I did. Do you think he'll talk after that? I do. I think he'll tell me everything. Everything you guys did, all the steps you took, who you dealt with, where the money went. Everything. He'll do that just so I don't kill him too."

Troy paused.

"Later, after all of that, I'm going to dump your body in a canal."

The man looked away, down the tracks. He made a sort of sniffling sound.

"Look at me, Peter."

Peter made a small head shake.

Troy pulled the Luger out of his jacket pocket. The gun looked great, but he had no idea if it even still worked. Again, he heard a gasp behind him from Dubois. "Stark…"

"I'm not kidding," Troy said. "I'm going to kill him. It's his fault. Last I heard, more than 40 people died at Hudson Yards. How many died last night in Belgium?"

"Four, at least," she said. "Another dozen in hospital."

Troy changed his footing, getting down on one knee. It gave him a more stable foundation from which to fire. He pointed the gun at the man's temple. The barrel was maybe six inches from his head.

"All those dead people. Why would I let this one live?"

The guy turned and looked at Troy. His face crimped like that of a child who wasn't getting its way. One thing was clear - he thought the gun still worked.

"We didn't know!"

Troy nodded. "That's a start. You didn't know what?"

"We didn't know that it would happen."

Tears began to stream down the kid's face.

"We didn't know," he said again, very low.

"You were gonna try to run."

Van Gent closed his eyes and nodded slowly. "Yes. I'm so sorry."

Troy shook his head. He felt nothing for this man child. If the world was fair, he really would kill the guy. He would just execute him right here, in cold blood, and it would make perfect sense, and no one would even bat an eye. But the world wasn't fair.

"No, you're not. You're sorry we caught you. And you're sorry we brought you out here to die on these train tracks and get dumped into a canal like a bag of garbage. But you're not sorry you tried to run, and you're not sorry you sold the drones in the first place."

"No!" the guy shouted. "You're wrong. I am sorry. You can kill me, but you cannot tell me how I feel. I'm sorry those people died. I didn't know what was going to happen."

"Peter, who did you sell the drones to?"

"I don't know."

Troy pressed the gun to the crown of the guy's head.

"Peter…"

Behind him, he heard a deep inhale and exhale from Dubois.

"I don't know. The sales platform is designed to guarantee secrecy. We delivered the product to a warehouse near the Port of Antwerp. They deposited the money into a numbered bank account in Switzerland."

"How much money?"

Peter said nothing.

"Peter, we're going to know anyway. We are going to know everything. You might be alive at that time, or you might be dead. But we're going to know…"

"Ten million euros."

Troy put a hand to his own head.

Behind him, Dubois said, "Oh my God," very softly.

"How many drones did you sell them?"

The kid hung his head. "Seven."

"Seven," Troy said. "Meaning there are five more attacks coming. You sold them seven high-tech drones, with swarms of nested, weaponized mini-drones…"

"They were not weaponized. There was no TNT or explosives mounted when we sold them."

Troy nodded. "But they are designed to accept explosives."

The kid said nothing. His head was still hanging.

"Peter."

It wouldn't take much for Troy to kill the guy. It really wouldn't. He wanted to do it. And the guy deserved nothing less than death. Or maybe… a philosophical person might say that a fate worse than death would be to live out his life in prison, carrying the weight of guilt, and thinking about all the people he had caused to die.

But Troy Stark was not a philosophical person.

"Yes," Peter said.

"Yes what?"

"Yes, the design can take explosives. But it can also take tiny cameras and be used for surveillance work. It can take tiny capsules of tear gas or an ambient sedative. There are a lot of things it…"

"Peter, you're hanging by a thread. I don't want to waste any more time. I want you to give me a name in the next three seconds. Or I'm done with you."

The gun was still pressed to Peter's head.

"Three," Troy said.

It was good to be done. They needed to get Peter back in the car pretty soon. Light was now beginning to fill the sky. Soon it would be daytime.

"Two."

Things were becoming visible. A dark wet spot appeared at the crotch of Peter's khaki pants and began to spread.

"One."

"Der Schatten," Peter said. He spoke just loud enough for Troy and Dubois to hear. "In German, it means The Shadow. That's the person we dealt with. That's what he called himself. That's all I know."

CHAPTER ELEVEN

10:20 am Central European Daylight Time
Interpol Liaison Office - Special Investigations Unit
Europol Headquarters
The Hague, The Netherlands

"You two are in trouble."

The four of them were in a small back room. It was Troy, Dubois, Miquel Castro-Ruiz, and Jan Bakker.

Jan was at a wide desk with a laptop on it and was facing away from the rest of them. There was also a small tablet computer, propped up on its own stand, and with a detachable keyboard. There were two tower CPUs under the table. He had a pair of headphones on. Practically all Troy could see of him was his broad back hunched over the screens, and the head with the headphones propped on top.

Troy, Castro, and Dubois were sitting at a round table. There was breakfast from McDonald's strewn all over the top of it. Troy had been to many parts of the world. A McDonald's always popped up sooner or later.

He was drinking a can of Red Bull he had gotten from a vending machine down the hall. Not his favorite, as far as energy drinks went, but he didn't see any Rock Star machines around.

"The Dutch National Police are already making noises that the prisoners were abused while in your custody. Especially your custody, Agent Stark, although Agent Dubois appears to have been complicit. And of course, you overstepped your mandate by taking them into custody at all."

"Miquel," Dubois said. "We also appear to have tracked down and captured three men who furnished drones that were used in terror attacks."

Castro shook his head. "Their rights were violated. It's possible that the cases against them won't hold up because of how the confession was obtained."

"We won't need the confession," Jan Bakker said. So he was listening, despite those big things covering his ears.

"We are following a trail directly from SymAero, through the dark web Bazaar trading platform, to the terrorists. It's already very clear that SymAero were building drones similar, and maybe identical to, the ones used in the attacks. It's also clear that trading high-tech tools on the dark web is the company's primary source of income. Their other activities are just to keep up appearances with government regulators."

"I don't care if there's a criminal case against those guys," Troy said. "I don't care if I stepped on the case or not, or what happens to them. I can always deal with them later. Right now, I want to find the terrorists. I want to stop another attack, and I also want to make them pay for what they did."

Troy didn't remember the last time he had been this tired. It could have been over a year ago, in Syria. He wasn't sure if he was divulging too much about himself. He wasn't sure if he was even making sense.

"All of these things are true, but it doesn't matter whether you're right or wrong. You're going to be called to the chopping block. If we were wise, we would repatriate you both to your home countries immediately, before the Dutch can think of charges to bring against you."

"Are we wise?" Troy said.

Castro shook his head. "No."

Troy smiled.

"Jan," Castro said. "Tell them what you've discovered."

The big man spun around in his seat. He was holding an egg and cheese sandwich on a croissant in one hand. Some of it was in his mouth. In his other hand he held a cup of McDonald's coffee.

"The Shadow. I found her."

"Her?" Dubois said.

Bakker nodded and smiled. "It's a woman."

Dubois shook her head. "I don't believe it. I don't believe a woman is capable of committing these sorts of…"

"Believe it or not, it's a direct hit. Her name is Aliz Willems. She's Belgian by blood, but she grew up in Luxembourg and Germany. She's an aristocrat, descended from one of the original medieval banking families. Over the centuries, they've had their fingers in every questionable thing, every dirty way that the European ruling class obtained wealth. They were large estate holders, with hundreds of serfs, until the Late Middle Ages. They were also slavers and gold traders, sending Africans to the New World, and bringing back gold looted from the South American interior. In the modern era, they moved seamlessly into diamond mining in Central Africa and arms dealing pretty much everywhere. As recently as the 1970s, they owned three landmine factories through nested holding companies in Bermuda and Panama, and their mines are known to have turned up in both Africa and Southeast Asia, particularly Cambodia. They've been bad people, for a long time."

"What have they been doing since the 1970s?" Castro said. The reading glasses on top of his head must be his trademark, Troy figured. He hadn't yet seen the guy take them down and attempt to read anything with them.

Bakker glanced at one of his screens. "The family has been moving toward respectability for a couple of generations. The father of Aliz Willems was Leopold Willems IV, who died of a heart attack in 1998, at the young age of 54. He was the owner of a Formula One racing team, and served as the Luxembourg Ambassador, first to France, and later to the United Nations. People used to joke that he wanted to live in Paris, and then decided no, he preferred New York City. He was on the European Board of Directors of *Medecins Sans Frontiers* and was also a major donor to UNICEF. While all this was going on, it is likely he was still earning millions from weapons, diamonds, and other precious metals smuggling, being conducted by companies that were mere facades, and were quietly controlled by the Willems family office. This may still be going on now. The family has been very good at playing the shell game."

"Why does the woman call herself The Shadow?" Troy said.

Bakker nodded. "That's been her internet handle for years. She has tried to distance herself from her family history. She studied philosophy and psychology at the University of Amsterdam, received a master's degree from the University of Cologne, and she's written a popular book in German about her idea of The Shadow, a darkness in human nature that compels people to commit evil acts. It isn't exactly an original idea, but she wrote it in such a simple way as to appeal to a large audience. Germans like that sort of thing, for obvious reasons. She's also begun a charitable foundation, apparently to do good works in the regions where her family has previously caused harm. She calls it the Willems Foundation."

"So the family name…," Troy said.

"Yes. It washes the name clean, now and in the future. They have hidden much of their past, and over time the pleasing reputation of the foundation will turn that reality on its head. They will be known only for their charitable endeavors. And for their efforts toward peace and understanding. After university, she spent three years as an EU diplomat in Belarus and then Lebanon."

"Russian mob," Troy said. "Hezbollah."

"Possible," Bakker said. "No evidence of that. But given her family's history of corruption…"

Dubois half-smiled. "You think she does charitable works, and also buys drones to commit terrorist attacks?" she said. "And as a young person just out of university, she was using EU diplomatic cover to establish networks with mafias and militant organizations?"

"Maybe," Bakker said. "Certainly, I don't think she commits the attacks herself. But perhaps she serves as a middleman. And the foundation provides a fig leaf to obscure her activities."

Dubois was shaking her head. "Seems like a foolish risk. She has more money than she can ever spend."

"The apple does not fall far from the tree," Castro said.

"And the data trail in the SymAero files, and on the dark web Bazaar platform, leads back to the Willems Foundation. It was well camouflaged, but I followed it and that's where the trail goes."

"Where do we find her?" Troy said.

"Usually, you don't. She keeps a low profile, and it's never clear which of her family homes she lives in. It's not obvious what country she calls home."

"Great," Troy said.

Bakker raised a large, meaty finger. "But it happens that the Willems Foundation is holding a fundraising affair in Luxembourg city tonight. It's a somewhat minor affair, a silent art auction. Hors d'oeuvres, not a full dinner. But they are expecting 200 guests. Apparently, Willems herself plans to attend. The foundation is her baby."

"I'd like to meet her," Troy said. "Can I go there?"

Bakker shrugged, then looked at Castro.

"It's complicated," Castro said.

CHAPTER TWELVE

6:50 pm Central European Daylight Time
The skies over Belgium

"It's ridiculous," Troy said.

He was sitting in the front passenger seat of a single-engine Piper Cherokee airplane, en route from The Hague to Luxembourg. The sky ahead was darkening. The pilot was none other than Mariem Dubois.

They were pressed shoulder to shoulder in the cockpit. The complicating factor was if he wanted to go to the fundraising event, he had to go with her. That little stipulation was disconcerting enough, but it wasn't the ridiculous part.

"You guys keep confiscating my guns. I've never seen anything like it."

"Apparently it bothers you to not have a gun at all times," Dubois said. "That's what I'm learning."

"Does it bother me? This is a mission. An operation. Whatever you people might call it. If it was our time off, and we were just going to play soccer in the park..."

"Football," Dubois said mechanically.

"What?"

"The sport is called football. It's the most popular game in the world, and the only place on Earth where anyone calls it soccer is America."

Troy nearly laughed.

"Whatever you prefer to call it."

She shrugged. "It's not what I prefer. Nearly eight billion people call it football. A couple hundred million Americans call it soccer."

"We already have a game called football."

Now she nodded. "Right. And because of that, you try to impose some other, odd name on the favorite sport of most of the world. Meanwhile, almost no one, other than you, cares about your football."

Troy looked at her. She was watching her instruments carefully. The night was nearly black outside of the windscreen. Her hands were small and light on the controls.

"Do you have an instrument rating to fly this thing at night?"

82

She turned and stared at him. "Of course. We wouldn't be up here if I didn't."

"Here's my point," he said. "If you people keep taking my guns away, you're going to get us both killed."

Troy had spent the late morning and much of the afternoon napping at his hotel. Interpol, or Europol, or maybe the Dutch National Police, had confiscated the gun he had gotten from the SymAero guy this morning as evidence. Evidence of what? That part he wasn't sure about. All he knew wasn't he didn't leave the Europol building with it.

They might have taken it to prove that his interview of Peter Van Gent amounted to torture. He didn't agree, but he wasn't a lawyer, and he wasn't European. The ordinary rules didn't seem to apply here.

They hadn't returned his other guns, either. What was he going to do, lodge a complaint? With whom? He wasn't going to fight them. He had to pick his battles here, and things seemed to be moving along.

Except when he reached his hotel room, he had no weapons there, either. They had taken those, too. It didn't make sense, this insistence on no guns. He could understand how they didn't consider him a police officer, and how he wasn't supposed to arrest anyone - even though he had already arrested three people. That was fine. He would continue to do things his own way but, generally speaking, he would need weapons to do that. He had picked up another gun this afternoon, but it wasn't much. And he wasn't going to tell her about it. Instead, he was going to pretend he had no gun at all.

"I don't want you to die," he said now. He had gotten about four or five hours of sleep, which was enough to rejuvenate him. That, combined with two Rock Stars, and he was feeling a lot better. Alex, his mysterious companion from the Brooklyn incident, brought him the Rock Stars. And the gun.

Troy had awakened at 3:30. He'd set a wake-up call with the front desk. At 3:35, a knock came at his door. He checked the peephole. A young, smallish Middle-Easternlooking man with a full beard, and wearing a bellhop's uniform stood there. He had a tray with a dome-like silver cover on it.

Troy opened and the door and Alex walked in with the tray. On one level, it was odd to see him there. On another level, it wasn't the least bit surprising. It already felt like he and Alex had been working together for a while.

"How are you feeling?" Alex said.

"Good. Got some sleep. You?"

Alex nodded. "Okay. Brought you some room service food from the kitchen. Also, a couple of Rock Stars. Persons told me you'd appreciate that."

"Thanks for not calling him Stu," Troy said.

Alex smiled and shook his head. He took the cover off the tray. There was a steak in some brown sauce, some rice, and asparagus on there. The food was steaming a little. There was a small extra plate with a big chocolate chip cookie. Also, two slim cans of Rock Star Zero. Troy took one of the Rock Stars and cracked it open.

He also ate the cookie. It was still warm. The cookie was soft, and the chocolate was sort of melted. It was good. Troy often ate dessert first. Life was short and sometimes ended abruptly. If he died five minutes from now, what would he have preferred - that he ate the cookie or the asparagus?

"And I do appreciate it."

He glanced around the hotel suite. It was a typical extended stay suite - nondescript, artwork from a department store, a living room with a couch and a chair and a TV bolted to the wall, a small functional kitchen, a bedroom, and a bathroom. He had barely looked at the place until now. There had been no reason to think about it. Now there was.

"How's this suite?" he said.

Alex shrugged. "It's clean. I swept it while you were out."

Troy nodded. "How did you get here?"

"Does it matter?"

Troy thought about that. "No. I guess not.

"We heard about the bust you did this morning," Alex said. "Nice work. We're getting closer. Only problem is you're in deep dip right now. You've pretty much worn out your welcome. I haven't seen an incident report, but I know they're annoyed. What happened?"

Troy shrugged. "One of the guys at the tech start-up pulled a gun. I don't know why he did that. Stupid."

"Was it a problem?" Alex said.

Troy shook his head. "No. None at all. You see that black girl I'm partnered with?"

Alex smiled. "Yeah. She's cute, man."

"I guess," Troy said. "If you like small chicks. Up close, she's tiny. I mean, a guy your height… okay, I could see it. Anyway, she pulled some Shaolin Temple, Crouching Tiger, flying fists of judo on the guy, and that's all she wrote. Then we took the boss to some old railroad tracks and now I had the gun, right? So I got the information out of him. It didn't take much."

Alex nodded. "All right. They made an inquiry to the NYPD about who you are and why you were sent. It's fine. Persons intercepted it. But there's some talk of bringing you up on criminal charges. Unlikely that happens, but it's very possible you could get arrested and kicked out."

"Of the Netherlands?" Troy said.

Alex shrugged. "Of Europe. The EU. The way you work, it doesn't fit. It's not how they do things here."

Troy nodded. "They took my guns. Can you get me some more?"

Alex went down on one knee. He pulled up his pant leg, revealing an ankle holster with a gun in it. He unclipped the entire thing, then stood up again. He handed the holster and gun to Troy.

Troy slipped it out. It was a very small gun. It had a small magazine loaded. Everything about it was diminutive. It was like a toy for a small child. Troy and the gun were not love at first sight.

Alex reached inside his jacket and came out with an extra magazine. "It's the old Belgian-made FN Baby Browning, .25 caliber. There are six rounds in each mag. You're not going to stop a tank with it, or an elephant. But it might buy you some time and get you out of a jam."

The gun was very light. The barrel was maybe two inches long. Troy pointed it at the TV set. "Thanks. Is it hot?"

"Yeah," Alex said. "Don't get caught with it."

"Can you get me more? Bigger? Better?"

Alex shook his head. "Not right away. But I'll see what I can do. In the meantime, you should get out of this hotel. Tonight, if you can. If you get picked up, they're going to deport you. We can't have that."

"I'm already leaving."

"Where are you going?" Alex said.

"Luxembourg. There's a lead on the buyer. Might be a woman named Aliz Willems. I sort of doubt it, but that's where things are pointing at the moment. She runs something called the Willems Foundation. They're having a fancy get-together tonight. That's where I'll be."

Alex nodded. "I'll pass it along."

"Good. Don't forget the guns."

"I won't," Alex said. "In the meantime, take this." He held out a small blue plastic box. It was about half an inch by half an inch on a side, and nearly flat.

Troy took it and held it up. He opened it. Inside were two smaller plastic wafers, lying one on top of the other.

"GPS units," Alex said. "Put one in some tiny pocket in an article of clothing or wedge it under the sole of your shoe - anywhere that it never leaves you. If you're on the move, it's the only way we're going to know where you are."

"What about the second one?" Troy said.

Alex shrugged. "If you find anything interesting, leave it somewhere for me with the second GPS. I'll pick it up and we'll check it out."

Now, on the tiny plane, Troy felt wide awake. And he also felt sincere concern towards this woman. She was crazy to be out here with him. She suspected he wasn't a cop, and she was right about that. But she was wrong in general. He wasn't who she thought he was. Alex's presence reminded him of this. He and Alex were black operators. They barely knew each other and had fallen into an easy working relationship almost instantly. This woman, and her bosses, had no idea Alex even existed.

"I've been an agent of Interpol for more than 10 years," she said. "I've felt threatened maybe half a dozen times, including this morning."

Troy shook his head. "Your career has just taken a radical change in direction."

She half smiled. "Because of your presence?"

"Because we're hunting terrorists," he said. "It's dangerous work."

For a moment, he almost felt like giving it to her straight. People got murdered in situations like this. She was a desk jockey, for the most part. Maybe she studied karate or some other martial art, and that was good. She had acted quickly and judiciously this morning, kicking the gun out of that guy's hand and taking him down. But you didn't kick people when they opened up on you with Uzis or MAC-10s. You killed them if you could, in any way possible.

What was he supposed to tell her, though? That he wasn't really a cop? She knew that already. But he couldn't tell her that he was a black operator. She would run and tattle on him again. This time they wouldn't take his guns away; they would kick him off the continent. And he couldn't allow that. He had a job to do.

"We're collecting information," she said.

Troy didn't want a debate. "Have it your way."

"Thank you. I will. Now, what's your name again?"

"Troy Stark."

She grunted, and a sound escaped her that was almost like a laugh. "At the fundraiser. What's your name?"

Troy sighed. She really didn't know him, or what she was getting herself into. He had memorized the details of the new identity in minutes. He could riff on it, and simply be the person. He could bluff his way past nearly anyone, except maybe a family member or intimate partner of the person. But that didn't matter, because the person they gave him didn't exist.

"My name is Ethan Garnatz. I'm American, and 35 years old. I grew up in Manhattan, on the Upper East Side."

They had given him an American from New York City, probably because they figured English was his only language. And he sounded like he was from New York, though not from the Upper East Side. Maybe the guy put on the accent to sound tough.

"I come from a real estate family. We're stinking rich. I've been mostly a party guy my whole life, a jetsetter, didn't get any kind of career going. Didn't even really try, to be honest. I flunked out of Yale after one year. Went to Brown for one semester after that but quit. College wasn't my thing. Work wasn't, either. I just live off a couple of inheritances and dividends from a family trust. We own more than 70 commercial buildings in New York, Philadelphia, and Baltimore, but I have nothing to do with that, other than collecting the payouts. I travel, hang out in places where the elite gather, meet gold-digging women. I'm a playboy, but I'm not entirely self-centered. I am pretty generous with good causes. That's why I'm going to the fundraiser tonight."

"Good," she said. "Now who am I?"

"You're my girlfriend, if you can call it that. We met in Ibiza a month ago. Your name is Giselle Toussaint."

He pronounced the name more or less correctly. He said it as *Too-SAHN*. Ethan Garnatz wasn't such an ugly American that he couldn't say people's names.

He went on: "You say you're from Paris, but I don't really believe you. You claim you work in online journalism, but you're between jobs. I can't be bothered to verify your employment. We've been having too much fun. Anyway, I'm not much of a stickler for facts. I have no idea how old you are. Mid- to late-twenties, at a guess, but I don't actually care. I figure this little affair will wrap itself up in the next few weeks. I'll give you maybe twenty or thirty thousand euros as a kiss off, and you won't get your greedy little claws on my real money. Then we'll go our separate ways."

She nodded. "Very nice."

"Will we be sharing a hotel room tonight?"

Dubois shook her head. She had close to zero sense of humor.

"We're going to be landing soon. They left us a car with our identities inside of it, and some clothes to wear in the boot. We won't be sharing a hotel room. We don't have hotel reservations at all. Miquel thinks it best that we attend the party, get as close to Aliz Willems as we can, speak to her, if possible, obtain whatever information we can, then leave the country immediately. We can drive into France easily. Personally, I would like to make it back to my flat in Lyon tonight."

"How far is that?" Troy said.

"Driving a car, maybe six hours."

Troy nodded. "That sounds good. I'll sleep on your couch."

Dubois sighed.

What he didn't tell her was he didn't care what Miquel Castro-Ruiz thought. If Troy got close to Aliz Willems tonight, and she was The Shadow, then in all likelihood, she was leaving the party with him. Where he ended up taking her didn't matter. Someplace secluded, where they could talk. A graveyard. An alleyway. A sewer system.

"We're about to land," she said.

Troy looked out the windows. Everything was pretty dark. Here and there, the landscape below was dotted with lights. It wasn't much to go on.

"Where?"

"There's an airstrip just a bit ahead. It's unmarked, and hard to find. It's in a heavily wooded area. It's not on a map, and there are no lights. It's fenced in and the gates are locked. It's just a place we use sometimes."

He glanced at her again. "You work for Interpol, right?"

She nodded but didn't seem surprised by the question. She was watching the monitors and working the controls. "Yes."

"And Interpol has a secret airstrip in Luxembourg?"

"Yes. We have secret airstrips all over the place. Sometimes we need to move people and material around without calling attention to ourselves."

"Ah. Because you're a data gathering and analysis organization."

"Yes. And we share that data with police agencies throughout the world. We keep enormous data sets, of everything under the sun. Crimes, crime scenes, individual criminals, criminal organizations, relationships between criminal organizations, drug trafficking routes, people smuggling routes, weapons smuggling and dealing, the illegal diamond trade. You name it, we catalogue it, and we share it with cops in dozens of languages in more than two hundred countries."

Troy noticed now that they were just above the trees. To be fair, he had felt them decelerating and dropping altitude for a little while now. The plane had no lights on. It was just about pitch dark. This plane was going to drop in and disappear.

Dubois watched the instruments. The plane touched down with a light BANG, and then it was rolling over a somewhat bumpy road. She brought it to a gradual stop.

"How was that?" she said.

"Smooth. No look landing. You're a good pilot."

She grinned and shook her head. "Let's go."

Troy opened the door and stepped across the wing to the runway. There was a car parked nearby. He had a small flashlight on him, and he ran it over the car. It was a silver Jaguar XJ8, very sporty looking, very James Bond.

Dubois had a key fob on her. She clicked it. The car made a chirp, the headlights flashing for a split second.

"Doors are open."

"How far are we from the city?" he said.

"About 50 kilometers," she said. "To you, maybe 30 miles."

"Thanks. I was in the military for a long time. I know what kilometers are."

She walked around to the trunk of the car and pulled it open. "There are outfits for us to wear in this boot. We should get dressed here for the most part and give ourselves a look over in the city before we go to the venue."

He watched her by the trunk light. She pulled out a shimmering, sequined blue dress wrapped in plastic. Then she took out stockings and shoes.

"I'll get dressed on my side of the car; you get dressed on your side," she said.

He pulled out a tuxedo, also wrapped in plastic. There were also nice striped socks and a pair of black wingtip shoes. He shrugged.

"Fine with me."

He had a gun strapped to his ankle that he didn't want her to see. It didn't bother him at all to dress away from her. Also, he was a gentleman and there was the whole privacy thing.

He went to the driver's side of the car. He pulled his boots off, then shrugged out of his jeans, t-shirt and jacket. He took his boxer shorts off. He was moving quickly, draping his clothes on the car. He put the ankle holster with his clothes. He put down a stack of zip-ties as well. He stood nude in bare feet in the darkness.

"Need any help over there?" he said.

"No!"

He nodded. Good. He carefully and methodically took the suit out of its plastic and put it on. He opened the car door and sat on the seat to pull on the socks, shoes, and strap the gun back into place. After a few moments, he was ready.

She was already climbing into the passenger seat. The blue sequined gown was form-fitting and hugged her curves. She was in terrific shape. She wore four-inch chunky heels. "You can drive," she said. She paused. "Can you even drive? I need to do my makeup."

"Yeah. I can drive."

There was a book on the floor by her feet. He glanced at it. *Der Schatten*, by Aliz Willems.

He gestured at it. "What's the deal with the book?"

"It's her book. I thought I might use it to get close to her, ask her to sign it for me."

He slipped behind the wheel and pressed the starter. The engine came to life. It was a beautiful car; everything seeming in tip top condition. The dash was nice, lots of fun readouts. The seats were deep, soft leather.

"Maybe I should be the one to ask her for an autograph," he said.

Dubois looked at him. "The book is in German. Do you even speak German?"

Troy nodded. "Spreche sie Deutsch? Ja. Ein bisschen."

"Okay. Give me some."

"Ubun macht den meister," he said. *Practice makes perfect.*

That was it. He was basically out of German.

Dubois pulled down the sun visor to get a look in the mirror. The mirror had its own light. She had a small makeup kit out and was already going to work.

She gestured with her chin. "The gate out is to your left, on the other side of the runway. We don't have all night."

"It's a nice car," he said. "And it's a nice night for a drive."

"Miquel said not to hurt the car."

"Oh, I wouldn't dream of hurting it," Troy said. He put the Jag in gear and headed for the city.

CHAPTER THIRTEEN

7:30 pm Central European Daylight Time
Europol Headquarters
The Hague, The Netherlands

"Is this to be a crucifixion?"

Miquel Castro-Ruiz sat in an office at the top of the Europol building. The office was used as a meeting room among the high-level officers. He was at an oval table, in the center of it.

Directly across the room were floor to ceiling windows giving a view of the city. It was night, and The Hague was lit up for the evening.

Around the table sat three men. Another man stood to his left, leaning against a wall and drinking a coffee. All of the men were dressed smartly, in suits, with close-cropped hair and clean shaves, as if they had just emerged from the bathroom.

Hans Jute, the Deputy Director of Europol, was here. Gregory Fawkes, of the Interpol Internal Affairs Department, was here. Had he flown up from Lyon for this meeting, or did he just happen to be in The Hague? A man from the Dutch National Police was here. He had identified himself, but the name had skipped past Miquel. The fourth man, who stood in the corner, hadn't identified himself at all.

"Miquel, this is far from a crucifixion," Fawkes said. "This is a statement of concern from interested partners."

Miquel pointed at the man in the corner. "Who is that person? Who are you, sir?"

The man smirked and took a sip of his coffee. "I'm an observer."

"And what organization do you represent?"

The man shrugged and smiled.

"Miquel," Hans Jute said. Jute was an officious man, very fit, who was balding and wore thin wire-rimmed glasses. It was never to be said, and probably inappropriate to even think, but looking at him always reminded Miquel of some Nazi accountant in World War Two, diligently calculating and recording the number of wretched damned sent to the ovens.

"It doesn't matter who that man is. He isn't the subject of this inquiry."

"And I am?" Miquel said.

Jute shrugged. "Your actions are. We are curious about how two agents under your charge came to involve themselves in torturing Dutch citizens during the course of your investigation into…"

"You and I both know those Dutch citizens sold military-capable drone technology to unknown persons through a dark web platform known as the Bazaar. And that the drones they sold…"

Jute held up a hand. "Miquel, please. You're embarrassing yourself. I'll remind you that the Internal Affairs Department of your agency has a presence at this meeting."

Miquel nodded. "I already know Agent Fawkes."

"Captain Fawkes," Fawkes said, his voice flat. Fawkes was a young guy, a Canadian, who was moving quickly up the ranks by landing with both feet on people who were trying to do their jobs.

"Of course you know him," Jute said. "This isn't your first dance with Internal Affairs. We are all aware of that. And therefore, we are aware that you well know the limits of your mandate here. We are aware that you know the Dutch citizens that your agents illegally detained today are to be extended the assumption of innocence. We are aware that you know there is circumstantial evidence…"

"More than… circumstantial," Miquel said. English, the language of Europol and Interpol, was his third language. He tended to trip over words like "circumstantial." He fought the urge to add "Mucho más!"

Jute held his hand up again: "There is circumstantial evidence that the men traded drones on the dark web, but there is no evidence that these were the drones used in the terror attacks in New York City and Bruges."

Miquel was silent. For a moment, he was back in Madrid, the morning of March 11, 2004. He was a 32-year-old commando of the Grupo Especial de Operaciones. He was married with two young daughters. His life changed that day.

The first bomb aboard the train inside Atocha Station went off at precisely 7:37 am, and then two more a minute later. Miquel's subgroup arrived on the platform about 7:48. The commuter train had giant round holes blown through it, from one side to the other, practically severing the train cars in half. There were bodies on the platform, smoke everywhere, the floor awash in blood.

There was a woman, Miquel thought middle-aged, who was missing below the waist. She was dressed in a white blouse and brown leather jacket. Her hair was pulled tight in a bun. She wore makeup.

Her eyes were open and staring. She had probably been an office lady, on her way to work.

Suddenly, there was a commotion. A rumor spread - another bomb was about to go off. Then everyone was running: all the first responders, police, emergency medical workers in their bright yellow vests, commandos from the GEO. Everyone running in terror, vaulting up the broken escalator, tripping over each other to get away, leaving behind the injured, the dying, and the dead. To Miquel, it was a disgrace that he might never live down. There was another bomb that did not go off. It was detonated hours later in a controlled fashion. But that did nothing to erase the animal panic that went through the men who had come there to save lives, and who were reduced to fleeing to save themselves.

Miquel had not been able to get the images out of his mind. Sometimes when he closed his eyes, he saw the woman again, the woman ripped from her family, who would never make it to her job, and whose face existed now only in Miquel's memory. Sometimes, he woke in the middle of the night, eyes wide, clawing his way up a broken escalator, smoke all around him, his heart pounding in his chest.

His girls were adults now and married. His oldest had a daughter of her own. His ex-wife was long gone, remarried, living the carefree life of an investment banker's wife in Barcelona.

Miquel had been separated from them by the events of that day. His mission in life, his reason for being, had become to never allow such a thing to happen again, if he could stop it. Had he broken rules here and there? Had he stepped on the supposed rights of terrorists? He supposed he had.

And now he had become marginalized, a pariah within his own organization. Director of the Special Investigations Unit of the Interpol Liaison Office at Europol. He had a tiny office. His best agents didn't even work here - they flew back and forth from Lyon as they were needed. He had been kicked to a place where he had little authority, and in the minds of his superiors, could do the least harm. That was what he was reduced to. He was a conduit for information, and little more. They had given him the American because no one believed the American had a lead worth pursuing.

"Miquel?" Jute said. "Did you hear me?"

Miquel nodded. "Yes. I'm sorry. What did you say?"

"How did this incident come about? What specific instructions did you give the agents involved?"

"The American, Troy Stark," Miquel said. "He came on loan from the New York City Police Department. He had acquired the information we acted upon, that SymAero had sold drones to the terrorists."

"Allegedly," the man from the Dutch National Police said.

Miquel shrugged. "I do not know this man. I sent Interpol Special Investigations Agent Mariem Dubois with him to interview the subjects at their headquarters in Rotterdam. Dubois is an exceptional agent. One of the subjects pulled a gun on them. Dubois disarmed the man."

"Then the American and your exceptional agent put all three of the men in the boot of a car, drove them to some abandoned railroad tracks, and forced an admission from one of the men through the use of a mock execution, now recognized as torture under international law. The man has since rescinded his admission of guilt, coming as it did under extraordinary duress."

Miquel didn't answer. In fact, Jute hadn't asked an actual question.

"Where are the agents now?" the man from the Dutch National Police said.

"Well," Miquel said. "The analyst Jan Bakker is here, and I expect he is working late, sharing the data he uncovered with analysts back at Interpol headquarters, here at Europol, and with the Dutch police."

"Bakker isn't at issue here," Greg Fawkes said. "Everyone knows Bakker is excellent, the best of the best. The other two. Where are they?"

Miquel shrugged again. "I sent Dubois back to France," he said.

Lying to them put his career in serious jeopardy. But this was his mission. He would stop the next terror attack if he could, even if that meant he ended up out of a job.

"And as far as I know, the American got back on his plane, and is en route to New York."

"You sent them out of the country, even though you knew they were wanted for questioning by the Dutch National Police?"

"No," Miquel said. "I sent them home after a job well done. This is the first I've heard that anyone wanted to speak with them."

The men were all staring at him. He raised his hands. "In any case, they're gone. Dubois can probably be interviewed tomorrow at Interpol Headquarters in Lyon. My understanding is she did not participate in any unauthorized activities."

"She also didn't put a stop to them," Jute said.

"I imagine that's a matter for Internal Affairs," Miquel said. "But with Dubois's service record, I hope that she will receive at most a reprimand, and perhaps some remedial training in the rights of suspects."

Miquel glanced at Fawkes.

Fawkes was starting to look bored. "That sounds about right."

Miquel went on: "As for the American, I cannot vouch for him. I never met him, nor heard of him, before today. He did what he did, but it appears that no one was injured, and perhaps some information of value was obtained. Now he's gone."

"Yes, he is," Jute said.

"I suppose that we don't have to worry about him anymore," Miquel said. "He's no longer a threat to anyone in Europe."

CHAPTER FOURTEEN

8:25 pm Central European Daylight Time
Cercle Cité
Place d'Armes, Ville Haute quarter
Luxembourg City, Luxembourg

"The Duchy of Luxembourg," Dubois said. "It's a giant money laundering operation masquerading as a country."

Okay. Troy would bite. "In what sense?"

They were walking slowly across the tree-lined plaza in front of a grand old building. The building was maybe five stories tall, with a tower, a very steep roof facing the street, a clock, and a few Roman-style columns on the ground floor.

There were valet parking attendants standing in front of the place, in white shirts and black pants, but in a pinch Troy wanted access to the car. So they had parked it along the street on the far edge of the plaza. Troy guessed that at a run, he could be back at the car from the front doors of this building in twenty seconds.

A small knot of people stood at the front of the building, waiting to get in. There was something, some obstruction, causing a little bit of a logjam there. Maybe they were collecting tickets.

"In every sense," Dubois said. "The tax laws are very favorable, and the banking is as anonymous as you want it to be. Everyone hides their money here. The Italian Mafia, the Russian Mafia, neo-fascist and neo-Nazi political parties from across the continent, the Vatican, corrupt dictators looting the coffers of every Third World tinpot. The bankers are more than obliging. Ten percent of the world's known billionaires make their legal residence here, in a tiny country of 600,000. Many international celebrities - pop stars, movie stars, sports stars - own Luxembourg-based companies. There are more than 125,000 companies registered here, ninety percent of which are held by non-Luxembourgers. The vast majority are shell companies. Meanwhile, the national trade register, meant to oversee the activities of these companies, has less than 60 employees."

"So they don't really want to stop it," Troy said.

She shrugged. "Why would they? Luxembourg has the highest standard of living in the world. And who would stop it? The powerful people shielding their money? The politicians? The former prime minister is now the First Vice-President of the European Commission. The former Central Banker works at the International Monetary Fund. The European elites are corrupt to their core."

He could hear the aggravation in her voice. This was where her pain was. She did not like the self-dealing, greedy, money-hiding rich.

Okay. That was something he could work with.

He glanced sideways at her. She looked good. The sequined mini dress hung exactly right. She had done her makeup perfectly on the drive here. She wore a hat, a touch askew, with a bit of a veil in the front. She was stylish. She looked like she belonged at an event like this.

"You clean up nice," he said.

She barely looked at him. "Thank you. So do you." She said the last part grudgingly, as if it was a requirement that she wasn't eager to meet.

It wasn't a requirement. He didn't care. He knew what he looked like.

Up ahead, a red Lamborghini Diablo pulled in. The gulf wing doors slid up and a couple got out. The valet took the key from the man and got behind the wheel. The doors slid back into place.

As the car pulled away, Troy watched the couple. They approached the columns at the front of the building. They raised their hands as men in suits passed wands along their bodies. The men were thorough. They reached down and ran the wands along the feet of the couple.

They had metal detectors. Those men were guards, looking for weapons.

What kind of gala was this?

Troy was suddenly very aware of the gun strapped just above his ankle. How to explain that? "Oh, hi. I'm just a guy pretending to be someone I'm not. I'm planning to get close to the host of this little shindig and take her prisoner, at gunpoint if need be. Then I'm going to scare her into divulging every dirty little secret she knows. Is that okay with you guys?"

He stopped short. Dubois walked on a couple more steps. Then she turned and looked at him. "Are you coming?"

He shook his head and smiled. "You know, I forgot my little breath freshener spray in the car. I left it in the little tray near the dashboard. It's been the longest day in recent memory; I've been going since I don't know when, drinking coffee and energy drinks like they're out of style. I'm a little embarrassed to say this, but I need to give my mouth a spritz. I'll be back in just a second."

She put a hand on her hip. "Somehow that doesn't surprise me."

He pointed at her hands. She had a small sequined purse in one hand, nothing in the other. "You don't have the book you wanted signed. Do you want me to get it for you while I'm over at the car?"

She shook her head, a very slight shake. "No. I decided to hold off. These are very refined and expensive people. I don't want to look like a silly girl with a crush. If the opportunity arises, maybe I'll get the book later, or bring Willems back to the car."

"Okay," Troy said. "I'll be just a minute."

He turned and crossed the plaza again, the way he had just come. It was night, and the plaza was well lit. But the trees cast shadows, and Troy moved into them. He took an angle that made him disappear from her sight. When he reached the car, he turned and could just see her, a tiny figure on the far side of the plaza.

He reached down and undid the holster. He took the gun out and slid it onto the front driver's side tire. He pulled the extra magazine from inside his jacket and put it with the gun. Then he clicked the fob to open the car door. He slid the holster in behind the driver's seat. The book was still on the floor on the passenger side.

He shut the door and locked it again.

Okay. No gun. Again. He probably wouldn't need it.

He walked back across the plaza. She stood waiting for him, her hand still on her hip. "Did you freshen your breath, Casanova?"

He shook his head. "No. I must have dropped that thing somewhere. It wasn't in the car after all."

She looked him up and down. "You blunder your way through things a bit, don't you? Bluff, make threats you don't mean, pretend you know more than you do? Forget things, then forget the thing you forgot?"

He nodded. "A bit, yeah. It's the secret to my success."

They walked together toward the stone pillars at the front of the building. Halfway there, she looped her arm in his. Of course. They were a couple.

"Talk about anything," she said.

He started in without missing a beat. "I come from a family of cops."

"Get out of here." She laughed as if he had said something funny.

He shook his head. "No. It's true. Well, one of my brothers is an emergency medical technician. He works for the fire department."

"I knew a fireman in Paris once upon a time. Good-looking guy. Can you imagine?"

"It can't be a coincidence," Troy said. "My brother is good-looking."

They approached the two well-dressed bouncers at the entrance. Big strong guys; Troy had a sense they would fold up quickly. Couldn't always be right about things like that, but he usually was. Dubois had the tickets. She held them out and one of the guys scanned their bar codes with a little X-ray gun.

"It's a small world," Dubois said.

They stepped between the pillars, through a brief tunnel, to the men wielding the metal detectors. Behind the men, three sets of tall wooden doors were thrown wide open. Beyond the doors was a grand staircase. The men ran their wands over Dubois and Troy's bodies, inches from touching them.

Troy nodded, keeping the nonsensical conversation going. "It's a very small world."

"Thank you," one of the men said in perfect English. "Welcome. Right this way. Up the central stair, then follow the corridor to the end, and up the spiral stairs to the third floor. Enjoy your evening."

"Thank you," Troy said. He was in, and weaponless. They walked across the marble floor. Dubois's shoes clacked on the stone just a bit. Troy could already hear the echoing buzz of conversation, punctuated by a piano. A few people moved ahead of them. Somewhere there was a cackling laugh, like a witch. The echoes of chatter and laughter reminded Troy of being at an indoor public swimming pool.

"This should be interesting."

A few people walked ahead of them. Troy and Dubois followed the parade, arm in arm again, up a flight of stairs, down a white marble hallway, then up another flight of stairs, which curved and gave you a choice of right or left. They both went right.

At the top, a grand rotunda opened above their heads. Now they had reached the crowd. Maybe a hundred people milled here in a sort of foyer area, where a bar was set up along the wall with five bartenders in white shirts and black ties ready to serve your drink of choice.

In the far corner was a man sitting at a black baby grand piano, letting out a steady stream of soft, tinkling sounds. Between here and there, small groups mingled, while women in black pants and white shirts, with a red sash around their waists, navigated through the people, carrying trays of finger food.

To the right, a set of wide double doors were open. Troy glanced inside. It was a wide-open space with a gleaming parquet floor, and tall windows with dark red curtains thrown open. A relative handful of people were in there so far, inspecting paintings that stood on easels at intervals of about ten feet. There was a white sign outside the room, also on an easel, with a message printed in several languages.

Troy found the one in English. *Please, no food or drink in the Grande Salle.*

That's why most people were still out here.

He leaned down to Dubois. "They're gonna have to shut the bar down if they want people to buy the art."

She threw her head back and laughed. She was good at faking it.

"Tell me if you spot The Shadow," he said.

Dubois nodded. "I'm looking at her right now."

"Where?"

The pinky finger of her right hand made a subtle pointing gesture. Troy followed it to a woman of about 30, in a red skater dress. She stood in a knot of four people, but Troy barely saw them. Something about the woman, or the light in this place, rendered her in Technicolor, while the people in her group faded into black and white.

In fact, everyone in the foyer began to fade into the background. The woman was a beautiful, voluptuous blonde, her hair long, but tied in such a way that it cascaded down over one shoulder. She was tall for a woman, and a pair of red heels that matched her dress added at least another two inches.

She listened intently to an older man in the group pontificating about some thing or other, something pointless, his old hunting lodge in 1968, the Fortune 500, some damn thing. How he made a killing in soybeans. The man barely existed. He would be dead soon. What was he going to say to Saint Peter at the Gates of Heaven? "Soybeans?"

The old man disappeared, fading backwards into the walls, becoming pixilated, indistinct. The woman's lips were painted red, dark red like her dress, and like the curtains in the Grand Salle. She sipped from a glass of white wine.

"That's her, eh?"

Dubois nodded. "Yeah. You can put your tongue back in your mouth now."

"I'm gonna get a drink. You want one?"

"No," Dubois said. "I'm working right now. This is my job."

Troy nodded. "I figured."

The lines at the bartender serving stations had thinned out. These guys were working quick. Troy got a bottle of Heineken and stuffed a five euro note in the guy's tip jar. The beer wasn't going to do anything for him. Which was good. He was starting to get tired again.

He came back into the center of the room and sipped his beer. Dubois had already attached herself to another group of people. She was chatting, feigning interest in whatever the people were saying. That was fast work. Good for her.

A man came out of the Grande Salle with a silver triangle. He began to knock a crystal swizzle stick against the inside of the triangle. It made a pleasant chiming sound. Gradually, the voices in the room began to die down. The piano stopped playing. Soon, all eyes were on the man with the triangle.

"Ladies and gentlemen," the man said. "Please finish your drinks and join me in the Grande Salle to review the beautiful, world-class, and significant works of art we are auctioning this evening. To whet your appetites, among many wonderful works for sale, I can tell you that we have a signed abstract pencil sketch of a horse, made by Pablo Picasso. We also have two engraving plates made by Salvador Dali when he was a 24-year-old engraver. Rest assured that everything you see tonight has been carefully authenticated. Our experts are prepared to take your questions. They are the two gentlemen, and the one lady, wearing the blue badges. Thank you."

People began to set their empty glasses down on the trays of passing waitresses, and then flow into the bigger room. Troy watched Dubois flow through the double doors with the other guests. She passed a tall, heavyset man in a blue dinner jacket. He stood near the doors. There was a bulge under his jacket. Troy marked him as security and carrying a gun. They didn't take anything for granted around here. You couldn't have a gun, but they still had theirs.

Willems said her goodbyes to the people she was speaking with. She still had about half a glass of wine and didn't seem in a rush to set it down.

That was good. Troy walked toward her.

Their eyes met. Troy couldn't read the thought behind those eyes.

He put on a big smile and raised his hands. "Aliz!"

She echoed his smile, but with a touch less enthusiasm. "Yes. I'm Aliz. Hello."

"You won't remember me," Troy said. "I'm Ethan. Ethan Garnatz."

Her eyes became big for a second. They did not remember him. But they were trying to. She was polite, had social graces.

"I was at the American embassy in Kyiv, what was it? Seven years ago?"

"Oh," she said, as if he was starting to ring a bell now.

"You were in Ukraine; who were you with? Luxembourg?"

Now her smile seemed more genuine. "The EU."

"The European Union, of course. We met a couple of times at embassy events. You're a beautiful woman, no offense, but I also never forget a face."

"Ethan," she said. "I remember you."

Smooth liar. Caught up very quickly.

She took a sip of her wine. She watched him over the rim of the glass. This was going fine. "What are you up to these days?" she said.

"Oh, you know. Finance, what else would I be doing? I'm with Chase."

"JP Morgan Chase?" she said.

He nodded. Is that what they called it now? There must have been a merger at some point. "Yeah. We have a presence over here. Geneva. Luxembourg. London. They sent me because of my Europe experience. I move around a bit."

That was it. He was out of bank talk. If she asked him what his job was, he had a choice of teller or manager. Or CEO.

They began to move toward the double doors. Neither of them had finished their drink. That was fine. He took a sip of his beer. They passed through the doors into the larger Grande Salle. The guard didn't say anything to them. He merely nodded his head politely. What do you say to Aliz Willems? Don't bring that wine in here?

"You're going to spill that wine on the Picasso," Troy said.

She smiled. He was breaking the ice like crazy. He had always been this way. But with people who were open. Not with people like Dubois. Poor girl had a wall up.

"I'm going to try not to," Aliz said.

Troy thought of her as Aliz now. He touched her on the arm. She was gracious. She didn't yank it away. She didn't act like her skin had been burned. They faced each other. He was going to get her. Around them, people were gathering in clusters near each artwork. But they were also alone.

"I want to tell you something," he said.

"Yes?" She seemed amused by him. She was half-expecting him to profess his undying, unrequited love from seven years ago. He could see it in her eyes. She probably got that kind of thing a lot.

"I know you're The Shadow," he said.

The eyes changed. A second ago, they were friendly, open, and just a little bit guarded, ready to gently fend off whatever advance was coming. But now they were confused. She opened her mouth, as if to say something.

"Don't talk," Troy said. "I know you're The Shadow who bought the drones on the dark web, on the Bazaar site. I also know something you don't know, which is who you bought them from. That's because we traced the transaction. And I know two of those were the drones used in the terror attacks in New York and Belgium."

Her eyes were wide now. He clamped his hand around her wrist an instant before she tried to pull it away.

"I have no idea what you're talking about. I'm going to talk to security."

Troy shook his head. "You're going to leave here with me, very quietly like we're old pals, and we're going to talk about this. It can go hard or easy for you. We don't think for a minute that you were behind the attacks. You can save your neck, and possibly your life, by giving up the terrorists."

"No," she said. "I really have no idea what you're talking about. Are you crazy?"

"Aliz, they have the death penalty in the United States. You know this, right?"

Now she did try to pull her arm away. It didn't work. Troy held it tightly. He was a lot stronger than she was. She wrenched her entire body backwards. She dropped her wine glass. It shattered on the polished floor. Somehow, even with all these people here, it made a sound like a bomb, cutting through the chatter.

"Guard?" she said. "Guard!"

* * *

"Anytime you're ready."

The man calling himself Antonio leaned on the low wall of the terrace outside the Grande Salle, smoking a Turkish cigarette. Antonio was a good name, and it said as much on his Italian passport. He was not Italian, though he could (and did) pass for it easily. His name was not Antonio.

He was dressed for the event, in a stylish and sharply cut dark blue Italian suit, with shoes of Spanish leather. His hair was short and curly, but well-controlled with hairspray. He was clean shaven and good-looking. His hands were neatly manicured.

103

It was a beautiful night, crisp and cold, with a hint of the coming winter in the air. He was from a warmer climate, so snow and ice were not for him, but he enjoyed the cool air of fall. Between the night, and the cigarette, and the two glasses of wine he'd had, it was a lovely sensation to just stand here, looking out at the buildings and the lights of the old town. But he was working.

In the darkness, it was not easy to see that in his free hand he was holding a thin but sturdy piece of rope. It extended away from him, off the side of the wall, and down three stories to the side street below him. There had been guards at the entrance checking for weapons, so they had been reduced to this.

Of course, it had been their fallback position all along. Abdyl had thought of this possibility ahead of time. Abdyl rarely got caught off guard.

Down in the narrow street, a man appeared. He was away from the stragglers at the front, who were still coming in. He was carrying a dark plastic bucket with a lid on it. As Antonio watched while appearing not to notice, the man tied the handle of the bucket to the far end of the length of rope Antonio was holding.

When the man was done, he gave the rope two yanks, then walked away down the street. He turned into an alleyway perhaps 20 meters further along. The streets around here were narrow, and each new turn was narrower and narrower still.

When the man was gone, Antonio put the cigarette in his mouth, and pulled the bucket up, hand over hand. He looked like a fisherman hauling a trap out of the sea. The bucket was heavy, a reasonable weight.

Antonio glanced around. There was a couple down the terrace from him, at the far end, smoking cigarettes and having what looked like an intimate conversation. They were paying no attention to him.

He brought the bucket up to the top of the wall, then set it down on the terrace in the shadow of the wall. He pulled the hard plastic lid off. Here were five loaded pistols from the Czech Republic. Good guns, clean. It was an innovative, simple solution to what could have been a difficult problem. Antonio reached into the bucket, took a gun out, and slipped it into his inner jacket pocket. He felt the weight of the gun there, making the jacket sag a bit.

Antonio glanced at the couple. They were making out now, pressed into each other's arms, their lit cigarettes extended out and away. If they had been ignoring him before, by now they had forgotten he existed. Antonio smiled as he took another gun out of the bucket. This was perfect. Leave it to Abdyl.

Antonio worked quickly, securing the guns in his various pockets, then lowered the bucket over the side again. The man was waiting in the alley he had turned down. As soon as the bucket touched down in the street, he would return, pick up the bucket and the rope, and disappear again. No bucket, no rope.

The men got into the building with guns, but no one knows how.

Antonio took a deep drag of his smoke before he went inside. He savored it, holding the smoke in his lungs for a long moment. This was going to be an outrageous, audacious display. A woman from a rich banking family, abducted at gunpoint from her own charitable event.

Normally, Antonio felt that public displays were not wise. He had learned this point of view from his father, and his grandfather before that, who for decades had run small gambling, liquor, and cigarette bootlegging, and prostitution businesses, even under the communists, who frowned upon things of this nature.

"Keep things quiet." That was Antonio's grandfather's mantra. "Don't talk too much. Don't make a stink about anything."

He had died a free man at a ripe old age.

But there wasn't much that could be done about this. Circumstances had changed, and it had become clear that Aliz Willems was going to be targeted by law enforcement, if not right away, then sometime soon. If not in Luxembourg, then in France, or Belgium, or Germany. If not in those places, the United States was sure to become involved, if they weren't already.

Willems tended to hide herself away. And when she was hidden, she was hard to find. But not tonight. Tonight, she had broken cover. And her puny attempt at security had all but guaranteed the night's outcome.

Antonio took one last drag of his cigarette then tossed the butt over the side. He looked down to where it had fallen. The bucket and rope were already gone.

He turned, without hesitation now, and carried the guns into the party.

CHAPTER FIFTEEN

8:45 pm Central European Daylight Time
Cercle Cité
Place d'Armes, Ville Haute quarter
Luxembourg City, Luxembourg

Two big guards in sports jackets converged on Troy.

He still had Aliz firmly by the wrist. He had the beer bottle in his other hand. "It's not gonna work," he said to her.

But he wasn't sure about that. He might have overstepped. Many people had heard the glass shatter. Easily 20 or 30 people were staring at them now, including Dubois, who had attached herself to a new group standing near a bright abstract painting in bold colors, red and blue and green.

It was nice. Troy liked paintings like that, paintings about nothing. He couldn't say why they appealed to him; they just did. Large, splotchy, cube-y colors, utterly meaningless. He liked to read their names, usually something like *Three Girls Dancing,* though only a maniac could see three girls there. He liked to read about what the artist was trying to get at, often something about living in the moment after the mass destruction of World War I, or something along those lines.

Here came the guards, both about to reach him at nearly the same time. They were large men, bulky, both with either guns or tasers in their jackets.

Troy wasn't sure what to do. His mind raced through the options. If he went limp, these two guys would grab him and probably walk him out of here. That would give Aliz the chance to disappear again, out another door, likely into a waiting car. He may never get this opportunity again. That was no good.

If Troy fought them, he was going to make a mess.

His grandmother had come to America from Ireland. He knew her when he was a child, and she had an old saying she was fond of.

"In for a penny, in for a pound."

If he was going to make a mess, he might as well make a big one.

He released Aliz's grip and threw his half-full beer at the first guard's head. The man ducked, the bottle soaring over his head. As he ducked, Troy hopped, gained momentum, and kicked the man in the face while airborne. The man's head snapped up and he flew backwards, hitting his head on the polished floor.

Ouch. Might have overdone that.

Troy spun, crouching low at the same time. The second guard was nearly on top of him, towering above him. Troy went down on one knee. He threw the right hand, the hard right, straight into the man's groin. Then he came with the left, an uppercut, into the exact same spot.

In his head, he heard his old white-haired cornerman Declan, when Troy was a 16-year-old Golden Gloves fighter, singing out:

One-two, Troy! One-two!

He hit the man in the balls. Twice.

The second one, coming as it did from below, ended the fight right there. The big man went down sideways like a heavy sack of rocks, his hands cupped to tender parts. He was out of it, maybe for a minute, maybe for five minutes, but he had a weapon in that jacket, and when he regained his composure, he was going to be eager to use it.

Troy jumped up to his full height again. Aliz was still standing there, nearly frozen. His left hand snaked out and clamped onto her wrist again.

"Listen to me," he said. "I need you to come with me."

Her eyes were large, like a child's eyes. "No!"

"Aliz…"

Suddenly, there was an even louder commotion behind him. A gasp, and then shouts and screams.

Troy spun, still gripping Aliz's wrist. He was half-expecting to see more guards coming, or maybe the first guard oozing blood onto the floor from a cracked skull. But it was neither of these things.

A group of men in tuxedos were moving through the crowd with guns in hand. They were dark men, sun-kissed, like Greeks or Italians. Or Syrians. Or Tunisians.

Troy counted four, then five, spreading out, like a bank robbery.

One stopped, pointed his gun at the grand chandelier, and fired.

BANG! BANG! BANG! BANG! BANG!

People ducked away and ran as crystal shattered, and then the entire chandelier fell from the high ceiling and crashed to the floor. If the wine glass had been a bomb before, this was the Hiroshima bomb. Tiny glimmering shards sprayed through the air as giant chunks of crystal slid outwards along the floor.

The man still had his gun raised. "Everyone! Get down! On the floor!"

Then he shouted in French. Then he shouted in another language, Troy thought German.

Troy looked at Aliz. "Kick those shoes off. We gotta go!"

Her eyes were wide. Blank.

"Your shoes! Get rid of them!"

There was no way to run in those things. She nodded, getting him now. She kicked one off, then the next.

Troy glanced at the crowd. Dubois was running their way, darting in and out of party guests, some frozen, some who couldn't get to the floor fast enough. Dubois had already kicked off her shoes.

"What is it?" Dubois said.

Troy shook his head. "I don't know. Maybe an art heist. I don't know. Grab her other wrist and let's go."

Dubois seized Aliz's wrist and the two of them dragged her toward the double doors to the foyer. Although she had kicked her shoes off, she was now dragging her feet across the parquet, sliding along. She didn't want to stay, but she wasn't sure if she wanted to go, either.

"You! Stop!"

Troy turned and one of the gunmen was pointing his way.

Then they all started moving, at once. This was not an art heist. This was not a shakedown of rich patrons at a fundraiser. This was... something else.

"Come on!" Troy screamed.

He stopped and slapped Aliz across the face. "Come on! Run!"

Dubois hiked her blue sequined dress up around her waist, freeing her muscular legs. Then they took off with Aliz again. She ran this time. The three of them tore through the bar area, stragglers diving out of their way.

A gunshot rang out!

BANG!

Troy didn't even glance back. They ran for the central staircase. It was a problem, because it spiraled back around. If the gunman was behind them, the stairs would take them back towards, and below him.

They were flying now. Suddenly Dubois let go.

Troy didn't even slow down. He and Aliz careened down the stairs, wrapping back around. He glanced up. Dubois was there. The gunman ran toward her. She had darted to the side, as if to let him pass. He didn't care about her. He was getting ready to aim his shots down into the stairwell.

Troy caught a glimpse of Dubois leaping into the air, her body nearly horizontal, like a high jumper in track and field. Her legs kicked

108

out and just about took the gunman's head off. They both fell to the floor.

Troy got a sense of Dubois up again and moving like a cat, but then he and Aliz were at the bottom of the stairs and running down the long hall. His mind pictured that, behind Dubois, more dark men were coming.

This is NOT an art heist.

"You're kind of popular tonight!" he shouted at Aliz.

The two guards who had been checking people for weapons appeared at the top of the wide main stairwell. They came running up the hall, their guns out.

"There are men with guns upstairs!" Troy said. "I'll take care of her."

The guards blew past, barely slowing.

Troy and Aliz barreled down the stairwell. Aliz slipped and fell, sliding upside down and on her side. They lost precious seconds as they slowed to a stop, and Troy dragged her to her feet again.

Behind them, gunshots rang out, then more gunshots.

It was the OK Corral up there.

Troy glanced back, and here came Dubois, hell bent, flying down the stairs like a missile. "They shot the guards!" she screamed. "Run! They're right behind me!"

Troy renewed his iron grip on Aliz's wrist. "You better run," he said.

They ran through the stone tunnel and out to the street. The plaza was deserted. Something about gunshots made people call it a night. They ran across the plaza, Aliz half-limping now. They weren't going fast enough.

"My feet! I have no shoes on! It hurts!"

"Run!" Troy said.

He dragged her along. He looked back. Here came Dubois. She was moving fast. In another couple of seconds, she was going to zoom past them.

Behind her, a man with a gun was also running.

Troy and Aliz reached the far side of the wide-open plaza. They ducked into the shadows along the tree-lined street. The car was right here… somewhere.

Troy reached into his pocket and pulled the fob. He clicked it and the car chirped, the brake lights blinking on and off. It was just ten meters ahead of them.

"Get in the back seat," he said to Aliz.

Dubois was moving along the passenger side.

Troy went straight to the tire on the driver's side and pulled out the small pocket pistol. He turned, and the gunman was almost on top of him. The guy was coming fast, full speed, his gun in one hand. He was going to crash into Troy.

Troy lifted the gun and...

BANG! BANG!

He shot the guy in the chest, which slowed him down, and then in the head, which dropped him.

Troy slid into the driver's seat and started the car. He handed Dubois the gun.

"Hold this. It might come in handy."

She stared at him. "Did you just kill that guy?"

Troy nodded. "Yeah."

He put the car into gear and pulled out into the street. For a second, he held out hope that this might be okay. They might just quietly drive away from here down some side streets, cruise out of town, and take the subject somewhere to question her. Dubois must know a place.

Then he looked in the rearview mirror. Across the plaza, two small cars had just roared away from the building. Troy watched them. Just before their headlights came on, he thought he identified them as Mini-Coopers. Small, fast, highly maneuverable.

"Okay," he said. "We still have a problem. They're coming after us. We need to find a way to ditch them. Aliz, this is your town. How do we get out of here?"

She didn't answer.

"Aliz?"

She didn't answer.

He was tearing down narrow, winding streets, the buildings standing right on the road. He zipped around an old man bent over a cane.

"Aliz!"

"What?"

"Where are we going?"

She answered a question with a question. "Who are you people?"

"We're the police," Dubois said. She sat with the small gun in her tiny hand, watching behind them. She had pulled her blue dress back down, making time for modesty.

They rumbled uphill across some cobblestones. A fresh produce stand was on the street, unattended. It was a little late for that, wasn't it?

He crashed through it, sending fruits and vegetables flying.

110

"Miquel said don't hurt the car!"

"That didn't hurt," Troy said.

The Minis were gaining. Troy could only go so fast. The last thing he wanted was to hit any innocent civilians. These streets were too narrow.

Up ahead, a small building seemed to sit in the middle of the street. The roadway flowed around it on either side. The first Mini was right behind him now. The driver put his brights on, filling the Jaguar with light. He was trying to blind them.

Troy skimmed along to the right of the building. It was incredibly narrow back here. The car was sandwiched between the building to his left, and a high stone wall to his right. There were doorways all along here. Anyone could simply step out into the street at any second.

The car scraped the wall, sparks flying.

"Stark!"

"I'm trying." He didn't really care about the car.

The Mini was right on his tail. He had a hunch that...

The building ended, and to his left, the roadway came back together again. The other Mini was RIGHT THERE. It had hightailed along the left side of the building. They were going to...

CRASH!

The cars bounced off each other.

A window was down on the Mini. A man with a gun aimed at the Jag. Troy veered left, this time intentionally. He drove the other car up onto the narrow sidewalk, and into the building. The gunman disappeared, thrown around the cabin of the Mini. Troy kept going.

He lifted the forefinger of his right hand. His left was still on the wheel.

"Don't say a word about this car."

He glanced in the rearview mirror. The one Mini was still right behind him, lights blinding. He adjusted the mirror, trying to see if the second car was out of commission. No. As he watched, it rolled off the sidewalk and rejoined the chase.

"Dammit!"

Somewhere, he heard sirens. He wasn't sure if that was good or bad. He and Dubois were cops too, but they weren't supposed to make arrests. On some level, this was an abduction. Or some kind of...

The Mini crashed into the rear of the Jag, nudging it hard while they drove.

Dubois groaned. Just behind Troy, Aliz shrieked. The sound sent a shiver through his body.

"Aliz! No screaming. We're not screaming right now, okay?"

"Okay," she said in a small voice. "It's just that…"

"No screaming," he said again. "I'm afraid I'm going to have to insist."

"All right."

"I'm with Interpol," Dubois said. "He's with the New York City Police Department. You're safe with us. There's no need to…"

BAM! The Mini bumped them again. That one was harder. Troy was jostled. He nearly lost his grip on the wheel.

Aliz didn't scream. She made a squeak like a frightened mouse.

The roadway made a steep drop toward an old stone bridge. Both Minis were right behind them again, three cars in a row, running fast through the night. They crossed the bridge at high speed. At the far end, the tight streets went right or left. An old building, painted in pastel blue, was right in front of them, coming fast. Troy checked the rearview. Still two cars right behind.

"Which way?" he said.

Aliz wouldn't commit. "Uh…"

He shouted it this time. "Aliz! Which way?"

"Right! Go right!"

The angle at the end of the bridge was sharp. He spun the wheel, the beat-up car sliding as he made the turn. It took him down another winding alley of a road, this one along the edge of the canal they had just crossed. The road dropped steeply to nearly water level.

And came to an end in a dirt parking lot.

"Left!" she shouted. "I should have said left."

"We have trouble," Dubois said.

Troy looked at her. "Thanks. I didn't know."

He rumbled across the lot, the two pursuing cars spreading out, behind and on either side of the Jag. They were all going to run out of lot in a moment and come to the water's edge. The town was above their heads now, the houses and buildings set back, and climbing up the hill. They could die down here.

"Mariem, I'm about to turn this thing around."

She nodded. "Okay."

"When I do, I'm going to put you on their side."

"Great."

"I want you to lay down covering fire as we slide around. Just light them up with whatever you got."

"Stark? I checked the gun. I have four rounds left in this magazine. I can't exactly light them up."

He nodded, sort of shrugged.

"In that case, use them judiciously."

He tried to think what he had done with the extra magazine. He had left it somewhere. Maybe it had been on the tire with the gun. If true, then they really only had four shots left. That mag was long gone now.

"Shoot at them. Take their tires out, if you can. Save us one round. We might need it." He looked at Aliz in the rearview. She looked bad. Her hair was mussed. Her eyes were wild. Her mouth was hanging open. "Aliz, I need you to get down low. Might be some bullets flying in a moment."

She crouched down, but not nearly enough.

"Down. Below and behind my seat."

She went a little further. It would have to do.

The end of the lot was coming right up. This was for all the marbles. "Are we having fun yet?"

"No," Dubois said.

"Get ready. Because here we go."

He turned the wheel hard. The car spun on the dirt and gravel. Dubois put the gun out the shattered window.

For a second, the car was straight perpendicular to the pursuers.

BANG!

A half second passed, then:

BANG! BANG!

Dubois got the three shots off. But now the Jaguar was facing the other two cars, headlights to headlights. The Minis slid to a halt, side by side, crashing into each other, then separating again. Their engines revved. Smoke and steam rose. Troy smelled a faint, wretched odor of raw gasoline.

One of those cars had an exposed gas line. All this jostling had ripped it open. He grinned. It was going to get real nasty sitting inside that thing in a minute. Raw gasoline would make you puke. It would make you pass out.

But they were blocking the way out. He was going to have to go around them somehow.

"Stark?" Dubois said.

"Yeah?"

"What are we doing?"

"We're figuring that out right now."

A passenger side door opened on the car on Troy's left. A man got out. He had a gun in his hand.

"Stark?"

"Yeah, yeah. I see him."

Suddenly the car's engine roared, wheels spinning on the dirt and gravel. It lurched forward, covering the small space between the cars in one second.

BOOM!

Troy's head lurched from the impact. The car had crashed directly into the front of the Jag. That was bad. They were going to use one car as a battering ram and beat this thing into the ground.

"Stark!" Dubois screamed. "He's coming!"

"Oh my God," Aliz said in the back.

The man who had gotten out of the car was running across the lot. He was dressed in a tux, just like Troy. He ran straight for the passenger side.

"Shoot him. Shoot that guy."

The man ran past her. Dubois didn't fire. Neither did the man. Instead, he used his gun to smash the rear passenger window.

Aliz screamed.

In front, a man was leaning out the window of the second car. He had a machine gun. These guys were not playing around. In another second, they were going to have the situation completely…

The first man was climbing through the back window.

They couldn't get taken prisoner here.

"Shoot that guy!"

Troy slammed the car into gear and stomped on the gas. The man was halfway through the window. From the corner of his eye, Troy saw him nearly lose his balance and fall out of the car. He dropped his gun.

Troy veered hard to the right and skimmed along the edge of the facing car. The guy with the machine gun was still leaning out of the window. He was sighted on the car. Too late, he realized Troy was coming right at him.

Metal scraped metal, loud, horrible as Troy shredded both cars against each other, like two cats rubbing their bodies together.

The man looked up.

Too late.

Troy took the top half of his body off. It made a thud against Troy's cracked windshield, the man's head and hands hitting the glass, the machine gun flying into the night. The head…

Never mind.

"Oh, man."

He kept going. They were past the two cars now and running for the road again.

"Stark!" Dubois screamed next to him.

Troy looked back. The guy was inside the car. He had made it. For a second, Troy thought he had fallen off. But no. Now he was in here.

He was in the rear seat. He was a dark man, not black, like an Italian. Dark hair, dark eyebrows. He was calm, a professional. He grabbed Aliz by the hair and pulled her close to him. Aliz made a low moaning sound deep in her throat.

A knife flashed in the lights passing overhead. He held the blade to Aliz's neck.

"Stop the car," he said. "We just want to talk."

"Drop the knife," Dubois said. She had the gun pointed at the man's head. By Troy's count, she had conserved that last bullet. Good girl.

"You put down the gun and he stops the car. And I won't kill her."

The man spoke English with an accent. It seemed like one Troy could nearly place, like he had heard that exact accent before. He watched the road approaching ahead. He looked back into the rearview. The other cars seemed to have issues back there. A dead guy cut in half was an issue. Half in the car, half in the parking lot.

Yeah, that was a major issue. Wouldn't want to drive around town in a busted-up car with a problem like that. You were just asking to get pulled over... by somebody.

"Just shoot that guy," Troy said to Dubois. "Kill him."

"I swear," Dubois said. "Drop that knife."

The guy in the back tried a new strategy. "Hand me the gun, and I won't kill her. You can all still walk away from this. You will be free to..."

"If you hurt her, I will shoot you in the head."

"Please," Aliz said. "Please! Make it stop."

The guy pressed the knife deep into the flesh of her neck. A little more pressure and he was going to cut into it.

Troy put his left hand on the wheel. They were going uphill now, back into the town. In another second, they would reach the bridge again. A right turn from the bridge was the wrong direction, so this time he would just go straight, as though he had made a left from the bridge in the first place.

"Give me the gun," he said to Dubois.

She looked at him.

"Yeah. Give it to me. Don't worry about pointing it at him. Just give it."

Now she handed him the gun. Troy was half-turned, one hand on the wheel, one hand extended backwards, pointing the gun at the man's forehead. The man's dark hair was curly, and short.

"You have a name?" Troy said.

The guy grinned. "Antonio, if you like."

Of course, it was an alias. No one ever had a real name.

"Well, Antonio. I'm only going to say this once. Drop the knife and I'll let you out of the car. I mean that. You can live through this and walk away."

The grin became broader. The guy was a rock star. This kind of thing clearly didn't bother him at all. He breathed in and out, slowly. One big hand gripped Aliz's hair near the scalp. The other had the knife pressed to her throat. Aliz's eyes were huge and round. They reminded Troy of cow's eyes he had once dissected in a high school biology class. Her mouth trembled.

"You won't shoot me," Antonio said.

BANG!

Troy pulled the trigger. It was close range. The shot went into the man's forehead and exited out the back. A spray of blood and gore went out the back of the man's head, splattering on the rear window.

He went instantly slack and fell over sideways. There was a dark hole in the middle of his forehead. Blood began to flow from it in a tiny rivulet and run down his nose.

"Oh my God," Dubois said. "Oh my God. Oh my God."

Aliz screamed. She scrabbled to get away from the man, as far away as she could while staying in the car. She didn't say anything. She just went from screaming to whining, squeaking noises.

Dubois had her hands on top of her head.

"Oh my God." She looked at Troy. "You just shot that man."

I guess you didn't see the guy I cut in half a minute ago.

"What were you going to do?" he said. "Wait until he killed her, and then shoot him? Does that make sense to you? It doesn't to me. Anyway, I warned him."

He looked in the back seat. There was blood all over the place, especially on the rear window. There were bits of hair and bone and brains as well. The guy was slumped against the seat, his head at a sharp angle to his body that no living person would tolerate. Aliz looked like someone walking through a horror movie. Her natural beauty wasn't helping her much at this moment. Everything was bad back there.

"We gotta get this thing tidied up," Troy said.

116

"Are you going to ask her for that autograph now?"

He gestured through the shattered window at the book on the floor, between her stockinged feet. Dubois was glaring at him, her eyes hard.

They were parked in a dirt lot, somewhere outside the city. The good thing about Luxembourg City was there was no endless sprawl of suburbs. The city limit came, and then the city pretty much ended. It looked like someone was doing some tree cutting here. There was this cleared area with a blue portable toilet. There were some tree stumps along the edge of the cleared area, and then deeper woods.

Troy opened the rear passenger door and pulled the body out. He dropped it to the ground. Steam was coming from the radiator, but it didn't seem that bad. The car hadn't overheated while they were driving. The car itself probably wasn't the issue. The bullet holes and the steam rising, and the smashed windows, were one thing. But the blood in the back was something else again.

"I know you don't like me very much right now," he said to Dubois. "That's fine. But we need to find a way to sop up some of that blood. The little bits of gore…"

Aliz Willems made a noise at the word *gore*. It was a low noise, not at all loud. It sounded like, "aaahhhaa…" She was evolving backwards, to a pre-verbal period of human history. She was going to be no help at all. She stared straight ahead, like she had seen a ghost, and was still seeing it.

"The last thing we want to do is try to explain ourselves to the local cops, right? We just want to get someplace tucked away, hide this car, and see what our subject knows. I don't know about you, but at this moment, I'm thinking she knows a lot."

"You want me to clean up the blood?" Dubois said.

"Yeah."

"What are you going to do?"

Troy kicked the corpse at his feet. "I'm going to get rid of this body."

Dubois was beginning to regain her composure. That was good. Her recovery time was quick. She probably hadn't been involved in anything quite like this, and she had frozen when the time came to kill, but she wasn't in shock. She was a tough lady, and she was bouncing back.

She nodded. "All right. But I want to know who you are. You're not a police officer. Who do you work for? The CIA?"

There wasn't a lot of time, but he supposed he owed her that much. "Clean first, and I promise I'll tell you. Okay?"

She sighed. "Okay."

Troy crouched down by the dead guy and went through his pockets. He had a fat money clip. Troy took that. He pulled the bills out and rifled through them - about three thousand euros. He put it in his own pocket. No sense leaving it behind. His hands roamed the guy's pants and jacket pockets. There was a pack of cigarettes, four or five smokes left in there. A lighter. Some keys. Not much else. No identification.

Troy grabbed the guy by his calves and dragged him backwards towards the woods. It took him about two minutes to reach the edge of the forest. Then he kept going. When he was about a hundred meters in, he stopped.

It was very dark back here. The woods were dense. Troy reached into his own pocket and found the little blue box with the GPS units. He took one out and slipped it in the breast pocket of the dead guy's jacket.

A little gift for Alex.

Troy stood over the corpse for a moment, looking down at it. Just another dead guy, a man of action who hit the wall before he saw it coming. The guy had dressed sharp tonight. He had three grand burning a hole in his pocket. And he had gambled big back there, diving into a moving car.

Troy remembered the guy's last words: *You won't shoot me.*

Overconfidence would kill you. Troy had seen it before, many times. Now the guy was dead, laid out here in the woods, waiting for the squirrels to come and eat him. Or the rats. Or the crows. Whoever came along.

Troy shook his head. "Oh buddy," he said to the corpse.

Maybe Alex would come here and bury the guy, or cremate him, or just… say a little Sikh prayer over him.

Troy turned and walked back out of the woods. In the clearing, Dubois had stripped down to her bra and panties and was sopping up the blood with her dress and her panty hose. Troy barely glanced at her body. If he did, he would end up saying something. This wasn't the time.

He looked in the back of the car instead. It was good. She was getting it clean. If they got stopped, and the car was impounded, it would never pass muster. The thing was a petri dish filled with the dead guy's DNA. But short of an impound, they might just get out of this.

The car had stopped steaming. It was a comfortable night, cool but not cold. The windows, instead of being shattered, might just be down. Okay, yes, there were bullet holes all along the side, and the windshield was cracked, but...

There was no sense thinking about all that.

Dubois backed out of the car, stood to her full height, not very high, and went face to face with Troy. Face to neck, actually.

"Okay. Tell me. Who are you? I have a right to know."

He kept his voice down. "My name is Troy Stark. It really is. I grew up in New York City, in the Bronx, just like I said."

"Who do you work for?"

"I'm employed by the NYPD, through a contract with the federal government. I'm part of a budget line item called Miscellaneous. They might have spent the money on paint for the precinct houses. They might have spent it on floor mats for the patrol cars."

"What does that even mean?" she said.

"I'm black operations, sweetheart. There was a terrorist attack in New York..." He thought about the timeline. It seemed he had been going nonstop and had barely slept. "...just over two days ago."

She nodded. "Yes. I'm aware."

"I was brought on to learn who did it, find those people, and make sure they can't do it again. So that's what I'm going to do, if I can. It's really that simple."

"Are you going to kill them?"

Troy shrugged. "It depends."

"On what?"

"On whether I find them or not."

There was a long pause between them. He glanced away from her, at the Jaguar. The thing was not in good shape. Troy didn't know this Miquel Castro dude from Mickey Mouse, but he did know one thing about him: he wasn't going to be happy about this car.

Troy focused on Dubois again.

"Is that okay with you?"

She shook her head. "I don't know."

He stepped past her. "Well, while you figure that out, we need to get moving."

He looked in the window at Aliz. "Aliz, we need a place to hide. A place where we can park this car out of sight, and where we can talk, and no one can find us there. Do you know of any place like that around here?"

She stared at him blankly. She was very pretty, but she seemed a bit hollowed out at this moment.

"I have a place we can go," she said.

CHAPTER SIXTEEN

10:45 pm Central European Daylight Time
Interpol Liaison Office - Special Investigations Unit
Europol Headquarters
The Hague, The Netherlands

"Why are you still here?" Bakker said.

Miquel looked at the huge back and skull of Jan Bakker. Bakker, true to form, was staring into three computer monitors at once. He was drinking a cup of coffee, even though it was the middle of the night. As he often did, he spoke without turning around.

"Why am I still here? I'm waiting to be fired. Why are you still here?"

Miquel had seen the security footage from the fundraiser in Luxembourg City. The video quality was not the best - grainy, black and white, and taken from a distance. It seemed that the Cercle Cité venue had not updated their camera equipment to align with the modern age. At the same time, it was clear to him that Dubois and Stark were in the footage. It seemed so obvious that no one could miss it.

He had told his superiors that Stark had gone back to New York, and Dubois had gone to Lyon. It would be obvious now that he had lied about this. Or they had lied, and he covered for them. Or he simply did not know where they went. None of these options boded well for his continued employment here.

And yet, the call to come upstairs and be let go had not come. Maybe that was because most people had gone home hours ago. His superiors might not even know about this incident, other than watching news of it on television. By tomorrow, it would become clear that Miquel had told the bosses one thing and done something else entirely.

"I would not assume you will be fired," Bakker said. "I've seen the video, and I've even cleaned it up a bit, improved the resolution. It is not clear to me that Dubois and Stark are the ones in the video. If you're predisposed to think Dubois went to France, then you would have no reason to think the Luxembourg incident is related at all."

He paused, but only for a few seconds. He used the time to spin slowly around in his chair and face Miquel. "We know it was them because we know they went there. Their names were not on the guest list, obviously. Most people think they went home. If Dubois turns up in Lyon in the morning…"

He raised his hands, palms upwards.

"What did you tell the other analysts?" Miquel said.

"You mean Europol, and the Netherlanders?"

Miquel shrugged. "Also, our own analysts."

"I'll be honest with you, Miquel. There are many leads being tracked. Thousands, in fact, all over the world. There are many possible conduits for drone sales, underground and normal channels. There are many bad actors. There are many state sponsors of terrorism. There are many terror networks and sleeper cells, certainly in New York City, but also in Belgium. The possibilities are nearly endless. SymAero did not have a corner on the so-called slaughterbot technology. They were not out ahead of the crowd. They learned about a well-understood technology, and then made it available for sale. Van Gent's own statements appear to incriminate them and suggest that they filled an order for seven such drones. But those statements were made under duress and have been retracted."

"What are you telling me?" Miquel said.

"That I am the only Interpol analyst currently working the SymAero angle. I shared the SymAero files I seized with analysts from Europol and the Dutch National Police, but it's a great deal of information, and there are only a few people even looking at it. Europol seems to view the SymAero raid as an embarrassment, and the Dutch Police are very sensitive to accusations of police brutality."

"So they're backing off this?" Miquel said.

His emotions were having a tug of war. On the one hand, he believed that SymAero was the best lead he had seen. But he had been in the field long enough to know how personal biases could cloud a person's reasoning. He wanted this to be the one. And why did he want that? Because his people had stuck their necks out and brought in this intelligence? Because he selfishly wanted the glory of stopping these terrorists? Because it would put him back on the map, and change the trajectory of his career?

No. He didn't think so. His motives were pure. He wanted this to be the one because of Atocha Train Station. He wanted to save lives.

"There isn't any hard evidence that a crime was committed," Bakker said. "Other than the man brandishing a gun, which was very foolish, but is unlikely to result in significant punishment. The gun itself was manufactured in 1939 and does not appear to be operable.

"Of course, there is the possible question of tax evasion. But the sale took place earlier this calendar year, so the company wouldn't even have been required to report it yet. They can say that the transfer took place to an opaque account to shield their own identity from the buyer, and it was always their intention to move it into one of the transparent corporate accounts at a later time. Selling drones and drone technology is not against the law. They didn't sell explosives, nor did they make it clear in any communications I've seen that the drones could be easily modified to carry explosives. Given how the admission of guilt was obtained, I believe those men are probably off the hook, and may have grounds for a lawsuit against this office, and against Europol for harboring this office. I'd expect to hear from their lawyers within days."

"Terrific," Miquel said. "They won't have to sell any more drones to terrorists. They can retire as multimillionaires from the lawsuit proceeds."

Bakker smiled. He didn't say anything. For someone so large, he was a mercurial man. In Miquel's experience, big strong men like this were usually more than happy to throw their opinions around. Often this was whether you wanted their opinion or not.

"So what did you tell them about The Shadow?"

Bakker shook his head. "Nothing. Outside of this office, I told no one about it. It is really a bit of a hunch. The trail goes in that direction, but the last few steps are more of an educated guess, maybe even a leap of faith."

Miquel frowned. "So you're not certain it was correct?"

That was worrisome, and not at all like Bakker. They had just sent two agents undercover into what was apparently a life-threatening situation. Miquel hoped that it wasn't based on a stab in the dark.

But now Bakker grinned. He lowered his voice and spoke just above a whisper. "Oh, I'm 100% certain. I know they sold slaughterbot drones to The Shadow, and I know The Shadow is Aliz Willems. I didn't share that information because I arrived at the conclusion in an eccentric, some might say unprofessional, manner. Also, I was afraid that if I did share the information, the subject might disappear. She has many places to run and hide, and she is very well-connected. With the intelligence agencies, you never know…"

Again, he put his hands up, but he was still grinning.

"…who really works for whom. I shared the information with you because I knew you would be willing to act immediately, and there was no danger of a leak. Also, we happened to have at our temporary disposal the American, Troy Stark. He elevates our enforcement game, you might say."

"What do you know about him?"

"Nothing I care to share at this time. It won't help you to be aware of a data breach of classified material. Let's just say I believe he will do a good job finding out whether the drones sold to The Shadow were the same ones used in the attacks. And I believe he will do this quickly and in the most efficient way available."

"Which brings me back to my original question," Miquel said. "What are you doing here now?"

Bakker gestured at the computer monitors behind him. "Stark and Dubois clearly took The Shadow with them. They appear to have escaped, but they have not tried to communicate with us. I'm trying to determine where they went."

CHAPTER SEVENTEEN

11:45 pm Central European Daylight Time
Engel Castle
Engeldorf-Pont
Luxembourg

"There was a Roman sentry tower here in the first century," Aliz Willems said.

To Troy Stark, her voice was like a songbird's call. A scientist could use it to categorize her, pinpoint her in a specific place and time.

She spoke with the clipped and refined voice of that golden class of people. She had lived in the best places, had gone to the best schools, and only fraternized with the best people. Troy could hear it. Somehow her voice let you know.

"The ancient keep is still there, at the center of the castle. The castle itself, as it stands now, was built on the remains of the watchtower, and later forts. That happened about the year 1200. Europe has a much longer history than America."

Troy was standing at a large bay window, looking up at the sprawling medieval stone castle that commanded the hillside above them. It was lit up in the darkness, lights positioned to make it dominate the night.

The place was a bit of a wreck. From here, he could see that parts of the roof were missing, and much of the castle was open to the elements. There was a wide stone wall around it, with a narrow bridge across to a gate. There were spiral towers with giant windows. Did they have glass in the Dark Ages? Troy had no idea.

Apparently, Aliz Willems owned the castle.

"Why do you have it lit up?"

"It's always alight," she said. "That's so people can see it. It's something of a national treasure."

They were in an old mansion at the base of the rocky outcropping the castle stood upon. They hadn't turned on any lights when they came in. That was good. The fact that the castle was always lit up was also good. Nothing was amiss. It could very well be that nobody was home.

There was a seven-car garage outside on the grounds. Only three cars had been in it when they arrived, all of them wrapped in showroom drapes. Troy had put the wreck of the Jaguar in there, and once it stopped smoking, he wrapped it in an extra drape he found folded and put away in a chest. He was satisfied, he supposed. They could be okay here. He hoped so.

He hadn't seen much of the house other than this room, but he could tell it was large, and very stylish. From the outside, it seemed like a Victorian mansion, or something along those lines. In here, it seemed the interior had been ripped out and replaced with modern everything.

He turned and looked at Aliz. The lights cast from the castle were shining through the window. It gave this large room a sort of ambient light and shadow effect that he enjoyed. They were in the gloom, but he could see pretty well.

She was sitting on a sofa, drinking a glass of red wine. She was still wearing the bright red dress that had caught his eye when he was at the gala. Her legs were folded under her. She had made no attempt to do anything since they came in here, other than pour herself a drink. Drink, and act as a stationary tour guide to the wonders of the Willems family, and their belongings.

"This property was a hideout for Luxembourg Resistance fighters during World War Two," she said. "There's a wine cellar, and beneath that, there's a sub-basement. The castle is very large, much larger than the house, and there are small, half-collapsed rooms deep inside of it that are difficult to reach. The bridge in town here, on the other side of it, is rural Germany. Fighters could take cover in the sub-basement, and inside the castle, and easily move weapons and men back and forth across the border. My grandfather was a terrible person in many ways, but I'll give him credit for one thing - he had no love for the Nazis."

Did Troy Stark care about heroic Willems family history? No, he did not. But this is what the woman had done since she finally started speaking again. Pontificate, basically.

Dubois, on the other hand, had taken her regular street clothes in a pile and had gone looking for a bathroom. Some people did stuff. Some people didn't do stuff. Troy had no judgment about that part. Sometimes the best, most effective thing to do was nothing.

Aliz seemed to be recovering from her shock. That was a good thing. It was probably the alcohol helping her along, combined with the familiar surroundings. This was her turf. She knew the house. They were locked inside. They were hiding. Very probably, no one could get her here.

126

Now it was time for her to talk. She had already started. Maybe it would be easy enough to keep her going.

"Who were those men, and why did they want you?" he said. "Why were there metal detectors at your fundraising event?"

She shook her head and took another sip of her wine. She had brought the bottle onto the couch with her.

"I don't even know who you people are. You crashed my event, evidently. And I'm guessing you're police of some kind."

"You're welcome," Troy said.

"I'm welcome to what?"

"We saved your life, Lady Jane."

She shook her head. "I don't know if that's true. I don't know what would have happened if you hadn't…"

"Intervened?" he said.

She waved a hand. "Sure. If you like."

"I'll tell you what would have happened," Troy said. "Those men would have taken you to a secluded place somewhere, they would have killed you, and then they would have made your body disappear. Depending on what kind of animals they are, and how pressed for time they were, they might have raped you before they murdered you."

"I don't believe it," she said.

He shrugged. "Okay. Believe what you want. But your life is in danger, some very bad people are involved, and right now I'm about the only friend you have."

She sipped her wine again. That was good.

Drink, baby. Drink.

"Who are you, please?" she said. "I gather you gave a false name at the party."

"My name is Troy Stark," he said. "I'm a special investigator for the New York City Police Department. The woman with me is Agent Mariem Dubois, with the Interpol Special Investigations unit."

"And what interest does the New York City Police Department, or Interpol for that matter, have in me?"

He watched her eyes over the top of her glass. It seemed that she was being genuine. This wasn't a game she was playing. Anyway, that was how it appeared. But he was about to find out how real that was.

"You don't know?"

"No."

"We tracked you," Troy said. "You purchased some high-tech drones from a small Dutch start-up company called SymAero. It's based in Rotterdam. You might not know where the drones came from because the transaction took place on an anonymous dark web trading platform called the Bazaar."

"I did this, did I?"

He nodded. "Yes, you did. Or someone at your foundation did. And those drones were used in the terror attacks in New York City and Belgium in the past few days. I'm not saying you carried out the terror attacks. But you were involved in getting the drones to the people who did. We know there are still five more drones out there."

She was staring at him now, staring hard.

"Oh my God," she said.

"Yeah. Oh my God. Here's the thing, my lady. I'm a good person. But I'm very angry about those attacks. I'm angry that we have to worry there might be even more attacks. And when I get angry, I do bad things. Did you notice tonight how I do bad things sometimes?"

She just stared. She didn't say anything.

"Yeah, you noticed. You saw it with your own eyes. So listen. I don't want to do bad things to you. But I will. You're pretty. You're rich. You're like a beautiful flower. You've had it your way your whole life, probably right up until tonight."

He came closer to her.

"But I don't care about things like that." His voice was just above a whisper. "People go on losing streaks. Even winners like you. And sometimes, when they do, they can lose it all in one night."

"You have the wrong person," she said.

He nodded. "We're going to find that out, believe me. If you're the right person, if you're the wrong person. We're here alone, out in the country, in the middle of the night. No one knows where we are. And I'm going to find out everything about you. Anything I want to know, I'm going to know."

She took another sip of the wine. "I know who the right person is. You won't have to torture me to get the information."

"Are you torturing people again?"

It was Dubois. She had come back from wherever she had gone. She was dressed in jeans and a sweater. She had scrubbed her makeup off. She had done her earlier transformation, in reverse.

Troy was still wearing the tuxedo. He noticed now that it was spattered with something dark. Blood, probably.

"I checked the house," Dubois said. "Entryways, exits, windows. The lights are out, except for a few small ones on timers. We didn't make much sound when we came in. I think we're okay for now."

128

Troy nodded. It sounded okay. "It seems the Duchess of Windsor here has something she wants to tell us. And I want to believe her. I'm hoping torture won't be necessary."

They both looked at Aliz.

"I think it was my brother," she said.

CHAPTER EIGHTEEN

October 18
12:10 am Central European Daylight Time
A clearcut in the woods
Outside of Luxembourg City
Luxembourg

"Come to Papa."

The man calling himself Alex pulled slowly off the road and into a dirt lot. The headlights of the car swept across dense woods, caught the yellow reflectors on a blue Port-A-San in their glare, then swept more woods again.

He piloted the car to the back of the lot and turned off the engine. It was dark here, and quiet. He waited a few moments, simply sitting still in the darkness. Out on the highway, the headlights of another car shone, lighting up the sky. The car approached, coming downhill from a distance. He let it pass.

On the seat next to him was a small tablet computer, sitting like a triangle, propped up by its stand. He tapped the screen. A map view appeared, showing him the blinking red light of one of the GPS units he had given Stark. The other one, on a smaller screen embedded at the top of this screen, was about 30 miles away.

But this one was *right here*. Stark had apparently left it here for him, then moved on. The map showed a sort of blue push pin, which was this computer. The red light and blue pin were very close. As a matter of fact, the red light looked like it was probably between 50 and 100 meters into these black woods.

"Okay," he said.

He took an LED flashlight out of the glove compartment. There was a small forensics kit in there, and he took that, too. He picked up the tablet computer, folded it flat, slipped it under his arm, and got out of the car.

He stepped into the woods, feeling the ghosts of the centuries. He got about ten steps into the trees, then turned on the flashlight. A hundred pairs of invisible eyes seemed to follow him as he picked his way through the dense forest. The skin across his body broke out in sudden gooseflesh. His breath seemed loud in his own ears.

The dead couldn't do him any harm. He knew that. It was the living who would hurt you. So he kept walking, ignoring the silent watchers.

He was very observant. Already he could see the underbrush pressed down as if something heavy had been dragged through here. He glanced at the tablet. He was very, very close to it now.

In a moment, he came to it. A dead man lay on his back among some bushes. As Alex approached with the bright light, something, some small animal, skittered away.

"They'll eat you quick," Alex said to no one.

This was what Stark left him. It was no surprise, he supposed. The disruption at the fundraising event, the fighting that spilled into the street, and the car chase through the old town - it had been all over the television news. Somehow, no one had been arrested, and the only bodies recovered after all that mayhem had been security guards for the event itself.

But here was a body. Not recovered. Left as a gift from Troy Stark.

Alex worked with the LED flashlight in his mouth, pointing at the corpse. The man had been shot in the forehead. Alex put on a pair of rubber gloves he took from the forensic kit.

He began to run his hands through the man's pockets. The first thing he found was the GPS unit. He put that in a small plastic box and slipped it into his own pocket. There wasn't much else. He found a pack of cigarettes and a silver lighter.

He held the smokes up to the light. It was a black box with a gold triangle on it, and gray letters. Merhaba. Turkish smokes.

But there was also a box on the cover, outlined in a thick black line, white space on the inside, with a warning in stark black letters: *Pirja e duhanit vret.*

Albanian for *Smoking kills.*

Turkish cigarettes sold in Albania. That was pretty funny. Turkey had the highest rate of smokers in Europe. The Albanians were second.

Alex put the flashlight on the ground. He shook a cigarette out of the pack. He popped the smoke in his mouth, flicked the lighter, and touched the flame to the tip. He took a deep inhale. God, that was good.

It was easy to quit smoking. He had quit a hundred times already. Nowadays, his rule was he would never buy cigarettes. But if someone offered him a cigarette, or if the Fates manipulated events so that cigarettes came into his possession through no effort of his own... so be it. He put the pack in his breast pocket.

He took another deep inhale, tilted his head back, and gazed up through the trees at the great sweep of stars across the dark night sky. It was beautiful.

He exhaled and looked at the body again. He needed to search the man's pockets again, then take his pants down and search his underwear. He would strip him to his underwear and take his suit, in case anything was sewn into his clothes. He would take the man's shoes as well, and for the same reason.

Then he would use the forensic kit to take the man's fingerprints, cut a few hair samples, and take some skin scrapings from inside his mouth for DNA. Alex didn't have the equipment here to take a dental imprint, but he probably didn't need one.

The dead man had already hinted at a lot about himself. He was a smoker, who had purchased his cigarettes in Albania. He had come to Luxembourg, the international money launderer's heaven, where he had been involved in what appeared to be a very public kidnapping attempt. During that kidnapping attempt, he had met Troy Stark somehow, and Stark had apparently killed him. Then Stark left him here for Alex to make sense of him.

Alex's first impression was this: everything about this man shouted mafia.

"Okay," Alex said, his mouth around the Turkish smoke. "But the only way to prove that is to identify him. So let's get to work."

Alex was his own hardest taskmaster. He bent to the job at hand.

132

CHAPTER NINETEEN

12:30 am Central European Daylight Time
Engel Castle
Engeldorf-Pont
Luxembourg

"My brother is not acknowledged as a Willems," Aliz said.

She was still on the sofa, still wearing the red dress from earlier this evening. She must be on her fourth glass of wine. She was beginning to warm up to them, and the wine was starting to loosen her tongue.

The mansion, and the castle looming above it, were protected by 16 security cameras, and a series of motion detecting lights. There was a laptop computer here on the coffee table, and Aliz had explained to Dubois how to use it to monitor the cameras. They'd been here for some time, and unless there were forces out there gathering quietly for a full-on assault, it seemed that they hadn't been followed.

That was good enough to allow Troy to help himself to a couple of beers from Aliz's large double refrigerator. He didn't ask permission, and Aliz scowled at him, but he ignored her. She was hardly in any position to complain. Prissy Dubois alone abstained from taking a drink. She was at work, according to her. Was she always at work?

Troy sat in an easy chair, sipping from his beer bottle. Sometimes he would watch Aliz as she spoke. Sometimes he would gaze out the bay window at the medieval castle on the hillside. It really was something else. Looking at it reminded him of the Legend of King Arthur. He could picture this region a thousand years ago, knights on horseback riding out of the mists, the sound of horses clop-clopping on the paving stones, flags waving on the battlements. The whole thing was out of sight. The fact that this woman sitting here *owned* that castle… How could a person own it? It was as if she owned Troy's daydreams. It was as if she owned King Arthur himself.

"He's my half-brother, just six months younger than me. My father, I think, was a good man overall. He tried to be a presence for good in this world, unlike his father before him, and so many of our line going back into history. But he was an incorrigible womanizer. That was his weakness. That was his shadow."

Troy sipped his beer. Neither he, nor Dubois, said anything. Dubois was watching those security monitors intently. She hadn't said anything about it, but Troy suspected that this night had scared her a bit. People had been shot. People had been killed. She had responded well, and held her own for the most part, but things were getting deep. Troy got the sense she wanted off this job before she was the one who got killed.

"While my mother was very pregnant with me, he impregnated another woman, Imane, an Algerian who worked as a domestic at our home in Paris. My father was at the embassy there at the time. Of course, he never acknowledged the child publicly, but he did provide for both mother and child. Luc was born Lucien Mebarak, and grew up in a Paris high-rise, a building full of doctors and lawyers and other professionals. Luc and Imane never wanted for anything - Luc went to very good schools. But they didn't have…"

She raised her right hand and gave a sweep around the room, taking in the living room, the nearby kitchen, and the towers of the castle outside the window.

"All of the comforts that come with being a Willems. The best schools, the best homes, the luxury, and the mingling with the elite of Europe. Luc did not experience these things. But he knew what he was missing."

"How did he know that?" Dubois said.

Aliz shrugged. "His mother was my father's mistress for many years. It was an open secret within the family. I met Luc for the first time when I was nine years old, or around then. We were on holiday in the Bahamas, at one of the grand hotels there. We were staying in a two-story suite of rooms, with views of the ocean from nearly every window. My father must have been tipsy one day - another of his weaknesses - because he took me to another part of the hotel, and we visited with Imane and Luc in their two-bedroom suite, with an eat-in kitchen and a terrace with a view of the swimming pool below. It was what a person might call nice."

"They were second class citizens in your world," Troy said.

She nodded. "Very much so."

"And he resents it." It wasn't a question.

"I'm afraid Luc hates me," she said. "And he has the meanness and the greed that has defined my family through the centuries. The Shadow. He has it. He is it. He began to get into trouble as a young teenager. He was expelled from numerous schools, at first for behavior infractions, later for selling drugs. He has the Willems ambition, and the sharp Willems mind. He wouldn't simply sell small bags of pot at school. He would set up networks to bring him the stuff from across the city and expand his wares to include whatever the other kids wanted or could afford - designer drugs, psychedelics, cocaine."

She took a long sip of her wine, finishing her glass. Then she reached to the bottle on the table at her elbow and poured herself another one. She was the one getting tipsy. Troy watched her. Her fundraiser had been blown to pieces tonight. She didn't seem particularly concerned about it at this moment. *The Willems ambition. The sharp Willems mind.* She seemed more interested in blowing gas up her own behind than in the fates of anyone who was at that party tonight.

"By the time he was 19, he was running a small ecstasy and ketamine empire in the nightclubs of Paris. We were nearly the same age, and I would spend time with him sometimes. He was outwardly friendly to me, but I knew what he was doing, and it frightened me. When he was 21, the Paris police shut him down."

"Did he do any time?" Troy said.

She shook her head slowly. "My father suppressed it. He had that kind of influence, the kind that purchases prosecutors and judges."

"Is this going anywhere?" Troy said.

Good looks only bought you so much slack, and no more than that. There had already been two terrorist attacks, and there was bound to be another one at some point. They were probably lucky the next one hadn't hit already. A group of men had tried to abduct her, and maybe kill her tonight. She had barely survived the car chase. And now she wanted to wax nostalgic about the specialness of the Willems family, and a kid who got busted for dealing drugs 15 years ago.

She looked at him with big pretty blue eyes. "What do you mean?"

"I mean, the clock is ticking here. Did your brother graduate from selling X to terrorism, is that what you're trying to tell us? Because he felt left out of the family fortune, and he got stuck with a last name that would make Muhammad proud?"

She shook her head. "My brother inherited money. Not as much as I did, but a lot by the standards of many people. He used it to further his criminal activities. He has the blood of his grandfather, and a long line of Willems men before him, running through his veins. He is the polar opposite of my father. Luc became involved in dealing weapons to North African rebel groups and warlords when he was still in his 20s. He branched out to smuggling heroin from Afghanistan into Europe, apparently using western troops as mules, carrying it on military transports. I believe he's been involved in prostitution and human trafficking of women from societies ravaged by war. And he has become a heroin user himself, if not an outright addict."

"Uh…," Troy said. "Heroin is one of those things. You use it for a while, next thing you know, you're hooked."

"He's a Willems," Aliz said. "He may have control over the habit."

That hurt Troy. It just hurt. Who were these people? These sharp-minded, ambitious, impervious to the effects of addictive drugs people. Clearly, they were super people. The laws of nature were put on hold when they walked in the door. They were rich, they were above the law, and they deserved everything that came their way.

Including Troy Stark.

"He tries to incriminate me, when he can," Aliz said. "I have never been online as The Shadow, not one minute, not one time. I wrote a book about the topic, but I did not name myself after it. I'm not that absorbed with myself. Luc has computer experts at his disposal who leave trails across the dark web, and the internet proper, that lead back to the foundation. He has mocked my work to my face, through his actions he makes a mockery of my desire to have our money help the world, and he mocks it even further by tangling up the foundation in his web of lies."

She shook her head. Tears began to form at the corner of her eyes. There seemed to be a lump in her throat. "If my father were still alive…"

Troy watched her closely. It could all be a lie, he knew that. It seemed like she was about to cry. But it could be a fake. She wouldn't be the first woman in the world to shed crocodile tears. Even so, Troy was content to let this story unfold for the moment. Maybe she really believed what she was saying. Maybe it was even true.

True or false, it might bring them closer to the answer.

"Let me get this straight," he said. "You think your brother bought the drones used in the terror attacks, may have been involved in the attacks themselves, all so he could incriminate and publicly humiliate you?"

Now the tears dropped down her cheeks.

"I don't know why he does what he does. Maybe he wants to prove something to himself. You say the computer trail leads back to me. I had nothing to do with it. He has tried to entangle me before. I would hope that he wasn't involved in these attacks, not even as a middleman for the weapon sale. But I just don't know. He has become involved with very dangerous people over the years. Sicilians. Russians. Mexican cartels. Afghan warlords. Maybe darker than these. He seems

136

to have a boundless appetite for dealing with the worst people on Earth."

She grunted, and half-laughed. "He goes by the name Luc Willems once in a while, did I tell you that? There are people who know him as this. He is pleased with himself when he can tarnish the family name."

"Do you think he's in trouble?" Dubois said. "Those are some heavy hitters that you mentioned."

"If he's alive, I think he probably is in trouble. I haven't seen him, or spoken to him, in over a year."

"That's convenient," Troy said.

She looked at him. "What's convenient about it?" It was apparent that she didn't get the joke.

Troy shrugged. "Oh, I don't know. Your brother gets mixed up with a bunch of shady characters, he may be involved in terror attacks, but you haven't seen him or heard from him in more than a year, so you have no idea where he is."

"I don't think I like what you're hinting at," Aliz said.

Troy stared into her eyes. "I'm not hinting."

"You think I'm lying?"

Troy thought about that, but just for a few seconds. In general, he thought the overall arc of the story was probably true, or something like true. Her brother was probably a bad cat. He was likely into all the things she said he was. Maybe he had even bought the drones.

Troy doubted very much that Aliz had bought them. Unless this was an Oscar-worthy acting performance, she was all wrong for international terrorism. She was smart, but she lived inside a bubble. She was a house cat. Terrorist masterminds tended to be alley cats.

The only thing that didn't ring true was the idea that she hadn't spoken to her brother in over a year. That was hard to swallow.

"No," Troy said simply. "I don't think you're lying. Not necessarily."

"Do you plan to kill my brother?"

"I plan to ask him who carried out the terror attacks. When he answers me honestly, I plan to move on to whoever those people are."

"And leave my brother floating in a canal somewhere?"

Troy stared and stared. He didn't have an answer for that.

"I witnessed how violent you are tonight. I will never forget it. If I knew where Luc was, and I was concerned that you were going to hurt him, why would I tell you?"

Troy didn't miss a beat. "To save hundreds, and possibly thousands of lives."

Now she was staring back at him. Tears streamed down, but she didn't look away. "He's so full of hate! Why is he this way?"

They stared at each other.

"Will you promise me?" she said.

Troy shrugged. "Promise you what?"

"That you won't kill him? I think he has goodness in him. If it's possible not to hurt him, if you can just bring him in, that you will do that? Maybe if he spends years in prison, if he can think about the things he does…" She trailed off.

Troy nodded. "Okay. If he surrenders, I will not hurt him."

It was a lousy promise to make, and he hated it. But it was also a reasonable trade-off. Maybe the guy was just a middleman, and he would go away for 30 years. Maybe smart, ambitious, super Luc was really just a dupe, being played for a sucker by much more powerful forces. Maybe when Troy walked in, the guy would lie on the floor and immediately recite the names of the real terrorists.

"Luc owns an old convent," Aliz said. "The nuns are all gone. The place is in champagne country, in northern France, near Reims. In the Middle Ages, the nuns made wine as their livelihood, so there's a vineyard and a wine cellar attached. There is also a house on the property. I don't know if Luc is there, but he has used it as a hideout before. For all I know, he has used the cellar as a place to store his weapons and drugs and whatever else. I visited him there once. It's a lovely place. The vineyards are rolling green hills, overgrown now. He was on the run from the Italians that time. I spent a week walking the grounds and talking with him. I told him I thought he should resurrect the winery and make that his business. He had me abducted and brought there, much like tonight. Which is why I think those men meant me no harm. They were probably just going to take me to him. But you couldn't have known that."

Troy nodded. It sounded okay. "How far is it?"

"About two and a half hours from here, by car."

"We're going to need a car," Troy said.

She gestured out the window. "There's a Porsche Cayenne in the garage. I never drive it. I don't like modern cars, and I don't like SUVs. It was a gift from a former boyfriend who was not a good listener. He was more interested in airbags, rollover reinforcement, and impact… how do you say it? Dispersal. He wanted me to be safe, I guess. You can use the car. Just try not to damage it. The impact is liable to disperse all around you."

Troy nearly laughed. Had she noticed the Jaguar when they pulled in here? Maybe not. The shock of the evening had worn off the more wine she drank.

"Thank you," he said.

This was interesting. She seemed to have anything and everything a man could want. He might as well take a stab in the dark here.

"Do you have any guns?" he said. Her eyes widened and he raised a hand. "No, I won't hurt your brother. But he might have henchmen with him, and I might have to deal with them first."

"I hate guns," she said.

"That doesn't really answer my question, does it?"

She paused for a long moment. Then she seemed to make up her mind. "In the castle. The ancient keep. It's full of guns. I'll bring you there."

* * *

"I don't like it," Mariem Dubois said.

Her voice echoed off the high ceiling, sounding childlike to her own ears. She stood in the formal dining room of the house. The room was cavernous. Hence the echoes. They reminded her of the gymnasium at her school when she was very young.

She held her mobile phone to her ear, waiting for her call to go through to the Special Investigations Unit office. It seemed like the call was taking forever to connect. She lowered her voice, mindful of the acoustics. She didn't want the Willems woman to overhear.

"We're already in an awkward position. We kidnapped that woman…"

"We saved her life," Stark said.

Mari watched him. He was a big man, and very handsome as men went, she supposed. He was too confident for his own good. Was it his looks? Were good-looking men prone to being overconfident? Or maybe he was just a psychopath. He had killed a man tonight, shot him in the head with no hesitation at all. Yes, it had ended the crisis of the man holding a knife to Aliz Willems's throat. But it was so sudden. Afterward, he had seemed to feel nothing about it at all. He had simply dumped the body in the woods as if it was some trash left behind.

And he had been confident! Confident that he was right, that it was the right thing to do. How could a man take a life so cavalierly?

She imagined it would take her months to recover from that one act. What about the man he had killed on the street?

The phone rang and rang.

"I need to talk to Miquel," she said. "If that woman has information about her brother, and he may be involved, then we should bring her in so she can give a formal…"

Stark shook his head. "No. I got no time for that."

And rude. He was rude. It was nearly impossible to finish a sentence in his presence. Mari had been identified as gifted and talented at a young age and had gone to schools reserved for the upper classes most of her life. Manners were important at these schools. Her parents were civil servants who had met in Senegal, her father French, her mother Senegalese. They valued decorum, respect for tradition, patience with bureaucratic processes - the wheel grinds slowly, but it does grind if you let it.

Troy Stark valued none of these. He spoke English in a garbled torrent of tortured syntax. He interrupted. He was sarcastic, almost caustic at times. He beat people. Instead of interviewing subjects, he put guns to their heads. He ended tense standoffs, what might even be considered a hostage negotiation, with a bullet to the brain.

"I just need to go there, check the place out. She says it's about two and a half hours away. If I leave soon, I can be there before dawn."

Over the phone, someone finally answered. "Hello?"

Mari raised a hand to Stark.

"Miquel, it's Mariem Dubois."

Miquel sounded far away somehow. "Mari. It's good to hear from you. We've seen the video. Much of Europe has seen it."

"This phone rang and rang," she said. "I think the phone might be compromised."

"Jan re-routed the office phone to my own mobile. He encrypted the calls and made mobile phone calls bounce around the world to mask their locations. He did in case you called. We can speak freely, and no one will know where you are."

It was a curious thing. "Why? I don't understand."

"I am under investigation," Miquel said. "They sent an Internal Affairs man up from Lyon. I was confronted by the Europol Deputy Director. Someone from the Dutch National Police was there, and someone else who chose not to identify himself."

"Oh, God. Miquel."

"It's fine. This has been coming. You're a good agent, Dubois. I told them you returned to Lyon this evening. If you don't turn up at Interpol tomorrow morning, you will probably have some difficult questions to answer, but as of now there's no talk of you being

140

investigated or suspended. Merely reprimanded, if that. You saved Aliz Willems. You did an exceptional job under intense fire. In normal circumstances, you would receive a commendation. You might still."

Mari took a breath. Miquel was her mentor. She had spent her entire career at Interpol under him. If he were fired…

"You should produce the woman unharmed, as soon as you can. Is she still…"

"Alive?" Mari said. "Yes."

"Did she have any information to offer?"

"She denies involvement. She thinks it may have been her brother. His name is Lucien Mebarak. He's really her half-brother, the bastard child of her father. He's been a drug dealer and maybe an arms dealer. He has ties to organized crime."

"If so, he'll be in the database."

Mari nodded. "Yes. But there's more. She told Stark…"

"Stark will be deported from any European Union country back to America, as soon as he's apprehended. He should know that. In fact, I told the investigators that he is already gone."

She looked at Stark. He was looming there, staring at her. It occurred to her that he was still wearing his tuxedo. Outside of the blood stains splattered on it, it looked good on him. The fit was excellent.

"I think he probably already assumes that," she said. "Willems gave him some intelligence on an old convent in champagne country, near Reims. She thinks her brother uses it as a hideout."

"No one is going to use our intelligence," Miquel said. "If the Willems woman has intelligence to offer, she's going to have to come in, and deliver it to Interpol or Europol directly, and in a formal setting."

"Stark wants to go there now."

There was silence over the line.

"Miquel?"

"I agree with him. Given the circumstances, I would say that we are not highly valued at this moment. Our mandate is on hold. Even if she wants to come in, it could be some time before anyone sees fit to interview her. By then…"

"Should I go?" Mari said.

It was a strange question to ask Miquel. It put him on the spot. Should she risk her life to follow the lunatic Stark into battle one more time? To what end? It wasn't even clear that all of this had produced anything of value. Men had died last night, Miquel was in trouble, the

Special Investigations Unit was disregarded, and the best they had come up with was a woman who thought her brother might be involved in some manner, and he might be hiding at an old convent in northern France.

"I think you should," Miquel said. "I think you and Stark are on to something. You are at the edge of acceptable behavior, but if this woman is correct and you stop the next attack, it will be the right thing, no matter what the career rewards or punishments are. You just have to approach it carefully and stay safe."

Had he seen the video? A shooting war had erupted in the middle of a fundraising gala. It was probably too late for careful and safe. The next one was liable to be worse.

"I would do it, if I were you. And I would stay dark until it's done. Don't talk to anyone. I don't know how long Jan will be able to hold this encrypted line of communication open. Interpol will probably notice it soon enough. If you tell a soul, it could be leaked."

She looked at Stark now. He was making hang-up gestures with his hands. Now he was slicing a hand across his own throat. Kill it. Okay, okay.

"I will do that," she said.

"Good," Miquel said. "You're a good agent, Mari. Exceptional."

"Thank you."

She hung up.

"Are you gonna come or not?" Stark said.

"My boss is under investigation by Interpol Internal Affairs."

Stark's brow furrowed. "Ouch. Because of what we did?"

She nodded. "Yes."

He sighed and shook his head. "In that case, why don't you go home before you get into more trouble? You're probably a good cop. You definitely have a lot of skills. If you come back into the fold now, I'm sure all will be forgiven."

"What about you?" she said.

"I don't work for Interpol. I'm not on the chopping block. I'm going all the way with this. If you continue, you've gone rogue and you're risking your career. If I continue, I'm doing what I was sent here to do. My superiors don't want me to stop. They don't want me to ask for permission."

"You're going to get killed if you go by yourself."

He smiled. "I doubt it."

"But you don't know for a fact."

His smile faded, and for the first time, he looked very tired. "No. I don't."

"In that case," she said, "I'm coming with you."

* * *

"Take this," Aliz said.

They stood in the courtyard between the house and the stone steps leading up to the castle. Aliz held a small lantern, that made a circle of weak light around them. She held something out to him, which flashed in the light.

"That's to the Porsche. It's on the far left as you walk in."

Troy looked at what she had put in his hand. It was the electronic fob to a car. He glanced at the doors of the garage where he had stashed the ruined Jag. There had been a few other cars, but they were covered with showroom drapes. Besides the Cayenne, he had no idea what kind of wheels she was sitting on.

"Walk this way, please," she said.

She held the lantern aloft. Troy and Dubois followed her up the winding stone stairway, which was hewn into the side of the hill. They passed through a low tunnel, the lantern sending shadows crazily against the walls.

They reached a tall, heavy wooden door, rounded at the top.

"We keep it locked, so that vandals and squatters cannot come in. Parts at the top are open to the elements, and so they could come in that way. But they would have to climb the walls to reach such a place."

She had a large key in her hand. She stuck it in the lock, cranked it, and pushed in the giant door. It swung easily. They kept the place maintained. Because of course they did. They were Willemses, were they not?

Now they moved through the old castle, following the lantern down dark hallways and then down a long, narrow flight of stone stairs. They were delving deep into the mountain. With each step, Troy felt like he was traveling further back in time, to the time of knights on horseback.

They came to another door, much smaller than the entryway.

"This is it," Aliz said. "This is the ancient keep."

She opened this door the same as before, with a heavy key, and this door swung inward easily as well.

"You would not believe the craftsmanship to make a working door that fits this doorway from so long ago."

143

They all ducked to step through the doorway. She held up her lantern to reveal a rough rectangle of a stone room, extending backwards into deep darkness.

"There are guns here," Aliz said. "Also, other supplies, which you will not need."

The place was some kind of apocalypse fallout shelter. There was a long gun rack, with rifles and shotguns slung along it. There were shelves with more guns, boxes of ammunition, and various types of non-lethal grenades - stun grenades, smoke and tear gas grenades. There were numerous bulletproof vests hanging like coats - old school heavy vests, not the more modern Kevlar or dragon skin body armor. Moving along from there, down the wall, there were shelves with hundreds of cans and packages of food, those boxes of irradiated long-lasting milk, bottles of whiskey and vodka, dozens of cartons of cigarettes, pallets of water on the floor, all of it disappearing into the darkness.

"Do you smoke?" Troy said.

"The cigarettes and hard alcohol are for trading," Aliz said. "Some things are always in demand."

"Is this your getaway, in case the world ends?" Dubois said.

Aliz shrugged. "This part of the castle has survived for nearly two thousand years. A hundred years after Christ is said to have walked the earth, this was here. It outlasted the Roman collapse, the Dark Ages, wars, plagues, and into the modern era. It's where my grandfather and great-grandfather hid Luxembourg Resistance members and re-supplied them with weapons in World War Two. They crossed into Germany three kilometers from here, carried out guerrilla attacks, and came back. Many of them died in the fighting, but the Nazis never found this place. Societies come and go, the centuries pass, and this suite of rooms has remained. If that day comes, yes. I will hold out here."

She gestured at the gun rack, and the table.

"Please. Outfit yourselves."

Now she was talking his language. Troy skipped over the rifles and the shotguns. He noticed that Dubois did the same. He picked an Uzi submachine with three 32-round replacement magazines. He took a couple of semiautomatic pistols of unknown vintage. He looked through the grenades. He took a couple of stun grenades and a couple of smoke grenades.

He glanced at Dubois. She had chosen two handguns and was mounting two holsters on her belt.

"Is that all?" he said.

"Before tonight, I never fired a gun on duty in my life. I rarely even carry one."

Troy nodded. It didn't matter. She was a decent partner. She was fast, she was light on her feet, and she didn't fall to pieces when the action started. She had those karate kicks. She could fly an airplane. She didn't have to shoot, and she didn't have to kill anyone. He would do it, if it came to that.

He looked through the heavy vests and found the smallest one. He picked it off the rack and held it out to her. "Wear this, though, if you don't mind."

She held it, apparently surprised by its weight.

"Just because you don't shoot, doesn't mean they won't."

Now Troy looked around the room again. A new thought occurred to him. Aliz was sending them somewhere a few hours away. She was willing to give them a car and guns. But she didn't want Troy to hurt her brother.

What if she was setting them up?

What if she wasn't setting them up, but got cold feet after they left and warned her brother they were coming?

What if she did something else that he couldn't predict?

He didn't like it.

Several meters down from him, there was something like a living area arrangement. There were three upright leather chairs, a sofa, and a table. He figured if you were going to live through the end of days, you might as well have somewhere to relax.

He went over and tried to lift one of the chairs. It didn't budge. He looked down at the legs. They were bolted to the stone floor. All the chairs, the sofa and the table were like that. There must be a rationale for it - earthquake?

No sense trying to figure it out. The ultra-intelligent and ambitious Willemses had their reasons.

"Aliz?" he said. "Can you please come here a moment?"

As she approached, he reached into his pocket and came out with the zip ties he'd had ready for the fundraising event. He hadn't found a need for them, until now. He separated two of them out from the bunch.

"Yes?" she said.

He gestured at one of the chairs. "Can you sit in that chair a moment? I want to see something."

Her smile said she was confused. That was good. Confused people often did things that weren't necessarily in their own interests.

She sat down. Instantly, he seized her right wrist, fastened a zip tie around it, then attached the other end to the arm of the chair. By the time she began to stand up again, he had secured her arm to the chair.

"What are you doing?"

He raised a hand and gently pushed her back down into the chair.

"Shhhhh," he said.

He crouched and quickly fastened her right ankle to the leg of the chair. Now she wasn't going anywhere.

"Stark?" Dubois said.

He raised a hand to Dubois. "It's okay. This has to be done."

He got up and went over to the food shelves. There was an immense quantity of items to choose from. He took two bottles of water, a large canister of mixed nuts, and a package of tea cookies. He brought them over and set them on the table in front of Aliz.

She was squirming in the chair, grunting, and groaning. It was sort of funny, but he didn't laugh. It had been a long night, and there was still more to go.

"I'm going to scream," she said.

He shook his head. "If you do, I'll friction tape your mouth shut. You don't want that, and I don't want to do it. So don't scream. Okay?"

She began to breathe heavily, hard eyes staring up at him.

"Listen," he said. "I can't have you calling anybody right now, least of all your brother. So you're just going to have to stay in here for a little while."

"I told you where I think he is. Why would I call him now?"

Troy shrugged. "Because you told me where you think he is. And I'm coming for him. After I leave, you might change your mind about my visit. Now, I'm not going to hurt him, because I promised you that. But I'm not going to let him hurt me, either. And I'm not going to let any goons he has around hurt me, or Agent Dubois. So you stay here for a little while, and once we conduct our little visit, someone will be by to let you out."

She stopped squirming. Maybe even she could see the wisdom in this. If she succumbed to temptation and warned her brother, she could find herself with big problems.

She pouted now, like a child. "What if I have to go to relieve myself?"

"Already thought of that," Troy said. There was a stack of large white buckets among all the supplies. He went over, took a bucket, and brought it back. He slid it next to where she was sitting.

"Instant ladies' room."

She shook her head. There almost seemed to be tears in her eyes again.

"You're a terrible person."

He nodded. "You're not the first to tell me that."

Dubois went over to a shelf and came back with a fat pill bottle. "This is the substance called melatonin. It will help you sleep."

"I know what it does," Aliz said. "Who do you think stored it here?"

Dubois shrugged. "So, take one. Sleep for a while. By the time you awake, it will be time for you to be free."

She opened the bottle and held it out to her. Aliz reached in with her free hand.

"Take two," Dubois said.

Troy watched Aliz take the melatonin out. They were gummies. "Yeah," he said. "Good idea. Take a nice long nap. Look! They're shaped like teddy bears."

Aliz put the two gummies in her mouth.

Troy picked up the lantern. "Nighty-night. We'll see you soon."

"Wait!" Ali said. "You can't leave me in the dark."

Troy sighed. "We need to find our way back outside. Anyway, the darkness will help you sleep."

They left, pulling the door almost, but not quite closed.

"She's a trooper," Troy said. "I think she'll be fine."

They wound their way back out through the castle, then down the stone stairs to the lower courtyard. As they came out of the staircase, a small man was just pushing an old scooter type motorcycle up the driveway and onto the property.

"Hello?" Troy said. He had the Uzi strapped to his back. For an instant, he considered taking it down. Where there was one, there could be more.

"Hello!" the man said. He raised a hand. "Good evening to you!"

Troy looked at Dubois. "Go inside and get your stuff ready. If Aliz has any bread, cheese, coffee drinks, anything good we might want to take, bring it along. I'll handle this guy."

"Who is he?" she said.

Troy shook his head. "I don't know. But I'll move him along."

Dubois backed toward the house, her eyes still on the man. Troy walked over to the guy. It was Alex.

"Can I help you, sir? This is my house. We don't get many visitors."

Alex gestured at the bike. Its headlight was dim and flickering. "Oh, I was just having some problems with my moto. I saw the gate and thought this would be a good place to repair it. I know what's wrong. It will only take a few moments."

Alex opened the storage compartment and pulled out a small toolbox. He opened the engine compartment and got down on one knee. He seemed to be playing around in there with something. Probably not, though.

"Sir, I don't have all night. I need to drive to France very soon."

"It's a nice night for a drive. A little late, though. Where in France?"

"Will you even remember, if I tell you?"

Alex shrugged. "I don't need to remember. I let tiny machines do my remembering for me."

Troy nodded. "In that case, I'm going to check out an old convent called Lumiere de Dieu. That's the Light of God in English."

Alex smiled up at him. "Your French is impeccable."

Troy nearly laughed. "Thank you. The convent is near the city of Reims, in champagne country. The man who owns it is a wealthy gentleman by the name of Lucien Mebarak. Sometimes he goes by Lucien or Luc Willems. Sometimes he goes by other names. Nice guy. Thought I might acquire the place from him. Or at least the stuff that's in it."

"What's in it?"

"I don't know yet. Could be drones, I suppose. That's going to be the big surprise."

Alex nodded.

"A man left me a gift in a forest last night. It was kind of a surprise, too."

"Oh? What was it?"

"It was an Albanian gangster by the name of Besnick Shkodra. He operates out of Brussels, normally. But not anymore. There are lots of Albanians in Brussels these days. They run the drug trade mostly, and in a big way. They also do some prostitution and gambling. It's hard to penetrate their little world. Family ties, and all that. They seem to have made friends with some of the Islamic extremists in Molenbeek, though. The two groups have some shared enthusiasms. Money. Weapons. World domination."

"That's very interesting," Troy said. "I'll tell you something else that's interesting. See that big castle up there? It was built a long time ago. Deep inside the oldest part of the castle is a rich lady named Aliz

148

Willems. She's a clever lady, wrote a book about something or other. I don't think she played any part in this, but I think her brother Lucien did. I think she might like to contact him and let him know I'm coming for a visit. But at the moment she's tied up with other things. It might be nice if someone checked on her for me. Not right away, but in a little while. Made sure she was still breathing or whatever. Also, it's good that we have her here, in our possession so to speak, on the off chance that she was involved."

Alex nodded. "See? It only took me a moment."

The flickering headlight had come back on full power. He stood and started to put his tools away. His hand came out of the storage compartment with a Rock Star Zero. He passed the slim can to Troy. It was warm, but that was okay.

Alex got on the bike. He revved the motor just a touch.

"There's security video of the little scrape you got into last night. Also, there's some mobile phone video, shot by terrified partygoers who were crawling on the floor. A man of your description is wanted for questioning pretty much everywhere in Western Europe right now. Two security guards died in the attack. No other bodies were recovered so far, but there's suspicion that a few of the kidnappers were killed."

"They were," Troy said. "Their buddies must have removed them."

"Persons says if you get busted, just clam up. You don't know anything. There are friendlies embedded who will pull strings and try to get you off the continent."

Troy nodded. "Understood."

"Nice talking to you," Alex said. He walked the bike so that it was pointing back down the driveway, put his feet up, and drove away. At the bottom, his turn signal indicated left. A second later, he was gone.

Troy turned around and Dubois was coming out of the house with their bags.

"Who was that?" she said.

"I don't know. Some guy who needed to stop here and fix his motorcycle. He spoke English, a little. I didn't find him the least bit suspicious."

She gestured at the Rock Star. "Where did you get that?"

Troy shrugged. "The guy gave it to me. He insisted. He wanted to pay me for letting him work on his bike here, but I said no. Then he gave me this. I tell you: life is like magic sometimes. This is just what I needed. You want a sip? It's warm."

She shook her head. "Let's just go, all right?"

He nodded. "Fair enough."

149

They headed for the garage and the Porsche Cayenne. Troy checked his watch. It was coming up on 2:30 am. With a little luck, they'd pull up to the convent in the hour before dawn. Maybe they'd catch whoever was there napping.

"You navigate," he said. "I'll drive."

CHAPTER TWENTY

4:45 am Central European Daylight Time
Lumière de Dieu Abbey
Outskirts of Reims
France

"People are there," Dubois said.

They were on a hill near a copse of trees, overlooking the medieval abbey, maybe half a mile away. It was quiet here, and dark. The only sounds were breezes rustling through the trees and the grasses, and what seemed to be the bell of a cow in a field somewhere nearby. The stars spread out above their heads, a billion of them, sweeping across the night sky.

They had ditched the car by the side of the road about a mile back and hiked up here with all their gear. Troy stood in shadow near a tree, not moving at all. The heavy bulletproof vest weighed on him. It was cumbersome. He watched the abbey, much of it a large dark spot looming darker than the surrounding darkness. To the left was a large house with a couple of lights on.

Dubois was on the ground, lying on her stomach, peering down at the scene with a pair of high-powered binoculars.

"How many?" Troy said, very low.

"I count two at the moment. Men. Each one has a rifle slung over his back. One is smoking a cigarette. See him?"

Troy looked across the distance. Now that she said it, he could see the tiny red end of the butt light up each time the man took a drag.

"Armed guards," he said.

"Yes."

He nodded. "No need to protect the nuns."

"The nuns are gone," Dubois said.

"It's them."

There was a long moment of quiet. Troy could hear Dubois breathing below him. He listened intently, trying to see if he could hear the men across the distance. Standing around, pulling guard duty, usually you talked. But he couldn't hear them.

"How do you want to play it?" Dubois said.

151

Her voice cracked, just a touch, giving away her nerves. Of course, she would be anxious out here. She was going into combat, again. Fighting to the death wasn't her forte. She could have died earlier tonight. She could still die. The fact that she was still here was a testament to her guts. Troy could respect that. It was enough for him.

"You don't have to come," he said. "You got me this far. You can walk back to the car, and drive to your flat in Lyon. Sleep until nighttime. I'm sure all will be forgiven, if not today, then tomorrow, or the next day."

"I'm coming with you," she said.

He nodded in the darkness. Okay. She had her reasons.

"Are they moving?" he said.

"The men?"

"Yes. Are they moving around at all?"

"Yes. They seem to be chatting a bit, moving around a little. One walked off before, then came back."

"Then there's no motion detector lights where they are," Troy said. "If there were, then they would have flashed on by now. So we come down the hill. We get into the trees there by the edge of the building. We take these two out silently. Then we go around to the other side. There will be more over there. Take those out."

"Take them out?" she said.

He could almost hear the gulp as she swallowed the frog in her throat.

"Yes."

"It's pre-meditated murder."

"It's war," Troy said. "They're the enemy. They've killed over 50 people in New York and Belgium."

"We don't know that," she said.

"You don't have to come," he said again. "You got me this far."

"I told you I'm coming with you."

He felt the urge to gesture down the hill, but he didn't move at all. He felt the urge to raise his voice, so he spoke even more quietly than before. "I believe the drones are down there, or the people who launched the drones are. It would be foolish to get yourself killed pretending those guys you see are good guys. They have guns because... why?"

He paused, letting total silence spin out between them. She didn't answer him or make a sound.

"Okay?" he said.

Slowly and carefully, she pushed her way back into the shadows of the trees, before she worked her way to her feet. "Okay."

Troy watched the red light at the end of the cigarette spark again. "Then let's roll," he said.

They headed down the hill, through overgrown fields where vines once grew. Troy took them on a path to the right, and further away from the abbey. They couldn't come straight toward the men. They needed to come from the side, from a place the men would never expect opposition to appear. Further, they needed to move like shadows, like wraiths, and to kill silently, without mercy.

He glanced at tiny Dubois beside him. This was not her job description. She was a good fighter; she kept her head in a tight spot. But a silent killer? Not her.

They moved through an area where the land dropped. There was a chill in the air at the bottom of the undulation, and a place of thick fog. He touched her shoulder, and guided her along the dip, staying within the fog instead of climbing out again.

At the far end of the dip, there was no choice but to move up to higher land again. The land was steep here, a perfect defilade if he planned to take a shot, but he didn't. He didn't have a sound suppressor, and even if he did, it wouldn't matter. The best suppressors in the world still made a sound. And some guys, when the man next to them suddenly dropped with a bullet in the head, they also dropped before you could line up the next shot. Then they started shouting for help.

No. This had to be done close quarters.

They reached the lip at the top of the drop-off. Troy poked his head over the edge. He was deep in the overgrown grass. The corner of the abbey was *right there*, looming in the darkness, maybe 50 meters away. The subjects were further away, along the front of the building. He could see them clearly now. He spotted the light from the cigarette again. He ducked down.

He and Dubois were lying along the edge of the dip.

"Listen," he whispered.

They sat and listened. There was the chirruping of crickets. Somewhere a night bird called. And there was the sound of two men talking in low voices. Their conversation carried across the night air. A man with gravel in his throat, probably the smoker, said something. The other one laughed and said something in return. The sound of their language was guttural.

"French?" Troy said, already knowing the answer.

Dubois shook her head. Not French.

"What?" Troy said.

She shrugged.

Okay. That ruled out several languages at once, languages she spoke, along with languages she might recognize by the sound. Two guys in France, with rifles over their shoulders, at a medieval abbey owned by a notorious weapons trafficker, and they weren't speaking French, or any language that a French person knew. That sealed it. If they weren't fair game before, they were now. These guys were either gangsters, terrorists, or aliens from outer space.

Troy put his head very near to hers. "We crawl," he whispered. "You follow me. The building is very close. We move along it."

He showed her two fingers walking. She nodded.

"I attack. You cover me. Don't shoot unless necessary. We need to be silent from here on out."

There was a pause between them, and he yawned. He was tired. He hadn't had real sleep in… he couldn't remember when. This job was for the birds.

Without another word, he turned and, very slowly, crawled out of the heavy grass. He got down on his belly like a worm. He looked across. The men were there. He turned his face away from them and began to move across the open gap, going so slowly, it was as if he wasn't moving, pressed so close to the hard ground, it was as if he was a low curb or some other feature of the pathway.

The bulletproof vest limited the mobility of his arms and shoulders, which might be a good thing. He reminded himself to go even slower.

Slowly, like a turtle, he glanced back. She was following, mimicking his movements, taking his lead. This was the hard part, being out in the open. The alarm could be raised at any second.

He slithered across into the darker shadows of the building. He sat up behind the corner, his back pressed to the wall, his hands feeling the cool stones. A moment later, she slithered up next to him.

He nodded to her and put a finger to his lips. It was good. She was doing well.

He gave them both a moment to catch their breaths. Again, he put his head very close to hers.

"Now we go quicker, but still silent."

She nodded.

He unclipped his knife sheath from his belt. He didn't take the knife out. The sheath was made of a dark fabric, not leather, and wouldn't reflect any light. The big hunting knife itself would practically glow in the dark.

154

"You follow me, right up the wall," he whispered. He made a gesture with his hands, one hand the wall of the abbey, one hand moving along it.

"I'll take them out. You cover me. We want to be as quiet as possible. There are more of these guys somewhere around. Don't shoot unless you absolutely have to."

She looked at him, eyes wide. He flashed back to her reluctance to shoot the Albanian gunman in the car earlier in the night.

"But if you do have to shoot, then please shoot."

She was still staring.

"All right?"

She nodded.

"Say it."

"All right," she whispered, very low. "I get it."

She took her pistol out of its holster, checked it, and kept it in her hand.

"Okay," he said. "Ready?"

"Yes."

"Here we go again."

He pushed himself up the wall. He glanced around the corner. The two guys were there, still talking. Just a couple of guys out in the cool night air, shooting the breeze. Rifles over their shoulders, guarding... something or someone.

Troy took a deep breath. He got low, turned the corner and moved quickly along the wall in a sort of half crouch. The shadows here were good, a darkness within the darkness. He felt her there behind him, fast and quiet, like a cat. Her martial arts training served her well.

They were closing, closing. The guys were ahead, and then increasingly, ahead and to the left, out on the flagstones of the ancient courtyard. In a second, two seconds, very soon, they had to become aware of his presence.

Closer... closer...

He was four steps away, maybe five. He was exquisitely close. He was too close.

NOW.

He broke cover, ripped the knife from its sheath, and darted out from the wall. He crossed the short distance between himself and the men. They caught a glimpse of him at the last second. They turned, eyes wide, guns not ready.

Troy slashed the knife across the throat of the cigarette-smoker. The knife cut deep, nearly beheading the man. He barely grunted in

155

response. His burning smoke fell to the ground, and a split second later, the man did as well.

Troy spun toward the second man, just in time to catch a punch in the face.

Troy's head snapped back, but he lunged in with the knife.

The man sidestepped and screamed something in a language Troy didn't understand, a deep guttural shriek. It almost sounded like the man was vomiting.

He did it again, backing away and trying to pull the rifle down from his back. He got it. He got the gun down. Troy lunged again, but the man leapt back. He grabbed the gun in both hands, pointed from his waist, and...

BANG!

A gunshot cracked and echoed across the surrounding hillsides. It was loud. It repeated itself as it rolled across open land, hit some hill or mountain, and echoed back again.

Troy stared at the man. The man stared back at Troy. The guy had a scruffy face, black, bushy eyebrows, and maybe three days' worth of sharp, thick beard. His eyes were dark. He dropped his gun and it rattled on the paving stones. He hadn't got a shot off.

His eyes went blank, no longer staring at Troy. The man's shoulders slumped. He leaked to the ground and lay still.

Near the wall of the abbey, Dubois stood, still in a shooter's crouch, both hands on her gun. Her eyes were wide.

Next to her was a doorway he hadn't noticed before - more of the opening to a tunnel than a doorway. It was darker than dark, and cool air was coming from it. Things were about to get hot. The tunnel looked about as good a place to go as any.

Troy reached for the machine gun strapped to his back.

"Did I kill him?" Dubois said. She gestured at the man on the flag stones. Her voice was high, and shaky.

Troy nodded. "Yeah. Thank you. He was about to shoot me. But now we have to move, and fast. Come on."

* * *

She had just killed a man.

Her mind was awash with thoughts, fears, and emotions.

Thou shalt not kill. The Fifth Commandment. It was a mortal sin to break. Ten years in law enforcement, and she had never broken this law.

156

She was numb, and she was crying now, and she was running. She plunged through the darkness, crouching low, running behind Stark, running in blindness, as she had been trained to do - her left hand on Stark's lower back, feeling him there, her right hand still holding the gun, the murder weapon.

They were running through a tunnel, or catacombs, part of the old abbey. It was cold in here. There were no lights, and they ran through pitch darkness. The tunnel was not straight. It curved around to the right.

Somewhere close, men were shouting, maybe up ahead. Dubois was breathing hard, not speaking, but she wanted to scream:

"WHERE are we going?! WHAT are we doing?"

It was crazy. They had just killed two men. She had no idea who those men were. Stark seemed to kill people regularly. Yesterday - it seemed like forever ago - he had threatened to kill the men at the small aerospace company. She thought he was bluffing. Apparently not. He had killed a bunch since then. Dubois was losing track of them all.

Without warning, he stopped short in front of her. She crashed into him.

He was completely still.

"Back," he said, under his breath. "Get back."

Suddenly, he opened up with the Uzi.

DUH-DUH-DUH-DUH-DUH-DUH-DUH-DUH

The noise was an explosion in the tight confines of the tunnel. The light of the muzzle flashes blinded her, then imprinted on her eyes. Darkness… light… a deafening wall of sound.

"Back!" he screamed. "Get back!"

She could barely turn around. He was against her now, looming large, shoving her back the way they had come. She turned, but then he tackled her. They hit the stone floor hard. His bulk landed on top of her.

She was screaming, but she almost couldn't hear herself.

Others were screaming as well.

TAT-TAT-TAT-TAT-TAT

More shrieking noise. Muzzle flashes lit up and down the hallway, wherever that was. Bullets ricocheted off the curving walls, throwing sparks.

Stark pushed off of her and slid along the ground.

"Close your eyes," he said.

He threw something, which bounced away from them along the corridor.

"Now! Close those eyes! Cover your ears!"

She did as she was told. There was a blinding flash behind her closed eyelids. Even with her fingers plugged into her ears, there was a loud, sharp…

BANG!

Instantly, somewhere ahead of her, Stark opened up the gun again, this time from the floor, the ugly blat of the Uzi blinding and deafening, once more.

DUH-DUH-DUH-DUH-DUH

Dubois pressed her hands to her ears. One hand was still holding the gun. She squeezed her eyes shut against the muzzle flashes, but it was too late. Lightning storms were inside the darkness of her vision. Close her eyes and there were lightning flashes. Open them, and there were more lightning flashes. All she could see were white explosions against black darkness.

His strong hand gripped the collar of her jumpsuit.

"Get up! Let's go."

He yanked her to her feet. She flew up from the ground automatically - she was lighter than air to him. Now they moved up the hallway again, more slowly this time. Her left hand was on his lower back again. She still had the gun in her right. She felt useless - dizzy, blinded, deaf, traumatized. She had killed a man. She had never done that before. Then she had almost died herself. She had never been fired on by a machine gun before. She was *an investigator.*

A night of firsts. A nightmare of them.

In a moment, a flashlight appeared in Stark's hand. It gave off a concentrated beam, nearly like a laser pointer. It searched the far curve of the wall, reaching ahead of them a few steps, keeping them out of the line of sight of any bullets.

Her ears were ringing. Her eyes were flashing. She could feel a headache coming on. The night had been too long already. If she lived through this, Interpol needn't fire her. She was going to quit.

A pile of bodies littered the narrow tunnel ahead of them. Stark's searchlight found them on the floor, three men, bloodied, battered, their clothes shredded.

"Don't look at them."

She could barely hear him. But anyway, how could she not look? She had to step on them, climb over them, just to get past. And she did, stumbling over their soft, immovable lumps in the darkness. If she could have, she would have stretched her legs like taffy to step all the way over them without touching. But they couldn't do that, so she stepped right on them, tripping, nearly falling, pushing blindly past.

Stark's light had already moved onward.

Three dead men in the tunnel. Two out in the courtyard. Five dead men so far. For what? What had these men done that warranted death? What were they doing here?

What if they were merely guarding the vineyards?

With machine guns?

The vineyards are fallow. There's nothing out there to guard.

Okay.

Her hearing settled down the smallest amount. Behind the ringing, she heard a new sound. Somewhere in the building, or on the grounds, alarms were going off. It was impossible to say how close they were to here.

Stark turned to face her. He put the light on his own face. He seemed like a gremlin, or a demon, his face half in shadow.

"We have to hurry."

She could barely hear him, but the opening of his mouth made it clear that he had shouted the words. Maybe he was as deaf as she was right now.

She nodded.

He turned and started moving quickly again. She touched his back and moved with him. He raced down the hall, crouched low, the machine gun poking out in front of him, the light probing ahead. A new hallway went off to the left and without a word, and with no reason she could discern, he turned and followed it.

Ahead was a solid wooden door with a heavy metal locking mechanism.

"Cover your ears!" he shouted.

She did as he said, jamming her fingers in each ear. The last thing she needed was to become even more deaf than she already was. But then he stopped. He let the machinegun hang on its strap. Gingerly he reached out and touched the lock. There was a long bolt. He slid it back. It seemed to move easily.

He grasped and turned the big knob. The door opened a crack. It wasn't even locked.

Stark stepped back, raised the machine gun again, and toed the door the rest of the way open. Dubois was ready with her gun. She was ready to die.

There was a large open space beyond the door, with a high ceiling. It was empty. There didn't appear to be anything in it at all. It occurred to Dubois that she could see again. The empty space - perhaps once upon a time there had been wine presses in here - opened to the outside,

159

the front courtyard of the abbey. Bright lights had come on out there, probably in response to their presence. There was a tall and wide wooden door on metal rollers, and it was all the way open.

"Do you smell that?" Stark said.

She did. It smelled like gunpowder, maybe, or some sort of explosive. There was also a faint smell of some type of petrol - gasoline or kerosene, or maybe even just an oil-based grease. The combined smells were sickening. But there wasn't anything here.

"They were making bombs," Stark said. "Or storing them."

"But they're gone now," she said.

He nodded. "Yeah."

He flicked off his light and walked across the open space to the doorway. She watched him. He took something out of one of his pockets and tossed it on the ground. Dubois just barely saw it - it seemed like a small sliver of plastic. She was about to mention it to him, but as he reached the open slider, a burst of gunfire rang out.

TAT-TAT-TAT-TAT-TAT-TAT

Dubois shrieked in surprise.

Stark fell back. He dropped to the stone floor, his gun sliding off his shoulder and out of his hand. He lay on his back.

"Oh my God," Dubois said.

She had seen Stark take the bullets. If he was dead, after all of this madness…

Outside, in the courtyard, she heard the tell-tale sound of a motorcycle engine roar to life. A headlight came on.

She ran to Stark. His eyes were open. He looked up at her.

"I'm not gonna lie. That hurt."

He put his hands to his chest. He ripped open his jumpsuit. Of course, the heavy bulletproof vest was there. His hands roamed up and down his chest.

He shook his head. "These old vests were great, you know. Cumbersome. Ridiculous. But they saved a lot of lives in their time. And they just did it again."

She looked out through the doorway. The motorcycle had turned and was tearing off up the long driveway that came to the abbey from the main road. There was another motorcycle parked where the first one had been, a low-slung racing bike.

Stark was looking in the same direction. He worked his way to his knees.

"They left us one. Let's go."

"Where?" Dubois said.

Stark gestured up toward the taillight of the first motorcycle. "Wherever that guy is going. Apparently, he knows something we don't."

"You were just shot," she said.

He nodded. "Tell me something I don't know."

He climbed to his feet and took a deep breath. He walked out on what seemed like unsteady feet toward the motorcycle. He seemed to feel along the ignition wire. She knew the trick well enough from her father. He was going to start the bike by popping open the wire socket, and filling both sides of it with something metallic, thereby closing the circuit.

As she watched, he opened his flashlight and took the battery out. He fiddled with the battery and a small knife. In a moment, he had peeled away the metal casing and plugged it into the wire socket. He sat on the bike and the engine roared to life. He worked fast; she'd give him that. In darkness. After a murder spree and being gunned down himself.

He looked back at her. "Ready?"

She walked toward him. Her entire body shook from adrenaline. If she had ever been this unsteady, she couldn't remember when it was.

"I don't want to ride behind you."

He shook his head. "There's only one bike. You either ride behind me, or in my lap. Unless you want to stay here and wait for the cops to arrive."

She looked back at the abbey. Now, with lights on, it appeared like a haunted castle, all the more haunted with five corpses on the grounds.

Dubois sighed. She holstered her gun, slid on behind him, and held his waist lightly.

"You're gonna want to hold a little tighter than that," he said.

He put the bike in gear, and they started moving. They rolled to the top of the driveway, Stark pointed it toward the road, and gunned the engine. Within seconds, they were accelerating, Stark revving and shifting gears.

Dubois reached around him and gripped his chest tightly. It was either that or fall off the back. Up ahead, far ahead, the taillight of the man who had shot Stark reached the road. His brake light came on for an instant, then he turned left, and rode hard.

The wind whistled past Dubois as they began their pursuit. She pressed herself against Stark's broad back.

She was alive. She had killed a man tonight, they had been in a battle of machine guns, and she was still alive.

CHAPTER TWENTY ONE

5:25 am Central European Daylight Time
On the road to Reims
France

Troy Stark liked motorcycles.

He liked them a lot. He liked this one in particular: some Yamaha dual-sport model that the owner had probably modified himself. Unless that guy up ahead was a professional racer in a previous life, there was no way he was going to outrun Troy Stark. Not out here, on wide open roads. It just wasn't going to happen.

But give the guy some credit. He had seen how things were going, and he had lain in wait. Troy had let his guard down, and the guy had pumped him full of lead, then taken off on his bike.

If not for the vest, Troy would be dead or dying right now. Would Dubois have taken off after the shooter? Probably not. She probably would have stayed and tried in vain to save Troy's life.

The shooter was clever. He was calm. He was patient. He did not get himself killed like some of the other guys back there.

And now he was making a run for it.

Troy gave the bike throttle. They zoomed forward. The engine whined. Troy's hearing was shot through, but they were already gaining.

"Get ready to take your shot!" he shouted at Dubois.

"Shot?"

Dubois had killed a man tonight. Troy was proud of her. The guy had the drop on Troy, maybe (almost certainly but you never knew), and she had taken him out. Of course, it had led to that whole mess back there, but it was probably unavoidable. You had to crack a few eggs to make a delicious omelet.

The kitchen was a disaster area right now. That much was true. It would take some explaining. Troy hoped the meal was going to be worth it. He also hoped Dubois didn't stand on ceremony every time she had to shoot someone. There's a first time for everything. But afterwards, that's it. You don't get to be a virgin anymore.

Her voice came back to him, small against the whine of the engine and the wind of the road.

"Why am I shooting him?"

"He tried to kill me, remember?"

"Oh. Right."

Up ahead, a hundred meters and closing now, the guy turned left and went off the road. Why did he do that? Troy marked the spot in the glare from his headlight.

A moment later, he was there. He slowed, almost to a stop. He went left, up a small barren cut in the land, like a hiking trail, or a trail for motocross bikes. This bike was dual purpose - it could take that trail. Troy killed his headlight, mindful of how the guy had set a trap before. The trail peaked quickly and headed steeply back down again.

There was a narrow canal below them. The guy was down there, speeding away along the edge of it. Troy could hear the guy's engine. ZZZZZZZZZ.

Troy turned his headlight back on and plunged down the trail toward the canal. At the bottom, the trail made a sharp right and followed the canal's edge. He and Dubois bounced along. She gripped his chest tighter, both hands.

Troy gunned it.

They tore off along the canal, the trail zigging and zagging through bushes and trees and tall grasses.

They passed under the roadway they had just left, zooming now.

A mile passed. Then two. The bikes raced through the early morning darkness. It was real country darkness - the only thing cutting it was the headlights on the motorcycles.

"You're not gonna lose me like this," Troy said. His voice was swallowed by the sounds all around him.

A house or building appeared above their heads and zipped by in the dark. Then another. They were coming into civilization.

A road appeared to their right. It was angling in toward them, two lanes, one in each direction. There was early morning traffic on the road. In a moment, this trail would end, and...

Ahead, the lead bike slipped between the end of two guardrails, and out onto the road. A truck coming the other way leaned on the horn. The bike zipped in front of the truck, and barely squeezed in front of a car going the same direction.

"Aaahhh," Dubois said.

"Don't worry," Troy said.

He cut right at the end of the guardrail, the way the other guy had done. There was no other choice. The trail was about to go into the canal. Up ahead, the road hugged the edge of the waterway.

He zipped right, then left, into the flow of traffic.

Okay. Okay. The guy was a daredevil. He was going to get himself, or someone else, killed. Time to put a stop to this. Here on a real road, Troy should be able to catch him. He accelerated, approaching the rear bumper of a car at high speed. The guy was about two cars ahead.

The guy zipped out into the oncoming lane again. A car horn shrieked. The guy went further out and passed the car on the far side.

"Jesus."

Troy went to the inside and passed the car in front of him on the narrow shoulder. Whoever was in the car laid on their horn, too. The drivers must think he and the other motorcycle rider were friends, out drag racing in the very early morning and putting the fear of the Lord into everyone.

"Stark, don't do this."

"Don't worry," he said again.

"We're never going to catch him."

They were stuck behind a delivery truck. Troy zipped out into the oncoming traffic. He accelerated, straight at the headlights of the next vehicle, some kind of bus or tall truck. The truth was he barely saw it.

"Stark! Stop!"

He leaned hard to the right and back into his own lane, out ahead of the delivery truck. There was so much commercial traffic out here. It made sense. Truck drivers were trying to get a jump start on their deliveries before most of the commuters appeared.

The outskirts of the city were appearing all around them now. Ahead, the bike peeled off to the right down a street that extended at a 45-degree angle from the road. Troy followed. It was good, just him and the other guy again, all alone.

Rows of warehouses and dark buildings slid by at high speed.

"We're gonna take him!" Troy shouted. "Get ready for your shot."

"Gladly," she said. "Anything to get this over with!"

Troy accelerated again. They were right behind the guy now. The road under their wheels became rough. They were bumping over cobblestones. There was a track alongside of them, something like an old cable car would run on. The track was gleaming, like it was new. In fact, there were two sets of tracks, one on either side of them. They were racing down the middle of a street with cable car tracks, barely feet apart.

Ahead, a cable car was coming. Two bright headlights shone below a giant windshield. The lights were blinding. The cable car conductor sounded some sort of alarm.

Ding! Ding! Ding! Ding! Ding!

It was too late to stop. The first bike roared forward, straight at the cable car. Troy crushed the brakes, his bike skidding to a stop. He nearly lost control, and tumbled in front of the cable car, but he held it.

Ahead, the first bike hooked right, leaning hard, a split second before the cable car reached him, and across the front of the thing.

"Son of a…"

The cable car whipped past. A second later, it was gone. Troy was at a dead stop. He looked to his right. The bike had turned down a side street and was already nearly a block away. That guy did not want to get caught.

"Stark. I really think we should…"

"Do you have that gun ready?"

She held it up. "Yes, but I don't want to fall off this bike."

He nodded. "One more try. I won't let you fall."

He looked both ways - the cable car was in the distance now, two or three blocks away, and receding - then he crossed the tracks. He settled in and got low. Dubois squeezed down behind him, her left arm tight around his chest. He popped into second gear, then third. The bike whined. Fourth gear. Fifth. Buildings flashed by, crowding in on both sides.

Here came the other bike, zipping toward him like it was coming backwards. The guy had to slow down and go around a truck that passed on a cross street. Streetlights shone down. Somewhere, a glimmer of dawn entered the sky. Troy could see the guy, and his bike, in exquisite detail.

The guy was wearing a helmet and dark riding leathers. His visor was down. Unlike Troy, who still had the Uzi strapped to his back, the guy had dropped his machine gun somewhere, probably ditched it by the side of the road in case he got stopped by the cops. Instead, the guy had some sort of satchel strapped to his back.

Troy zipped through the cross street without slowing down. A car skidded to a stop to his left. Behind him, Dubois let out a breath, but didn't scream or ask him to stop. She was getting it. She was climbing on board his life.

They were half a block apart now. Troy was focused on the man. He was crouched on his bike, leaning forward, willing it on.

They were open all the way now, both of them. Tiny cars were parked along the right side of the street, whooshing by. Sssp. Sssp. Sssp. Sssp.

An old man was out walking a small dog. He was a flash, there and gone.

That bike was everything. There was a green space ahead, maybe a park, something green and large. It seemed to take up all the space in front of them. The bike and its rider were superimposed on the green.

"Ready?" Troy shouted. His eyes never left the bike.

The throttle was balls-out.

"Ready!" she shouted.

Troy nodded.

They hit another cross street, then straight at the green. It was a park. There was an opening, a paved walkway, something straight ahead. The guy knew exactly where he was going. An escape plan, a route, to keep trying to give Troy the slip. It didn't work. Now a public park.

They zoomed across the street and right up onto the walkway. It made S curves. Troy leaned low into each curve. People were out, early morning types. They jumped off the path as the bikes blew past.

The guy took a left, up and over a small hillock. Troy was right behind him. It was a wide-open field here. A bandstand was at the far side. Concerts. Sunday in the park.

The guy went straight up the middle of the vast lawn.

Troy slipped back, just a touch and to the left. That should give Dubois a shot with her right hand. The bikes were running together now, the lead bike just ahead and to their right. The helmet turned and looked at them. He was reaching inside his jacket, reaching for something.

The grass was wet with dew. Troy's bike slid, skidded, threatened to drop out below them. It was heavy. If they slid…

"Dubois! Take him!"

She grunted. There was hesitation. She aimed the gun. This was no time to go soft again.

"Dubois!"

BANG!

The shot echoed across the field.

The other bike's rear tire popped and shredded. The guy held it for a second, lost control and went flying off. Troy blew by him but turned his head to watch the guy thrown clear. He slid and tumbled along the wet grass as the bike bounced end over end.

Troy hit the brakes and skidded to a stop. He took a deep breath and grunted. It was almost a laugh. Then it was a laugh. He smiled.

"Nice shot, Dubois. Did you see that guy bounce? Man!"

"I couldn't look," she said.

Troy turned the bike around and rolled slowly back toward the man.

"Ready with the gun, Dubois. In case he wants to test us."

The guy was face down on the grass, not moving. One of his arms was under his body, and out of sight. Troy rolled the bike to a stop ten meters away.

He put the kickstand down and climbed off. Dubois climbed off a second later.

"Is he…"

Troy shook his head. "I don't know. Don't think so."

He reached inside his jacket to his holster and took his own pistol out. He glanced around the park. There was a glimmer of pale light, nearly dark, just enough to see by. They were out in a wide-open field. Some buildings were off to the right, the way they had just come. He could picture kids out here in the afternoons, kicking a soccer ball around. There was nobody here now. His hearing was a bit wrecked at the moment, but as far as he could tell, there were no sirens coming. They were all alone.

Two motorcycles ripping through town at high speeds in the early morning must be a normal thing around here.

"Watch him," he said. He approached the man warily, his gun in a two-handed grip. The guy looked like a spaceman in his helmet and leathers. His wrecked bike was behind him, a little further in the distance. This guy had nearly killed Troy a little while ago. It should be a fundamental rule - be careful of people who nearly kill you.

Troy gestured to his left. "Take an angle on him. Come at him from two sides. Force him to make a decision."

Tiny Dubois moved to the left, gun pointed at the man.

Troy was two steps away. Suddenly the guy rolled over, his hand inside his jacket. Troy crossed the small distance in a heartbeat. He stepped on the man's chest, squashing his hand inside the jacket.

Dubois was there, a few feet away. "Arret!" she shouted. "Arret ca!"

Troy pointed the gun at the man's throat.

"Don't make me kill you."

The man went limp and lay on his back. He was done.

Dubois spoke to him in rapid fire French, her voice commanding. She was back in her element, maybe more so than ever before.

The man raised his hands. He opened them and showed them to Troy. Empty. Then he reached slowly to his head, removed his helmet, and threw it aside. It bounced a few feet away. The man let his head fall back onto the grass.

He was a bald man with a black scrubble of beard and dark eyes. He was in his late 20s, maybe early 30s.

"Speak English?" Troy said.

The man shook his head.

Troy reared back and kicked him in the ribs. HARD. The man writhed.

"Then how do you know what I said?"

"Little," the man said. "I speak a little."

Troy crouched down next to him, reached inside the man's jacket, and pulled out the gun the man had been reaching for. He tossed it away onto the grass.

"Then don't say no. Say yes. How hard is that?" The guy was such a reflexive liar he couldn't answer a simple question in a straightforward way. Troy had met too many people like this in his life.

"Lucien Mebarak," he said. Then he asked a question to which he already knew the answer. "Is that you?"

The man shook his head. A harsh sound escaped from him. It sounded almost like a laugh. "No. Of course not."

That was right. The Lucien Mebaraks of this world didn't hang around at night guarding stuff, getting in gunfights and high-speed motorcycle chases. They loomed over the top of all that, pulling the strings.

"Where is he?" Troy said.

"How would I know that?"

Troy smiled. "Who are you?"

The man shook his head again. "Nobody."

This line of questioning was going nowhere. It was time for a little forward momentum to begin. Troy wedged the muzzle of his own gun up under the guy's chin. "Well, Mr. Nobody, I'm gonna blow your brains out. Right out the top of your head. I killed all your friends. I'm gonna kill you, too. Okay?"

The guy's hands wanted to do something. They clenched, then unclenched. The man's eyes were hard. His jaw was set.

"Try it," Troy said. "Please."

The guy said nothing.

"You know what's going to happen to me if I kill you? I'll tell you. Nothing. I've been killing guys like you all over western Europe the past couple of days. That's why they sent me here from America. New York City. That's where I came from. Understand?"

The guy's eyes did something now. They changed. They might have softened just the tiniest bit. He understood, all right. He understood vengeance all too well.

"Stark...," Dubois said.

Troy raised his hand. He got it. He understood. It was one thing to kill a bunch of guys in a gun battle out in the countryside. It was quite another to kill a guy in cold blood in a public park in the middle of the city as the light of dawn came into the sky.

She was a good partner. She didn't hammer the issue. She didn't beat a dead horse. She didn't say another word.

Troy took a breath. "Let's see what Mr. Nobody has on him, shall we?"

"Okay," she said softly.

Troy kneeled across the guy's chest. He took his knife out and cut the black leather strap holding the satchel the guy had been carrying all this time. He yanked the satchel out. He watched the guy's eyes carefully. They didn't change. The bag wasn't booby-trapped, that much was clear. People who are about to explode tend to become alarmed.

Troy unzipped the bag and looked inside.

There was a laptop computer in there - the heavy metal, watertight, shockproof, nearly indestructible type of laptop that military people used to call "toughbooks." This one was further encased in a thick layer of rubber, making it even more impact resistant. The data inside had probably survived that wipeout just fine. The man had survived. The computer was built to survive things that would nearly liquefy the man.

"What's in the computer?" Troy said.

The man shook his head. "I don't know."

Troy sighed and shook his own head.

"They don't tell me," the man said. "They say protect it. So I do."

"Who are they?" Troy said.

The man shook his head again. "Kill me."

Troy nodded. Of course, the guy wasn't going to say who he worked for. He'd probably do ten years in prison before he named anyone. It occurred to Troy that neither he, nor Dubois, had the power to arrest this man. Even more, if Troy tried to hand the guy over to anyone, they were just as likely to arrest Troy.

The day was lightening by the second now. There were no cops around, but that could change at any time. There were buildings right on the edge of the park, with dozens of windows facing this way. Troy couldn't beat the guy, mock execute him, or do much at all to get him talking. Unless Alex turned up here with a paddy wagon in the next few minutes, they were probably just going to have to let the guy go.

That was frustrating.

Troy worked quickly now. He reached inside the guy's jacket and came out with a wallet. There was no identification inside, of course. Just a bunch of money in euros. Troy sifted through it. A few thousand in various bills.

"Thanks." He tossed the guy's wallet on the grass and pocketed the money.

He patted the guy down, head to toe, looking for more weapons. He made the guy unzip and remove his boots. Nothing in there. Troy took each one and tossed it away. That was it, all the guy had - a machine gun, a pistol, and a laptop computer. Those things, and a motorcycle, currently out of commission.

The guy had nothing, basically.

Troy stood with the leather satchel. Dubois went over and picked up the guy's pistol. The weak gray light of dawn was really in the sky now.

"Nice doing business with you, Nobody."

"Is that all?" the man said.

Troy shook his head. "No."

Then he kicked the guy in the head. The man writhed again, this time in real pain. Troy hated guys like this. He would kick him again, kick him until his skull cracked open and his brain slid out onto the wet grass. But it was time to go.

He and Dubois walked over to the motorcycle. He handed her the satchel, and they climbed aboard the bike. Troy reached in, turned the ignition with his fingers, and the engine roared to life.

"Hey!' the man shouted. He was on all fours on the grass, his head against the ground. "You stole that cycle!"

Troy shrugged. "I guess you better call the cops."

He and Dubois rode off toward the edge of the park.

CHAPTER TWENTY TWO

7:45 am Central European Daylight Time
Interpol Liaison Office - Special Investigations Unit
Europol Headquarters
The Hague, The Netherlands

"Where are they?"

Miquel had just arrived with his coffee and a sweet roll. As usual, he walked in to find that Jan Bakker was already here, perched in his normal place, computers and various blinking devices lined up in front of him. Jan should probably just pull a cot in here, so he never had to return home. It would have to be quite a large cot, however.

"They're in Reims," Jan said. "At a guest house."

"Together?" Miquel said.

"Agent Dubois expensed it. They booked two rooms."

Miquel smiled. That wasn't what he meant. He had known Dubois her entire career. Stark wasn't her type.

"We can afford the extra room."

Miquel did a quick calculation in his mind. Reims to Lyon was perhaps five hours by car, four hours by train. It was nearly 8am now. Clearly, Dubois was not going to arrive at Interpol headquarters bright and early this morning.

"There was an incident," Jan said. "In the night."

Miquel glanced out the glass walls of the office at the corridor. People were beginning to arrive. He had not yet been called in to speak to any more concerned officials, but he assumed it was coming. He had this office swept for listening devices every week, so they were probably free to talk. But the incidents were starting to pile up. Jan was a master of encrypting communications, but it was not out of the question that their hosts here at Europol were attempting to break those encryptions.

"What was its nature?"

Jan shook his head. He still hadn't turned around. "They didn't say, and I didn't encourage them to. They did acquire a laptop, which they have turned on, and which I am attempting to access remotely. It is going to be a bit of a job."

"Can we speak with them?" Miquel said.

Now Jan spun around in his chair. He raised an eyebrow. "Of course. We were merely waiting upon your arrival."

Miquel smiled. Jan Bakker never seemed to sleep and did not seem to have a personal life beyond hobbies nearly as intricate as the paid work he did. He processed mountains of information much like a computer, and at lightning speeds. He also couldn't seem to understand people who did not live as he did, which was nearly everyone else on Earth.

"Now I'm here," Miquel said.

Jan nodded. "Good. I can make an encrypted call directly to Dubois's room. Unfortunately, it will be wide open for interception on their end, but at the moment it's the best we can do."

"Okay. We will try not to divulge too much."

A device on Jan's long table was serving as a telephone. It was a nondescript thing made of black plastic, with a speaker embedded on top of it, and a microphone built in somewhere. There were no lights on it. It seemed like a device from an earlier era.

From the speaker came the sound of a phone ringing.

"Yes?" a female voice said.

"Mariem, it's Jan. I'm here with Miquel."

"Good," she said. "And I'm here with our friend from abroad."

"Very good," Miquel said. "Good morning to you both. Before we begin, Mariem, please make sure that you call headquarters this morning, and inform them you are taking a personal day. It's highly unusual, given the questions lingering about yesterday's interrogation, but it is your right to take a day off. You can always provide further information tomorrow. Just be sure to inform them that you are in Lyon and returned there yesterday evening."

"Understood," Dubois said. "I will do that as soon as we end this call."

Miquel nodded. "All right. Now please give me the update but be careful about the details. Only what is crucial to convey."

Stark came on the line. "Lucien Mebarak," he said. "We have a military grade laptop computer that we believe belongs to him. It's what we used to call in my combat days a toughbook. You can kick it around without breaking it. Jan is working on accessing it now."

Miquel glanced at Jan. Indeed he was. He had returned to his computers and seemed to be lending only half an ear to the conversation.

172

"We had a confrontation with men we believe work for Mebarak," Dubois said.

"Was anyone injured?" Miquel said. This was a concern. If either Dubois or Stark had been wounded, and they were out in the field, then it instantly became more pressing to bring them back into the fold.

"No one on this side," Dubois said.

"Witnesses?" Miquel said.

"Hard to say at this time."

"We need whatever we can get on Mebarak," Stark said. "He seems to be an unwanted member of the wealthy and wonderful Willems family, and sometimes uses that name. But given our discussions with his half-sister, I'd guess he goes by other names as well. First and foremost, I need to know where he lives. He's probably got a bunch of houses, but I need the one where he is right now."

It was interesting to Miquel what a hard charger Stark was. He didn't work for this agency. He had become something of an unwelcome guest in Europe. His time here was running out. And yet, he sounded like he was issuing orders, or thought he was.

Miquel looked at Jan. Jan must have eyes in the back of his head, or perhaps he saw Miquel in the reflection of the computer screens.

"We should be able to find something," he said.

"And if we do," Miquel said to the telephone, "what do you plan to do with that information?"

"I'd like to pay the man a visit," Stark said.

CHAPTER TWENTY THREE

4:50 pm Central European Daylight Time
Fleur-de-Lis Hotel
Reims, France

"Mind if I smoke?"

Troy Stark opened his eyes. He stared up at the light blue ceiling of the hotel room for a long moment. His head rested on a fluffy pillow. The soreness in his chest where the bullets hit him had settled in completely. It hurt to breathe.

He had slept like the dead. He didn't even remember lying down. If he had dreamed, he remembered nothing of it.

He looked across the room. Alex was sitting in a wooden chair at the small table the room came with. The table was by a window, and Alex had the window cracked open. The smoke from the cigarette in his hand mostly wafted to the outside. Faint city sounds of traffic and distant voices wafted in - a fair exchange.

Alex sat with his right leg folded over his left in an exaggerated manner. He was quite skinny, something Troy supposed he had noticed before, but not to this degree. Alex almost looked like he was made out of matchsticks.

For once, he wasn't dressed in any particular costume. He wasn't a hotel busboy or a Sikh from the Midwest, or a man with scooter problems. He was just some guy. He wore dark blue jeans and a blue and yellow soccer jersey. There were nice, zippered, suede boots on his feet. They looked like they would be soft to the touch.

There was a white ceramic ashtray on the table. Alex deposited some ashes into it and regarded the butt between his fingers.

"It's no big deal to quit," he said. "I've probably quit a hundred times. But these Turkish cigarettes…" He shook his head. "Once you get going again, they're hard. It's like that girl from the past. You know the one? You'll always go back, if you can."

Troy didn't bother to ask him how he got in here. By now he knew that Alex would always find a way inside.

"How are we doing?" he said instead.

Alex shrugged. "We're just about out of time, I'm afraid."

Troy wasn't ready to sit up. The pain in his chest was too much.

Of course, Alex noticed that, too. He gestured at the tiny bedside table. This hotel was nice. It was old but renovated and well maintained. The bed was big and comfortable, but everything else was like a miniature version of the real thing. The room itself was small. The bathroom was for less than one person. The bedside table's surface was maybe five inches across, with a tiny lamp perched on it.

Also, there was a small glass of water and a couple of blue pills.

"I brought you some naproxen sodium tablets. In the States, they call them Aleve. They're the best."

"How did you know I was hurt?"

Alex shook his head. "I didn't. Given all the bodies piled up out at the abbey, I just guessed."

Troy reached across and gingerly took the pills and water. He gulped the pills and washed them down. Then he put the glass back.

"Is that why we're out of time? The dead guys?"

Alex sucked in some smoke, held it, then exhaled it out the window. "Persons," he said. "He wants you home. The situation has gone from uncomfortable to untenable. Interpol, Europol, the Dutch Police, and the Luxembourg Police are all asking questions that can't be answered. They all either want you in custody, or off the continent. If the French knew you were here, you'd already be gone."

Troy shrugged, just barely. It hurt to move his neck. And his shoulders. "He should be able to weather that kind of scrutiny."

"He has a cover story to maintain," Alex said. "You're supposed to be a cop, remember? So is he. By my count, you killed three guys in Luxembourg, and another five out at the abbey. All in one night."

Troy nearly shook his head. "Four. My partner killed one."

Alex raised an eyebrow. Then he smiled. "Is she your partner now?"

Troy didn't say anything. He just wanted to get to the point of this meeting. Was he being recalled, or wasn't he?

"Popped her cherry, did she?"

"Crude," Troy said. "But if that's how you want to put it."

"This trip is getting expensive," Alex said. "When you leave a pile of bad guys behind, it has to be cleaned up. That requires calling in a chit. We had to disappear the guys, and clean up the building itself, which was a mess."

"They had explosives there, not too long ago," Troy said.

Alex nodded. "No doubt. There's also industrial grease on the grounds, evidence of high-tech batteries that were used there, and a cache of AK-47s still in their boxes, buried under some hay in an outbuilding. Every one of those dead guys is a career criminal, three from Albania, one from Serbia and one from Sicily. They all had rap sheets as long as my arm in multiple countries, and three of them had active warrants. Nice work finding that place. But prove something about it, if you don't mind. Prove who owns the place. Prove who those guys were working for. Prove there were ever drones there, and if there were, that they were involved in the terror attacks. And tell me where the drones went, again if they were ever there in the first place."

He paused for another inhale of the smoke. Troy didn't say a word.

"Face it, Stark. You've been stampeding across the continent, and that's cool, but so far, you've come up with nothing. And I'm hustling along behind you, cleaning up your messes, while pretty much every police organization has your picture hanging on their wall. You're the bad guy right now, not the terrorists. And it's becoming a distraction."

He shook his head. "I had to crush that woman's Porsche. It was a nice car, but what else was I going to do with it? Sell it? Drive it back to Luxembourg? I couldn't leave it there, like you did, full of your prints and DNA. And food crumbs."

An image of Aliz Willems appeared in Troy's mind. She was a beautiful woman. There was also something interesting about her. Troy didn't usually go for the vastly wealthy, jet-setting types. But in this case...

"Aliz," he said. "How is she doing?"

"The heiress?" Alex said. "That's very thoughtful of you to ask. I couldn't keep her locked away in cold storage forever because I had other matters to attend to. We had a doctor and nurse come in, who work for some friends of ours. Aliz is up in her bedroom sleeping off her adventures until we can get you back to the United States. She's very comfortable, well-hydrated, and well cared for. She's going to be fine. She just won't remember much of what went on since you left."

Troy nodded. "Good."

"It's fine," Alex said. "But let's not pretend it's good. We have an heiress on ice. We have eight dead gangsters. We have a shootout and car chase in downtown Luxembourg associated with a charitable event, which was filmed on about 60 different cameras, and has gone viral all over the world. And we have three guys who own a small high-tech company that are suing anyone and everyone and are hoping you're put on trial in The Hague for human rights violations. You and Ratko Mladic can hang out together. Won't that be nice?"

176

Alex paused again. "Your work here is supposed to be a secret. Secret agent. Are you familiar with that concept?"

"Yeah," Troy said. "You know what else we have? We have the identities and location of the guys who made the drones. We have the likely buyer, or agent of the buyer, Aliz Willems's brother. We have the laptop computer I took off the guy who was at the abbey, a place where the drones may have been stored."

"We don't have the drones, and we have no idea where they are," Alex said.

"We've only been at this for three days," Troy said.

Alex nodded. "I agree. It's actually a lot of progress. But there's no time. The next attack could happen today, tomorrow, any minute, and we have nothing to show. Meanwhile you've been burning bridges."

"Do we know what's on the laptop?" Troy said.

"Your man at Interpol has been working on it all day, while you and your partner were asleep. He has something, but everything he does with computers is encrypted from end to end. He's a clever character. We don't know what he has."

"He said he'd get me an address for Aliz Willems's brother. Lucien."

Alex nodded. "Phone calls are easier to intercept. We do know he got you that. The guy works fast, multi-tasks. It took him half the day, but we think he got a good pinpoint. It's a big house in Amsterdam. It's not registered to Lucien, but he owns it through a series of shell companies, and your man believes he's there. At the moment, Lucien appears to be living under the name Charles de Klerk."

"Well, give me that much," Troy said. "Let me go hit the guy and see if he squawks."

Alex shrugged. "It's not up to me. You know that. I just work here. But Persons figured you'd want that, and he's willing to stretch things out a bit longer on the off chance it will bear fruit. But you're out on a limb now. If you get picked up, pretty much by anybody, you'll get deported at least, and you might face criminal charges. We can get you off, but you might sit in stir for a while."

"If that's the least of my worries…," Troy said.

Alex took one last drag of the cigarette and pitched it out the window. Then he stood. Troy noticed another thing that was odd about him. This was the first time when he didn't seem to have any accent at all.

"Don't get yourself killed over this, Stark. We're nearly out of rope. And don't get your little partner killed either."

He was on his way out of the room. As he passed the bedside table, his hand reached out and deposited an unopened silver can there.

Rock Star Zero. Troy reached out and touched the can. It was cold as ice.

CHAPTER TWENTY FOUR

10:35 pm Central European Daylight Time
The Gouden Bocht (The Golden Bend)
The Herengracht Canal
Amsterdam, The Netherlands

"I don't think you'll find anything here," Jan Bakker said. "The recordings will be inadmissible as evidence because of how they are obtained. There is no warrant, so this is a home invasion. But you already know that."

They were sitting in a small sedan along a canal, less than a block from the home in question. The neighborhood was upscale, with mansions, centuries old, right on the water and behind stone walls on the street.

"Any admissions or hints of guilt will give me some context, though," Bakker said. "Some clues of what to be looking for, and perhaps where. So recordings could be helpful in that way."

Bakker was at the driver's seat. His giant bulk did not belong in this car. He took up nearly the whole front. Miquel, the leader of this motley crew, was not here. He couldn't risk being seen with, or knowing the whereabouts of, Troy Stark. Bakker didn't seem to care who saw him, or with whom.

Troy and Dubois were stuffed in the back seat with their gear. Their gear included, among other things, the tiny recording devices they were both wearing, wired into their black jumpsuits. The microphones were embedded on their collars, and not visible to the naked eye. The actual recordings would go on devices no larger than an American penny, also embedded in their clothes. Jan Bakker was a master of technology. And technology was reaching a level of miniaturization where pretty soon it was just going to disappear altogether.

"So he's definitely in there?" Troy said. "Lucien Mebarak?"

Bakker nodded. "Yes. Almost certainly he is."

"Almost?"

"Well, Charles de Klerk. Almost certainly, he is Lucien Mebarak. And I've been tracing communications by him, from inside that house, all day. Charles de Klerk is not hiding. But he's not saying anything confidential, either. He could be mistaken for a rich man leading his normal day-to-day life."

Troy shrugged. "Well, then I guess we'll just go in and talk to him and see what he says."

Bakker shook his massive bald head. It swiveled at the top of his tree trunk of a neck. Troy marveled at the sight. It was like watching a nature special on TV. The birth of a hippopotamus. Twins. He almost couldn't understand what he was seeing.

"He will say he knows nothing about it," Bakker said. "That's what I predict. I hope I am incorrect."

It, in this case, was the information that Bakker had managed to glean from the laptop computer thus far. He had been accessing the computer remotely, and it had been time consuming and difficult work. He felt that now, with the computer in his possession, things would proceed more quickly and easily.

He had found no identifying markers of ownership within the computer. All of that data had been scrubbed by someone sophisticated. There might be some remnant of that information left, but it could take days to undercover it.

What he had found were maps, drawings, plans and specifications that seemed to indicate coming attacks in five places - the London Stock Exchange, the New York Stock Exchange, the Chicago Board of Trade, the Frankfurt Stock Exchange, and the Tokyo Stock Exchange. But these weren't drone attacks. They were suicide attacks, with men simply walking into the buildings, going to particularly crowded and vulnerable areas, and blowing themselves up.

The attacks didn't seem realistic. The amount of explosive they would require would be nearly impossible to smuggle into any of these buildings. Further complicating matters, they were supposed to take place simultaneously, in an attempt to crash world markets all at once.

Troy didn't like it. Bakker didn't, either. In Bakker's case, he felt that these plans might be hiding or blocking access to files layered beneath them. The two attacks so far had been less spectacular than these but had been carried out successfully. Did it make sense to build on easy, low-hanging fruit drone attacks with a series of difficult, if not impossible suicide attacks?

It didn't, and even if it did, what about the missing drones? SymAero sold seven drones to someone. Two had been used. Five were still out there.

The man who might be able to clear up these mysteries was inside a house, right up the street from here. By now, he would know that his abbey had been knocked over, if it was even his. Bakker hadn't been able to verify the name of the true owner - a holding company in Singapore was the owner of record. But that Singapore holding company was in turn held by a partnership of three companies, two in Bermuda and one in the Bahamas. Each of these were then held by other companies, or partnerships, or consortiums. On and on and on, one nested Russian doll after another.

That didn't really matter to Troy. He was confident that the abbey was owned by Lucien Mebarak. Aliz Willems had told him as much. She had no reason to lie.

Mebarak would also know that the laptop had been seized, and a bunch of his men had been killed. All of these setbacks, and he hadn't moved a muscle. He was hiding in plain sight, just a law-abiding rich guy, a citizen of the world, who happened to go by different names at different times.

"Shall we?" Dubois said.

Troy nodded. "I think we shall."

Dubois was surprising him. She never did make it back to Lyon. She had called in sick, and slept in all day at the hotel, just like Troy. When they got together in the late afternoon, she was as eager to come get Mebarak as Troy was.

"He's the one," she said. "I get it now. It's not even that he got tangled up with the wrong people, as his sister seems to think. He is the wrong people."

Troy got out on his side. He and Dubois had taken a commercial flight here, in both cases under false identities. See? He had known all along there was more to Dubois than met the eye. They had to leave the weapons they'd gotten from Aliz Willems behind. Now, he had a grappling hook, carabiners, and rope that Bakker had brought.

Bakker had declined to bring him a gun, and Alex hadn't turned up again. So Troy was going in without a weapon.

Bakker's window was down. Bakker seemed wedged inside the car. He would need the Jaws of Life just to get out the door. God help him in a rollover.

Troy stuck out his hand and Bakker took it. His giant hand swallowed Troy's large hand completely. Like a snake swallowing a rodent.

"Jan, if I don't see you again…"

"You'll see me again."

Dubois leaned in on the passenger side. She said something in French. Bakker said something back to her.

181

"I'll never make it back."

"Okay, see you tomorrow."

Who knew what these people said to each other?

Troy and Dubois moved down the street. There were security cameras all along here. Troy could spot a couple of them without even trying. The camera system for this neighborhood was run by a private firm.

Bakker had hacked the entire system earlier and replaced the live footage with 20-minute loops of non-activity from the early evening. That was nice, but to Troy it didn't matter. He wasn't trying to hide himself. His run here was almost over, and he knew it.

Behind them, Bakker pulled the tiny car out of the parking space, turned around, and disappeared up the narrow street. His headlights splashed over them as he turned.

There was a high wall around Mebarak's place. A right-of-way or an alley ran between that wall, and the wall of the mansion right next door. Troy and Dubois casually turned down the alley and walked between the two walls. The space was narrow, perhaps a meter across. The walls were high enough that it was impossible for anyone in either house to see down here.

They walked the entire way. At the end, it opened onto the canal. Across the water were more mansions, decks overlooking the water, and boats docked. A few of the properties were strung with colorful lights. They stopped here for a long moment.

Jan Bakker was headquartered in France, but he often worked in the Europol office as well. He also worked on loan to the Dutch National Police from time to time. He had kept his old flat here in Amsterdam, about ten minutes' drive from here this time of night. He had a flat in Lyon, and one in The Hague as well. The guy was in demand, and he got around.

He was headed home to his Amsterdam flat, but not to sleep. In a few moments, at precisely, 11:05 pm, he was going to take down the electricity to several square blocks in this neighborhood. A minor blackout, caused by an overloaded transformer which then blew out. It was no one's fault. These things happened. The utility would get it back up and running in no time.

It should give Troy and Dubois plenty of time to cross Lucien Mebarak's grounds, enter his house, and surprise him with their sudden presence.

So for the moment, they waited.

"It's been quite a ride so far, huh?" Troy said.

Dubois nodded. "Quite a ride."

"Was it worth it?"

She shrugged. "That I don't know yet."

"But you're going to see it to the end?"

"Yes."

Troy nodded. It was everything he could ask for in a partner. She had risked her job and her life. She had killed a man. She was left with an uncertain future, and this next move had an uncertain payoff. But she was still here, still with him.

"Then let's roll," he said.

He tossed the metal hook up and over the top of the wall. It was heavy, but he reached it easily. The hook was padded with rubber, and barely made a sound. Slowly, he pulled it back, and it caught at the top of the wall. He yanked it; he took two steps up the wall. The grip was solid. It would hold their weight.

She was putting on a pair of dark leather climbing gloves. He did the same.

He glanced at his watch. 11:03.

"Here we go."

Dubois went first, springing lightly up the rope, like a pixie, her feet kicking off the wall. When she reached the top, Troy followed, a little heavier, but nearly as quickly. At the top, the wall was about two feet across. Little pieces of sharp glass were embedded in the concrete at the top, jagged edges up.

Dubois was perched nimbly on top of the wall, in a deep crouch, her small feet wedged between the shards of glass. No way could Troy pull that posture off. He would have to impale his big feet on the glass, and even then...

He simply hung on the rope. They looked across at the house. The second-floor study was as Bakker had described it - an add-on to the elegant old home, basically a glass box that opened to a terrace overlooking the canal. The lights in the study were on, and for an instant, Troy could see the man, Lucien, sitting at a large desk, appearing to pore over some paperwork in his hands.

Then the lights went out. Beautiful. Perfect timing.

"Go," he said.

Dubois slipped off the wall, her fingers gripping the very edge as she lowered the rest of her body down. She hung there for a few seconds, then let go and was gone. Troy heard a thump as she landed on the grass on the other side.

He heaved himself over the wall, strategically placing his hands between the pieces of glass, pressing hard, then vaulting over like a gymnast. He flew through the air, one second, two, then hit and rolled forward, letting his momentum carry him, taking the impact off his knees. The grass was soft, and he rolled all the way over and into a crouch.

Dubois was beside him.

"Hit it."

They moved across the lawn like shadows, no motion sensor lights suddenly coming on to disrupt their progress.

They reached the bottom of the terrace, and now Dubois had her rope and grappling hook out. It was a similar, but somewhat smaller version than the previous one. The hook was still metal encased in rubber, though.

She handed it to Troy, and he tossed it over the top. Same as before, it caught, almost without a sound. It must be hooked on the low parapet wall that went around the terrace. This time, there was no waiting. Dubois went straight up the rope. When she reached the top, Troy followed. In seconds, they were both standing on the terrace.

"Careful now," Troy whispered. "He could have a gun."

He looked at the glass box. The door to it, a slider, more glass, was already open. There was no breaking and entering required. All they needed to do was walk right in. Low lights were on, a weak yellow, recessed somewhere that wasn't immediately visible. They must come from an emergency power source.

They moved across the stone terrace to the doorway. Troy could see Lucien clearly. He was standing at something that looked like a bar, his back to them. In the gloom, it was hard to say anything about him. He was a decent size, maybe around Troy's own height, but slimmer.

Troy walked in first, in case the man turned around with a gun in his hand. If that happened... Well, it would almost qualify as justifiable homicide, wouldn't it? Yes, he was in the man's house uninvited, but even so.

"Good evening," Lucien said, without turning around. His voice was somewhat deep, and pleasantly musical. The devil must have a similar voice when he took human form. "I've been waiting for you. Can I mix you a drink?"

Troy smiled.

"Clever to knock out power to the whole area," Lucien said. "I can't say I was expecting that. But once it happened, I knew you'd be along any moment."

He turned, and all he had in his hand was a glass.

"Scotch," he said. "McCallan. Thirty years old. With one cube of ice."

"The ice cube kills it," Troy said.

"Sixteen-hundred euros a bottle," Lucien said, as if that explained anything.

His hair was dark - his mother's influence. His eyes appeared to be a pale blue or gray. It was hard to tell in this light. He had a light stubble of dark beard on his face. He wore a light blue dress shirt, open at the collar, and a pair of loose-fitting khaki pants. He looked like he was ready for business casual day at the office. He was handsome, Troy supposed. Of course, he was. He was descended from that superior genetic line, the Willems family.

"I'm glad to finally meet you," Lucien said. He regarded Dubois. "Both of you."

"Who are we?" Troy said.

Lucien shook his head. "I don't know. Something that became stuck to the bottom of my shoe, I guess. But you will come right off."

There was a button on the bar. He reached over and casually pressed it. Behind Troy and Dubois, the door to the terrace slid closed. It moved quickly, but not shockingly so. They could have jumped out, if that was their plan. But they had no intention of leaving, and the door engaged with the lock.

"The house has an emergency power supply, of course," Lucien said. "It's separate from the urban grid. This room is a panic room, if you like. Both doors are locked. The glass isn't glass at all. It's a modern shatter-proof composite. No man alive can break it. You could shoot it with an AK-47, and it wouldn't even crack. So we're trapped together, until the police arrive. Yes, the switch also alerts the police. The panic room feature is to be used in the event of intruders. In this case, I thought it would be more amusing to lock myself in with the intruders, instead of locking the doors against them."

"You're a big talker," Troy said. "That much is clear."

"You're a small thinker," Lucien said. "That much is clear, as well."

"Did you find the mess I left out at your abbey?"

Lucien shook his head. "I don't have an abbey. You must have left a mess for someone else."

"That's not what your sister told me."

The words were out of Troy's mouth before he quite knew it. Beside him, Dubois seemed to gasp. It was the first sound she had made since they walked in here. Troy had put his foot in his mouth - he did that sometimes.

It was a mistake because it could place Aliz at risk. There was no way of telling whether this man was depraved enough to kill his own sister. He had certainly attempted to kidnap her. And he seemed happy enough to leave a trail of evidence that if anyone found it, would lead back to her.

Either way, the statement hit home. Troy could see it. Lucien's eyes changed. They sharpened, and hardened. His mouth opened the slightest amount. Then it closed again. He was the bastard son, and Aliz was the darling daughter. Those facts had never left him. All these years, he'd been taking insane risks to prove he was the real Willems. Maybe he was always a monster, or maybe he had made himself into one. But all Aliz had to do was exist. It still hurt.

"My sister," he said. He seemed to ponder her for a moment. "She has a remarkable imagination."

"I get it," Troy said. "I understand. You're the black sheep of the family."

Lucien shook his head. He smiled ruefully and considered the drink in his glass. "You will never understand a man like me."

Troy shrugged. He was getting somewhere. This guy wanted to tell on himself. He wanted to brag about the things he had done.

"Okay," Troy said. "I don't understand you. I don't understand a cockroach, either. But I don't need to. When I see one, I just step on it."

"Step on this," Lucien said. He flicked his glass, his drink flying at Troy. The amber liquid splashed across Troy's chest.

Troy stepped forward and delivered a right hand to Lucien's jaw. He didn't put all the mustard on it. Lucien's head snapped sideways, but he didn't go down.

"Stark!" Dubois said. It was an odd time for an exclamation. She had watched him kill four men this morning. What? He wasn't even supposed to hit this guy?

Lucien smiled. "That's assault," he said. "Mr. Stark."

Troy shook his head. "No."

He feinted with the left, selling it more with the head bob than the hand itself. At the same moment, he brought the right fist straight forward, HARD this time, driving the punch through the target. Lucien went down like a straw doll. His glass went flying out of his hand, shattering on the floor behind him. His head made a soft BONK on the polished stone of the study.

"That's assault," Troy said.

For a long while, Lucien's eyes were closed. He was out. Troy looked down at him. He had promised Aliz he wouldn't kill the guy. He'd never said anything about not punching him.

"Oh Stark," Dubois said.

"I know. I shouldn't have done that."

They both stood over Lucien's prone body.

"The police are going to be here any moment," Dubois said.

Troy squatted down next to Lucien. The man was snoring lightly. Troy tapped his face, giving it little pats. "Hey. Buddy. Wake up a minute."

Then he slapped it.

Lucien's eyes popped open. For a few seconds, they roved from place to place, trying to make sense of what they were seeing. Lucien looked like a man who had no idea where he was. Then his eyes focused on Troy. To Troy, it seemed that Lucien was coming back to reality. But then Lucien spoke.

"I will have your job," he said.

Well, not quite reality.

Troy shook his head. "No you won't. You don't even know what my job is. So I'll tell you. My job is to be a good guy, by being a bad guy. My job is to massacre your henchmen. My job is to beat a punk like you into a coma with my bare hands. How am I doing so far?"

Lucien stared at him but didn't speak.

"I took a computer off a friend of yours this morning. The last man standing at your abbey."

Lucien opened his mouth as if to say something. Probably, he wanted to issue another denial about owning an abbey.

Troy raised a hand. "Don't talk. I don't have a lot of time, so if you interrupt me, I'm going to hit you again, but for real the next time. Your man took off like a frightened bunny rabbit, and we ran him down. We confiscated a laptop computer from him."

"A person might say you stole it," Lucien said.

That was good. It was an interruption, but it was also nearly an admission of guilt. Troy didn't hit him for it. He wanted to encourage that sort of thing.

"However we obtained it, there was information on it suggesting five more attacks. London, Frankfurt, New York, Chicago, and Tokyo. They look like suicide attacks, not drone attacks. Before the cops get here, you're going to tell me when they'll happen, how they'll unfold, and who will be involved on the ground. You're going to give me everything I need to stop them from happening. If you don't, I promise

I'm going to kill you. Not tonight, obviously, but the next time I see you. The only reason you're still alive is because I need this information."

A strange thing happened then. Lucien laughed. It wasn't a hearty laugh or a mad cackle - nothing along those lines. After all, the man was lying on his back, and had been knocked unconscious for a minute or two. The laugh was more like a weak hydraulic system wheezing and running down. It only lasted a few seconds.

"You fool. You're talking about a strategy game I play with other men like myself. You wouldn't know it because it's not open to the public. It was developed specifically for a group I belong to. There are perhaps 90 of us in total, worldwide. We call the game *Conquest*. What you're so excited about is merely a strategy for collapsing several markets at once, through terror attacks, then cornering certain investments at low prices. Yes, terrorists and businessmen can sometimes find common cause. Terrorist attacks often spark panic selling, and the markets come back to their previous highs within several days. A perfect buying opportunity. But in this case, it isn't real. It's just a game."

It clicked. Of course it did. Simultaneous suicide attacks on world stock exchanges were never going to work. But then why did the guy run with that laptop? Why was he told to protect it? There must be more on that computer. There had to be.

"It's a game," Troy said. "That you play."

Lucien nodded. "Investing is a game, my friend. Trade is a game. World conquest is merely a game. Geopolitics: a game. You don't see it because you're poor. You don't have a bird's eye view of the board. You only see what people like me show you."

"Stark," Dubois said. "They're here."

Troy looked up. On the other side of the glass door leading into the house, a couple of big Dutch cops stood. He glanced back at the terrace outside the glass box of the study. Cops were climbing over the low wall. It looked like they were coming up the rope that he and Dubois had left there.

Troy sighed. "Might as well let them in."

He stood, and watched Lucien slowly work his way to his feet. The guy was going to be groggy for a while. He held his wide desk for balance, went around it, and reached underneath. There must be a control under there, because the slider to the terrace opened again, and the door to the house clicked open.

An instant later, the cops were inside. Troy and Dubois were both handcuffed within seconds. There was no sense fighting it. This was the end of the line. What did it even mean? Troy was certain, damn near 100% convinced, that this man was behind the drone attacks. The abbey was his. His men defended the place with their lives. There had been explosives stored there. The laptop had something secret on it.

But this was it. He and Dubois were under arrest, about to get walked out of here. Meanwhile, Lucien Mebarak or Charles de Klerk would be free to do as he pleased. Lucien was the upstanding citizen, who lived in the fancy waterfront home. Troy Stark was the violent criminal, the home invader.

The cops were saying something to Troy now. It was in English, but he couldn't understand it anyway. He was too focused on Lucien.

Lucien watched him and smiled. Then he came around the big desk again. He came close to Troy. The cops didn't try to stop him. He gripped the side of Troy's head, not hard, not gently - just firmly. Their faces were inches apart.

Lucien spoke in a whisper. "You're so stupid," he said.

Troy nodded. He whispered back. "I know. And so are you."

"It's going to happen," Lucien said. "But all concentrated in one location, and sooner than you think. Your precious downtown, your financial district, your stock exchange... Boom. Just like in the game, but it'll be real."

Lucien took half a step back. He smirked. Troy could see the glimmer of mirth in his eyes. "There's nothing you can do," Lucien said.

Now he shrugged. "There's nothing anyone can do. It's too late."

It might be too late. Troy wasn't sure. They were going to lead him away in a minute, and then this guy was likely to evaporate into thin air.

But there was something he could do.

He and Lucien were still close. Troy took a step closer. They were almost body to body. "Hey now!" Lucien said. "Careful."

He looked at the big cops. "Gentlemen?"

Troy brought his right knee straight up into Lucien's groin. He drove it all the way, savagely, as if he were trying to push the knee through Lucien's groin and up into his lungs. Air hissed out of Lucien's mouth into Troy's face.

Lucien grabbed himself and bent over in pain - more than pain, the weird sort of nauseating agony that engulfs a man taking a direct, brutal hit to his balls.

189

Troy's right foot was back on the floor. The cops were dragging him backwards now. As he fell back, he kicked out with the right again, his foot connecting with Lucien's face. Lucien snapped up and backwards, falling toward the floor. Nothing slowed his fall. The back of his head hit the stone for the second time.

THUD.

Troy almost felt the impact, head against stone, in the bottom of his feet.

"I can do that," he said.

Lucien wasn't moving at all. For a second, Troy thought he might be dead. It happened that way sometimes.

The cops pulled Troy toward the doorway. Troy pushed against them, impeding their progress.

"Stark!" Dubois said. "Stop fighting!"

A cop was kneeling next to Lucien's body. He checked Lucian's pulse. It was clear, even from Troy's vantage point, that Lucien was breathing. The cop looked at the others and nodded. He said something in Dutch. Troy didn't understand the words, but the sentiment was clear enough.

"He's all right."

Troy stopped resisting and went limp as they dragged him out the door.

CHAPTER TWENTY FIVE

October 19
2:15 am Central European Daylight Time
A Small Airfield
Near Amsterdam, The Netherlands

They wanted him out of here.

Out of their country, and off this continent. They'd probably kick him off the planet at this point, if they could.

They'd run him out to this airstrip in another Dutch National Police car, two guys in the front, practically twins, same set up as before. They even had a teddy bear with a cute yellow ribbon around its neck on the dashboard. The last time the ribbon was purple, he seemed to recall. So that was different. And Troy was handcuffed this time. Also, Dubois rode out in the back seat with him.

They made a convoy of three cars - tiny, energy-efficient Dutch police cars, with five cops in total. Troy guessed they were taking no chances. If they had to, they would tackle him and restrain him. As he stood on the tarmac, it occurred to him that they weren't planning to remove the cuffs until he was on the plane.

The dark blue jet was behind him, the stairs to the passenger cabin down. It seemed to be the same plane he had taken here. A fuel truck was topping it up. Lights flashed in the darkness. A stiff breeze blew across the open runways.

Somewhere nearby, there was the sound of a plane taking off into the sky. He glanced in that direction. FEDEX. Those people never slept.

He and Dubois were facing each other. Her hands were free. She was tiny. Her hair, which she normally kept pinned down tight, was up in a large Afro-style. She was still wearing the black jumpsuit from earlier tonight, as was he.

She was fit. She was tough. She was brave. She was a rock star.

"I'm suspended for two weeks," she said. "I just found out. It was a voice message left at my office telephone this afternoon. A very cordial phone call, with a harsher punishment than expected. And of course, they didn't know about tonight's little adventure yet."

There wasn't much Troy could say about any of that.

"I'm sorry." It was all he had.

She shook her head. "Don't be. It's a paid holiday. I'm more concerned about Miquel. He was hanging by a thread before any of this. I think they may..."

She made a slicing motion across her throat with her hand.

"Off with his head," Troy said.

She shrugged. "Maybe. Or if he's lucky, maybe they will find something even more..." She made a gesture with her hand, like a bird flying away. "I'm tired. It's an English word."

"Irrelevant," Troy said helpfully.

She nodded. "Yes. Irrelevant. For him to do."

A crazy idea came to Troy. Ideas like this were usually the good ones. They were just hard to sell.

"You know this isn't over yet, right?"

"I know," she said. "But what can I do? I'm on suspension. What can anyone do?"

"Come to New York with me," Troy said. "Mebarak told me New York. That's the target. I doubt anyone will believe us. But we'll keep going. You're getting paid anyway. So keep working. Keep pushing."

She shook her head. "We don't know any details. He could have been lying. He could just send us on a chase for his own amusement."

Troy considered that. He doubted it, but sure. It was possible.

"I need you, Dubois. It's really that simple. Look, if I'm going to do this, I need you with me. You can stay at my place."

Now she was shaking her head and smiling. She looked at the ground between her feet. A dark shade of red seemed to creep up her neck.

"Stark, it could never be..."

She looked up at him, in the eyes.

"I like girls."

Now Troy smiled with her. The air seemed to go out of him. What a world! For the first time in a while, he felt pretty good.

"Oh, I don't mean like that. I mean my mom makes chicken and potato pies. Lasagna. Weird tater tot concoctions that are hard to describe. She's a pretty good cook. She might put a little meat on your bones. Not for nothing, but you could use it."

Now Dubois was really smiling. "You live with your mother." It wasn't a question. "YOU. Live with your mother."

He shrugged. "I'm in a transition phase."

She was grinning ear to ear. She shook her head. "I should have guessed that."

192

"Look, have you ever even been to New York?"

She smirked. "Of course."

"Where have you been?"

She shrugged. "Everywhere, more or less. The Empire State Building. The Guggenheim. The Met. The Statue of Liberty. I saw *Jersey Boys* and *Hamilton* on Broadway."

Now he really did think he would laugh out loud, here on the tarmac, surrounded by cops, about to get thrown out of the country.

"Ah, hell. You've never been to New York. Okay, listen. Get on the plane. I'm sure these guys don't care."

He looked at them. They were a bunch of cops, standing around, chatting quietly in their own indecipherable language. If they had been speaking English, the New York American version of it, they could be standing around outside Yankee Stadium before a ball game. Their job was to put Troy on an airplane, and watch it take off. They didn't care what Dubois did.

"We'll work the case. We won't give up right away. I've got people in New York. It's possible we'll find something. If we don't, okay. I'll show you around town. It's an adventure either way. And you'll be back here before they miss you."

"You'll show me the real New York? Is that it?"

"Uh... yeah."

She was on the line, about to tip one way or the other.

"I don't have any clothes, make-up, toothbrush."

One of the cops, the biggest one, took Troy by the arm.

"They're ready for you," he said.

Troy looked at Dubois. "Don't worry about that stuff. We'll get you some. You have your passport on you? Interpol credentials?"

She nodded. "Of course."

The cop was pulling Troy, steering him toward the airplane door. Troy didn't resist. It had been a long couple of days. Resistance was futile.

"Then let's just go," he said to Dubois. "It looks like I'm leaving right now. Last chance."

He was going to lose her. There was no way she was going to get on this plane. It was okay. If she didn't come, he would keep working on his own. Missing Persons would have something. Alex would turn up at some point. This couldn't be the end. The drones were out there. The next attack was coming.

"Dubois," he said. His back was to her now. She was behind him somewhere. "There's more to do and you know that. Be a hero, Dubois. Be my hero."

He was sandwiched between two cops, the original cop guiding him from behind. The plane was just ahead. He could see the pilots in the cockpit, going through their checklists. The stairs were in front of him now. Another cop stood at the bottom. The cop did a funny arm wave, as if to say: *right this way.*

Suddenly, Dubois was walking along with the group.

"All right," she said. "I'll get deported with you."

CHAPTER TWENTY SIX

6:35 am Central European Daylight Time (12:35 am Eastern Daylight Time)
Interpol Liaison Office - Special Investigations Unit
Europol Headquarters
The Hague, The Netherlands

"Are you still here from last night?"

Jan heard the voice, but it seemed to come to him in a dream. He had fallen asleep with his head on the desk. He knew he was asleep, and yet he knew the voice was not part of his sleep, and at the same time, he seemed to be dreaming it.

He had come here... where was here?

The office in The Hague.

Yes. He had come here after he knocked out the electricity to the area around the Herengracht. Why had he done that? It was a crazy risk, but something about Troy Stark made people take risks. The man seemed willing to die at a moment's notice. If he was willing to die, then what was it to take down a small part of the power grid?

Dubois had gone to New York with Stark. She was suspended, and now she was headed to America. It was crazy. Stark did crazy things, and he made the people around him temporarily lose their minds.

"Jan?"

He had come here because it was here that he had the tools to fully analyze that laptop. Lucien Mebarak had as much as admitted guilt to Stark and Dubois. Jan had heard it on the listening devices. Mebarak had as much as admitted the laptop was his. He had threatened the New York Stock Exchange.

What else had he done?

"Jan?"

Jan was dreaming along in dreamland. Mebarak... he had buried encrypted files in the laptop. There was a hidden directory. Jan had cracked it in the night, as he was drifting off. The specs were there for the drones. They would do a sort of dance in the sky - five drones would release thousands of tiny slaughterbots.

Once the cloud was in motion, they would be impossible to stop. Jan could picture a swarm of the creatures, each one artificially-ntelligent and independent, but commanded and brought together by a central brain. When they came together, interlocking in the air, they would become a flying bomb powerful enough to destroy a city block. No one could stop it because no one would see it coming.

What else had Mebarak done?

The worst thing... In the middle of the night, he had left. Jan had watched the house with commandeered street-level security cameras, and with satellite surveillance cameras. Late, he didn't remember when (though he would have the data saved) a sleek, dark gray Rolls Royce Silver Shadow, one of the very modern ones, had pulled up to Lucien Mebarak's house. Mebarak himself came out with two bags, placed them in the trunk, then climbed in the back.

The car had left Amsterdam and driven south and west into Germany.

Lucien Mebarak was gone.

Because he was under suspicion.

Because he was involved in the attacks, and possibly was the mastermind.

And because...

The next attack was coming.

Oh my God.

"Jan!"

Jan snapped awake and sat up straight.

The office materialized in front of him. His three laptops, and the heavy-duty laptop confiscated from the abbey, were on the long table in front of him. The computers had all gone dark to conserve energy. A large mug of coffee was to his right. He picked it up and peered inside. It was empty. At some point, coffee stopped keeping you awake.

He spun his chair around. Miquel stood there. He wore a light jacket and corduroy pants. His hair was combed back, and he was clean shaven, but his eyes said he was a man who hadn't slept.

Jan nodded. He knew the feeling. His tongue felt like it had grown a coat of hair on it. His contact lenses had dried out and become glued to his eyes.

"Miquel. Hi. Why are you here? I thought..."

"I did, yes. Indefinite suspension. Likely disciplinary action. Possible termination. Suspension of the activities of the Special Investigations Unit, with possible permanent disbanding. So everything is a disaster. But they haven't disabled my entry card yet. They have so

196

little respect for me, it seems that I'm not even considered a security risk. So I came to collect some things I will need."

Jan thought about that. If the activities of the unit were being suspended, then it was possible these computers would be locked down whenever the IT department people began to arrive. Jan needed to migrate what he was doing to his own devices, his own satellite communications, and his own power sources. He would begin to do that in the next several moments. But he needed something from Miquel.

"How much pull do you have left?" Jan said.

Miquel shook his head. "Precious little, I'm afraid."

"Stark was deported. Dubois went with him. They're on a jet I think is owned by the New York City Police Department. Or maybe the American government. I'm not certain."

Miquel nodded. "I know. Dubois texted me in the middle of the night. I told her vaya con Dios. She deserves a holiday."

Jan shook his head. "Her holiday is over. We need to find their plane in the sky and get in touch with them."

Miquel was staring at him.

"The attack is coming," Jan said. "I think it will be New York City. And I'm very concerned that it will be today."

Now they stared at each other. There was much left to do, a terrible amount. Yes, Jan had cracked the encryption, but there were so many things he didn't know. He had no idea where the central navigation computer might be - it was likely to be a mobile device. If he could find the drones, he could probably back trace to the navigation device, but... he had no idea where the drones were, or how to find them. He had no idea who would be launching and controlling the drones, or where that person might be right now. Clearly, it wasn't Lucien Mebarak. Men like him did not get their hands dirty.

Jan had found at least nine aliases for Mebarak, and more than 20 shell companies in five countries that he suspected were associated with Mebarak. By the end of today, Mebarak would be somewhere far away, living under an assumed identity.

A yacht in the Seychelles.

An island in the Caribbean.

A high rise in Dubai.

Who could know?

Jan needed to forget about Mebarak and concentrate on the matter at hand. But finding all these things, the drones, the computer, the perpetrators, in a place as large as New York City… it seemed an almost impossible task. Where to even begin?

"We need to contact that airplane," he said again.

This time Miquel nodded. "That much I can still do."

CHAPTER TWENTY SEVEN

5:45 am Eastern Daylight Time (11:45 am Central European Daylight Time)
A distant runway
John F. Kennedy (JFK) International Airport
Queens, New York City

"We're here. Let's hit it."

The plane landed far away from the passenger terminals. Troy had been in this part of the airport before, coming in on military transports, landing on distant runways. They were way out in the swamps somewhere. Sometimes, he would get off a plane and ride in a bus what seemed like miles back to the actual airport.

He opened the cabin door. The stairwell had already folded down. Dubois was right behind him. If what Jan Bakker and Miquel Castro had been saying was true, Troy and Dubois would have to act fast.

It was a rainy, misty early morning. Lights from the plane were flashing. There were lights on the horizon in the distance - probably the terminals. They had left at night, and the time zone change meant they were landing in New York just a few hours after they left Europe.

Troy could smell the salt of the ocean in the air. He looked out across the dark airport grounds, half-expecting to see... what? Someone here to intercept him. Corrupt cops on Lucien Mebarak's take. A phalanx of Russian fighter jets. Something.

Lucien was rich and powerful. He had pull. He knew Troy had been deported. He could try to stop Troy, right here at the plane. But so far, he hadn't tried.

He thinks you're not good enough.

Maybe Mebarak hadn't tried anything here because he didn't want to break cover. He wanted plausible deniability. Maybe he didn't even have any reach in New York. But maybe it was none of those. Maybe the plan was far along, hard to uncover, and he really didn't think Troy could do anything to stop him.

He doesn't respect you.

Troy hoped that was true.

Rain swept the tarmac, blown by the wind. A black Town Car was parked out here, its engine idling, waiting for them. He and Dubois walked toward it, carrying nothing. They had no luggage.

As they approached, the driver door of the car opened, and Alex stepped out. He wore a dark sports jacket and a chauffeur cap. He had a sense of humor, anyway. But now Troy's little worlds were colliding. It didn't matter. It was time to stop pretending.

Alex opened the rear door and stood next to it. Troy walked up to him and gestured to Dubois to get in first. She ignored him.

"How did you get here ahead of me?" Troy said.

Alex shrugged. "I left yesterday afternoon. I didn't see any point in staying." His hands appeared. In each hand was a silver can of Rock Star. "Here. You'll probably need these."

Troy took one. It was cold. He was tired. He would definitely need one.

Dubois took one. "What is it?"

"Rock Star," Troy said. "You drink it. Bottoms up."

She cracked the pop top open and took a sip. Her eyebrows raised. She smiled, just a touch. "Hmm. It has citrus."

"It has more than that," Alex said.

She took a long gulp. "It isn't bad."

"We got big problems," Troy said, trying to change the subject back to slightly more important matters.

Alex nodded. "I know. I heard."

Troy looked at him sharply. Alex shrugged again. "It's our plane, Stark. You think we don't listen to what's said on our own plane?"

Dubois slid into the passenger cabin, all while looking up and studying Alex. There was a glimmer of recognition in her eyes. "Stark, who is this man?"

Troy answered truthfully. "I don't know. He's some guy. He likes it when you call him Alex. I doubt that's really his name, though."

"Have I seen you before?" Dubois said.

Alex ignored her question. "Stark, what do you need from me?"

"I need a helicopter," Troy said. "We need to get up in the air, free to move around the city fast, at a moment's notice, and not get stuck in traffic."

Alex nodded. "I can get you a helicopter. We can go straight there. There's a chopper pad about a mile from here, straight across that wasteland." He pointed out at the open, pitted tarmac they had just landed on.

"I need a pilot, too." Troy looked down at Dubois. "Can you fly a helicopter?"

She shook her head. "Just small planes."

"You have a pilot," Alex said. "I can fly a helicopter."

Troy shook his head. "Of course you can. Everybody around here has magical powers except me. Dubois, meet Agent Alex. He's a helicopter pilot and a master of disguises. Alex, meet Agent Dubois. She's an airplane pilot, a Kung Fu master, and speaks about a dozen languages. You two should hang out."

Dubois looked up at Alex. She shook her head. "I like girls," she said.

Alex nodded. "I know."

"What?"

Alex looked at Troy. "Can we get out of the rain, please?"

Troy looked at Dubois, still sitting right in the doorway. "Do you mind sliding over so I can get in? Or would you like me to go around?"

She scooted over, Troy slid in, and Alex went back to the driver's seat. In a moment, they were driving across the vast open land of the airport.

"You gotta keep an eye peeled when you're out here," Alex said over his shoulder. "You don't want a plane to come down and land on your head."

His dark eyes met Troy's in the rearview mirror.

"No," Troy said. "I suppose you don't."

He looked at Dubois. She was leaning back in the seat, her eyes closed. He got it. He understood. She was tired. He was tired. But this wasn't the cab ride to the hotel.

"Dubois, can you see if you can get Jan or Miquel back on the phone now that we're on the ground? I'd love to hear if they came up with anything else."

She opened her eyes. Without a word, she nodded.

Troy looked at Alex.

"What are the odds of us getting some help here?"

Alex raised an eyebrow in the rearview. Ahead of him, in the windshield, was more wide-open darkness, rain coming down, and distant lights, coming closer. The car bounced over pitted and humped asphalt.

"Help?"

Troy nodded. "Yeah. It's a big city. It'd be nice to have some help looking for these drones. I don't know. The cops. Homeland Security.

The fire department. The PTA. Doesn't really matter. Somebody could help us."

Alex shrugged. "It's not like everybody suddenly starts looking for the drones just because you're back in town. The city is practically locked down. Security is as tight as it's been in 20 years. There are cops posted everywhere. The National Guard is out in force. Everyone who gets on the subways and the commuter railroads gets searched. Bags on tables, everything taken out. Bomb-sniffing dogs, metal detectors, pat-downs. Random searches and seizures on the streets. Persons told me there's been about 300 no-knock warrants executed in the past four days. That's a pretty good pace for the NYPD."

Troy nodded. "Yeah, but we've got..."

"You have hearsay, Stark. You got a guy who told you something, probably to get your blood up because you hit him. You got a laptop that belongs to nobody, and there are a couple of computer strategy games on there."

"You know it's more than that," Troy said.

Alex nodded. "Of course I do. And so does Persons. That's why I'm out of bed at this ungodly hour, and that's why we're about to commandeer a helicopter. But you don't have anything, right now, that's going to interest the larger powers. They have thousands of cops and FBI agents breaking down doors. They have hundreds of analysts at the CIA, NSA, Department of Defense, Homeland Security, all sifting through millions of data points. You roll into town after a European vacation, claim you have THE THING everybody is looking for, you found it, it's here somewhere, only you need some help. And they're going to drop everything, right? You're the guy getting kicked out of the Navy SEALs for insubordination, remember?"

Dubois was next to him, murmuring into her mobile phone. But that got her attention. She turned and looked sharply at Troy.

His worlds were really colliding now.

"And, not to pile on here, but you just got deported from The Netherlands. You've got both Interpol and Europol entangled in a civil rights violation legal case. You managed to get an entire investigative unit suspended from their jobs."

"It's a small unit," Troy said. "It didn't take much. It's not like a hundred people got suspended."

Alex shrugged. "There's a lot going on here. That's all I'm saying. Resources are maxed out. And your reputation isn't exactly reaching its pinnacle right now. You probably would have been indicted for several murders, except I was over there, going around, cleaning up your..."

Troy raised a hand. STOP.

"I get it."

Alex nodded. "We're gonna look. I'll help you."

"We're close, man," Troy said. "We're real close."

Alex's eyes were there in the rearview again. "Okay."

"I have them," Dubois said. She held the phone out. "Do you want to speak to them?"

"Can you put it on speaker?" Troy said.

Dubois looked at Alex. She didn't put it on speaker.

"He's all right. He's just a little weird."

Dubois hit the button.

"Stark?" a male voice said. "Stark?"

"Jan?" Troy said.

"Yes. Agent Dubois said you are safely in New York."

"We are."

"Good," Jan said. "We've been crunching information here. I've resurrected photos that appear to show the drones being loaded onto a small freighter, the kind that might normally ply coastal waters. The photos are not well taken and may be a decoy in any event. The meta data for the photos suggest they were taken in early September. For now, I think a good place to start looking would be small freighters in the harbor."

That was interesting. Jan was a smart guy, and he was making a good, educated guess. Troy wondered if Jan had ever seen New York harbor. It was big. There were a lot of boats out there. And there were a lot of docks where you could hide a small freighter. Brooklyn, Staten Island, Lower Manhattan, New Jersey, along the Hudson River, out along the Long Island Sound.

"Did the freighter have a name, or any kind of numbers on it?"

"Uh... impossible to see, I'm afraid. I've brought the resolution to a point as good as it's going to get and cannot pick out anything like that. It is a rusty green freighter, let's say, less than half as long as a football pitch. It appears to be quite old."

"Why would they take an old freighter across the ocean?" Troy said. "I mean, they've got a sizeable investment riding on this."

"I wish I could answer," Jan's disembodied voice said. "I would guess that underneath the exterior, the engines and seaworthiness of the freighter are in excellent condition. Probably the aged hull is meant to render it invisible to investigators. I think few people would search for high tech drones on a decrepit freighter."

It was a good point. But it brought them no closer to finding the boat. Troy sat back and looked at Dubois. An image came to him. It was of Dubois doing a flying drop kick and taking out one of the gunmen upstairs at the charity event in Luxembourg. The guy was so focused on Aliz, he never saw that kick coming. It just about clotheslined him.

Troy almost laughed. He loved stuff like that.

"Let me ask you a question," he said. "Are there any freighters on the water registered to the foundation that held the gala in Luxembourg? The Willems Family Foundation, I think she called it. When trouble comes this guy's way, he likes to divert it towards his sister. Assuming he's the culprit, which personally, I do. Is that something we can find out about?"

There was a pause over the line. "Yes, I think so," Jan said. "Maybe. But I must hang up for a few moments." Jan's voice sounded like that idea hit the jackpot in his mind, and he was already working on it.

Troy shrugged. "Sounds good."

The line went dead. In the meantime, Alex had pulled the Town Car up to a high fence. At the top it was ringed with razor wire, the kind that came in loops, and was nearly impossible to climb over. They were stopped at a gate. A chain was looped in the gate, with a heavy lock.

The rain seemed to have stopped. Now there were just patches of fog blowing over their heads, and at ground level.

Alex got out of the car and went around back to the trunk.

Troy looked at Dubois. "What is this guy doing?"

"He's your friend," Dubois said.

"I met him on Sunday," Troy said.

Alex crossed to the front of the car with a large pair of bolt cutters. They seemed nearly as big as he was. He put the slicers on the chain, and cut it, just like that. He pulled the chain and it fell away to the ground. Then he pushed the gate on its rollers, retracting it so the car could come through.

He climbed back into the car and tossed the bolt cutters on the floor on the front passenger side.

"What are you doing?" Troy said.

Alex put the car in gear and drove slowly through the open gate. "I'm getting you a helicopter. This is an NYPD helipad. There are a bunch of choppers out here that don't see day to day use. I'm sure they're in working order, though."

"Oh yeah," Troy said. "They're sticklers for maintenance at the NYPD. And I can see that security is tight as a drum."

204

"Yeah," Alex said. "And Persons told me to take whatever I need."

"I bet these things work great," Troy said.

"He didn't mention helicopters specifically," Alex said. "He just said whatever I need, take it. I'm going to treat that as open-ended."

"If you need a Patriot missile battery…," Troy said.

Alex nodded. "Yeah. Take one."

"Why don't we requisition a helicopter from the police department?" Dubois said. "Wouldn't that be easier?"

"You mean easier than just stealing one?" Troy said.

Now Alex was looking at Dubois in the rearview. He seemed surprised by what he saw there. "No, it wouldn't. Not if we want a helicopter before next Wednesday. We do want one now, right? You guys want a helicopter, now, this morning, today?"

Dubois nodded. "Yes. I think so."

In the gloom, several small helicopters appeared, their rotors hanging down the slightest amount, like the drooping ears of depressed dogs.

"Well," Alex said. He put the car in park. "These are helicopters. So let's go."

CHAPTER TWENTY EIGHT

12:25 pm Central European Daylight Time (6:25 am Eastern Daylight Time)
Interpol Liaison Office - Special Investigations Unit
Europol Headquarters
The Hague, The Netherlands

"Miquel, you need to leave. You're only making this worse on yourself."

Hans Jute was here, in Miquel's office, sitting right on the other side of the desk. The Deputy Director of Europol had made an appearance at the Special Investigations Unit, a very unusual place for him to turn up.

Jute was here, not to play the gracious host, but to play the angry landlord, kicking out an undesirable tenant. The reflection of the light off Jute's glasses made it seem as if the man didn't have eyes.

"Hans, we have intelligence to suggest that the next drone attack is today, in New York City. We are working to…"

Jute shook his head. "Miquel, you don't have anything. You lied to your superiors and your police partners about the activities of Mariem Dubois and Troy Stark. You appear to have condoned an extralegal home invasion of a prominent citizen. You are under indefinite suspension, with possible termination in your future. Your unit is disbanded, and no longer has an office here at Europol. A case can be made that you are trespassing inside this building. I haven't made that case yet because I do like you, and I do care about you. But if you remain here much longer, I am going to have you escorted off the premises, with all the public embarrassment that will entail, and with a note to your file that such a thing was necessary."

Jute raised his hands as if to say, "There's nothing more I can do."

Miquel thought about it.

"If I leave, can Jan continue the work he is doing?"

Jute shook his head. "Agent Bakker has been reassigned. He is on loan to Europol. He is to surrender any Interpol materials and equipment he has, and report to my office upstairs. We are looking

206

forward to working with him and want to get him up and running as soon as possible. He'll be assigned new equipment this afternoon."

That was perfect. It was just like Hans Jute not only to kick Miquel out onto the street, but also to poach his data analyst and technology expert.

"You don't understand," Miquel said. "The intelligence we have…"

"Agent Bakker can submit any intelligence he has to his superiors at Interpol. I am sure they will provide it the attention it deserves."

Jute stood briskly.

"I'll give you 15 minutes to pack up what you need from here. In the meantime, I'm going to take Agent Bakker with me."

"He can't be interrupted."

"He can and will be interrupted. As I indicated, he has been reassigned. To me."

Miquel was about to do a strange thing. It was nothing he had ever considered before. But there was no way Jute was simply going to shut down this office or put a stop to what they were doing here. They were very close to disaster now, another one, worse than before. But Dubois and Stark might be close to stopping it. And they needed Jan to help them.

Miquel was beside the point, except as a way to make their work possible. And as such, he could destroy himself, if it meant they could continue on.

"Can I show you something Hans?"

Jute's shoulders dropped. He likely thought Miquel, reaching the end of his career, was going to pull out something sentimental, even maudlin. An award for bravery he had received as a young man, or maybe his first badge. A picture of his children as toddlers. Something that a rational man would be mortified to show in this situation.

"Of course." Jute's tone suggested he was exasperated but demonstrating the infinite patience of a superior officer.

Miquel opened the drawer of his desk. Inside was a silver Walther PPK pistol with black grips. Yes, the same gun James Bond carried in the early films. It was a beautiful gun, all steel, heavier than most guns its size. And it was loaded.

He pointed it at Jute.

"Get out of my office."

To his credit, Jute showed no fear. He just shook his head in disapproval. "Now you've done it. Do you know that? You were finished a minute ago, but they probably would have let you retire. Now you've pulled a gun on a fellow law enforcement officer. Inside a police building. You're going to be arrested. This will be the most humiliating end to a mediocre career that I can think of."

Jute gestured at the gun. "Why do you even have that in here?"

Miquel stood and came around the desk. "I have it so I can walk you out of here, and so you cannot disturb the important work my people are doing. Now turn around, hands in the air."

Jute hesitated.

"Hans, I swear to Jesus, I will shoot you where you stand."

Something got Jute moving. Maybe it was something in Miquel's eyes, desperation or cold-blooded calculation. Miquel wasn't sure what his eyes were showing. He just knew that he would shoot Jute if he had to.

Jute turned around and headed for the door.

"Do not stop. Do not talk to Agent Bakker."

Miquel walked Jute through the outer office, and then out into the hallway. Jan didn't even turn around as they passed. Miquel stood on the catwalk with Jute for a long moment, the gun held low now, hard for passersby to see.

"It's over," Jute said. His balding head gleamed in the overhead lights. "Your career, your freedom, your very life, I guess. Expect to be arrested in the next ten minutes. That will give you enough time to take that gun and do the honorable thing, if you can find the courage."

Miquel shook his head. "I won't kill myself. You know that. But I also won't let you obstruct this work. I promise you're going to have a lot to answer for."

Jute smirked. He began to say something, but Miquel was already going back into the office. Inside, he went immediately to a cabinet and came out with a pair of handcuffs, the real kind, steel manacles. He clipped one to each of the two handles of the doors. Cuffed together, they would not open all the way. It was better than the digital lock, which Jute could easily have someone override. But it wouldn't last forever.

He looked at Jan.

"Jan, I think we're going to lose access to our computers. We will probably lose network access. We might even lose power."

Jan didn't take his eyes off the screens, or his hands off the keyboard. He nodded. "I know. I anticipated that a little while ago. I've moved to auxiliary power. I've created a strong networking hotspot here, with redundant internet and satellite access. And I'm using my own computer, which I cannot be locked out of."

Miquel nodded. He went over to the large filing cabinet, got to its side, placed the gun on top, and began pushing the cabinet toward the door. This was going to be primitive. He was just going to blockade the doors with heaviest office furniture he could find. If Jute wanted to break in here and arrest him, he would have to smash through thick glass, and shove cabinets and a conference table out of the way.

He would probably do it anyway, but it was going to take a while.

"What's the update?" Miquel said.

Jan stared at his screens. "We're looking for a ship."

CHAPTER TWENTY NINE

7:30 am Eastern Daylight Time (1:30 pm Central European Daylight Time)
The skies over New York Harbor
New York City

"We're lying a lot," Alex said. "It's going to catch up with us."

They were in the tiny police helicopter, high over the lower harbor, south of the Verrazano Narrows Bridge. It was like being inside a plastic soap bubble, in the bright sky. The rain had cleared. Behind them, to the south and east, was the vast ocean, and the morning sun. In front, to the north and west, were the towers of Manhattan, and behind them, the smaller towers of Jersey City. Somewhere up there, invisible now, was the Statue of Liberty.

Directly below them were dozens of ships, a mad scatter, like dark grains of rice that had fallen from a bag. Alex was keeping to the most distant part of the harbor because air traffic control had them on radar now and was wondering who they were. Each time they asked, he told them something subtly different.

"We are a police helicopter, engaged in water traffic surveillance."

"I see that you're a police helicopter. Identify yourself."

"Classified information, control. We... uh... it's a need-to-know situation."

"Right. And I need to know."

It went on and on like that. Eventually, Alex just turned off the radio.

It was taking Jan Bakker a lot longer to find a ship registered to the Willems Foundation than one might imagine. The answer had come quickly enough - yes, there was such a ship, and it was in New York Harbor. But where? Jan was trying to get a satellite positioning read on it, so far to no avail.

Also, cell phone calls were junk up here. They had dropped calls from Jan and Miquel repeatedly. Now it was getting late. The day was here, and the morning commute had started. For no good reason he could think of, Troy was peering out at the world with a pair of binoculars. It wasn't as if he was going to spot a sign scribbled on the deck of one of those ships below him: HERE ARE THE DRONES.

What he did see was the morning traffic picking up. There were cars everywhere, and all the thoroughfares and highways were slowing down, congealing.

"The traffic is worse than ever," Alex said, as if reading Troy's mind. "No one wants to get on the subways or commuter trains, in case they explode."

The phone rang again. Dubois's cell phone ring tone was a driving techno-pop beat, something you'd hear in a packed dance club or at an all-night rave, and completely out of character for her. Or was it?

Troy didn't know her at all. There were moments when he thought he did, but he was wrong. He supposed he could admit that to himself.

She answered the phone, mumbled something in another language.

"He's got it," she said. She said listened for a long moment as Jan made caveats in her ear. "He thinks he might have it," she corrected herself.

She paused to listen again.

"It's called *Fortunate Daughter*."

Troy smiled. "Boy, he loves his sister, doesn't he? Never misses a chance to take a crack at her."

"It's in the upper reaches of the harbor, just below the tip of Manhattan, moving very slowly north, at three or four knots. Barely moving at all. It's on a heading to enter the mouth of the East River. It is indeed green in color, though very rusty along the outside. He has coordinates for it."

Alex raised a hand. "Not necessary. The description should put us right on top of it. We'll be up there in a few minutes."

The chopper moved up the harbor now at a good clip. They passed the Verrazano Bridge. Up ahead, Troy could see the Statue of Liberty now, also green, looking very small against the towers of Manhattan.

"What do you see?" Alex said.

Troy was scanning the water with the binoculars. The chopper was dropping altitude. Two Staten Island ferries were passing each other, going in different directions. Lots of boats were out here - small freighters, a Coast Guard cutter, pleasure boats, a large sightseeing boat, yachts, a few sailboats. The harbor was crazy with boat traffic.

"Too much. I see too much."

"What are those coordinates?" Alex said over his shoulder.

"The call dropped," Dubois said. "I'll try to get them back."

"Okay," Alex said. "Never mind." He pointed to his right, and down. "What's that. It's green, isn't it?"

Troy followed Alex's hand. In the circle of the binocular sights, a ship appeared. It was green, a rusting hulk. For a split second, Troy's heart seemed to skip a beat. Well, well, well. The ship was really here. They had gone on what seemed from the beginning like a wild goose chase. And yet, here was the ship, right below them. Now if the drones were on board...

"Stark?"

"That's the one," Troy said.

"Sure?"

"Looks like it. Old, small, slow-moving freighter. Rusty. Green. Headed toward the East River. But there's only one way to be sure. We need to get down there."

Alex shook his head. "Ah, negative Stark. That thing doesn't have a helipad. It's in motion, and it's way too small to freelance a landing on the deck. If there are guys with guns on there, we'd get chewed up in seconds anyway."

Troy didn't like the sound of what he was hearing. Not even a little bit. "So, what are you suggesting?"

Alex shrugged. "I don't know. It might be time to call the cops. Or maybe we just monitor its progress?"

Troy looked at Alex. "Fast rope. There's two in the back. They must use this chopper as a training vehicle. We can't let the NYPD come in and surround this thing with police boats. If the bad guys see that coming, they'll just launch the drones. Why wouldn't they? And if we monitor, what are we supposed to do, monitor until the drones take off? We need to go in there, Alex. At the very least, I do."

Troy turned and looked back at Dubois. "You ever fast roped out of a helicopter before?"

Dubois nodded. "When I was young, and first joined Interpol. We did cross-training with an elite French military unit."

"When were you young?" Troy said.

She shook her head. "I was young until yesterday. But this was several years ago."

Troy looked at Alex. "She's good. I'll go first. If I make it, she comes after me. I'll cover her descent." He paused. He might have forgotten one thing. "You have a gun on you?"

Alex sighed. He reached inside his jacket and came out with a Glock 19, matte black, nine-millimeter semiautomatic. This is where Troy had come in - Missing Persons had handed him a nearly identical

212

gun on the first day. Troy took it in his hand, checked the chamber, slid out the magazine, then popped it back in.

Alex shook his head. "She's going to fall, and her head is going to splatter open like a watermelon."

Troy looked back at Dubois. She was smiling now. She looked like a little kid on a field trip to the firehouse. They were going to let her slide down the pole.

"No, she's not."

The chopper was behind the freighter now and dropping down. Troy put the binoculars on it again. No one was on the deck. No one was visible at all. At this height, he could see some sort of clear tarp or awning, covering what looked like a deep well, an open-air freight hold.

"I don't see anybody down there," he said. "Might just be a skeleton crew, running an automated boat. Could be we catch them napping."

"Or not," Alex said.

"Thanks for the gun," Troy said. He slipped out of the seat and squeezed into the back with Dubois. She was already separating the ropes. They were thick, heavy things, both tied and knotted to rungs at the very back of the chopper.

There were several pairs of thick leather gloves back here. She handed a large pair to Troy. He wrestled them on. They were tight, but he got them there. She slid on a pair that were a touch too large for her.

Alex's hand reached back, holding a small hand-held radio transceiver. "Don't forget to call me. That is, if you need me to pick you up."

Troy took the radio. "You're a peach."

Alex nodded. "I know."

They were getting low, very low, now. Troy watched that deck. Still no one had come out to play.

"It's time," Alex said. "Don't leave me hanging here."

Troy looked at Dubois. "Ready?"

She nodded. "Ready."

"Wait until I hit. Wait until I've cleared the deck. Then go, as fast as you remember. Straight drop. But if I don't make it, don't go. It's that simple. You reading this, Alex?"

"Buddy, if you get shot down there, I'm at a thousand feet before you draw your last breath. Let these cavemen try to shoot arrows at the sun."

Troy slid open his door. Dubois did the same on her side. He tossed his rope out, watching that deck. Still nobody there. He was calm. He was more than calm. He felt nothing at all, just a small amount of excitement in his belly. It was that place he went to. He might die in the next several seconds. He might not. He saw Dubois's rope snake down next to his. He had his rope in his left hand, turned, and...

"Cowabunga," he said.

He pushed out with his legs, cleared the chopper, and dropped like a rock. It went as fast as he remembered. Do not cling to the rope. Simply ride it down, all the way to the bottom. A few seconds, and his feet hit the deck, a little harder than he intended. The impact went up his legs and spine. He felt that. He was out of practice.

He turned, gun already in hand, looking for a target.

Nothing. No one was waiting. He looked up at the pilot house. No commotion coming from there. He ran and took cover behind a thick steel stanchion. He crouched. His head was on a swivel, scanning the environment, 360 degrees. Where was everybody?

He watched as Dubois came down. She didn't ride the rope like she should. She climbed down, arm over arm, her legs entwined in the rope. It gave him the willies just watching her.

But then she was down and running toward him. She threw herself to the deck and slid up against a shaded metal wall.

Troy was still scanning. "Out of sight, Dubois. That was out of sight."

Above their heads, the rotors thumped as the chopper took off into the sky, trailing the ropes behind.

"What do you think?" Dubois said.

"The deep hold," Troy said. "There's some kind of cover over it."

She nodded. "Okay."

"Head on a swivel," Troy said. "We'll make this quick. Ready?"

"Ready," she said.

Troy got up and ran for the stairs, watching everywhere at once. He could hear her two steps above him. The stairs were a naked iron spiral, vertical, like dropping down a well. He pounded down, making a right turn every ten stairs.

He reached the bottom and stopped. An instant later, she was there, touching his back. There was a doorway here, which afforded them some cover. He took a pause before making another move.

He looked out into the freight hold. It was dim, shielded from the light of day by the mesh covering at the top. No one appeared to be around.

The drones were here, though. There were five of them, just as promised. Each one was sitting on its own platform. They were all black, fat and bulbous, about six feet long, with multiple rotors and landing gear mounted. They looked like giant, silent insects. None of them were doing anything.

No. They were doing something. They were waiting.

"Oh man," Troy said.

"Incredible," came Dubois's voice from behind him.

* * *

"There's nobody here."

Troy was talking into the radio, communicating with Alex, who was somewhere up there in the sky above their heads. Next to Troy, Dubois was murmuring into her phone, probably telling the same thing to Jan Bakker and Miquel Castro.

"Nobody at all?"

Troy shook his head. He didn't know that for a fact, but it was beginning to look that way. There could be someone hiding in a deep hold, someone asleep in a bunk somewhere, someone locked in a bathroom. He didn't know.

"We've been up to the pilot house," he said. "We are down in the main hold right now. No one has asked us what we're doing. No one has come out to play. No one seems to be guarding these drones at all."

Indeed, he was looking at the drones right now. Each one was showing a prominent red LED light, which was on. Next to the red light was a green light, which was off. Red light, green light.

Next to both of them was a black switch. To Troy, it seemed like the easiest thing in the world to simply flip that switch, but it wasn't clear what would happen then.

Above their heads, two stories up, was the mesh tarp or covering. It was sheer, nearly see-through, letting some visual of the sky in, and some bit of the daylight, but otherwise protecting this area of the ship from the elements. The covering rested on a steel platform, which looked like it could retract into the wall. Troy had touched the material of the covering when he was up top. It was strong, but had a springiness to it, almost like a trampoline.

"I think they must have ditched."

It made some sense, he supposed. If the cops came, that meant they probably knew what was on board. Who would want to be around for that?

"Who's driving the boat?" Alex said. His voice crackled with static. "I mean, someone had to steer it toward the river. It's on a heading that someone had to pick."

"I don't know," Troy said. "The pilot house is super high-tech. Not sure I've seen anything like it before. Either the boat is driving itself, which I think is possible in this case, or someone is driving it remotely."

Dubois was gesturing with her telephone.

"Alex, I gotta run. I'll call you back in a bit."

He clicked off. Dubois held her phone up. The speaker phone feature was on.

"The connection is better here," she said.

"Stark?" a male voice said.

"Yeah. Jan. Hit me."

"I am in touch with the drones, and I am in touch with the onboard computer that serves as the brain for the ship. It's located in the pilot house, where humans would normally be. Both the drones, which are not very bright after all, and the boat, which is very intelligent, are resisting my attempts to access them. They are all in touch with another computer, a master navigation controller, which is not on the ship, but appears to be steering it."

Troy met Dubois's eyes. She nodded. She must have already heard this.

"Where is it?"

"It appears to be in Manhattan, moving south along the Bowery, possibly in a car. If it continues in this direction, it will approach Canal Street soon. If you map this from the sky, what I see is the navigation controller coming south, possibly to the banks of the East River, or maybe taking the Manhattan Bridge or Brooklyn Bridge. The boat you're in is heading slowly north and east, up through the southern reaches of the East River. In other words, it looks like a rendezvous or near-rendezvous is going to take place."

"What if we try to turn off the drones?" Troy said.

"I don't know," Bakker said. "My concern is that any attempt to interfere with them will cause them to either launch, or self-destruct."

"What if we tried to hack them apart, break them in some way?" Troy could picture doing that easily enough. There were plenty of heavy items on a ship like this. Dubois and he could take turns dropping anvils from the deck down into this hold, crushing these things like bugs.

216

"Same," Bakker said. "I imagine they would launch a group self-destruct sequence."

"Big explosion?" Troy said absently. He ran a hand along the length of one of the drones, but then Dubois slapped his hand.

"At least five times bigger than the one that hit Bruges. Possibly much bigger, as I believe that attack was actually practice, and wasn't intended to hurt anyone. I'm guessing the slaughterbots inside these drones are more numerous and weighted with a more devastating payload."

"So what do we do? Turn them over to the bomb squad?"

Bakker sighed. Troy felt like sighing. They had the drones now. This thing should be over. But the boat was driving itself, the drones were resisting Jan's advances, and somewhere nearby, someone who could launch these things was on his way.

"No. I'm afraid not. We need the master navigator. I believe it will know the launch sequence or command and may teach me how to disarm the drones. But I need that computer, I need it in our hands, and under our control."

He paused. There was silence over the phone. Troy and Dubois stood in this shadowy, ghost ship hold, with these black tarantulas on platforms around them, all of them quietly waiting for the order to attack.

"So we need to get that computer," Troy said. "And take it away from whoever has it, before he gets the chance to launch these drones."

"I think so, yes."

"Then what?"

"Then we see," Bakker said. "I may be able to understand how to disarm the drones simply by what is on the readout of the navigation computer. You may be able to grant me access to that computer. I may be able to relay the directions to a person standing by near the drones."

"Those are a lot of maybes," Troy said.

"It will help to have the navigation computer in our hands."

"But you also need someone here with the drones."

Troy could almost see Jan Bakker nodding. "Yes."

"What if they self-destruct?" Troy said. "What if the guy orders them to self-destruct?"

"Right," Bakker said. "It will be helpful to subdue and incapacitate whoever has the navigation commander in their possession."

Subdue and incapacitate. That was a formal way of saying it. Beat to a pulp, and potentially kill. That sounded like Troy Stark's department.

"What if we sink this ship?" Troy said. "Just punch a hole in the hull somehow, and put it at the bottom of the river?"

"Same problem as before. During the delay between punching a hole, as you describe it, and when the ship actually goes down, the drones could launch or self-destruct. My hunch is that all the drones self-destructing at once will be a significant problem. All of them managing to launch will likely cause a catastrophe."

Troy nodded. "All right. Dubois and I need to talk about this for a minute. We're going to hang up."

"Please hurry," Bakker said. "The rendezvous we discussed is less than ten minutes away, by my reckoning."

Nice. Dubois clicked off the phone without another word. They looked each other in the eye.

"You good?" Troy said.

"I'm fine."

"You're okay hanging out here with these things for a few minutes? I gotta go see a man about a computer."

Dubois nodded. "I know. It's cool. It's the right way to do it."

Troy nodded in turn. He reached inside his jacket and brought out Alex's gun. He held it out to her. She took the big gun in her tiny hand.

Troy pointed a finger at his own temple as though it was a gun. "Any bad guys come, don't stand on ceremony. Just put one in their head."

She nodded. "You're going to need this to talk to Jan."

She handed him the cell phone. She was going to be completely incommunicado. It was what it was. He gave her a hug. It was awkward as hell, not least because he was a foot taller than her. They broke it off quickly.

"Okay Tiny Dancer," he said. "Be careful. I gotta go."

She nodded. "Good luck."

Within seconds, he was racing up the iron stairwell towards the deck. He was back on the radio as he ran. "Alex, I need a pickup. And we need to hurry."

"Both of you?"

"Just me. Dubois has to stay with the drones. You and I need to intercept a guy. Probably a guy."

"I'm coming down. Right above you as we speak."

Troy reached the deck, and there was the chopper, the thick ropes dangling down. He slipped the radio in his pocket with the cell phone and grabbed one of the ropes. As soon as he did, the chopper jerked back toward the sky again.

218

Troy inch-wormed up the rope as the chopper gained altitude and zoomed north toward the bridges of Lower Manhattan. In a moment, he climbed through the open door into the cabin.

"Thanks for waiting until I got in," he said.

Alex shrugged. "I thought you said we're in a hurry."

Troy nodded. He began to yank the ropes back up.

"We are, buddy. We are."

CHAPTER THIRTY

**2:05 pm Central European Daylight Time (8:05 am Eastern
Daylight Time)
Interpol Liaison Office - Special Investigations Unit
Europol Headquarters
The Hague, The Netherlands**

They had cut power to the office.

The lights were out. So was the air conditioning. Without airflow, it was amazing how quickly it became hot in here. Miquel had sweat through his shirt.

He sat on the floor, leaning against one of the cabinets. He had piled all the cabinets, one on top of the other, in front of the doors and the glass wall. Jan had taken a minute and helped him place the heavy conference table across the top. The view from the corridor into this office was now completely blocked.

The story went that he had taken Jan hostage and was holding him at gunpoint. It made Miquel seem as if he had gone insane, but that was what he wanted them to believe. If they knew the truth, which was that he wouldn't shoot Jan Bakker for any reason, then they would simply crash through the glass and storm the office.

He had called up to Jute's office and raved like a lunatic. A man whose career was ending ignominiously was also suffering a breakdown. He might kill someone. He might kill his own staff member.

Across from him, Jan plunged on, using satellites to follow the device that controlled the drones. It was clear now that they had found the drones. It was clear that Stark, and by extension Miquel, had been right all along, that the right move was to push everything to the limit.

But no one was going to believe that, not yet.

So Miquel was reduced to this. The building was being cleared. There were two snipers on the catwalk opposite from this office, across the open space. They must have high caliber rifles to shoot through this glass. Or maybe they were just for show. But Miquel was taking no chances. He was staying down.

He was guilty of multiple major crimes, he supposed. And as soon as his opponents finished clearing the building of personnel, very soon, they would have a host of options available to them. For example, they could turn the air conditioning back on and send a sedative gas through the vents. Once he and Jan passed out, Jute's men would be free to don gas masks, break down the wall and doors, and walk right in here.

If they were more vindictive, they could put tear gas in the system instead. Miquel wouldn't put it past them. There was no reason for them to take it easy on Jan. They must know he was in on this.

Miquel sighed. He watched Jan from behind. Jan had gone to that highly concentrated place he went to sometimes, where the surrounding world seemed to drop away from him.

"How is it going?" Miquel said.

Jan nodded. "I have it in my sights."

"And?"

"It is moving onto the bridge."

CHAPTER THIRTY ONE

8:15 am Eastern Daylight Time (2:15 pm Central European Daylight Time)
The skies over the East River
New York City

"It is moving onto the bridge."

The chopper was skimming about ten stories above the Brooklyn Bridge, the pointed arches of its gray stone towers an astonishing sight against the backdrop of the city. The bridge was almost like a church, Troy decided, with spires pointed up toward heaven.

They were moving west from the Brooklyn side to the Manhattan side. Car traffic was a snarl, slowed to a crawl on the Manhattan-bound side. Not even a crawl. It was like sludge. Traffic was a little better on the Brooklyn-bound side. At least it was moving. On the far side, upriver a touch, the southbound FDR was at a standstill. How did people live like this?

"The device must need to be in some physical proximity to launch the drones," Jan said. "So he is driving it closer."

To their south, the freighter was moving upriver. It would be here in a few minutes. Air traffic control was trying to radio them again. The chopper had been reported stolen from a police helipad storage area out at JFK airport. Whoever was on the radio was becoming increasingly aggravated. He insisted they take the chopper to the stadium on Randall's Island and land it on the soccer field there immediately. Armed police units were already waiting.

Now Jan Bakker was telling them the car with the navigation computer had entered the bridge roadway. Things were coming together nicely.

"What does it look like?" Troy said. He was scanning the roadway with the binoculars, trying to spot anything out of the ordinary.

"The car?"

Troy shook his head. What did Jan think he was asking about, the helicopter? The bridge? Troy knew what those looked like.

"Yes."

"On my screen, it looks like a red dot."

Terrific.

"Wait. I will try to superimpose a satellite feed onto my map."

People got excited when events were in motion. Troy knew that. They didn't do things they should have done several minutes ago. They didn't even think of them. Even a genius like Jan Bakker could fall into the trap.

Troy waited several seconds. Then it didn't matter anymore.

Down on the bridge, a car had stopped in the right-hand lane, near the edge of the bridge. It was a dark blue car, a late model sedan, completely nondescript. It could be anything, any make, any model. All cars looked the same nowadays.

Troy looked downriver. The car was stopped right where the boat would pass under the bridge. Instantly, the stopped car caused a backup, as traffic tried to flow around it in the left lane.

"Never mind," Troy said into the phone. "We have it."

Bakker was saying something, but Troy didn't hear him anymore. He slipped the phone into his jumpsuit breast pocket in the middle of Bakker's sentence, then clipped the pocket shut.

He nudged Alex. "We gotta get down there."

Alex looked at him. "Get down where?"

Troy pointed. "On the bridge. He's right there. It's the guy. It has to be him. The boat's coming."

"It's the Brooklyn Bridge, Stark. We can't go down there."

"That guy's about to do something," Troy said. "Just put the chopper down on the roadway ahead of that car. I'll work my way back."

"Stark, are you crazy? We won't fit. It's a suspension bridge. It's got these… what? Suspenders hanging everywhere. They're made out of metal. If one of these rotors hits on of those things…"

"Put the chopper down!" Troy shouted. "What the hell are we doing up here if we can't land on the bridge? You didn't tell me we can't land on the bridge. If I'd known that, I would have walked."

He pointed at the car again. A man had exited the car. He had what looked like a small laptop open on the hood of his car. He pressed some buttons on the laptop. There was a bunch of gear at his feet. He seemed to have a couple of packs with him. He glanced downriver at the arriving boat. It looked like he was planning to just leave the car behind.

Why would he do that? It was the middle of rush hour. Traffic was backing up all the way to Manhattan behind him.

"Down there! Right there! That guy!"

"I might be able to fast rope you to the pedestrian walkway. Even that…," he shook his head. "I don't know, man. It's tight in there."

Suddenly the mysterious Alex, he who disposed of corpses, and gave people knockout shots of God-knew-what, and stole helicopters, was punking out. Out of nowhere, there was something he could not, or would not do. It wasn't going to stand.

"There's no time for that, Alex. Put the chopper down or I'm going to do it. You won't like it if I do it."

"Stark…"

"Alex…"

Alex sighed. "All right. You asked for it."

"Yes I did. Today, please."

The chopper dropped altitude. It passed below the top of one of the suspension towers, moving along the thick sloping metal supports. The rotors whipped around, very close to the supports. Below them, the pedestrian walkway was coming, the roadways below and on either side of it. Alex winced, his breath suddenly coming in gasps.

"I'm not a professional helicopter pilot," he said. "I know how to fly a helicopter, but this is…"

"Land it!"

Below them, traffic was flowing around the stopped car. Troy could hear the horns of irate drivers. Now the chopper was coming down.

Several cars sped under the helicopter, trying to beat it. Typical New York drivers. Then two cars crashed into each other. The cars following crashed into them. Now traffic was piling up. The bridge was becoming blocked. The roadway in front of the accident was open.

"Right there," Troy said. "Perfect."

"We won't fit," Alex said. "There's no way we're going to…"

A rotor hit one of the supports and sheared off. The sound of shredding metal was almost impossible to understand. The chopper spun around and crashed sideways into the support, right outside Troy's window.

Troy squirmed to his left, practically into Alex's lap. The right side of the cabin was crushed in. Glass sprayed inward on them. Another rotor hit and sheared off. From the corner of his eye, Troy saw it fly away toward the river.

"Mayday, mayday," Alex said. "This is mayday."

Troy looked down. They were ten feet above the roadway.

The chopper dropped out of the sky without warning. Troy's stomach flew up into his throat.

BOOM.

They hit the roadway HARD.

The impact went straight through their bodies like a wave. Troy's head snapped backward at the top of his spine. The front of the windshield exploded. Troy heard the landing gear crushed under the chopper, heavy metal crunch.

The rotors, all of the blades gone now, continued to spin.

Shooop, shooop, shooop, shooop, shooop…

"That hurt," Troy said.

He looked at Alex. Alex was staring out through the wrecked windshield. In front of them, the roadway to Brooklyn was wide open.

"You okay?" Troy said.

Alex's whole body turned slowly toward Troy. It didn't seem like he could turn his head using the neck. His face was sad. Very, very sad.

"No. I don't think so. I think I'm broken."

Troy raised his hands. "My fault. Okay? I own that. But something like this… Helicopter crash on the Brooklyn Bridge. It's big news."

He gestured down the road. "There's no traffic on this side. I'm sure ambulances will be here in a couple minutes. And you look fine. I think you're going to be all right. But I can't wait around. I gotta go."

"Good luck," Alex said. His voice was somber. He didn't sound like he meant it.

Troy nodded. "Thanks."

He unclipped from his belt and climbed through the shattered windshield onto the road. He stumbled away from the helicopter. From this vantage point, it looked like some weird modern sculpture, making a bold statement about the human tendency for destruction. Alex stared out at Troy, watching him leave.

Behind him somewhere, on the Brooklyn side of the bridge maybe, Troy could already hear the sirens approaching.

Ahead, there was a blonde-haired man near the railing. His hair was so blonde it almost looked fake. He was somewhat, but not very, tall. He had what was clearly a parachute strapped to his back. He was strapping a satchel or knapsack to his front. He clicked in the straps, then tightened them. When he was done, he looked almost like a paratrooper, saddled with gear.

Well behind him, his car was now on fire. He had set the car on fire. The man ignored the horns blaring and the shouts from people who'd just had their morning commute ruined. Red and orange flames raged, and black smoke jetted toward the sky. The gas tank was going to blow any minute. The man didn't seem to notice the car at all.

He looked up and saw Troy advancing toward him.

Suddenly, the guy had a gun in his hand. He conjured it like a magic trick. It was a small pistol. He waved it in Troy's direction.

"Don't even think about it."

Troy raised his empty hands but continued to walk toward the guy.

"Hear me out, buddy."

The guy shook his head. "There is nothing to hear. The codes are launched. It's already too late." The guy had a faint accent... from where?

To Troy's left, the freighter was almost here, far below them. It was quite a leap. No wonder the guy was going to do it with a parachute. He must be one of these low-altitude BASE jumpers.

"What's your name?" Troy said.

The guy almost grinned. "You can call me Sven."

"Well, Sven. Why did you set your car on fire?"

Sven shrugged. "It's part of the plan, of course. It traps people on the bridge. Then the bridge collapses with more people on it."

The target is the bridge. Mebarak said...

"The bridge?"

Sven nodded. "The bridge, the city. Multiple strikes at once increase the terror factor. An American commando man like you doesn't need me to explain about causing terror among civilians. You must know a great deal."

Sven gestured at the downed chopper with his chin. "Of course you do. Your helicopter did a better job blocking the road than my car."

The bow of the boat was passing the edge of the bridge. The man leapt up on the railing. He was going to do it. He was going to jump.

"I'm leaving now," he said. "Goodbye."

Troy ran at him. He couldn't get his body to work. Everything had stiffened. It was a shuffling, shambling wreck of a run. He reached the guy just before he leapt and grabbed him around the knees.

The guy pitched forward. Troy reached with one hand and gripped the waistband of the man's pants.

Sven. Sven spun in the air. He still had his gun out.

He pointed and...

BANG!

BANG!

BANG!

Three shots, fired straight into the sky.

Troy let go of his knees and gripped the satchel across his chest. Sven was upside down, trying to kick away. Troy unclipped a strap. One of Sven's legs was tangled over the top of the railing.

Troy gave up on the waistband and gripped the satchel with both hands.

Sven fell away, the satchel ripping free from his chest.

Far beneath them, the deck of the freighter was passing. Sven fell backwards towards it, his gun flying away now.

He reached behind him as he fell. He must have found the parachute because it flew out and around him. It wrapped around his body. It didn't slow him at all.

BOOM.

Sven's body hit the deck of the freighter with the force of a bomb. Troy caught an image of a tomato hitting a concrete wall, but then the carnage was mercifully covered by the parachute.

"Oh, man."

Troy was hugging the satchel.

The boat was flowing by. The deep freight hold was about to pass. Troy had to get down there. He had the laptop - it must be the laptop, right? The navigator. Maybe it could stop the drones. He didn't know.

He glanced back at the wrecked helicopter. It was surrounded by police cars. More were coming. Two ambulances were there. They were bringing Alex out. He was on his feet. His hands were in the air. The cops had their guns out.

He had to go. There was no time for talking to the cops. He climbed up onto the railing, not the leap that Sven had made. Troy was too sore for that. And he was about to be a lot more sore.

He looked out at the city. Brooklyn to his far left, Manhattan to his right, the wide expanse of the East River everywhere else. It was dizzying. Below him, the hold of the freighter was coming. He remembered touching the mesh covering above the hold. It was like a trampoline he had thought at the time.

He shook his head and sighed. This job was the pits.

"Hey!" someone shouted behind him. "Hey!"

Troy didn't even look. He leapt out into nothing.

He turned in mid-air, so he would land on his back. Was that good or bad? He didn't know. At least he wouldn't have to see it. The bridge fell away above him. Two heads appeared at the railing, cops who would have tried to save him from himself.

He fell and fell.

How far was it?

Too long. Could he have missed the boat entirely?

Then he hit. The mesh covering was springy, just as he remembered. He sank into it, his fall slowing, slowing... He had a bad thought. It was going to launch him back into the air again.

No. Please no.

He slowed... reached the end of the tarp's give...

And it shredded. He heard it go, like the world's largest pair of slacks splitting. He hugged the satchel with his right arm and reached madly with his left, grabbing for some piece of the tarp to hold on to. He got it, and dug his fingers in.

The thing ripped again. His body fell through the torn fabric, and he swung with one arm on a long, thick strand of it. It was heavy. He swung, the world spinning around him. Then he crashed and slid. He stuck his head up at the end of his neck, like a turtle sticking it out of the shell. It was an old trick for falling - keep your head up so it doesn't bang against the surface.

He came to a stop, flat on his back, wrapped in weird, metallic, fabric-y mesh, his right arm crushing the satchel to his chest. He stared up at the hole he had just made in the sky. He was passing under the bridge now. The underneath world - the pipes and nets and catwalks and steel girders - were all far above him.

Dubois's face appeared, much closer, looking down at him. Her eyes were wide. Her mouth hung open. She seemed concerned.

"Are you alive?"

He tried to shake his head. Not much movement there.

"No. I don't think so."

Dubois nodded. "That was probably the stupidest thing I've ever seen. I mean, I thought running through a narrow tunnel while getting machine-gunned was stupid. I thought riding a motorcycle into oncoming traffic was stupid. I thought stealing a helicopter was stupid. Each time, it's like you break your own world record."

She paused. "For stupidity," she said, as if that needed clarification.

Troy sort of gestured with his right arm. It was little more than a hand flap. "The navigator. Command module. Whatever he called it. I think this is it."

"Oh my God," she said. "I need that. The drones came on a couple of minutes ago."

She yanked the satchel away, and then was gone.

Troy reached to the breast pocket of his jumpsuit. He couldn't seem to work the button, so he just tore it open. He pulled the mobile phone out and held it up above him.

Suddenly Dubois was back. She took the phone out of his hand.

"Thank you." And was gone again.

Troy just nodded.

* * *

"Take the navigator up to the deck," Jan said. "I need a better satellite connection, and we don't want to lose this phone call."

"The drones are on," Dubois said. She started running toward the metal stairway to the upper level. "Their rotors are spinning. They are all making a whining sound."

"Yes. I understand. They've been activated. We have to try to deactivate them."

"They could take off any second."

"Yes. Please go to the top level."

How many times was he going to repeat himself?

"I'm doing it, Jan." She reached the stairs and took them two at a time, the satchel pressed against her chest, the phone to her ear.

"Mari?"

"Yes?" She sounded breathless to her own ears. The stairs spiraled upwards. She was halfway to the top. It had been a surreal time, the moments she had spent on this boat by herself. She had moved from room to room, gun out in front of her, half-expecting to run into the ghosts of pirates, dead men walking.

No one. Pigeons that scattered as she startled them.

Then a man had fallen from the bridge and hit the deck like a bomb. Then, seconds later, Stark had done the same, only he didn't explode like the first man.

"Mari! Please hurry."

She crested the stairs and looked around. Up near the front, she could see the blood-soaked parachute wrapped around the corpse of the man who had landed here. She didn't want to look at that.

Closer, there was a long sheet metal table mounted to a gunwale along the edge of the ship. The table was once white, and now had the old paint flaking off of it, and rust showing through. She put the satchel down on it, and unzipped it, half thinking Stark would have brought the wrong satchel. No. There was a small computer in here.

"I got it."

She pulled it out, opened it and placed it down on the table. It was already on.

"What does it say?" came Jan's voice from thousands of miles away.

"I don't know. I'm trying to understand it."

There wasn't much to the readout. Against a black background, there was a series of five long identifiers, letters and numbers. Each identifier was lit up in green.

Each identifier was trailed by several columns of... what?

"Can you hack this thing?" she said. "Can you look at this?"

"No. I'm afraid not. I believe I have found it through satellite positioning, but it is blocking any attempt at communication. It is communicating with the drones, though. I am trying to simply block their interactions, also to no avail. They are wedded together in a tight network."

His voice washed over her. Okay. The identifiers were the drones. Five identifiers, five drones. That made sense.

There was a digital number at the top of the screen in red.

0:57.

What was that, minutes?

0.56.

0.55.

0.54.

Not minutes. Seconds.

"Oh my God!"

"What is it? Mariem, speak to me."

"It's counting down. There's less than a minute left."

His normally deep voice was rising. "What does the readout say?"

"There are five identifiers in a column on the left side. Those are probably the drones. Then there are other columns. Status. Connection? A couple that are just numbers and are not clear. Abort? There is a column for abort."

"What are the options under abort?"

She looked down the column.

"Y/N. Those are the only options. The Ns are lit up in green all the way down. Is that it? Abort? Yes and no?"

"It would seem like it," Jan said. "Try it. Simply go down the line and click on Y. Yes for abort."

The keyboard was not a typical laptop keyboard. There were only a handful of keys. There was no mouse or pointer device.

"Mari?"

"There's no way to go down the line."

She was on the verge of a panic. Suddenly, she felt like she was going to cry. She wanted to run away. She suppressed the emotions, pushed them down. She had to stay rational. She had to focus.

She looked at the clock.

0:22.

"Twenty-two seconds. Oh my God. Twenty-one seconds."

The whining from downstairs seemed to be getting louder. Maybe it was the bomb. Maybe that countdown clock was the bomb, and this ship was about to erupt in a firestorm. She had to get Stark up here from downstairs, away from the coming explosion. There was no time to do anything.

"Are there arrow keys?"

"Yes," she said.

"Use them to scroll across the first line. Change the N to Y."

She tried it. It worked! Relief flooded her system.

0.16.

She scrolled across to the first *Abort?* column. She was in the cell. The Y lit up in green, and the N turned gray. Now what. There was an ENTER button. She pressed it.

The Y blinked several times. It was taking too long.

And now the cursor had dropped to the *Abort?* cell on the second line. She changed it and hit RETURN. The Y blinked and blinked.

"Come on!" she shrieked at it.

"Is it working?"

"Yes, but each one takes several seconds."

She was on the third line.

0:04.

The Y blinked several times, then stabilized. Three rows done, two more to…

0:00.

She grunted and tried to drop another line. It didn't work. The screen went blank. Something else was happening. They were out of time. She braced herself for the ship to explode. Her whole body tensed. Her fists squeezed. She wanted to squeeze her eyes shut. But she had to get Stark.

"Mari?" Jan said.

She turned to race back down the stairs, but Stark was behind her. He was at the landing. He was a big man, but he looked somehow… *diminished.*

"Mari!" Jan's voice squawked.

Stark walked towards her. "How did it go?"

Behind him, the wrecked covering had detached and was retracting backwards in two different directions, opening like a giant mouth. The sliders made a crunching sound as the shredded mesh was sucked into the slots. An instant later, two large objects suddenly zipped by, emerging from the deep hold. They moved fast, passing in a blur. The sound was like: WHOOOOOSSSSSSSHHH.

Stark flinched as they passed. She had never seen him do that. She turned and watched them take off.

"Oh, man," Stark said.

In the sky, the drones stopped and hovered together. As she watched, both drones seemed to crack apart, and fall toward the water in pieces.

"What in the…?" Stark said.

But something remained in the sky. There was a sort of swarm of tiny flies up there, the slaughterbots that Jan had talked about. They were dark, clouds, like a plague of locusts from the Bible. They swirled around each other like twin tornados, going higher and higher. Then the two tornados melded and became one, a giant, swirling, dancing mass of insects. It was beautiful in its own way.

"What am I witnessing?" Stark said behind her. "How can they do that?"

Now they were coming together, seeming to climb all over each other. A seething, wriggling mass, remaining in the sky, defying the law of gravity. The mass was vibrating now, taking some shape. Outlying bots were circling it, waiting to attach themselves. It was growing bigger and bigger. It was horrifying. It was from another world.

"We gotta stop them," Stark said.

She shook her head. "How can we?"

It was a disaster. They had come all this way, fought through everything, and they were seconds too late.

Her jaw hung slack. There was no way to stop it now.

"It's the computer!" Stark said. "It's this damn computer!"

She turned to look as Stark lurched toward the navigation computer. He picked it up and brought it down on the table. BANG! He did it again. BANG!

He started hammering it against the table. A seam cracked along the edge of the device.

"Stark! You're going to make them explode! Stop!"

He held the device with both hands and heaved it off the side of the ship. They both watched as it spun, around and around like a Frisbee, and dropped toward the dark water of the river. In a few seconds it hit, paused, then went under the surface.

For the first time, Dubois noticed that the river was full of police boats. She saw a couple of boats that said FDNY. There was one that said US COAST GUARD. They were all converging on this ship.

The navigation controller was gone. Dubois glanced at the table. Her mobile phone was still on there. Far away, Jan was yelling something.

"Look!" Stark shouted. He was pointing at the sky.

Dubois looked up. The giant mass was doing something. It seemed to lurch north, then back south again, moving very fast. Suddenly, the outlying bots started to drop away from the mass. They fell toward the water. The first ones hit.

BANG! BANG! BANG! The water rippled with small explosions.

The freighter was almost directly beneath the mass. Now the entire mass started to fall apart.

They were all falling down. The slaughterbots. Instead of joining together into a giant flying bomb, they were falling down like rain.

"Get down!" she screamed. She grabbed Stark by the collar. He was hard to pull down. She threw herself off her feet and used her weight to pull him down. They both hit the deck. She crawled under the metal table. Now he got the message and followed her. They both squeezed under there.

The bots, each one a tiny bomb, hit the deck like a rain of fire.

BANG! BANG! BANG! BANG! BANG!

Dubois covered her ears, rolled into a ball, and screamed.

After a long moment, it was all over. She opened her eyes. Stark was lying next to her. He smiled. All around them a few final bots were hitting and going off, like the last few kernels of popping corn.

BANG!

"We better stay under here a minute," Stark said.

BANG!

"Looks like you saved my life," he said.

BANG! BANG!

She nodded. "Twice."

Stark stared at her. He seemed honestly puzzled.

"I killed that gunman at the abbey. He had the drop on you."

Then he smiled again. "How could I forget?"

BANG!

Stark crawled out from under the table. He stood. Dubois just watched him, not ready to expose herself yet.

Stark looked down at her. He was grinning now. Behind him, a NYPD helicopter hovered. Behind that one, another one was coming.

Men were dropping down the ropes toward the freighter, like she and Stark had done earlier.

"What a day, huh?" Stark said. He looked out at the blue sky all around them. "It's a great day."

Dubois gestured with her chin. "Choppers coming in."

Stark nodded. "I know. I saw them. They're the good guys. If you have that gun I gave you earlier, I'd toss it away now. And when they get here, just go limp, like a slab of meat. These guys mean business."

She watched as the first wave of police commandos reached the deck of the freighter. Stark put his hands in the air, as high as they would go.

"I'm a cop!" he shouted. "We're both cops!"

CHAPTER THIRTY TWO

2:30 pm Eastern Daylight Time
A holding cell
The 1st Precinct
Lower Manhattan
New York City

"What do you think is going to happen?"

Troy sat on the bench next to Dubois. He was tired. His body hurt. All of it. His spine, his head, his legs, his shoulder, especially his right shoulder. He'd probably need a hip replacement and Tommy John surgery after this.

He had no idea how to answer Dubois's question. He had been optimistic earlier, but that was much earlier. The cops had left them sitting in this cell for an awful long time now. They hadn't gotten a phone call. They hadn't seen a lawyer. No one had even come down this hallway in hours. They were lucky that the cops had at least deigned to jail them together.

There was a guy in a cell across the hall. He stood at the bars, looking at Dubois. He kept sticking his tongue all the way out and making licking motions at her. He pantomimed running his tongue along one of the bars. It was a long tongue.

"Buddy," Troy said to him. "When I get out of here, I'm going to rip that tongue out of your throat, and I'm gonna strangle you with it. Okay?"

The guy looked at Troy, saw that he wasn't joking, then turned and went back to the bench in his cell.

Down the hall came a sudden loud buzz, and the sound of a heavy door unlocking. Someone was coming into the block of cells. Footsteps echoed on the floor, coming this way. It sounded like two pairs of feet. Troy sighed. He didn't even want to look.

"This should be interesting," he said.

Two men appeared at the cell. One was a uniformed cop, desk jock, a little overweight, with close-cropped hair. The other was Colonel Stuart Persons, or whatever title he went by now, dressed smartly in a dark jacket and red tie. His eye patch even seemed formal.

The cop unlocked the cell and slid open the bars. Then he stood aside as if to let them out. Troy didn't move off the bench. He wasn't sure if he even could move. Dubois stayed with him.

Persons nodded to Troy. "Agent Stark," he said. "Agent Dubois, it's a pleasure to meet you finally. I've heard great things about you."

"Dubois, this is Colonel Persons," Troy said.

Persons shook his head. "Please don't call me Colonel Persons. I'm retired from that job. Stuart will be fine, or Stu."

Troy cringed at the thought of Dubois calling him Stu. He leapt in to put a stop to it before it happened. "Some people call him Missing Persons."

"No one calls me that," Persons said.

"Not as far as you know."

Dubois stood and extended a hand. They shook. "Nice to meet you, Stu."

"Thanks for coming so soon," Troy said. "Stu."

Persons shrugged. "I didn't know where they were holding you. I came as soon as I found out. You're both free to go."

"That's nice," Troy said. "Since we just spent the past several days saving this…"

Persons raised a hand. STOP. There weren't many people in the world who could cut off Troy Stark with a hand gesture. Persons was one of them.

"That's classified," Persons said. "Understand that you both have my respect, and the unending gratitude of many people, even if none of them know that."

"Thank you," Dubois said.

Troy waved a hand.

"Agent Dubois, you've been recalled to Europe. Your presence is required within the next 24 hours, both to receive commendations for bravery and initiative, and to testify at an internal affairs hearing about your own actions, the actions of other Interpol personnel, and international personnel, if any, who were working with Interpol. It seems that certain jobs are on the line, and the powers-that-be want your input. There's a car waiting outside to take you to a small airport in New Jersey, where you'll leave the country with a minimum of red tape. The plane is already waiting for you."

Dubois looked down at Troy. Then she looked back at Persons.

"I was going to go to Stark's house. His mother was going to make lasagna."

Persons looked at his watch. "Is her cooking that good?"

Dubois looked at Troy again.

He shrugged. It didn't matter. She had to go. That was okay. The job was done. "I don't know," he said. "Maybe it improved over time. I grew up eating Cap'n Crunch for dinner, to be honest with you."

Troy worked his way to his feet. Everything hurt. His teeth hurt. His eyes hurt. The hair on his head hurt. It felt like he was made of broken glass.

"How is Alex doing?" he said.

Persons's one eye looked at Troy with meaning.

"Who is Alex?"

Troy shook his head. "Nobody."

"Agent Stark," Persons said. "Let this be verbal notification that you are relieved of duty as a New York City police officer, effective immediately. You will receive formal, written notification by mail in the weeks ahead. Expect that notification to include allegations of broad misconduct, civil rights violations of private citizens both here and abroad, assault, kidnapping, theft, including unauthorized use of a police helicopter..."

"You know I don't know how to fly a helicopter, right?"

Persons raised his hand again. "...unauthorized weapons use, including possession and discharge of automatic weapons in countries that forbid the same, and a host of other allegations and potential charges that this department is still trying to fully understand. As far as we can tell, your conduct has been beyond deplorable, and we are working hard to repair valuable relationships with our international law enforcement partners that you've damaged to a degree that's hard to estimate at this moment."

"Oh my God," Dubois said. She looked at Stark. Her eyes were watering. Was she going to cry over this? Troy certainly hoped not.

He glanced at Persons again. This was the same man who just claimed he didn't know who Alex was. Troy could see the smirk in Persons's eye, if not on his lips. It was all for show. Of course Troy Stark had to be fired. You couldn't let someone run amok around foreign countries, stomping on toes everywhere, without bringing the hammer down. This whole thing needed to be swept under the rug. One way to start that process was like this:

Troy Stark doesn't work here anymore.

Dubois stepped into his arms and hugged him fiercely. She was stronger than she looked. He knew that already, but his battered body was finally getting a taste of it.

"Are you okay?"

Troy shrugged. "Sure. I'm okay. I never really liked this job anyway."

CHAPTER THIRTY THREE

9:30 pm Eastern Daylight Time
A hotel room
Big Apple Suites
Times Square
New York City

"How was Tennessee?" Persons said.

Troy stared at him. Persons was dressed casually now, in a tight sweater and jeans. The sweater hugged his upper body, showing that Persons, whatever his age, was keeping himself in good shape. The eye patch seemed to be the same one he'd been wearing earlier today.

They were sitting in two easy chairs across from each other. On the table in front of them were cans of beer, a couple of empties, a couple of new ones that Persons had just taken out of the mini-fridge.

When Troy had gotten out of jail, a car had taken him here. The driver had given him a key card to this room and sent him upstairs. Troy had slept for a few hours, then ordered up some room service. Steak. Potatoes. A shrimp cocktail. A slice of apple pie. The food wasn't bad.

After that, he had simply sat and waited. He knew the deal. They didn't just release you back to the wild after a trip like this one.

"Is this the debrief?" Troy said.

Persons grimaced and shook his head. "There's no debrief. Just play along, okay?"

Troy shrugged. He picked up his can of beer and took a sip. He was moving slowly. His entire body was stiff. He had ordered a bottle of Aleve with the room service, but it didn't seem to do much.

"Tennessee was fine. Some rural mountain town I never heard of. Mostly it was a surveillance gig, hanging out with some ATF guys, watching a couple of trailers on a property out in the middle of God's country. At the end, we took down an illegal distillery. There was also a small methamphetamine lab on the property, so we got a two for one deal. Not bad for a few days' work."

Persons nodded. "How did you get hurt?"

"Ah, you know. There was a good ole boy, made a run for it on foot. He was a big guy. I chased him and caught him, but he fought, and we went tumbling down a hillside together. We bounced over a few stumps in a clearcut. It hurts."

"Does it still hurt now?"

Troy sipped his beer. "What do you think? In real life, I was in a helicopter crash and then fell off the Brooklyn Bridge."

Persons smiled. "I heard you jumped off."

"Same difference," Troy said.

Persons reached into his jeans pocket and came out with a pill bottle. He tossed it across to Troy. Troy caught it in his free hand. There were a lot of pills inside.

"Those are strong," Persons said. "They should clear up that pain for at least a while. But don't get hooked on them, okay? The last thing I need is a junkie on the payroll."

"Am I still on the payroll?" Troy said.

Persons shrugged. "Sure. Of course you are. Not the NYPD payroll. I mean, that ship has sailed. But people like what you're doing."

Troy didn't bother to ask who "people" were.

"I'm thinking more of a consulting thing," Persons said. "You know, we've got all these charitable efforts abroad. USAID, things of that nature. They've got these little kids in a lot of places, they have this thing where their upper lip is split, something along those lines. Ever seen that?"

Persons gestured at his own face, around the lip and nose area.

"Cleft palate," Troy said.

Persons nodded. "Yeah. It's easy to fix. Except they don't have doctors in a lot of these countries. So we send doctors and nurses in, do a bunch of surgeries at once. We change a lot of lives for the better like that. Also, old people and their cataracts. Same kind of thing. One minute you're blind, the next minute you can see fine. It's low hanging fruit."

Troy didn't say anything. He wasn't a doctor or a nurse. That should be apparent to Persons by now.

"This kind of thing interest you?"

Troy shook his head. "I don't know. I've never done anything like that."

Persons snapped his fingers a couple of times. "Hello, are you home?" he said. "I don't mean doing the actual work. Obviously, you're not going to be performing surgery. I mean conceptually, as an abstract thing, an ideal. Charity work. Doing good in the world. It's a cover story, Stark. You represent our efforts in that regard. That's the payroll you're on."

Troy nodded. He finally got it. "Oh. Oh, yeah. I like that kind of thing. Helping kids. What's not to like?"

Persons took a long sip of his beer. "Exactly."

"So that's what I'm going to be doing?" Troy said.

Persons shook his head. Now he slugged the beer and looked at his watch. "In a sense, but not really. You know this guy over in Europe, Miquel Castro-Ruiz?"

Troy nodded. "Yeah. Decent guy. Seems like he's on the hot seat."

"We're following his situation. They don't like him over there, but we do. Still, it looks like they can't get rid of him after this. He gambled big and won big. So we think they're going to spin-off his little office into its own thing. Free of encumbrances. That way they can disavow him if he paints too far outside the lines. If he's part of Interpol, they can't do that. But if he's an independent agency…"

Persons shrugged. "You see my point."

"Okay," Troy said.

"We have our methods for knowing things. He was in jail earlier today, but now he's out."

Troy nodded. "Like someone else we know."

"You know he held his bosses off at gunpoint? They were going to shut him down, so he pulled out a piece. He took it to the edge, and then over the edge. Also like someone we know. They're going to give him what he wants. They have to. Right now, he's talking to his number two over there, the computer guy, about trying to hire you."

Persons's eye looked at Troy closely.

"If he offers it, we want you to take the job."

"What about the charity thing?" Troy said. "Didn't we just…"

"That's a consultancy," Persons said. "We think he's going to offer you a job. A job-job. We need a man like you in a job like that. A lot goes on in Europe. A lot goes on with European interests in Africa, and Asia, and even South America. There are a lot of moving pieces - guns, people, drugs. There are emerging threats that impact us. Radicals of every stripe. Leftists, neo-Nazis, Islamic terrorists. Illicit money flows, and I mean a lot of money. There are oligarchs in Eastern Europe who stole entire industries after the communists bit the dust. These are sensitive industries, oil and gas, coal, steel, and they're owned and managed by criminals. That's not good. And then there are the politicians who we think are our friends, but they're secretly dirty, and compromised. In American politics, we know who has their hand in the cookie jar. Half the time, we're the ones holding the jar. In Europe, we fly blind a little bit. These governments are our friends, the EU as a whole is our friend. But they aren't us. They don't tell us everything. I think you understand."

"You want me to spy on the Europeans?"

"I want you to work for them. And tell us what you see."

"And the consultancy?"

Persons shrugged. "Keep it. You'll do good things."

"Is it double-dipping?"

Persons shook his head. "There's no such thing as double-dipping among spies, Stark. Come on. You know that. You're a big boy."

Persons stood and polished off the last of his beer, crushed the can, and dropped it on the table between them.

"I'll be a double agent, though," Troy said.

Persons pointed a finger at him like a gun. "Bingo. Listen, thanks for the beers. Keep the room until morning. It's paid for."

He went to the door. "Goodnight, Stark. It's been a real pleasure."

Troy looked at the pill bottle in his hand. It had no markings of any kind on it. He turned to the door. It was closing slowly, slowly... and then clicked shut.

CHAPTER THIRTY FOUR

October 24
5:15 pm Eastern Daylight Time
E. 239th Street
Woodlawn, The Bronx
New York City

"I hope you don't mind me calling like this."

The voice on the other side of the line was deep, sultry, and feminine, almost in a cat-like way. Troy pictured the person attached to the voice. He certainly didn't mind her calling, but...

"How did you get this number?"

He was standing in his mother's kitchen, at the old phone attached to the wall. Outside, the fall day was fading. The trees in the neighborhood were starting to go bare. The remaining leaves were rust-colored now. A good rainstorm would bring the last of them down.

On the one hand, it was odd that she had this phone number. On the other hand, Troy could remember standing at this exact phone, looking out at the fall leaves when he was in high school, and when he was a child. This number hadn't changed in decades.

"I have a great many resources available to me, Mr. Stark," Aliz Willems said. "I think I may have explained that to you."

"Well, it's nice to hear from you," Troy said. "How's your brother doing?"

Five feet away, Troy's mother was puttering around, pretending not to listen to his conversation. She really had no other reason to be in here. She had put a tray of lasagna in the oven 15 minutes ago. It wasn't ready yet. The scent of it was only just beginning to fill the room.

"Oh, Lucien. He's disappeared, like he always does when he's caused me trouble. I'm sure he'll turn up again at some point."

Troy nodded. Lucien was going to turn up again, all right. Troy was going to dig him up, like a rat terrier digging vermin out of a hole.

"But he's not why I called."

It occurred to Troy that Aliz really had no idea just how bad a man her brother really was. She thought he got himself in over his head sometimes. It wasn't true. Lucien was the deep depths of the ocean, where no sunlight reached, and he was also the great white shark swimming down there.

"Do tell."

"It's just that... I don't think I've ever met anyone like you. You're certainly the first man to lock me in a dungeon, and then leave me there."

"Are there men who lock you in a dungeon, and then let you out again?"

She laughed. It sounded incredibly awkward. And Troy realized she was nervous. "No. No one has ever locked me in a dungeon at all. It was a radical move, and I needed it. I needed to be locked away. For my psyche. Do you understand?"

Troy shook his head. No. He didn't understand. He had locked her in there, not as an exercise, but so she wouldn't tell her brother he was coming.

"Sure," he said. "I get it."

"If you ever find yourself in Europe again, I'd like you to give me a call. I'll fly to wherever. I want to see you again. I'd really love to take you out to dinner."

There was no mention of the missing Porsche. There was no mention of an abbey full of dead guys. Lucien had disappeared. He did that sometimes. None of this, in Aliz's mind, seemed to have anything to do with the terrorist attack that had been thwarted less than a week ago.

And she wasn't the only one. The whole thing had been swept under the rug. The first attack was bad, certainly. But in the second attack, the drones had malfunctioned. and the inept terrorists had fallen off the Brooklyn Bridge, after being cornered by quick-thinking cops from the NYPD.

No one in America seemed to remember the attack in Belgium. If they did remember, it must have been something unrelated.

"Who was that?" Troy's mother said as he hung up the phone. "A new girlfriend?"

"I think it was a wrong number, Ma."

He kissed her on the forehead.

"Dinner is gonna be ready in 20 minutes," she said.

He nodded. "Thank you."

He gimped past her, heading for the couch and the TV news.

"You know, your brother made Inspector recently," she said. "It's a big deal. It would be nice if you got him something, a bottle of champagne maybe. And it would also be a good idea if you took some pointers from him, maybe get your own career on track a little bit."

She waved her hand at the telephone. "Instead of playing around with all these women. You're not a teenager anymore."

Troy nodded. "I know."

* * *

In the evening, Troy walked over to the Michael Collins.

It was a quiet night. Kenny Dolan was not perched on his customary stool. The bartender nodded to Troy, poured him a beer, and left him alone. A handful of people were throwing darts.

The jukebox was on, playing something low that Troy couldn't hear. His hearing was taking a little while to come back. It felt like he had cotton balls stuffed in his ears sometimes.

A boxing match was on TV behind the bar. The sound was all the way off. Troy looked at it for a second, then did a double-take. It was Mike Tyson and Buster Douglas, live from Tokyo, 30 years ago.

"Talk about a rerun," Troy said.

A man slid onto the stool next to him. "I won about 800 pesetas on that fight," he said. "The odds were 40 to one in favor of Tyson. I thought if all the people believe Tyson is that good, there must be something wrong with him."

Troy looked at the man. He was a small guy, middle-aged, probably. He had a thick head of mostly black hair spotted with strands of gray. The last time Troy had seen him, he also had a bushy mustache. Now he was clean shaven. He wore a long leather jacket, jeans, and black shoes. The guy looked good, almost like he was aging backwards.

It was Miquel Castro-Ruiz. Of course it was.

"Pesetas, huh?"

Miquel nodded. "I was in Spain. They hadn't introduced the euro yet. I guess you didn't watch the fight at that time."

Troy shrugged. "I was probably in diapers."

Miquel looked around the nearly empty bar. "It's a nice place. They told me I would find you here."

Troy didn't bother to ask who "they" were.

"I like it," he said.

"I came a long way to talk to you," Miquel said. "So I'll get right to the point. We're men of a similar mind, I think. There are a lot of challenges in this world, but I believe we can rise to meet them."

Their eyes met.

245

"I want you to come work for me."

Troy hesitated and took a long sip of his beer, like a man thinking something over. What was he thinking about? He pictured Aliz Willems in the dress she wore to her charity event. He pictured the two of them at dinner somewhere, maybe in the Alps, clinking glasses of wine, a fireplace burning nearby. He pictured Missing Persons in a hotel room, reciting all the reasons why America needed Troy Stark in Europe.

He smiled and put his beer down on the bar.

"Sold," he said.

EPILOGUE

October 25
7:05 am Eastern European Daylight Time
Foinikion, Island of Carpathos
The Greek Islands
The Aegean Sea

"Stark just left the pub," a male voice said.

Lucien Mebarak held the mobile phone to his ear. In a sense, it was amazing that a man was talking to him in New York City, thousands of miles away, while standing on a street corner, in the middle of the night. It was probably cold there, and overcast, and the man was probably wearing a coat.

Here, Lucien was sitting shirtless on the patio of his remote, modern white stone house, overlooking the crystal waters of the Aegean, while sipping a cup of coffee. In front of him, a young dark-haired Croatian model was completely nude, swimming laps in the blue infinity pool. Behind him, the first rays of the day were rising above the rugged hillsides to the east. It was warm here, and beautiful.

It was amazing that technology had leapt so far that Lucien and this man could speak in this way. During Lucien's youth, speaking to anyone from this location would have been close to impossible. Cellular technology barely existed in those days, it certainly didn't reach here, and the local telephone utility would have been a paragon of dysfunction.

And yet, as amazing as it was, it was now the most mundane thing in the world.

"It's late," Lucien said. "Isn't it?"

"Just after midnight."

"What about the Spaniard?" Lucien said.

"They talked closely for a quite a while, but the Spaniard left about two hours ago."

"Where did he go?"

"He got in a taxi," the man said. "I assume he returned to his hotel."

Lucien nodded. The man made an assumption. It was fine. This wasn't a critical moment. It didn't really matter where the Spaniard went.

"And Stark?"

"He seemed to meet some people he knew from before. So he stayed and celebrated his homecoming with them. Now he's walking to the house."

Troy Stark. Walking home to his mother's house.

It was almost too amusing for words. The unstoppable killing machine, the man who had derailed Lucien Mebarak's best-laid plans, had a mother. And he lived with her.

Lucien had a soft spot for mothers.

But not for Troy Stark.

Stark had made trouble for Lucien. He had placed himself on Lucien's radar. That much was certain. And what did it accomplish in the end?

The near disaster in New York had caused a minor stock market crash anyway. Events of that nature always did. Lucien, like all the smart money, had bought while the panicky herd sold. Next week, or the week after, the market would come back. Lucien's profits would not be what they could have been, but he still stood to make a tidy sum.

Stark had saved some lives. So what?

And he had killed some gangsters. But he had been lucky more than anything. And his luck wouldn't last forever.

"What do you want me to do?" the voice on the phone said.

Lucien watched as the Croatian lovely emerged from the pool. She was perfect. He followed her with his eyes as she went to a lounge chair, picked up her plush white towel, and wrapped herself in it.

Lucien sighed. Everything was beautiful here. Everything was perfect. The girl, yes, but not only the girl.

Lucien pictured the man he was speaking to. He was a middle-aged Albanian criminal who lived in New York. Overweight, a heavy smoker. He was passably good at surveillance because he was easy to overlook.

All he would do against Stark was get killed and call attention to himself.

"What do you want me to do?" he said again, more emphatically this time.

"Nothing," Lucien said.

He took a sip of his coffee and gazed out at the water, which was becoming clearer every moment.

"For now."

NOW AVAILABLE!

ROGUE COMMAND
(A Troy Stark Thriller—Book #2)

"Thriller writing at its best. Thriller enthusiasts who relish the precise execution of an international thriller, but who seek the psychological depth and believability of a protagonist who simultaneously fields professional and personal life challenges, will find this a gripping story that's hard to put down."
--Midwest Book Review, Diane Donovan (regarding Any Means Necessary)

"One of the best thrillers I have read this year. The plot is intelligent and will keep you hooked from the beginning. The author did a superb job creating a set of characters who are fully developed and very much enjoyable. I can hardly wait for the sequel."
--Books and Movie Reviews, Roberto Mattos (re Any Means Necessary)

From #1 bestselling and USA Today bestselling author Jack Mars, author of the critically-acclaimed *Luke Stone* and *Agent Zero* series (with over 5,000 five-star reviews), comes an explosive new, action-packed thriller series that takes readers on a wild-ride across Europe, America, and the world.

Although elite Navy Seal Troy Stark was forced into retirement for his dubious respect for authority, his work in stopping a major terrorist threat to New York did not go unnoticed. Now part of a new, secret international organization, Troy must hunt down all threats to the U.S. and pre-empt them overseas—bending the rules if he has to.

In ROGUE COMMAND, a group of European terrorists have a new, unexpected target, with nuclear-level consequences. With the clock ticking for Troy to stop them before they set off a global war, Troy, partnered with an Interpol agent whom he grudgingly respects, is up against the enemy of his life.

But there is only one problem: no one knows exactly what the target is.

And as Troy's investigative work leads to a discovery, he realizes it may not be the target—or the enemy—they all think it is. Just how deep do these terrorists' connections run?

An unputdownable action thriller with heart-pounding suspense and unforeseen twists, ROGUE COMMAND is the debut novel in an exhilarating new series by a #1 bestselling author that will have you fall in love with a brand new action hero—and turn pages late into the night.

Book #3 in the series—ROGUE TARGET—is now also available.

Jack Mars

Jack Mars is the USA Today bestselling author of the LUKE STONE thriller series, which includes seven books. He is also the author of the new FORGING OF LUKE STONE prequel series, comprising six books; of the AGENT ZERO spy thriller series, comprising twelve books; and of the TROY STARK thriller series, comprising three books (and counting).

Jack loves to hear from you, so please feel free to visit www.Jackmarsauthor.com to join the email list, receive a free book, receive free giveaways, connect on Facebook and Twitter, and stay in touch!

BOOKS BY JACK MARS

TROY STARK THRILLER SERIES
ROGUE FORCE (Book #1)
ROGUE COMMAND (Book #2)
ROGUE TARGET (Book #3)

LUKE STONE THRILLER SERIES
ANY MEANS NECESSARY (Book #1)
OATH OF OFFICE (Book #2)
SITUATION ROOM (Book #3)
OPPOSE ANY FOE (Book #4)
PRESIDENT ELECT (Book #5)
OUR SACRED HONOR (Book #6)
HOUSE DIVIDED (Book #7)

FORGING OF LUKE STONE PREQUEL SERIES
PRIMARY TARGET (Book #1)
PRIMARY COMMAND (Book #2)
PRIMARY THREAT (Book #3)
PRIMARY GLORY (Book #4)
PRIMARY VALOR (Book #5)
PRIMARY DUTY (Book #6)

AN AGENT ZERO SPY THRILLER SERIES
AGENT ZERO (Book #1)
TARGET ZERO (Book #2)
HUNTING ZERO (Book #3)
TRAPPING ZERO (Book #4)
FILE ZERO (Book #5)
RECALL ZERO (Book #6)
ASSASSIN ZERO (Book #7)
DECOY ZERO (Book #8)
CHASING ZERO (Book #9)
VENGEANCE ZERO (Book #10)
ZERO ZERO (Book #11)
ABSOLUTE ZERO (Book #12)

Printed in Great Britain
by Amazon